D0873642

Choose to Rise: The Victory Within is a work of fiction based on documented historical events with mention of actual historical persons and sites. All additional characters, places, experiences, and events are created from the imagination of the author and are used fictitiously. Any resemblance to actual experiences, locales, or persons, living or dead, is entirely coincidental. Please refer to the following letter for more information.

Choose to Rise: The Victory Within

Edition 1

First Printing, 2015

ISBN-10:
0692385169
ISBN-13:
978-0692385166

Choose to Rise:
The Victory Within

M. N. Mekaelian

My Dearest Readers,

Long ago, I knew I wanted to write a book, not necessarily publish one, just write one. I didn't know what about and I didn't know by when; it was a vague life goal of mine, and one that I was sure I'd never accomplish. However, through a set of perfect events over a decade later, I found myself holding the first proof copy of my completed book in my hand. It was a moment that will forever sit with me in mystery, and one that I'll forever look back on in awe.

In January 2011, when I first considered the possibility of achieving this now forgotten goal, I remember telling myself that, having no major writing experience, I should at least write about a topic that I knew *something* about. It only made sense. Thus, being Armenian, I figured I should write about the Armenian Genocide.

Using my own history, I began with Kharpert, the province of Armenia where my ancestors once lived. After researching the area, now in Turkey, I couldn't ignore the abundant mention of grapevines and apricot orchards. So, as a way to reflect the simplicity of life I continually try to achieve, I created the Hagopian family who lived on a farm in the Armenian province of Kharpert in the Ottoman Turkish Empire.

After creating a few more characters and adding more family history, I quickly realized this book would only work if I could properly capture the realism in a way that you, the reader, would believe. To accomplish this, I created a rough outline, a timeline of events based on historical research, that I would eventually intertwine with a fictional story. It was during this research phase that I further realized that I had picked a topic I *thought* I knew something about, but in fact, didn't know *anything* about. I had inadvertently transformed my driving force from one of mere completion to one of profound curiosity: Why did the Armenian Genocide happen? How did it happen? Why didn't anyone stop it? From there, the questions kept building, and I quickly found myself wanting details, so many, in fact, that I wanted to feel as though I had actually experienced the genocide myself. I felt this was the only way I would truly be able to understand it enough to deliver it to you. Early in my book, I even quote my struggle while searching for this realistic experience. I write:

> I now had an infinite number of questions racing through my mind. So many detailed questions. I wanted to know more. I wanted to know about [my grandmother's] emotions. I wanted to know what she was thinking, what she *saw*, what she *heard*, how she *felt*. I wanted to see my grandfather's footsteps, his actions, the moves he used, the jabs he made. I then wanted to see the soldiers, their faces. I wanted to know what they wore. I wanted to hear their conversations, hear their voices. I wanted details. So many details. I wanted to know because I needed to understand. I needed to be there with her. After a quick thought, however, I bit my tongue.
> Did I *really*?

So, in an effort to find exactly what I was looking for, I dove deeper and began reading books and newspapers of the time, interviewed families of survivors, and searched online, realizing along the way just how shockingly similar the individual stories were. Unfortunately, I never found what I felt was a complete picture with the details I wanted. Thus, as an effective solution, I placed myself in the Ottoman Empire, living as my characters for the next three years, and used my imagination to fill them in. For those long years, I relived every situation, perilous or not, in order to re-create the circumstance of the time. I did it to ensure that I met my criteria of capturing the realism and producing the most authentic interpretation of the Armenian Genocide that I could write. That was the only way I felt I could truly grasp and deliver the reality of what is arguably the worst emotional experience a human can go through.

By the time I finished in 2014, what I ended up with was a narrative, written through the eyes of an old Armen Hagopian, that not only explains the events through my own artistic freedom, but one that allows you, the reader, to feel as the victims felt. You'll notice that this book is as descriptive as I thought could be tolerated, using every sense and every emotion, even using my own struggle as a means to rediscover a lost generation. This book is intense, it is moving, it is promising, and it will sit with you long after you put it down.

Before you begin, though, I'd like to thank you for taking the time to read my work. It means more to me than you'll ever know, and regardless of how you ended up with my book in your hands, I'm evermore grateful. And if, by the time you finish, you enjoyed it, please pass this copy or recommend this title to someone who might enjoy it as much as you.

Please know that the goal of this book is to educate, inspire, and reignite an old hope. Hopefully, you'll agree with me. I present to you *Choose to Rise: The Victory Within.*

Enjoy,

M. N. Mekaelian

Based on Actual Events

May 1971

Chapter 1

It was a pleasant day. The sun was shining, and the birds were singing in celebration of another victory over the brutal winter. Even the curious spring flowers found their way to gaze at the surface of their new world. What a beautiful day in Chicago. The pale stone buildings of the university towered over the students like an old fortress as they walked to and from class, happy that the sun was finally out. The scene was picturesque, and to many people, this was home.

The old professor sat in his office, taking a moment from the world to himself. His day seemed longer than usual. Coffee wasn't much good for him anymore in his old age, and the consistently empty mug in the corner of his large wooden desk reflected it. With a shallow raise of his hand, the old professor carefully removed his glasses and set them down atop a stack of crinkled papers. He then leaned back in his worn, tufted leather chair, cupped his hands over his face, and stretched his body out like a lion in the wake of the new day. Quickly, the blood rushed through him like a river of molten lava.

This felt better.

He felt more awake.

He then leaned forward in his chair and peered outside his first-floor window, narrowing his eyes against the strong sun beating through.

"What a gorgeous day to have a terrible headache," he thought to himself, as if he, too, were celebrating bittersweetly with the birds.

It was true. Of all the days to have a headache, it had to be on the most beautiful day of the year.

Peering back into his office, the old professor placed his glasses back on his aged face, bringing the walls back into focus. He looked at cherry shelving, the many color-bound books on advanced science. The old professor had many honors and degrees and was proud of each one. He was a smart man, a well-respected man, a logical man. So he sat, reflecting on his life.

The beauty of it all.

With his still sensitive eyes, he peered outside once again, and once again, he thought, "What a beautiful world God has created—the green of the trees, the rich blue of the skies, and the sweet song of the birds. How was it possible to put so much beauty into one world?"

Such a peaceful thought, yet his headache still pounded.

With a casual reach, the old professor then picked up the stack of papers. His hands were thick and strong. He had working hands. The top page revealed the subject of his next lecture—gravitational lensing. Having taught it so many times over the past thirty-four years, he wasn't sure he needed his handwritten notes anymore. He then glanced at the plain, oversized clock above the door and noted the time.

2:30 p.m.

Time for class.

Papers still in hand, he slowly stood up, using the arms of his chair for support. From all the years of use, the hardwood floor creaked under the old professor's weight as he shuffled his feet. Complemented with a long sigh, he then staggered his way out of his office and into the corridor, locking the frosted-glass door behind him.

The university hallway was wide and quite dark. From the high-set windows, patches of light beamed down radiantly at distinct intervals, exposing the dust in the air. The old professor walked slowly through each pass, through each piece of heaven, closing his eyes, feeling the heat energize his body.

His headache had grown worse.

Along the way, old friends, fellow professors, and students greeted him warmly. Everyone who passed did so with a smile. His strong character and genuine personality made anyone feel comfortable from the moment they met him. This was the way the old professor carried himself—a man no one could hate.

Farther down, the dark wood and detailed trim of his classroom door came in sight and began moving closer, though not nearly as fast as before. It was uncommon for the old professor to express dislike, but as a worn man, he hated his old age.

Just at the door, the old professor stopped and reached for the tarnished brass knob. He didn't turn it, but instead closed his eyes, inhaled, then slowly let it out. He needed to get rid of his headache. Something had to be done. Owning up to the challenge, the old professor opened his eyes and rolled them around. He then tightened his grip, turned his wrist, and leaned slightly into the door. Inside, the students' chatter quickly stopped. With his short few steps over the pale tile floor, the old professor looked at them, seated as if at a sporting stadium, wondering again why there were so many students for such an advanced course as astrophysics. Whatever the cause, he was happy to be there.

"I apologize for my tardiness," he began with his raspy yet booming voice, slightly marinated with an accent. "I'm happy everyone is still here."

The class laughed slightly as the old professor smiled to himself and walked to the head of the class behind a long counter.

"And so, what is the topic for today? Does anyone know?" he asked, looking around, examining the future.

The class sat in silence as he waited for a response.

"Interesting," he began a moment later. "Hopefully, then, I know what we're supposed to do, because otherwise, we are all lost."

He smiled again, and the class laughed slightly more.

The old professor enjoyed taking his time with things. There was no reason to rush. For him, life was happier when it wasn't hectic.

"Today, I'd like to take the time to introduce a new—"

"Professor Hagopian?" a female student asked, interrupting him.

"Yes, Sasha. How are you today?" he replied.

She smiled. "I'm fine; thanks, professor. Don't we have to turn in the homework?"

"Ah, yes, thank you for reminding the class. Will everyone please bring up their assignment for today?"

The students immediately shuffled through their papers;

some even threw glares of annoyance at Sasha. She smiled regardless, feeling confident and justified in her actions. Professor Hagopian might have been old, but his memory was still sharp, just like his grandmother's. Today, though, he blamed his forgetfulness on his terrible headache, which only grew worse.

As they stood in a line, the students placed their papers, one by one, in a single stack on the counter. Professor Hagopian stood humbly with his hands near the stack and looked at each passing student, wishing only for his own youth. He remembered a time when he was their age and even younger, and his jaded eyes told it all. Tiredly, as a way to ease his mind, he shifted his attention to the growing stack of papers and quickly became mesmerized by the repetition of each passing assignment. His eyes then turned stale, and he began to daydream. A vivid memory of his childhood home by the hillside flashed through his mind, becoming as real as the classroom in which he stood. He saw his two oxen, the stone well, the barn, and the many livestock that provided his family with everything they needed to make a living. Standing in the doorway, just on the porch, he then saw his mother, watching him fight with his brother, Armen, younger by barely two years.

She yelled for their father.

"Tevos," she gasped. "Tevos, come quick!"

Remembering the seemingly insignificant argument prompting this unwarranted match and the much greater lesson to be learned after, Professor Hagopian then saw his father, a farmer like the rest. He peered over from the barn and noted his teenage boys wrestling on the ground. With a careless throw, he dropped the tools in his hand and sternly paced his way over. After making a quick decision, he raised his right hand into the air as if petting an animal and wrinkled his face to ease his wife's worries in his own way.

"Hasmig, let it be. Let them get it out of their system. This is the only way they're going to solve this."

The old professor's father was always a calm but merciless man. Always being tough with boys, he reasoned that one day he wouldn't be there, and it would be up to them to work the fields and watch over the women.

As she stood nervously, the old professor's mother, realizing that nothing would get the boys to stop, tried once more.

"Tevos, but they're going to break a bone!" she exclaimed.

Standing calmly still, he crossed one arm across his body and twirled the tip of his long mustache with the fingertips of the other—his signature move.

"If they do, then they must deal with the consequences of a broken bone," he reasoned.

By this time, the students had finished placing all their papers on the counter. Forty-five in all. In their seats, they patiently sat, waiting for the old professor as he stood, staring at the stack.

Still mesmerized by his youth, however, he kept to his flashback.

It was a different day. His mother now sat on the porch. The sun was shining, and its warmth made her feel better. Next to her, a beautiful girl stood majestically. The light of his path. Her long brown hair flowed gently in the wind, and her pale green eyes sparkled softly under the sun. Her long fitted dress, sewn as a gift from his mother, waved as gracefully as ripples in a pond. She smiled, slowly. There was no reason to stop. There never was.

With the moment of that smile, as if struck by a bolt of lightning, a stream of shivers traveled down the old professor's spine. A small tear then fell from the corner of his eye, guided by the wrinkles in his face.

"Nadia," he whispered.

The classroom was silent. There was no one named Nadia in the class.

"Professor... Professor?"

"What? Yes," he said, subtly waking from the daze.

"Professor, is... everything all right?" a student asked.

"Yes, honey, everything is just... fine," the old professor

responded as he took off his glasses with one hand and wiped away the tear with the other, his head now pulsating. The students looked at each other, having never seen this from him before.

As if nothing was the matter, Professor Hagopian quickly dismissed his dream by turning to the chalkboard behind him.

"Excellent," he said. "Now, today we will discuss gravitational lensing," he explained as he buttoned his tan corduroy jacket.

Still in a moment of awe, the students didn't know what to make of the situation, and their confusion persisted even as the old professor began writing on the board and the sound of the chalk echoed through the quiet room.

Suddenly then, as if hit in the head with a hammer, the pain of his headache intensified. The old professor stopped writing and massaged around his left eye with his free hand.

The flashback continued.

It was early in the afternoon, the two boys, still in their church clothes, arrived back home, out of breath and in a crying panic.

"They're all dead!" screamed the elder, wearing his new suit. "Oh my God, they're all dead! I don't care what you say! We're going to leave!"

His father ran from a short distance to understand the nonsense he heard. Suddenly then, in the distance, the haunting sound of a machine gun echoed through the farm. Still seated in her chair, the old professor's mother jumped, shocked by the surprising sound, and turned her head towards the direction of the shots. Soon after, a woman's deafening scream traveled through, followed by two more separate gunshots. With each one, his mother blinked and jumped a little more. Nadia did the same. Even the remaining farm animals scurried out in different directions, sensing that something wasn't right.

After running a few more steps, his father then stopped again. He, too, gazed into the direction of the shots.

The boys, still catching their breath, stood in their dirtied clothes and listened.

His mother looked around and eventually focused on the hill to the south. "Tevos!" she yelled to her husband. "Soldiers!"

A few hundred meters out, two soldiers sat on horseback, and five stood on foot, all of them in full uniform, complete with their red cylindrical fez hats, each armed with pistols and daggers at their waists. The five foot soldiers began marching towards their house, and the ones on horseback stayed behind. The old professor's father narrowed his eyes and examined the situation. He was quick to make judgments, but he usually ended up being correct.

"Hasmig, Vartan, Armen, go inside, now!" he yelled. "Nadia," he turned, "you should go inside, too. We don't know what these soldiers want."

In distress, the old professor closed his eyes and shook his head, quickly returning to the classroom. He was dazed as his students looked on. Waiting. Watching. Realizing that his flashback must have lasted only a few seconds, the old professor focused on the chalk still in his hand and tried writing again, only to realize that he'd forgotten what about. Turning towards the counter, he thus scrambled to find the handwritten notes from his office. He grabbed the pages and looked at the title.

"Oh, yes," he murmured to himself, "gravitational lensing."

Turning back to the board, he finished writing, papers now in hand. Just as he turned back to face the class, his headache throbbed now with an agonizing pulse. He raised his right hand, still holding the chalk, and put pressure on his head once again, trying desperately to ease the pain.

The students looked on.

"Professor, are you sure you're all right?" a student asked.

"Yes," he answered softly. "It's just this headache. I cannot get rid of it."

"Well then, maybe you should cancel class," said another with a smirk.

The professor chuckled as he looked at the floor, not wanting to lift his head. His eyes had grown increasingly sensitive to the light. He felt sick. Something wasn't right, and he knew it.

This was more than just a headache.

"Nice try," he said, keeping his composure.

The students laughed, sending away their worries, and the professor, once again, forgot the day's lecture, and again, he looked to his notes. However, before even reading another word, the flashback continued.

"I need to go home and warn my family," Nadia responded.

"It's not safe. Please, Nadia, just go inside," his father responded with his stern voice.

He was serious, and the boys knew it.

"I need to warn them," she repeated. "I'm sorry."

Then, as the soldiers continued their march and moved only faster, Nadia picked up the bottom of her dress and started running west towards her house, merely a thirty-minute walk from theirs. Seeing this, one soldier pointed to her direction, signaling to the others. He then unholstered his pistol and cocked it back.

"Nadia!" his father screamed. "Nadia, run!"

Without hesitation, the soldier shot his weapon.

He missed.

Two soldiers then quickly broke away from the formation, including the one who'd shot, and began pursuit after her. Nadia turned to look and gasped, then ran faster than she'd ever run, as if she'd been given wings to fly. His father then quickly ran into the house and emerged immediately after. He ran out towards the soldiers to try to intercept them and give Nadia a head start. Vartan, realizing his father's plan, also ran towards the soldiers. His brother, Armen, on the other hand, simply stood at a distance, frozen with indecision.

The old professor shook his head, bringing the chalkboard back into focus. He had no idea where he was standing. He felt disoriented, and his mind was cloudy. Without mercy, the pain then attacked his head harder than before and became unbearable, now with pressure like a bomb ready to explode. In that instant, he closed his teary eyes tightly and sprung both his hands up, clutching his head and sending the chalk crumbling to the floor and his notes flying through the air.

With nothing left to do, the old professor lowered his pulsating head towards the tile floor. Then, with an emotional burst from a saddened plea, he cried out her name.

"*Nadia!*"

Unsure of how to react, some students sat, some even stood up, but they all looked at each other confusedly and in a disbelieving shock. Then, with a hobbling spin, the old professor turned to face them, lost his balance, and fell to the floor.

2

"Professor!" the students yelled as a handful leaped over the counter and knelt at his side.

"Someone get a glass of water," exclaimed a male student next to him, "and call an ambulance!"

A female student immediately rushed out the classroom door to find a glass of water and a telephone. A few students followed. Lying on the floor, the old professor's entire body was now in serious pain. He blinked repeatedly and searched in all directions, falling in and out of consciousness. He saw everything that was happening, every occurrence, but only tiny pieces at a time.

A severely fragmented reality.

"Professor, can you hear me?" asked the male student.

The female student who left returned to the classroom. "The ambulance is on the way," she informed as she lowered the glass of water to him.

The rest of the students now crowded around the old professor, wanting to help in any way they could.

"Professor, did you hear that? There's an ambulance on its way," repeated a student sitting next to him.

"Can you drink this?" the girl asked.

The old professor didn't answer. He continued falling in and out of consciousness, returning to the same blurry vision.

"*Nadia*," he whispered sullenly.

The students at his aid looked at each other, still confused as some girls began to whimper, fearing the worst.

"There is no one here named Nadia, Professor Hagopian. Did you mean someone else?"

The old professor heard their voices, but they were muffled and spoke too slow.

"Nadia," he repeated. "I'm going after Nadia."

The students looked at each other again and understood by now that he must have been hallucinating.

"D-Don't worry, professor, the ambulance is here. Just keep talking to us."

The old professor, however, closed his eyes and kept them shut.

He was back at his house, eating dinner with his family. His father sat at the head of the table across from his mother. He sat next to Nadia, across from his brother, Armen, and the family friends. There were two cooked ducks on the table, prepared in a moment's notice, baked with asparagus and carrots. Next to the ducks was the lavash, thin Armenian bread. In a separate bowl, the aroma of sweet baked potatoes, sprinkled lightly with pepper, quickly filled their senses. He smiled. His mother was the greatest chef in the world, always preparing the best. Before anyone ate, however, his father raised his wine glass and made a toast, then began the celebratory meal with the *Hayr Mer,* the Lord's Prayer in Armenian.

They were so happy. Everyone was so happy.

"Sir… sir," a voice echoed faintly as if in a deep cavern.

The old professor opened his eyes, just enough to see beyond the darkness. The classroom was gone. Above him, the paramedics, flashing red lights, and beautiful sky painted a bittersweet scene. Barely lifting his arm, he saw the IV in him as the paramedics wheeled him on the stretcher towards the waiting ambulance. His students followed alongside.

"Sir, can you tell me your name?" the female paramedic

asked.

The old professor didn't answer. There was no point to answer silly questions. He didn't have enough energy. His body was numb, and his head felt like someone had struck it with an ax.

"One! Two! Three!" the female paramedic counted just before she, with the help of her colleagues, lifted him into the ambulance. She then climbed in herself, closing the doors behind her. As the ambulance drove away, the students stood in the parking lot and watched helplessly. They knew, however, that this wasn't the end of the journey.

"Sir, can you please tell me your name?" the female paramedic asked again as the ambulance drove over the bumpy road.

Noting his surroundings, the old professor looked at the interior of the ambulance and closed his eyes once more.

"He's lost consciousness again!" she announced.

Following strict protocol, the paramedics immediately hooked him up to the EKG and listened as it began its rapid succession of beeps, echoing throughout the ambulance, pacing faster and faster. The sound of panic. Quickly then, just as the beeps couldn't beat any faster, everything in the old professor's body stopped as if hit by another blunt hammer. In that moment, his lungs stopped breathing, and his heart stopped beating. There was only the sound of one steady note.

Without pause, the male paramedic grabbed a pair of scissors and cut away the old professor's jacket and underlying shirt, exposing his broad shoulders and sagging muscles.

"One, two, three, four..." said the female paramedic as she began the chest compressions.

She gave him a few short breaths.

A second passed.

Nothing.

The male paramedic took over, "One, two, three, four..."

And yet, the sole, drawn-out, steady note lingered. She looked up at her partner.

"Stay clear!" the male paramedic yelled as he leaned over with the paddles of the cardiac defibrillator. The powerful electric jolt caused the old professor's body to jump in the air.

The paramedics waited.

Nothing.

"I'm trying again," he exclaimed. "Clear!"

He jolted the old professor one more time.

And once again, they tried CPR.

Nothing.

After another few seconds, the male paramedic jolted him one last time.

Nothing.

Finally then, he set the paddles down and looked at his watch.

"Time of death—"

Just then, an interruption.

As if not yet his time, the old professor's heart returned through one miraculous sound—a beep.

"We have a beat!" exclaimed the female paramedic as she wrapped an oxygen mask around his face, stabilizing his condition.

And then, another beat.

Followed by another and another.

The beat slowly, yet continually, repeated itself.

Allowing for a partial moment to relax, the paramedics eased their stance and leaned back, watching over him cautiously. The old professor was alive, and the ambulance drove on.

3

On the bare, light-green wall was an old clock.

7:30 p.m.

The old professor now rested on the uncomfortable hospital bed, not awake, breathing shallowly. On a cart next to him, the EKG beeped steadily. The doctor on call stood in the room with a clipboard, monitoring his vitals.

"My God, Vartan!" exclaimed an old woman in her late sixties as she entered the hospital room.

A large brown purse hung from her bent elbow, and she wore a white floral dress, tied lightly at the waist. Her first instinct was to hug the old professor or at least sit next to him. The doctor, however, seeing this scene too many times before, stopped her short.

"I'm afraid you can't talk to him right now, ma'am. He's just come out of surgery, and unfortunately, he's currently in a coma. The good news is that he's in stable condition."

The doctor hated this part of his job, when he delivered the news, good or bad. Over the years, though, he'd become immune to the sense of misery. This was nothing to be proud of, but nonetheless, this was his life and his profession.

"Oh my God," the old woman whispered, placing her hand over her mouth.

Her eyes began to tear up as she, once again, remembered the fragility of life, something she desperately wanted to let go of. With her glazed eyes, she turned to face the doctor.

"What happened?" she asked in English with the same foreign accent as the old professor's.

"Well, ma'am," he explained emotionlessly, "he's had a stroke."

"A stroke?" she cried.

"Yes, ma'am. He's been falling in and out of consciousness for a while and eventually showed signs of intracranial hypertension, increased pressure in the brain. We had to operate on him, and during the surgery, he unfortunately slipped into a coma."

"My God," she whispered under her breath.

"We are monitoring him constantly and waiting for the pressure in his head to decrease. Otherwise, he could have another stroke. At this point, all we can do is wait and keep him comfortable."

At the door behind them, a young female nurse peered into the room. "I'm sorry to interrupt, but all visitors must please sign in. Ma'am, may I have your name?"

"Yes," she responded, using a tissue to wipe the tears from her eyes, "my name is Anahid Hagopian. I am Vartan's sister-in-law," she clarified.

The nurse handed Anahid a clipboard, and she signed her name below the others. The nurse looked at it when she finished.

"Thank you, Anahid," she said.

As the nurse turned to leave, two boys and a girl, all in their teenage years, rushed in. They wore bell-bottom pants and tight colorful shirts—a sign of the times.

"Grandma!" the teenage girl exclaimed.

The overwhelming emotion in the room brought everyone together. Anahid hugged her granddaughter, and the two boys stood by the door.

"Oh, *hokis*," she responded in Armenian, meaning "my soul."

The parents of the teenagers soon followed, also signing in one by one, then let the door close behind them.

"Hi, Mom," said the mother of the teenagers.

"Hi, *hokis*," responded Anahid.

"What happened?" she asked.

"Vartan… has had a stroke, and now he is in a coma," she replied, slightly rolling her *r*'s.

The family looked at him helplessly. So much had changed for the old professor in the past five hours.

In the hallway, just outside the room, an old man stood, also in his late sixties. He stared at the old professor through the window in the door, gently rubbing his fingers over a gold crucifix hanging around his neck. Every wrinkle and every hair on the man's face was filled with anguish. His broad shoulders and intimidating height told a story of greatness. This was, however, a humbling time, even for a man of such importance— the lowest point in a family's journey together. As the parents, the teenagers, and Anahid consoled each other, he looked on. They hadn't noticed him yet. The old man's heart couldn't bear any more sadness. With the other hand in his pocket, he thus looked at the floor, not wanting to see any more; then finally, he removed his hand, silently opened the door, and like a ghost, stood just inside.

The doctor, still in the room, then remembered a detail.

"By the way," he began, "Vartan's students told the paramedics that he kept asking for Nadia. Is she a family member? Will Nadia be here soon?"

At that moment, the old man in the doorway raised his head, and his eyes swelled. No tears, however, dared to show themselves.

With a quick shift to eyes of rage, he scrambled through the family towards the doctor. Grabbing his white jacket, he stood in his face.

"What did you say?" he whispered with a stern voice.

Stunned, the people in the room looked at him.

"Armen!" gasped Anahid.

"Um, I… the students said that he asked for Nadia—"

The old man interrupted the doctor: "I don't *ever* want to hear you say that name again—do you understand?"

The doctor trembled, not knowing what he'd done wrong. Silence riddled the small room. "I'm sorry. I just thought that she might be a family member."

Confused, Anahid took her husband's arms off the doctor.

"Armen, please calm down. Who is Nadia?" she asked.

The rest of the family looked on, just as confused. There was no one in the family named Nadia, nor had anyone heard of her. Armen turned and faced them, examining the situation. It was a long, terrifying silence. No one spoke.

No one dared.

"Nadia does not exist. Forget her," exclaimed Armen. "My brother was talking nonsense."

"Armen, please. Who is Nadia?" asked Anahid again, knowing by now when her husband wasn't telling the truth.

"Leave it alone!" he repeated, slightly raising his voice. "I mean it!"

It was obvious that the mere mention of the name had

made poor old Armen angry. He thus made his way back towards the door and left, letting it close loudly behind him. In the hallway, he stood, breathing heavily. His heart raced, his mind narrowed, and he carefully planned his next moves. He thought about what to do, what to say, even how to say it. He thought, understanding the effect his actions could deliver. Then, he made a decision.

He had to do it.

Without explanation, the rest of the family exchanged glances of bewilderment.

A few moments later, Armen then reentered the room, armed with the greatest kept secret of his life. He glared at each of the family members individually—his granddaughter, his two grandsons, their parents. He studied their faces, analyzing the situation.

"Vartan, my brother, your great uncle, and I," he pointed to the teenagers, "made a promise, an oath, to never speak these words."

He was nervous and spoke deeply.

"With the telling of this story, I, unfortunately, am going to break that oath," he curled his lips and breathed through his nostrils, "because at this moment in our lives, I believe it is fitting for the circumstance."

There was another long, distressing silence. The family members stood as stone statues with faces as solemn as the old professor's condition, gawking at this man speaking with such control. They opened their ears, not once blinking, and provided him with their fullest attention, unknowingly preparing themselves for the story they didn't want to hear.

Part I
June 1913

Chapter 4

"The best place to begin a story, I suppose," old Armen said slowly, "is at the beginning. The day was June 21st of the year 1913.

"I was fourteen years old.

"I lived with my family in a small, clay-brick house at the base of a large hill in the ancient Armenian province of Kharpert. As farmers, we lived several kilometers west of the main city, also named Kharpert, in just one of over three hundred fifty small villages. Surrounding us were the Taurus Mountains, placing the main city on a large hill and making our province very mountainous with frequently rolling hills and deep valleys. The Eastern Euphrates River, or as we called it, the Murad River, flowed through from the east, and its many tributaries provided the many farms with an everlasting fertility.

"At the time, the entire region, including five other Armenian provinces comprised of two million Armenians, was part of the Ottoman Empire. Together, we shared the same land—Turks, Armenians, and Kurds, living just as neighbors.

"June 21st, 1913.

"I remember this day as if the Lord never wanted me to forget. The sun was shining, the air was warm, and to me, it was perfect." Old Armen shrugged. "I can still remember it.

"My schooling for the year had ended, and the summer had begun, so I occupied myself by helping my father with work around our farm. We owned typical animals for farms in our area—two oxen, rabbits, cows, goats, horses, and a few sheep. We also grew typical crops—wheat, some vegetables, but mostly early harvest grapes and mid-season apricots. I particularly loved the apricot trees," he said, raising his pointer finger in the air, emphasizing the word *particularly*.

"My God, I loved those apricots. It seemed as though I would end up eating more than I picked, and all it did was infuriate my father. As you might expect, on this day in June, I was up in an apricot tree, enjoying the view of our land, eating those delicious orange fruits. With an apricot in one hand and another loosely gripping a horizontal branch, I relaxed, scoping out the farm. I watched as the sheep roamed collectively, as the oxen spun their tails while eating their feed. I heard a horse neigh and the goats speak freely. I saw the rabbits jump and the birds fly. Feeling empowered from my vantage point on the southwestern corner of our land, I smiled, then took a bite, and leaned the back of my head against the tallest branch to relax, to take a break from the dry heat of the afternoon. As I stared up at the white cotton clouds, I filled my lungs with the crisp summer air and slowly let it out." He slowly shifted his eyes to the floor.

"If I had known that that would've been one of the last great summer days I'd spend there, I would have taken that breath a little slower," he finished, looking back up.

"Then, as if a mirage, I saw my brother, Vartan, galloping in the distance, coming back from college. With his head wrapped to protect himself from the scorching sun and his old canvas bags draped across the horse's body, he sat high on that horse as it galloped steadily. The way he sat with his back straight, reigns in hand, confidently looking in all directions, fully aware of his surroundings, made him look just like a hero. Yes, just like a hero, like the ones we read about in our folk tales. I never told him that, but indeed he was."

"Mama!" I screamed from the tree as I hurriedly climbed my way down. "I see Vartan! Vartan's here! Mama, Mama! Vartan's back!" I screamed again as I ran to the house.

My mother, who was preparing dinner with my younger sister, little Margaret, as we called her, stepped outside and peered into the distance. Little Margaret followed closely behind.

"*My God!* Vartan! He's a day early, just in time for his birthday!" she said in Armenian as she hugged little Margaret.

"Tevos, come quick! Vartan's back!" she said, turning her head while keeping her eyes fixed on her son.

My father calmly walked over from behind the house to his direction. He slowly nodded his head in approval and started wiping his hands with a rag from his back pocket.

"Mom, did you hear that?" my mother yelled to my grandmother inside the house. "Vartan's back!"

My grandmother, on my mother's side, peacefully sat in her chair, wearing her one-piece nightgown, with her wrinkly hands lying across her lap. Always a source of great wisdom, her emotions were hardened, yet she was very sincere. She would tell us her stories of the wars before so that we'd never forget. We never bothered writing them down, but by God we never forgot those stories. At seventy-two years old, however, the summer heat posed too much of a threat to her health, and so she spent most of her summers under the roof.

"*Ayo, ayo*, I heard you," she acknowledged in Armenian with her raspy voice, feeling insulted that everyone thought that she had a hearing problem just because she was old. "Tell him to come and give me a kiss."

With a grandiose smile, Vartan rode the horse to the edge of the porch, then promptly jumped off. As his feet hit the ground, his worn leather boots made a deep imprint in the soft dirt, and he unraveled his head wrap, revealing his long dark-brown hair.

"Hi, Mama!" he said with his low voice as he kissed our mother on both cheeks, a customary Armenian greeting.

"My son, happy birthday! It's so good to see you!" she exclaimed.

"Margaret!" said Vartan as he kissed the top of her head.

"Are you hungry, Vartan? Margaret and I made *lavash*, *pilav*, and lamb."

"Yes, it was a long ride from the college," he answered as he turned around to his father and respectably shook his hand.

"Hi, *Hyreeg!*" he said.

"Vartan, *dughas,* my son, happy birthday! What happened, they don't give you razors at school?" he joked as he pulled the hairs of Vartan's thickly bearded face.

"I spent a long time studying and didn't have time to shave," he said with a smile.

"And what's with this hair?" my father continued mercilessly.

"Vartan!" I screamed as I ran in for a hug. "Nice beard!" I laughed. "You look like a castaway!"

We all laughed together, enjoying the wonderful surprise of his arrival. It was at least six months since anybody in my family had seen him.

"*Medzmama* wants you to give her a kiss. She's inside," my mother mentioned.

"All right," Vartan agreed as he began to untie his bags from the horse.

"Vartan, don't worry, I'll get those," I volunteered, wanting to help him out, understanding that his journey from school wasn't exactly comfortable.

"Thanks, Armen, you really are useful!" he responded with a smile as he patted me on the back and boldly took his steps into the house.

We all followed him inside.

"Today," I thought, "is Vartan's day."

"*Medzmama!*" Vartan said cheerfully as he went over to kiss our grandmother.

"Vartan, my grandson, I've missed you dearly," she said. "Happy birthday. How was school?"

"It was great! I had a great time!"

"Good," she affirmed.

"Okay, please, let's sit down and celebrate!" started my father, making it obvious that he was hungry.

Hurriedly, we situated ourselves at the dinner table—a gift. We then bowed our heads, and my father began with the *Hayr Mer,* the Lord's Prayer. When we finished, Vartan gazed up at the food. Like a wolf stumbling upon a herd of sheep with broken legs, his eyes grew hungry. He didn't know where to begin.

"This amazing smell, Hasmig," started my father, "is enough to attract the neighbors. But if they come over, there won't be anything left for hungry Vartan!" he finished with his way of saying thank you.

"It's good for the body and soul," my mother answered with a smile.

She then stood up and grabbed the plate of lamb, offering Vartan the first piece. She then poured him a glass of fresh milk I'd taken from the cows earlier that day.

"So, I want to hear about school," began my father. "What did you learn?"

"Well, I don't even know where to begin," responded Vartan with a full mouth. "I had this astronomy professor, Dr. Green, who came over from America. He's a bit on the heavy side, but, man, is he smart! He taught me everything there is to know about the sky and the stars, and he made it so interesting. Most of my classmates complain about him, saying he's boring, but I think he's so interesting."

"Aha! That's my boy!" said my father in Armenian.

He looked over at my mother, who smiled at Vartan.

"Why do you look homeless?" asked little Margaret.

"Margaret," interrupted my mother in annoyance, "don't be so rude! He always has a home here, and he knows it." She turned back to Vartan. "Vartan, that is very good news."

As we sat, enjoying each other's company, we continued to eat. At that meal, like every meal, we laughed, we told stories, and we argued, just as any big, happy family would, sharing the moments that made life worthwhile. At that healthy young age, I even remember thinking that the only thing missing from my life was an array of beautiful women.

Old Armen's grandsons in the hospital room smiled, knowing that he had hit the nail right on the head. Anahid, his wife, glanced at Armen with a face of disapproval.

"Anyway," old Armen continued, "at the end of the meal, my father sat back in his chair, unable to stand, and placed his napkin on his plate."

"*Park Asdoodzoh*," he whispered, meaning "thanks be to God."

"Hasmig, that was incredible," he continued.

"*Ayo*, Mama, that was delicious. Thank you," I elaborated, with Vartan and little Margaret soon following my words.

"*Tserkerut talar, akhcheegus*," complimented my grandmother, meaning "may God bless your hands, my daughter."

"You're welcome, but little Margaret did most of the work," she explained, passing a smile to little Margaret, who was only nine.

"Armen," my mother asked, "would you please bring a towel from the kitchen?"

I looked at her, confused, not knowing why she needed a towel, soon realizing that she had said *the code*.

I immediately sprung up and left the table. A few moments later, I returned behind Vartan, with a decorated pie and two brightly lit candles on top.

"Well, well, what's this?" exclaimed my father.

Vartan turned around and saw the pie. Surprised, he smiled a large, wondrous smile. Happily, we then began singing Happy Birthday in Armenian.

"Vartan! Happy birthday, my son!" my father chirped after we finished with a pat on Vartan's back.

We all clapped our hands, cheering in celebration, as Vartan, for a moment, closed his eyes to make a wish, then blew out the candles. I never knew what his wish was, but knowing him, I could've made a pretty good guess.

"Tevos," my grandmother reminded, "his gifts."

"Oh, yes," said my father as he stood up and walked to the back room.

A moment later, he came back with two gifts. One large and one small. One formless and one rectangular, each wrapped with brown paper and tied with twine.

He handed the larger, formless one to Vartan.

"Oh, wow!" he exclaimed.

"Open it!" I said excitedly, not knowing about the second.

As if it were going to wither away into ash if he didn't do it fast enough, Vartan ripped through the brown paper. Throwing it aside, he revealed the contents: a black suit jacket with matching black pants, both made of wool.

"Oh, thanks!" he said to everyone.

As we smiled and laughed, my mother gently rubbed his back as a way to congratulate him.

At the time, to own a suit was the true mark of a gentleman and professional, and Vartan knew this. Standing up, he put the jacket on over his shirt; it fit him better than his shoes. I had to admit, he looked pretty good in that jacket.

"*Parov vayleh*," said my mother, meaning "enjoy it well."

"And now open the second gift, Vartan," said my father.

Apparently, only my father and grandmother knew about the second gift because the rest of us helped with the suit.

Vartan looked at my father, then began tearing open the brown paper wrapping of the rectangular box.

"Ah, ah," my father instructed, stopping Vartan, "slowly."

Trying to contain himself, Vartan finished unwrapping the gift, tuned to a speed that satisfied my father. Beneath the paper, he exposed a box, maroon in color, about a forearm's length. Confused, Vartan and I leaned in, filled with growing curiosity. Vartan then lifted the lid and placed it to the side. He turned to my father, who stood collectively, twirling the tip of his mustache—a sign that he knew what he was doing. Finally, as Vartan removed the thin wax paper that covered the object, I instantly locked my eyes on something shiny.

Something powerful.

Something that I didn't fully understand.

A dagger.

My mother took one good look at it. Her eyes also widened.

"Tevos!" she exclaimed. "How did you get this? What if they find ou—"

"Hasmig, don't worry about that. He's sixteen now. He's old enough. I think it's about time," my father replied.

My mother sighed worriedly, but trusted his judgment.

"Whoa," breathed Vartan as he partially took the dagger out of its darkened leather sheath and held it up with both hands, examining the unique design. Suitable only for a man of high stature, the polished steel blade, razor sharp on both edges, and its intricately carved, ivory-colored handle echoed in the light of the room. I couldn't unlock my eyes from it.

"With that dagger, my son, you will be a great man," prophesized my father. "But, before you are," he continued, "someone has to teach you how to use it," he finished as he grabbed the dagger and sheath away from him.

"Hey," said Vartan.

"Soon enough, my son. Soon enough."

<u>5</u>

The following morning, I awoke and dragged my tired body into the kitchen. With one eye open, I peeked at the brightness of the morning as the rays of light shone in through the small kitchen window to where my father and Vartan sat at the table, eating breakfast. Having shaved off his beard, Vartan wore a new bald face, his new black suit, complemented with a white underlying dress shirt, and a black tie.

"He looks very sharp," I thought tiredly, "but why is he wearing his new suit?"

"Aha, good. You're up," my father began. "Hurry and eat. We're leaving now."

"Where are we going?"

"Church!" he replied. "Now hurry up."

My eyes widened. I had done it again. Not only had I failed to wake up in time, but I still wasn't dressed.

"Where's everyone else?" I asked, hoping that they shared my carelessness.

"They're waiting outside," Vartan answered.

Peering out the kitchen window, I confirmed the ladies were seated patiently on the porch on that beautiful Sunday morning, simply waiting, ready in their church dresses.

In an immediate state of panic, I thus grabbed a large piece of bread from Vartan's plate, quickly stuffed it into my mouth, then jumped out the door and ran the thirty meters to the stone well outside and splashed my face and hair with water, all in an attempt to get ready. Dripping wet, I ran back inside and back to my room, passing the kitchen table along the way. I then slipped on my black socks, jumped into my black cotton pants, spun into a tan shirt, and snapped over a pair of suspenders just as the bread fully dissolved in my mouth.

"All right, let's go!" I said out loud as I ran out the door for the third time, passing little Margaret on the porch, who, annoyed that she had to wait for me, watched me run back and forth. In the time that it took me to get ready, my mother, father, grandmother, and Vartan had moved onto the ox-drawn cart—a shallow, rectangular box with four wooden wheels and two rows of old boards nailed to thin, vertical pieces of the same wood.

I jumped onto the cart from behind, joining the rest of my family, thinking for sure that my tardiness was going to be the topic of argument on the way. Little Margaret, who had caught up behind me, extended her little arm, and I leaned over and helped her up. I then sat on the right side next to my brother, facing my mother, grandmother, and now, little Margaret.

"Good. *Now* is everybody ready?" my father asked, sitting at the front like a concierge.

"Yes, finally," said Vartan as he turned to look at me.

"All right then. Let's go."

Lifting the leather harness, my father snapped it down, sending the signal to the two oxen to begin walking. With that, the cart jerked forward, and we began to move.

Ears still wet, I slumped my posture and took in a few breaths, trying to settle the chaos within, even feeling my heartbeat mellow to an acceptable rate.

Vartan leaned in towards me.

"You smell like the oxen," he commented.

When Vartan was away at college, it was my responsibility to safeguard the well-being of our two oxen. Fully understanding their importance to our family's livelihood and to our survival, I took great care of them, ensuring they were always fed, healthy, and comfortable. I even personally groomed them twice a week. These horned beasts, both about the same massive size, were crucial to the efficiency of our farm; they pulled the plow, carried heavy loads, and took us into and out of the city, since our only horse wasn't capable of pulling all six of us for a half-an-hour's ride. Each of us, therefore, owed it to them, and for that reason alone, I took Vartan's statement as a compliment and smiled.

"So, are you excited for church?" I asked Vartan, quickly turning the tables and putting him on the spot.

"What? Why would I be excited for church?" he replied, playing dumb.

I looked at him and just smiled. "Isn't someone going to be there? Someone you haven't seen in a while? Someone you know?" I finished with a wink.

"Who? I know a lot of people," he generalized while resisting the urge to return the smile.

I laughed as I nudged him with my elbow.

"Be quiet, Armen. I know what you're doing," he whispered as he looked at the rest of our family, who were engaged in their own conversations, except for my grandmother, who looked back at Vartan's rugged yet refined character—his dark and youthfully long and wavy hair, combed sloppily to the side, and his slightly chiseled cheekbones.

"Vartan, you look so handsome without a beard." She smiled.

"Thanks, *Medzmama*," he replied. "It's the suit."

"I agree," I commented, "because it's definitely not his face!"

My grandmother laughed and looked away to the distant horizon.

"You're cutting it close, Armen," Vartan warned me.

"Big deal if *Medzmama* finds out. What's she going to do?" I asked.

"She won't do anything," he said. "It's just private."

"Whatever, all someone has to do is look at you to figure it out. I'm sure everybody already knows, but nobody is saying anything."

Vartan looked at me for a few seconds. "That's not true. The oxen still smell better."

I didn't respond. If that was the best he could do, I

decided to abandon our lazy argument. Now uncaring and distracted, I occupied myself at the back of the cart and watched as the dirt road to church lengthened as we crawled over it, creating a small trail of dust that would eventually settle over the rolling green pastures. Like a net, the natural scenery around it captured my fullest attention. Something about the beauty mesmerized me, the soft, dancing slopes, the green grass, the dark-blue sky above. The peace of it all. For that moment, as the uplifting and warm breeze moved around my body, I closed my eyes and listened as the wooden wheels turned and felt each rock we passed over.

Simplicity.

I had found it.

Once I opened my eyes, I faced forward and watched as we neared the landmark of the area—an old bare tree, uniformly thick, that, long ago, bore fruit. Stocky and twisted, it stood alone near the edge of a pasture where a herd of sheep flocked with their shepherds—five Turkish boys that I knew.

I stood up, keeping my balance, and waved to them. From atop their donkeys, with their long, thin sticks in hand, they waved back, smiling, happy to see us once again.

As Armenians who spoke the Armenian language, ate Armenian food, partook in Armenian culture, and lived in our own granted state of Armenia, it was still common for us to also speak the Ottoman Turkish language and adopt parts of the Turkish culture. This came as a direct result of the Moslem Turks and Christian Armenians readily intertwining their everyday lives within the Ottoman Empire.

Thrilled to have seen my Turkish friends once again, I sat back down with satisfaction as we continued to crawl over the scattered stones of the road until we arrived at the edge of the churchyard, to *Soorp Asdvadzadzin*, our church.

"Ohh-kay," said my father as the ox-cart came to a halt.

He then stepped off and attached the harness to a wooden post. Vartan and I also leaped off the cart, then helped our ladies down.

"Armen!" I heard from the distance.

I turned around and focused my eyes.

"Hey, hey, Tavit! Good to see you!" I said as I greeted my closest friend with a hug.

"Good to see you too, Armen!" he replied.

Tavit was a shorter kid, not too skinny, but not yet fat. He had a loud, slightly high-pitched voice. He and I had been friends since we were children, and he quickly became the best friend I had. His father, Garo, and my father were also in the wine business together, inheriting it from their fathers and their fathers' fathers. For generations, my family would grow the grapes, and Tavit's family would turn them into wine to make what most considered the best wine in Kharpert.

"*Parev,* Garo," said my father to Tavit's father, saying "hello" in Armenian.

"Tevos, my good friend, how's everything? You look healthy," he noted as he looked up at my father.

Garo was a man of short stature. He was stocky with a very rich personality, always warm and inviting, making it uncommon to feel out of place or uncomfortable around him. Just as with his personality, he was also smooth with his words and was quick to compliment you. I always liked to blame the wine for that, but I knew his charisma came straight from the heart.

"What can I say? God has been good to me," my father responded.

"Good! Hi, Hasmig." Garo turned to greet my mother as he respectfully removed his rounded top hat and gave my mother a kiss on each cheek. "Hi, Taqoohi, you look gorgeous!" he said with a smile to my grandmother.

"Ohh, stop it!" She blushed. "Thank you, Garo!"

"So, everyone is doing well then?" he asked collectively, as he placed his hat back onto his thinning hair.

My father nodded.

"Yes, everyone is doing very well, thank you. How is Ana?" asked my mother.

"She's doing great. She's around here somewhere, most likely inside. Shall we go find her?"

"Let's go," agreed my father, pointing the way.

With Tavit next to his father, me next to Tavit, and Vartan next to me, we all began walking in a straight line over the plush grass of the churchyard towards *Soorp Asdvadzadzin*. The dark-blue sky and bright green of the hills fell in perfect contrast with the stained gray stones of its walls. Der Kourken Hovagimian, our priest, organized the task of building it entirely with his hands from the rocks of the region. At each approach, I marveled at its boldness and complexity, the flawlessly rounded steeple of remarkable height, the glass inlay above the carved wooden doors, and the spacious setting. It truly was a great accomplishment of our people—a structure made to be impenetrable.

"Vartan, come here," my grandmother said from behind us, "let me hold your arm."

With a quick step back, Vartan extended his left elbow for her. She lightly grasped his upper arm.

"She loves me more," Vartan whispered to me up ahead.

"I heard that," said my grandmother, "and I love both of you equally. Armen, let me hold your arm as well," she continued wittingly.

I ran to her left side and extended my elbow. She grabbed it, and I gave Vartan my winning smile just as my father approached Der Kourken.

"*Ohrnyal Der, Der Hayr!*" my father said, expressing the words of respect to clergy, meaning "bless me, father."

"*Asdvadz ortneh*, my son," said Der Kourken, responding with "let God bless you," as he extended his arm through the long, black sleeve of his long, black cloak, firmly shaking my father's hand.

We then all greeted Der Kourken in the same respectful fashion.

"Welcome, everybody, I'm happy to see you all again today," he said as his long, black beard moved with his chin as he spoke. "And welcome back, Vartan!"

"Thank you, *Der Hayr*," responded my brother.

Just then, I felt a small tug on my shirt from little

Margaret. She wanted to tell me something, so I leaned down to hear what she had to say.

"Armen," she whispered into my ear, "his beard scares me."

I laughed. "Okay, just don't say that out loud."

"School is good?" Der Kourken asked, not hearing my sister's remark.

"Yes, school is going great," explained Vartan. "I still have a few years left; then I'll get my degree."

"Very good!" he responded. "Come now, let's begin the service."

<u>6</u>

"Armenian church services were, and still are, very customary and extremely traditional. As devout Christians, Armenians had, and still have, the utmost respect for their religion and clergy. In 301 A.D., Armenia became the first nation in the history of the world to adopt Christianity as her national religion," old Armen explained as he looked at each of his grandchildren seated in the hospital room. "Did you know that?" he asked one of the boys.

Old Armen's grandson nodded, "Yes."

"You did?" he asked with a smile. "Wow, I just learned that yesterday."

They laughed as he picked up a small foam cup and took a sip of water.

"Good," he expelled. "So, where was I?"

"You were walking with your grandmother and Der Kourken to the church," summarized one of his granddaughters.

"Very good, yes," he responded excitedly.

. . . .

We followed Der Kourken to the entrance of the church. There, Vartan and I left our grandmother with our mother and held open the two heavy wooden doors to allow the congregation of people, all from various neighboring villages, to fill its walls, which held about three hundred people comfortably. As each person passed, we noted their exceptionally proper clothes and tastes in fashion, the perfectly fitted suits, the ornate dresses, the jewelry, and the gold, so much gold. Finally then, as the last person entered, we, too, stepped inside and made the sign of the cross, slowly letting the thick brown doors close behind us.

Inside, the sanctuary was a well-respected and dimly lit space echoing with the angelic hymns of the service already in effect. We had no electricity, and there were no pews, so we all sat on simple cushions on the solid stone floor. The only source of light came from the high windows and hanging candles that painted the inner gray stone of the walls with an elegantly dull glow. On each side of the solid marvel, just under the windows, were two large fabric murals of Christ—one of him bearing his cross and the other of his birth. And facing east, opposite the entrance, hung a crucifix directly above the altar where Der Kourken stood with his deacons.

The ambiance, decorated with a lingering scent of rose incense, humbled even the anxious spirit. It was a church built to last forever.

Near the front, I helped my grandmother at her spot, making sure she was comfortable by supporting her with additional cushions. My mother and Ana, Garo's wife, sat next to my grandmother, happy to have found each other. Over the years, they too had developed a friendship as secure as the structure in which they sat. I then took a seat between Vartan and Tavit near the carpeted aisle down the center and exhaled as I sat and peered over to Vartan, who was looking around the congregation as if he had lost something.

"She's not here yet?" I whispered with a lean smile on my face.

"Who's not here yet?" he asked, playing dumb still.

"Why are you looking around so much?" I asked.

"I just want to see who's here and who's not."

"Are you looking for anyone in particular?" I asked.

"No, I just want to see if my friends are here."

"Vartan, do I have to remind you?" I said. "You don't have any friends."

He looked at me, unamused, as the service continued.

For that entire first half, until the sermon, Vartan continuously and subtly searched around the church, clearly not paying attention. Indeed, at our age, church was tiresome, and with the start of the sermon, nearly an hour later, I, too, had become just as restless as him.

"My friends, my family," Der Kourken opened, "I welcome you once again to the house of the great Lord, our God.

"Today, I would like to emphasize the importance of God and what we call His plan, what we identify as fate—the ill-perceived notion that makes your life predetermined and thus unchangeable. So what then, if not that, *is* fate? What is it *really*? Fate, I answer you, is simply a fresh canvas that God has issued to each of you, an unfilled, blank map upon which He allows you to draw your own *personal* direction, your own *unique* course, to live your life and *build* who you want to become. He does this by providing, by planting, only the tools that you *need*, nothing more, nothing less, to fulfill the person you were always meant to be. So, look around you, and ask yourself, which tools can I use today to make myself better for tomorrow?"

At the time, with other things on my mind, I wasn't exactly sure what Der Kourken said or what exactly he meant by "tools." What did these tools look like? I tried focusing on the rest of the sermon to gain a further understanding, but as curious as I claimed to be, I couldn't do it. I couldn't sit still any longer. My attention was spent. So, I began peering around the congregation instead as the sermon now lingered in my background. I looked around at the people. I saw their faces. Their focused, attentive faces. As cynical as it seemed, I quickly realized that I had grown tired of the same, mundane pace. It then dawned on me that I needed something different—an unachievable adventure.

I thus peered at Vartan, who, miraculously, seemed to be paying attention. I then peered to my right, again towards the elderly and their families. I peered up at the domed ceiling of smoothed stone and down to my feet. Then, with a slight turn of my head, I peered at the entrance, just as a glowing sliver reflected into my eye, catching my intrigued mind. The door was opening. Someone was late. The sliver then grew as the gap widened, spilling the natural white light into our church.

"Vartan," I whispered as I tugged on his shirt, excited to have found something different to focus on. "There she is."

"Who?" he asked.

Covertly, I pointed towards the entrance. Vartan turned his head around like an owl to the newcomers. A family of five. Among them, a girl of just fifteen years, walking in with her parents and two younger sisters, obviously flustered. It didn't take long for my brother's world to stop spinning. His eyes became as if he alone had discovered a ship of gold, and he didn't blink, not even once. Knowing her faults, the girl walked with her family through the church looking for an empty spot on the floor. Vartan's eyes followed her every step until they sat down on the other side, at which time he continued to stare. Then, as an ironic meeting, she peeked our way, briefly making eye contact with my brother. Upon the awkward exchange, he quickly spun his head back around and faced the altar, feeling his rapid heartbeat as he swallowed his saliva. Vartan wasn't scared of anything, yet this one girl made his knees tremble.

I leaned in to him. "Vartan, she looks good today," I whispered.

He didn't respond.

"Are you going to talk to her?" I asked.

"Yeah, when are you going to ask her to marry you?" asked Tavit, joining the conversation.

"Where did you come from?" Vartan asked.

"He has to talk to her first, Tavit," I reasoned, answering his question.

"When the time is right, I will," Vartan answered cautiously.

"But you said that last time," I responded.

Vartan grunted. "I know what I'm doing."

"Boys," my mother whispered sternly, "listen to the sermon. It's important."

My father leaned backwards to let her speak.

"Stop talking," she finished as she placed a finger over her lips.

We looked at each other in silence as Der Kourken continued. Thus, Vartan sat, relieved that he didn't have to succumb to any further interrogation by Tavit and me. From that moment until the end, there was absolutely nothing else on Vartan's mind. Each time I glanced at him, he wore the exact same expression—a blank face, head cocked to one side, eyes wide open, body not moving. He wasn't looking up; he wasn't looking down; he was simply staring… into nothing. As life's novice, I figured that this was how people looked to the rest of us when they were in love—crazy. Only God knew what Vartan was planning in his head or how far he'd taken his imagination. As old Armenian tradition had it, we all knew that when a man found a woman of interest, it became customary for him to focus all his efforts on anything that would impress her, seldom leaving room for dating and moving straight into marriage. Thus, deep down, Vartan knew that I was right; if he wanted to get something, he needed to say something as a start.

I didn't blame him, though. She really was gorgeous.

7

At the end of the service, the families of the congregation slowly began to spill outside. We were, as all Armenian villages were, a very tightly knit community. Everyone enjoyed everyone else's company, and for the most part, we all knew each other fairly well.

"Tevos!" I heard someone say from across the church. "Tevos, how are you?"

The distinct voice grew louder. It was Ara, another

family friend, and I immediately knew, with the sound of his voice, what the future was going to hold; he was going to come over with his wife and three daughters, and Vartan was going to panic.

"I'm great, Ara, thank you," answered my father.

"Good," he responded. "Hasmig, how are you today?" he continued, kissing my mother on both cheeks.

"Good, Ara," she replied, then turned to Ara's wife. "Mary, good to see you," she said.

Waiting next to my parents, watching them socialize, I felt abandoned without Tavit, who had wandered away with his family somewhere in the churchyard, leaving me with Vartan, the man of hopeless romance, the man of a simple desire, the man who was in love with Ara's eldest daughter.

"Wow, look how beautiful your daughters are!" my mother complimented Mary.

"Oh, thank you," she responded as she put her hand on the head of her littlest one, younger even than little Margaret. "They're a handful, though."

Ara, hearing his wife's remark, cut from the conversation with my father and peered over, rolling his eyes.

"I think I'm going deaf!" he explained. "Where's my dress? Who took my shoes? The drama! It never stops!" he acted out comically. "God gave me one brain, and that's barely enough for me," he finished, pointing to his head.

We laughed easily, knowing he spoke only the truth.

"But they all help out in their own way," Mary added.

"That's true," Ara agreed. "They do help to cook the meals. I thank God for them every day because I figure that eight hands are better than two," he finished as he held out his hands. "They're actually quite good. Especially Nadia."

With that name, Vartan immediately awoke from his trance and shifted his attention to her like a wildly instinctual animal.

"That's very nice!" my mother praised with a smile. "Little Margaret helps me cook as well."

"Oh, Margaret!" said Mary.

Little Margaret smiled with a strong blush.

"Well, Tevos," said Ara, "it's time for us to move along. I'll be over later this afternoon. Please ready some bushels of apricots for me."

"Of course," my father reassured. "Why don't you bring the whole family over this time? Garo's will be over, too. The weather is ideal."

"Sure, that's a great idea. Mary, will that work?"

"Certainly," she agreed, smiling.

"Excellent then," he concluded as he extended his hand. "Come when you can."

"Of course." Ara shook my father's hand and turned around. "All right, ladies, let's get going."

"*Gu desnuveenk*, Hasmig," said Mary to my mother, meaning "see you later."

"*Ayo*, I'll see you soon."

They waved farewell to each other, and Ara commanded his troupe to their own separate beat. The best part about Ara was that he looked just like my father, except that he had small, gold-rimmed glasses. He had a long mustache just like his, and he would also twirl the tips to a point. He was definitely not as serious as my father, but he came pretty close. It was clear that the girls in his family had softened him up.

Thus, after the parting, we made our way towards our ox-cart, ready to go back home. By this time, the sun was directly overhead.

Mid-day.

At the cart, I helped my mother and grandmother up, then pulled up little Margaret. Vartan, my older brother, the lover, then climbed in and sat, not saying a single word. My mother looked at him, smiled, and then looked at my grandmother, who also smiled. They weren't dumb; they knew exactly what was going on. Then, after unhitching the harness, my father climbed in the front, exhaling as he sat down. He turned to look at me.

"Armen, when we get home, I want you fill three bushels of apricots for Ara and his family. And Vartan," he continued, followed by a pause, waiting for a response. "Vartan," he repeated, turning his head more to get a better look.

"Huh? Yeah," he replied, slowly coming back to life.

"I know that Garo will want a sample of the grapes, so I want you to get two bushels for him. Do you hear me?"

"Yes," he responded. "I understand."

"Okay, good. I won't tell you twice."

He then turned back around and snapped down the leather harness. With a small jerk of the cart, we started moving. On the ride back home, there wasn't much talking, simply an admiration of the scenic route, an absorption of the beauty, until, a while later, Vartan broke the silence.

"Armen!" he said in an unnaturally excited tone as if coming to an epiphany. "I have an idea! I'll pick the apricots, and you can pick the grapes!"

Surprised by the request, I looked at him, confused by his severely delayed, sudden outburst of energy.

"What?" my father asked. "What did you say?"

"Nothing, *Hyreeg*, I just told Armen that I want to pick the apricots," he repeated.

"Listen, as long as I have two bushels of grapes and three bushels of apricots ready before Garo or Ara get to the house, I don't care who does it. Work it out with your brother," he replied.

"Armen, I'm going to pick the apricots, all right?" Vartan reiterated.

"What? No! *Hyreeg* said that I'm picking them, and so that's what I'm doing," I responded sternly.

"Yeah, but he said he doesn't care who does it! The grapes are fun!"

For the obvious reason, Vartan wanted to pick the apricots. Nadia loved them and I knew that. I honestly wanted to help him, but now, for me, for my own sake, it had transformed into a matter of principle. Vartan couldn't just tell me what to do. He knew that I loved the apricot trees, and so did my father. That's why he'd asked me to do it. Besides, picking three bushels of apricots was the same amount of work as picking two bushels of grapes, minus the flies or the mosquitoes, or whatever those annoying insects were.

"You can pick the grapes this time. It's not a problem, just once!" argued Vartan.

If he had said please or even asked me nicely, I *might* have considered it. I, however, stood my ground evermore stubbornly. "No, I'm picking the apricots, and you're picking the grapes. So stop asking me!"

"Why won't you let me?"

"Why do you want to pick the apricots all of a sudden, huh?"

"I just want to!" he explained unconvincingly. "It's different."

"Well, I just want to, *too*!" I retorted with sarcasm, hence perpetuating the argument back and forth until our voices grew louder.

From the lead, the oxen let out their long grunts of dissatisfaction, and little Margaret laughed as a result. Even they were growing tired of our childish bickering. Having just turned sixteen, Vartan should *not* have been acting like this.

"Why don't you both pick the apricots and you both pick the grapes?" little Margaret intervened.

"What? Why would we do that? That's double the work," Vartan responded.

"You fool, you're in school, and you don't know that it's not double the work?" I yelled.

"It's double the work because I know I'll be picking and you'll be eating!"

"I… that's not…" I stuttered.

With nothing to say to that, with no logical rebuttal, I knew he had me. I couldn't argue it because it was true.

My mother laughed a little. "He's got a point, Armen," she said.

"Whatever, I'm still picking the apricots," I mumbled.

"No, you are not!" Vartan argued relentlessly, prolonging the endless argument.

Growing tired of this, I nobly decided to be the bigger

man and sat, biting my tongue, even as we passed by the Turkish boys herding their sheep. I was so angry that I didn't even want to say hello. For the rest of the way to our house, this was how it played out. Little Margaret sat under my mother's arm, my grandmother sat next to her, and I sat across from them, next to my mortal enemy, who also happened to be my brother.

"It's so silent back there!" said my father some time later, trying to bring some light on the argument he could've resolved but didn't.

"They ran out of things to say," commented little Margaret, throwing in her day's worth.

My father laughed. "Oh really? Vartan, Armen, is this true? Have you come to an agreement?"

"Yes," I stated firmly, "I'm going to pick the apricots, and Vartan is going to pick the grapes!"

"No, you're not!" Vartan exclaimed.

"Oh boy," said little Margaret as she turned to my mother. "Mama, do something. They're not going to stop."

"*Hokis*, they're big boys. I think they can come to an agreement like adults," she explained as she turned to us when she said "adults."

We got the hint. Well, at least *I* did.

As the ox-cart came to a slow halt at our home, my father jumped off to secure the leather harness to the wooden post near the barn. He began to detach the oxen, and I quickly jumped down to help my mother, grandmother, and little Margaret. Vartan, though, I noticed, sat suspiciously quiet in his spot. Not knowing what to make of it, I assumed that I had won and that he'd given up.

I should've never assumed that.

Casually, with the three ladies in front of me, I began my walk towards the house. I wasn't tired like I usually was after church; the argument had gotten my blood to boil. I was on edge. My plan for the day was to go inside the house to change into some work clothes and begin picking. Simple. After all, my father wanted the apricots as soon as possible. We had guests coming over. Barely passing the front door, I thus stopped to look at the rows of apricot trees not even fifty yards in front of me. Taking in a breath of fresh air, I closed my eyes in an attempt to calm down so I could relax in the comfort of those magnificent trees. A faint screaming sound, however, approaching from behind me, interrupted my serene moment. Opening my eyes in confusion, I realized that the scream was growing louder, and it sounded angry... very angry. I curiously turned around just in time just to see Vartan lower his shoulder into my gut and tackle me to the ground.

"Uff!" I exhaled as my back hit the dirt surface like a sledgehammer.

"I'm picking the apricots!" he yelled as I tried to catch my breath.

"Vartan!" I screamed. "No!"

The winning principle had now completely changed.

"Mama! They're fighting!" little Margaret notified my mother.

Turning around, my mother saw us on the ground, rolling in our church clothes. My grandmother put her hands over her mouth in disbelief.

"Tevos!" my mother gasped. "Tevos, come quick!"

My father looked over from the barn and saw us on the ground. He threw down the tools in his hand and sternly paced towards us.

"Tevos! Do something!" my mother exclaimed, pointing to us.

Calmly, my father raised his palm in the air and shortened his face as if the sun had suddenly become too bright.

"Hasmig, let it be. Let them get it out of their system. This is the only way they're going to solve this," he said.

"Tevos, but they're going to break a bone!" she exclaimed.

My father crossed one arm across his body and twirled the tip of his mustache with the other.

"If they do, then they must deal with the consequences of a broken bone," he answered, "but if it gets out of hand, I will take care of it."

Rolling and twisting on the ground, Vartan and I kicked up the dust as our appendages intertwined like noodles.

"You fight like a girl!" I mocked as the fight intensified.

"Shut up," he responded. "You're as weak as a worm."

Up until this point, we weren't throwing punches, just wrestling. We were young and inexperienced in nearly all aspects of being a man, especially fighting. Admittedly, I hadn't even planned to throw a punch, either, until Vartan's elbow hit my face. Whether or not it was intentional, I didn't care. It happened. So, with my back to the ground and Vartan on top of me with his head next to my shoulder, I tightened my right fist and punched Vartan square in the eye. From my angle, the impact didn't seem very strong, but it was enough to wake him up.

"You call that a punch?" he taunted, trying to intimidate me.

I didn't respond. At the current and unchanged position, with Vartan on top, I felt increasingly more vulnerable, so I decided to switch directions. Bringing my right knee up to his chest, I slid my hips out. I then grabbed his right wrist with my left hand and pulled it towards my body while moving my legs like a pair of scissors. This caused Vartan to roll over, and his weight pulled me on top of him. Our roles were now reversed. As soon as I gained the dominant position, overconfidence caused me to let down my guard.

Not knowing what to do next, I grabbed Vartan's collar, extended my arms, and lifted my head away from his body. This was a mistake because, before I had time to react, Vartan's fist was on a direct path straight to my nose, and I did nothing to defend it. I felt the fury of the punch rock through my head, and my brain froze the moment of impact, permanently etching the image of the scene into my skull. My eyes quickly felt like they were going to jump out of my body. My nose began throbbing, and I felt disoriented. I then rolled over onto my back and felt the blood dripping over my lip. Vartan then followed me and straddled my torso, firmly planting his knees on the ground. He then reached down and grabbed my collar just like I had grabbed his before. He raised his right fist to punch me again, and I raised my arms to defend myself.

"Stop!" I screamed. "Vartan, stop!"

Then, a terrifyingly familiar and burly arm, much more dangerous than my brother's, fell into the mix. With one hand, my father grabbed Vartan by the back collar and, with one effortless tug, forcefully lifted him up to his feet.

"Stand over there!" he yelled. "Don't you dare move!"

"Armen punched me!" he shouted, trying to blame me.

"You elbowed me!" I retorted, defending my actions.

I stood up and brushed the dirt off my body. There was blood on my shirt, and I wiped my face with the back of my hand. At that moment, to say that I burned with anger was an understatement, not because I'd lost the fight, but because Vartan had an obvious tactical advantage.

"Now *I* have had enough of this!" my father continued as he stood between us.

Vartan stood, breathing heavily. His face was swollen. His new suit, with the collar now raised, was covered in dirt. The white shirt underneath had drops of blood on it, probably mine. He looked like a herd of donkeys had trampled him.

Despite the circumstance, I smiled inside knowing that I was looking at the product of my defense system. I even remember imagining Vartan on display in a museum behind a caption that read *Armen's Wrath*, up until I felt the sweat drip down my face and a drop of blood fall from my nose, making me realize that I was in no better condition.

"Now, who can tell me why this is *still* an issue?" my father boomed.

"*Hyreeg!* The oxen aren't tied!" little Margaret screamed.

My father glanced behind him to the tired beasts and didn't really seem to care for the moment.

"The only reason Vartan wants to pick the apricots is because of Nadia!" I defended.

"That's not true!" Vartan exclaimed.

"I don't care what's true and what's not! I don't want any arguments, anymore! Vartan, *you* pick the apricots, and,

Armen, *you* pick the grapes," he pointed. "And before you do, Vartan," he continued, "I want you to get the oxen into the barn. And tie them up—*now!*"

"What? That's not fai—"

"Not another word, Armen. All you'll do is eat the apricots! Now get changed and go," commanded my father. "And don't eat the grapes, either!"

My father only yelled when he meant business. I knew I had gotten the short end of the stick, but I let it go and began my way towards the house while Vartan walked sternly in the opposite direction after the oxen. As I walked past the ladies, I kept my head down, sensing them gawking at my beaten face.

"You've really done it this time," little Margaret said as she shook her head.

"Armen, let me clean that up for you," offered my grandmother as she tried to examine my nose.

"No thanks, *Medzmama*," I murmured as I walked past her straight into my room. "I can do it."

Just inside, I took off my ruined church clothes and slipped on my work pants, then started towards the stone well outside, even forgetting to grab a shirt. It was too hot outside, and I was too angry to care. All I needed to do was get my work done before the guests arrived, and then I was free. That was my motivation. So, after I fully turned the crank to raise the bucket, I dunked in my hands and splashed my face, feeling the water drip down my face and over my mouth. It tasted like blood, and I watched as the pale red droplets fell from my chin.

"So, was it worth the fight?" my mother asked from behind me.

Surprised, I turned my head, wiping my face in the process.

"Yes," I defended. "I wasn't going to let Vartan walk over me for some stupid girl."

"Armen, that's not nice. You shouldn't judge someone. Later tonight, I want to speak to both of you," she said as she handed me a towel.

"Thanks."

"Don't worry, I'm going to tell Vartan the same thing," she reassured.

"Fine," I responded angrily.

"And put on a shirt, please," she added.

After a light pat on my back, my mother walked back to the house. I then turned around and placed my hands on the edge of the well, leaning my weight on my arms. I stared inside through the darkness and imagined the crisp, clean water at the bottom, wishing for its purity to somehow transfer into me. I then closed my eyes, took in a deep breath, and focused on the beat of my heart, followed by a small prayer to myself. Deep inside, I knew we could have avoided this unnecessary disturbance, but perhaps there was a reason to it. For the moment, though, it was over, and I felt good about that.

<u>8</u>

Our farm's vineyard grew opposite the apricot orchard, just before the base of a large hill to the north, with our house sandwiched in the middle. When we wanted apricots, we would leave from the front door and walk straight out, passing the well. The trees would be on the right, lining the southwestern corner of our farm. When we wanted grapes, we would leave from the back door and walk straight forward, passing the barn on the east.

After leaving the well, that's exactly what I did.

I had just made my way out the back door, lugging a small wooden ladder not much taller than me and two empty bushels that rested against the northern wall, when the low murmur of the oxen from the barn to the east caught my attention. I turned my head just in time to see Vartan walking out wearing his ugly work clothes and suspenders. For a moment, our eyes awkwardly met. Neither of us said anything, though. By the way he casually picked up the chain and locked the barn door, and by the way I kept on walking, it was apparent that our nerves hadn't yet settled.

"That fool," I thought. "What a selfish kid," I thought again, as I neared the vineyard, making me hate him even more.

With our fight still fresh in my head, I imagined the different things that I would have done to win. If I had the ladder and the two bushels when he attacked me, I would have used the ladder to knock him down, and then I'd put a bushel over his head to confuse him. That might have distracted him for a little while, but I couldn't help but think about his skill. At the end of every scenario in my head, Vartan pulled a quick technique on me and I lost. It was a terrible thought, but I knew it was something I needed to work on.

Just at the outlying grapevines, an early harvest, I momentarily stopped with my loaded arms to inspect the grapes. I then placed the bushels on the ground and opened the wooden ladder near a healthy-looking bunch, pressing the ladder down into the ground to test its stability. With two short steps up, I picked one solitary grape and held it carefully between my forefinger and thumb. I examined the size, color, and firmness. It was about the size of the tip of my finger, dark red in color, not very hard, and not very soft. I then opened my mouth, threw it in, and bit down. Its sweet juice proudly echoed inside, and my mind sensed it immediately. *Perfection.* My father would have been proud and disappointed at the same time. After all, he was the one who taught us how to accurately test for and harvest the best grapes, and yet he was also the one who warned me not to eat them.

After stepping back to the ground, I grabbed one of the bushels and placed it against my hip with a grunt. Without a shirt, the buzzing insects instantly began eating away at my bare skin, and as a result, I began slapping them away. The more I slapped, however, the more they bit. Using my free hand, I then climbed up the ladder. In this position, it was nearly impossible to slap away the insects without either falling or dropping the bushel. Therefore, I decided to endure the pain of the bites as a way to discipline myself for losing the fight and to remember to wear my shirt next time. With the picking of each grape, each bunch, I welcomed the pain under that scorching sun until I placed down the last of the two bushels, each filled to the top. Accomplished and satisfied, I sat and leaned against a tree, using its shade as a safe house, sweating heavily. My back, arms, and shoulders pulsated a vibrant red and swelled like small balloons, itching ever so deeply to the point that it felt like I was lying in a bath of ice. However, before I made it worse by scratching myself, I simply sat under that tree, clenched my teeth, and resisted the urge the best I could, blaming Vartan for my torturous ordeal.

As I sat, sweating through the urge, I turned my head to the bushel of grapes next to me, then looked to my right to the other one. In that instant, I imagined one of the grapes jumping up and speaking to me.

"Look how delicious I am," it said, waving its arms. "Eat me."

I shook my head and wiped the sweat from my face. Thirsty and overheated, even in the shade, I quickly shut my eyes tightly to fight the temptation. It didn't take long, however, for me to weigh the odds and make a decision. It was hot outside, I was sweating, I was thirsty, and my face was bruised. I was covered in bug bites, my entire body itched, and I was supposed to be picking apricots instead, where there were no bugs! With my father's policy clear in my head, I quickly overruled his words and gave myself the right to some grapes. I deserved it. And so, taking the law into my own hands, I braced my right elbow against the ground and lazily extended my left arm across my body to the bushel. I wiggled my fingers deep inside and pulled out a handful. I then closed my eyes, readying myself to taste their beauty. Just as I was about to toss them in, of course, my father yelled at me from the distance.

"Armen!" he screamed.

His echoing voice scared me enough to drop the grapes down onto my lap.

"Armen, they're here!" he yelled again.

For a moment, I thought he had caught me succumbing to the temptation of self-fulfillment. On high alert, I looked through some trees to the dirt road and focused on a small ox-cart, wobbling ever slightly. With a cigarette hanging from his mouth, Garo controlled the wagon from the east as he sat next to Tavit. Coincidentally, Ara, Mary, and their three daughters rode in from the west at the same exact moment.

I sprung up, grabbing a full bushel, then began running towards the house. Wanting to impress my father with my punctuality, I ran around the west side, put the bushel on the porch next to the front door, and ran back for the other. The sweat on my face had dried from my recess, but the drops hiding in my hair fell into my eyes with each step, burning them in delight, and I did nothing to stop it. I then grabbed the second bushel and ran it over, placing it next to the first one.

"Armen! Hurry up!" my father yelled again from the side of the house, thinking that I was still in the vineyard.

"I'm here, I'm here," I said as calmly as I could. "I've been here for fifteen minutes."

He walked to the front and peeked around the corner.

"Oh wow, *abrees*," he said, congratulating me on a job well done. "That was fast."

"I know," I agreed, hoping that he'd be satisfied with my achievement. "I worked quickly so that I could help you with other work."

"Is that so? Well, in that case, I want you to help your mother fill glasses of water for the guests," he responded. "But before you do, wipe all that sweat off your face. And put on a shirt. It'll help with the itching." He smiled, knowing that I was lying about my timeliness.

I grunted, feeling defeated, and went inside, passing my mother and little Margaret in the kitchen.

"Mama, do you need any help?" I said as I stood in the house, shirtless.

"Armen, what happened to your back?" my grandmother asked from her chair.

"Nothing, *Medzmama*. The mosquitoes just bit me, that's all."

"Come here, let me see," she said. "My God."

Unwillingly, I stepped closer to her. My grandmother

took my arm and gently pulled me closer. I bent down as she inspected the bites on my shoulders and she then spun me around to examine my back.

"Armen, what happened?" she asked again. "Did you *let* them bite you?"

Caught off guard by her ability to dissect the situation as fast as she did, I brushed it off.

"*Medzmama*, I'll be all right, trust me."

"You should wear a shirt next time," she suggested.

"Yeah, wear a shirt next time," repeated little Margaret.

"I understand!" I uttered in annoyance. "Thanks!"

"And yes, Armen, I would like some help. Could you put the small table and three chairs onto the porch and fill twelve glasses of water?"

"Yes, Mama."

With a casual stop to my room, I finally threw on a shirt and moved the small table and chair from the kitchen onto the porch, adding two dining chairs. Grabbing two jugs on the way out, I made my way over to the well, where, in the hazy distance, Vartan came stumbling back with three bushels of apricots—two hanging from either end of a large wooden rod, slightly bent, draped across his back shoulders, and a third worn as a backpack.

"What a jerk," I said to myself as I watched him trying to time his steps perfectly so that he would get to the house just as Nadia would.

As he passed, once again, we made eye contact. As focused as he seemed to be, he walked past me without saying a word, and I pretended to be busier than I actually was. Our paths, as much as I resented it at the time, kept crossing, making it impossible to stay mad forever. Eventually, it would work, but for the time being, as my body itched and burned, it reminded me just how much I hated my brother.

With a sigh, I turned the crank at the well, lowered the bucket deep into the water, then raised it back up. Detaching it from the thick, braided rope, I poured the water into both jugs and carried them to the house. I then filled twelve glasses and neatly arranged them on the porch table, just as my mother had asked.

2

"Welcome, welcome! How was the ride, Garo?" my father asked as he shook Garo's hand, then shook Tavit's. "Ana couldn't make it?" he continued.

"No, no. Unfortunately, she's not feeling well. It's nothing serious, but she didn't want to get anyone else sick."

"That's too bad. Please, give her my best."

"I will. Thank you. Other than that, the ride was pleasant. I think one of my wheels needs to be looked at before I leave today," explained Garo. "The cart felt wobbly."

"Good, we'll look at it. Please make yourself comfortable. Ara is joining us now."

"Ah, good," he said with a smile as he peered over my father's shoulder.

Then, with a hooked thumb, he pulled out his gold pocket watch attached at the end of a chain, connected to his front pocket. With a weak push of a button, the round watch clicked open, and he peered at the time. Quickly, he snapped it back up and stuck it back inside the pocket. He then pulled out a chair from the porch and sat down.

"Wine?" my father asked.

Garo looked up at him, opened his arms, and cocked his head a little to the left. He looked at my father for a second without saying a word.

"Tevos, do you really have to ask me? Of *course* I want wine!" he laughed a moment later.

"Very well," my father obliged.

"That reminds me; I brought over three kegs of my latest batch. I'll go get some bottles right now, and we'll unload the kegs later," said Garo. "Tavit, go get the crate of wine bottles from the cart and give them to Mr. Hagopian."

"Okay, but have you seen Armen?"

"No, I haven't," his father said.

"Yes, he's inside washing up," answered my father. "He should be out soon."

"Okay, great," Tavit acknowledged before running to the ox-cart.

"*Parev tsez!*" said Ara, meaning "hello, everybody," as he walked onto the porch behind my father with his wife and three daughters.

My father turned around.

"*Parev,* Ara," he welcomed.

"Ha-ha! Hello, Ara!" said Garo as he stood up and gave Ara a hug as if they hadn't seen each other in ages.

"Please, make yourselves at home, all of you," my father said. "Mary, what would you like to drink? We've set up water here for all of you."

"I'm fine. Thank you, Tevos. I'm actually going to go inside and help Hasmig," she said, smiling. "Girls, have some water and help around if anyone needs it."

They nodded shyly as Ara sat down across the table from Garo and let out a sigh. The three girls then each grabbed a glass of water when suddenly, as if from nowhere, Vartan stepped up onto the porch and appeared at the front door just as Nadia was about to enter the house. He had three bushels of apricots on him—one still attached to his back like a backpack, and the others still hanging at the ends of the long wooden rod across his back. After placing down the two bushels hanging on the wooden rod, he gazed at her, trying to catch his breath. Her eyes momentarily returned the gaze, only to fall back upon the bushels.

"*Hyreeg,* where do you want me to put these perfectly delicious apricots that I just handpicked?" he asked with one shallow breath.

Immediately, Vartan's rotten appearance caught my father off guard. His clothes were filthy, he was very sweaty, and his hair pointed in all directions. Normally, my father would have said something to him, but he decided to stay silent; he didn't want to embarrass his son in front of the guests.

"Uhh, go to the well and wash them and then put them

in the smaller baskets we have in the barn. Get a basket or two ready for Ara's and Garo's families."

"Yes, right away. I love apricots!" he said with a quick glance at Nadia.

Forgetting about the bushel attached to his back, Vartan leaned over to lift one of the others to take to the well, immediately dumping the contents over his head. With a firm grasp already on the filled bushel in front of him, he leaned back up with it and took a step to gather the newly fallen apricots. As if the ground had moved from under him, however, he lost his footing over the edge of the porch and stumbled off, waddling like a drunkard, unable to recuperate. My father, Garo, Ara, the three girls, and I all watched helplessly. Thus, in order to maintain his balance, he thrust the bushel out of his hands, also sending those apricots flying through the air, and threw his arms in front of him, trying to save himself. Ultimately, Vartan fell, and the bushel attached on his back swung over his head, dumping the remaining contents, and ended up on him like an oversized knight's helmet all the way down to his shoulders, while the apricots, as if in a parade, bounced freely on the ground around him.

It all happened so fast, and I saw all of it just as I stepped outside.

Not being able to see, Vartan then tried to stand but smashed his hand into an apricot. It oozed through his fingertips as he slipped back down onto his side then ripped the bushel off his head and tried again, finally succeeding to his feet.

"Ha-ha! Sorry!" he exclaimed as his face turned bright red.

We simply stared at him, baffled, as he looked around at his mess.

As giddy as a baby monkey, Vartan was completely out of character, smelled like a donkey, and had successfully and thoroughly embarrassed himself in front of the girl of his dreams. Thus, as with any victory, I celebrated with a loud and uncontrolled hysterical laugh, enough for my mother, grandmother, little Margaret, and Mary to turn their heads outside and see why.

With my laughter in full bloom, Vartan got down on his hands and knees and began picking up the apricots.

Laughing hard still, I clutched my stomach in pain and placed my hand on the wall to keep balance. My eyes began to water, I couldn't breathe, and my body fell numb, so I slid to the ground, bringing my knees to my chest, just so I could laugh some more. At this moment, nothing brought me greater joy than to see Vartan fail.

I didn't feel sorry for him at all.

As I wiped the tears from my eyes and my laugh slowly began to fade, my father looked at me and then to Vartan. I remained stationed against the wall, and the two younger sisters walked inside with their glasses of water, smiling. Then, against my most devious thoughts, Nadia did something that quite possibly changed the course of my predicted history.

Something that defeated me.

Despite wearing a clean dress, she put down her glass of water, stooped over, and began helping Vartan. Speechless and demoralized, I looked around from the floorboards of the porch for someone to verify what my eyes were showing me.

Vartan paused momentarily.

"Thanks," he said.

Without response, she picked up each apricot with him, one by one, placing them neatly in the bushel, until together, they'd picked them all up. Every last one. Then, without even another word, Vartan simply walked the bushel to the well, and Nadia went inside the house.

My father turned to Ara and raised his eyebrows.

Ara smiled.

"Glass of wine?" my father asked, not skipping a beat.

"Yes, Tevos. Thank you," he responded.

"*Hyreeg*, where should I put this?" asked Tavit as he came back with a wooden box containing six unlabeled bottles of Garo's Best.

"Ah, okay, just set it down here."

Tavit placed the box next to Garo's chair and sat down

at the edge of the porch away from the table.

"Tavit, you just missed what happened!" I said from the floor of the porch as I began laughing again, but this time, bittersweetly.

"What? Tell me," he asked enthusiastically.

"Armen, boys, please, just go inside," directed my father.

"All right, Tavit, follow me," I said as I led him inside.

My father let out a sigh of relief before setting down three glasses and filling wine for Garo, Ara, and himself.

"Finally," he mentioned, "we have some peace. So, tell me, Garo, how is the business?" he continued as he pulled a chair for himself.

"It's great; sales are rising! That new batch—you're going to like it."

"Good," said my father as he raised his glass, "to family and success."

Garo took off his rounded top hat and placed it on the table. He then quickly shuffled his thinning hair with his free hand and joined his glass with my father and Ara.

"Yes," he repeated, "to family and success."

Their glasses clinked, and the three men sipped their wine. As they placed their glasses back on the table, each took a moment to savor the taste and feel the warm breeze of the June afternoon.

"Garo, this is delicious," started Ara.

"Wait until you try the new stuff! The other day alone, a man came in asking for thirty cases," explained Garo. "Thirty! In the twenty-two years since I've been in this business, I've never sold so many cases at once. People are going crazy for it! Each case has sixteen bottles in it. Imagine how many bottles that is. It took me three days to prepare that many for him. My thanks to the Lord I had enough. I've lowered the price because I'm selling so much. Even the taxes have no effect on me!"

"Speak for yourself!" snickered Ara.

My father looked at him.

"What did he need so many bottles for? Did you ask him?" asked my father.

"He said he was going to ship most of it to his relatives in America. He told me I make the best wine in Armenia, so I gave the man a discount."

"Must be the grapes," Ara laughed as he patted my father on the back.

My father smiled. "Must be. That reminds me, Garo," he added, "I have the grapes you wanted behind me. When we fix your wheel, we can load them up."

"Yes, I saw them. Excellent. That sounds excellent. They look good from here," he responded as he stretched his neck and glanced at the bushels I had set down earlier.

"They're very sweet this season. Take the bushels and test them out. Let me know if you want to harvest the rest."

"I already know that they'll be nothing *but* the best, Tevos."

"Forget it. I don't need the sweet talk."

The men laughed as they sat, enjoying each other's company.

"And how are other things, Ara? How's business for you?" my father asked.

"Believe it or not, but I've been selling a lot of dinner tables," he explained.

"Oh yeah?" said Garo. "Dinner tables, huh?"

"Yeah, of all things! Here is my theory if you want to hear it," he began.

Garo leaned back and crossed his arms.

"I can always assume the prosperity of our people based on the number of dinner tables I sell."

"How so?" asked Garo.

"Well, if people have enough money to buy dinner tables, then they have enough money to buy a dinner to put on top of them!" he explained.

Garo nodded in approval.

"It makes sense, right? Why else would you need a dinner table? The more I sell, the more I make! The more I make, the more people eat!"

My father laughed while looking at his glass, slowly

turning his finger around the base. "It does make sense, indeed."

Ara laughed, too.

"Let the government tax me all they want. Rob me and make the taxes as unfair and as injurious as possible. As long as I sell my work, I can prove their plan for us will be foiled."

Garo rolled his eyes, reached into his jacket pocket, and took out a small white carton of cigarettes and matches. He threw the matches onto the table and bumped the end of the carton against his palm. He then pulled out a cigarette and placed the end between his lips. "I think we're learning to live in peace," he said as he lit it, predicting the ensuing conversation. "Cigarette, Ara?" he offered, extending the carton.

"Yes, thank you, Garo," Ara responded as he slid one out.

Garo leaned over and helped him light it. "Tevos?"

"No, no. Thank you, Garo."

Garo sat back and took a puff from his cigarette, then put the carton back into his pocket.

"Not one Moslem in the Ottoman Empire, be it Turk or Kurd," Ara expanded as he blew out the cigarette smoke, "pays the taxes we do. Not even close. We are Armenian. Why are taxes for us so high? They say it's for what? Schools? Hospitals? Exemption from the military? Religious freedom? I am still in disbelief that we have to pay to be Christian! They're trying to tell us that if we don't pay our special tax, on *top* of the Ottoman tax, we have no schools, no hospitals; we must convert to Islam and then join the army? Is that correct? That's absurd. This isn't freedom. It's to drive us out of the empire! And don't roll your eyes at me, Garo; you just mentioned the taxes yourself."

"Listen," my father stated, "the Lord knows I agree with you, and I know we've all had our share of mistreatment, but if we're going to continue to fight for our rights and for our freedom, we must do it peacefully. That is the only way we'll live in harmony."

"Peacefully fight? How can you say that, Tevos? We've been peacefully fighting for decades!"

"Ara, please," said Garo. "I came here to enjoy the

afternoon, not argue."

"Just seventeen years ago, Sultan Abdul-Hamid killed nearly three hundred thousand Armenians with his Turkish hands. How do you explain that? This is exactly why the world labeled him the Red Sultan—because of his sole objective to completely eliminate all Armenians from the Ottoman Empire and his undying thirst for blood. *Armenian* blood!"

"Ara, they treat us unequally, but we cannot retaliate with violence," elaborated my father. "We cannot do as they do. It's as simple as that."

"Tevos, I'm not saying that violence is the answer, but I am saying that peace is not. Let me remind you of the massacre at Sasun, a place where Armenians have lived for *over* two thousand years, where Armenians were butchered by the thousands, regardless of age or gender. Just ask your mother-in-law, Taqoohi! She described the Armenians as being hunted like wild animals!"

"Ara, enough. Why do we keep discussing this? We know what happened. It's in the past already," Garo expressed.

"Like wild animals! It gets me so angry. We contribute far more to society than they do, and this is how they treat us, with *planned* massacres during times of *peace*. Of peace!"

My father glanced at Garo.

"After Abdul-Hamid's cavalry slaughtered those Armenians in Sasun over the protest of exactly what I'm saying—unfair taxation—the Armenians planned a *peaceful* demonstration at Constantinople denouncing the massacre, the awful treatment of Christian Armenians in the empire, and basic civil rights that we *still* do not have."

Ara blew out the smoke from his cigarette and extinguished the rest in the ashtray.

"The protest, during that summer of 1895, included a petition that was detailed plainly with a list of fair and simple requests, including the freedom to practice our own religion, the freedom to follow our own moral beliefs, equality under the same law, the right to worship, the preservation of our life and land, honor of our women, an end to torture, the right to bear arms, and a *fair tax system*, not only for us, but for *all* Christian minorities. They were, and are, basic attainable rights, simple liberties granted to us by God Himself, and here is a government that has taken them away from us."

My father and Garo continued to listen.

"And then, in broad daylight, in response to the protest, the Turkish soldiers, and even their police force, opened fire on the crowd of over two thousand *unarmed* Armenian demonstrators. The Armenians dispersed to avoid another massacre and hid in the villages around the area. For that entire month of October to the rest of the year, the soldiers surrounded those nearby villages and killed anyone inside whether or not they had paid their taxes and whether or not they had partaken in the demonstration.

"Well into June of 1896, in the province of Van, the Armenians fought back in self-defense. After days of fighting, the two sides eventually came to an agreement, a promise, that if the Armenians would put down their arms, the Turks would safely escort them to the Persian border and denounce accusations of planning a revolution against the government, which, I might add, was never the case. And do you know what they did?"

"Ara, I beg you, this has become more than just your thoughts on taxes."

"I'll tell you, Garo. You've got me on a rant, now. As soon as the thousand Armenians marched to the Persian border, the soldiers killed every single one of them, *after* they were promised safety and peace. Does it sound like peaceful demonstrations work?"

Ara leaned in and lowered his voice.

"*This* is the kind of people they are. The Turks are rats. To them, we are the parasites of the Ottoman Empire. Nothing more. And we are treated as such."

My father cut in: "Yes, but, Ara, this was all the sultan's doing. He was overthrown in 1908. That was *five* years ago. We're in 1913 now. There's been relative peace between us and the Turks since then."

Ara reached to his face and adjusted his gold-rimmed glasses. Behind my father, Vartan returned for the second and third bushels to take to the well. The three men turned their heads.

"Tevos," continued Ara, "they still burn our houses, rape our women, steal our livestock—all in the name of what? Religion? Land? Jealousy? They do *not* see us as equal. As Christian Armenians, we are less than minorities! We're dirt!"

My father crossed his arm across his torso and twirled the tip of his mustache with his other hand, allowing his elbow to rest upon the crossed arm.

There was silence among the three men. The tension in the air was dense.

"Uff, Ara, don't be insulting. The Turks are not rats," Garo defended. "While I cannot argue the facts, I still feel that they've changed for the better. The sultan, like Tevos said, is gone. That story you told us was *his* doing. His time is now over. The Young Turks overthrew and replaced him with their revolution. They have established a new government and are giving back the rights he took from us!"

"Rights?" interrupted Ara. "Where are these rights? Every day they take more away. We're the educated! The academic elite. We're the merchants. We boost their economy. We even fight in their wars. We work so hard and this is how they repay us? They're draining us out!"

"Ara, these things take time. They restored the parliament that the sultan took away in 1878."

"It was given to us and then taken away because the sultan feared a revolution."

"It makes no matter. That was then. We now have a voice in government! This is progress! They are looking to a new future, a new beginning. Since 1863, we've had our own constitution. The new Committee of Union and Progress that these Young Turks formed has declared the constitutional government with equal rights for *all* the empire's citizens— Greeks, Bulgars, *and Armenians*!"

He paused.

"We are on the correct path. Some of my relatives have emigrated from here to America, but it's unnecessary. The economy here is strong, and it's because the new government sees us as a prospective contribution to an even *stronger* economy. Business is good for us like you said. Am I wrong? I will stay here optimistically, hoping for continued reform for Christians and Armenians."

"Don't be fooled, Garo. Of *course* we contribute to the economy, but again, where are the equal rights? Where is the peace? Just four years ago this new Committee of Union and Progress organized and slaughtered nearly twenty-five thousand Armenians in Adana," Ara continued. "Do you realize how many people that is? Bulgaria has already declared their independence. Why are *we* still part of the empire?"

"I believe it because it's promising," Garo explained. "It's hopeful. There was a reason the sultan was overthrown. He was corrupt and didn't see it the way the Young Turks do. The Young Turks are here to *help* us. You will see. Turks and Armenians will live side by side as brothers, backed by a government that respects this bond."

"How can you trust the Young Turks after they killed twenty-five thousand Armenians? Tell me, how can you trust them? You'd have to be crazy! That's why your relatives left!"

My father interjected. "Ara, I understand your frustration. I am equally as disturbed, but there has been *harmony* since," he explained, "and we must strive to preserve *at least* that much—"

"Of course there's been harmony! The Turks are learning that living in peace is the best way to live," Garo rephrased, "and I see a future where the peace will flourish with more deserving rights!"

"I'm just saying that we should be grateful to God that things have not grown worse. That's all."

"How can it get any worse?" asked Ara. "Is it possible?"

No one answered, not even Garo. Each man had his own beliefs and thus basked in the silence. There was no need to say more.

My father coldly studied the hand-built table where they sat and shifted his eyes towards his wine glass. He reached for it, never taking his eyes off it, and brought it close to his lips. Just as he was about to take a drink, a thought passed through his mind.

"Perhaps the storm has passed," he said, trying to stay positive. He then shrugged his shoulders slightly and continued his drink.

Ara sat, noticeably more uncomfortable. "I hope you're right, Tevos, because if you're not, we are all in trouble."

10

Vartan stood by the stone well next to a bucket of water on the ledge, the three bushels filled with apricots to his left and five small wicker baskets with large rounded handles to his right—two for Garo's family, two for Ara's family, and one for Nadia, ready to be filled with the cleaned apricots. In his mind, he vowed to fill Nadia's basket with only the best ones, ensuring that every apricot was perfect, free of any imperfections, just as he saw her.

With a short lean, Vartan bent down and picked up one fruit from the first bushel. Gently then, he dunked it into the bucket of water, brushed off the excess dirt, and placed it into the first empty basket. He then grabbed for another, repeating the process. Just like my father had taught us how to test for the ripeness of a grape, he also taught us how to properly clean the soft apricots as to not damage them.

As soon as he had filled the first basket, he pushed it to the side and began again, this time slowing the process. After gently wiping his palms on his pants, he picked up the first rounded fruit, slowly lowered it into the water, and thought about his embarrassing stunt just moments before as he softly scrubbed its delicate skin. He analyzed and replayed the scene over and over again, focusing on details he didn't want to remember—everyone's reaction, the sounds he made, the voices he heard. He thought about it and sulked when he saw himself.

"Stupid, stupid, stupid," he muttered. "I've lived here my whole life, and I've never done that before. What was I thinking?"

He then glanced at his leg and noted his bleeding knee—a scrape he acquired from the fall. He did nothing for it. With an extension of his stinging forearm, he then looked at the three long scratches, also bleeding, but only slightly. He shrugged at his small misfortune. The wounds would heal. There were bigger things to focus on at the moment, so he exhaled and finished cleaning the remaining apricots.

Satisfied with Nadia's share, he finished stacking the small orange fruits inside the basket into the shape of a pyramid and smiled at his creation. He then gently placed her basket to the side on the ledge of the well, careful not to confuse it with the rest, and filled the remaining four.

Vartan then glanced back towards the porch and saw the three men suddenly burst out into laughter. They were having a good time as expected. Garo took the cigarette out of his mouth, still laughing, and patted Ara's back. Vartan then picked up the four baskets and walked them over, leaving the fifth one behind.

"Hi," he said as he handed them to the guests. "Garo, these baskets are for your family."

"Ah, thank you very much, Vartan!" Garo smiled as his eyes followed the basket, and his thick cheeks followed the shape of his smile. "These look stunning!"

"You're welcome. And these are for you, Ara," Vartan continued as he handed over two more baskets.

Ara took them and placed them near his feet, nodding his head in approval. My father watched Vartan, pleased with his work.

"Thank you, my son," he said. "Now please, wash yourself before dinner."

Vartan obliged, and as he walked to the well, the three men resumed their conversation. Garo took out his pocket watch and checked the time. With a click, he snapped the lid back down and snuck it back into his pocket, keeping the chain exposed.

"You know, Tevos," Ara began, folding his arms,

"you've raised a very respectable, well-behaved son. Both of them, including your daughter. Very respectable."

"Thank you, Ara. Yours as well," my father replied.

Hearing the compliment, Vartan continued walking but didn't acknowledge it, secretly hoping now his chances with Nadia might have improved with her father's observation.

At the well, he raised the full bucket of water and placed it on the ledge. With a swift move upwards, he then took off his shirt to wash himself, but instead of picking up the bucket, he picked up the fifth basket of apricots. With a newfound confidence, he stood tall and lowered his voice.

"Hello, Nadia," he said as he extended the basket, "you look beautiful. Would you like to taste my apricots?"

Vartan shook his head. "No, no. That doesn't sound right."

"Hello, Nadia," he tried again, changing the tone of his voice and standing up a little taller, "why yes, these apricots are for you. Oh, you love apricots? Well, I love *you*!

"No. Too much."

He cleared his throat.

"I picked these delicious bites, so we can eat them together."

He shook his head, unsatisfied still.

"Hello, Nadia, I want you to have these apricots," he practiced as he picked one up from the bunch and held it out in front of him. He studied it curiously and examined it, staring at that small mid-season fruit, ditching his prior efforts. Like a knife, he cut deep through its flesh with his eyes all the way to the core. He envisioned his future—a promising and hopeful future. He saw himself running with Nadia through the meadows, holding hands. He envisioned them laughing together, dancing together, and just *being* together. He envisioned a future where their paths in life converged to become one of the same. Perfection. He strived for it. He imagined speaking to her and explaining his life's story so that *someone* would understand who he was and what he stood for, to sympathize with whatever his plight might have been. If anyone could understand, it would be her. He imagined them living together in a house, waking up to hot cups of tea. He imagined their many livestock and their perfect harvests on perfectly sunny days.

Vartan even imagined how their love, even at an old age, would still be as strong as the day they first succumbed to the lure. He thought about that day, the day that he would propose to her. He imagined himself getting down on one knee and asking her the question, to which she would immediately say yes. He imagined a relationship where he would do anything for her, and she would do anything for him. He thought about their wedding, all the people standing in neat rows, watching the holiest of all bonds. He saw his parents, his friends. They were all happy. He saw Der Kourken, the priest who would unite them. And then he saw Nadia, wearing her traditional dress, slowly walking towards him down the aisle, their eyes never leaving each other until they stood side by side. He then heard Der Kourken finish with the final blessing and announce the completion of their marriage with a great smile. He then saw them leave the church to prepare for the three-day celebration but saw them escape together to a private getaway, a place only they knew about. He saw them standing, looking still into each other, she at him and he at her, becoming evermore anxious for the inevitable kiss. He then readied himself for the moment, closed his eyes, and leaned in for it—her soft lips. He wanted to kiss them more than anything. He then felt it—her lips on his. She tasted as sweet as an apricot. He kissed her more. She felt like one, too.

He then heard a man's voice—a voice that didn't belong.

"Hey, ugly, what are you doing?"

Vartan opened his eyes, severely confused. He looked at the barren, grassy fields in front of him and the apricot in his hand.

"Huh?" he questioned as he licked his lips free of the juice.

Quickly accepting the absence of his dream from the reality in which he stood, Vartan looked to his left as I approached him, and focused beyond me to where Nadia stood inside the kitchen window. With a dish in her hand, his dream of a perfect life was still just that—a dream.

Vartan frowned and set the apricot back on top of the stack.

"What do you want?" he asked as he turned his back to me.

"Mama wants to talk to us," I answered.

"Now?"

"Yes, now."

Vartan let out a grunt and grabbed his shirt. "Fine, I'll be there soon," he said sadly.

I turned around and walked back towards the house, and Vartan let out a sigh, still not convinced that it was all a dream. He set down the basket of apricots and picked up the bucket of water, indefinitely postponing his thoughts. He closed his eyes, held his breath, and finished what he set out to do.

"Whoa, that's cold!" he exhaled after dumping the water over his head, fully coming back to reality.

In the kitchen, my mother stood like a general.

"Okay, I want to get this over with quickly," said Vartan as he appeared in the doorway, wiping his wet hands over his wet face.

"Hi, Vartan!" said my grandmother with Vartan's blood-stained button-down shirt and dusty suit on her lap.

"Hi, *Medzmama*," he said, smiling barely.

"Go to the back room and wait for me. Right now. Both of you," my mother commanded sternly.

Being given no choice, Vartan and I walked to the back room and sat, waiting for my mother's mending.

"Mary, I'll be back soon. Do you have everything you need?" she asked Ara's wife in the kitchen.

"*Ayo*," she affirmed with a smile, "thank you."

From the back room, I listened as Mary further taught her daughters how to prepare the dinner for the night. I also heard my mother's footsteps approaching our location as we sat in anticipation. In the cases of detailed and personal values, my mother hit it much harder than my father, who, more or less, viewed the situation from afar. Where my father saw large boulders, my mother saw grains of sand. She had a knack for those details, consistently staying true to her word, rarely allowing for the slightest exception, even realizing traits and weaknesses about us that we, ourselves, didn't even know or take the time to see. Because of that, there really wasn't much we could do in our own defense.

To me, that was dangerous.

Without a moment's hesitation, my mother's footsteps became more than just a sound. She had welcomed herself inside.

"First," she began unremorsefully, "Vartan, apologize to Armen."

"What! Why me?"

"Do it."

"We're too old for this!" he exclaimed as he stood up to leave.

She blocked his path. "If you don't want to be treated like a child, then maybe you shouldn't behave like a child. Sit down," she demanded. "Right now."

Defenseless, he acknowledged her request and did as he was told, only to begin his measly attempt at an apology shortly after.

"No, no," my mother interrupted. "Start again. Look into his eyes."

Vartan raised his head and looked into my eyes. Immediately, I smiled, and so did Vartan. We even began to laugh a little.

"Armen, I'm sorry I yelled at you and hit you," he said.

"Now, Armen, apologize to Vartan."

"Vartan, sorry I yelled at you and hit you really hard in the face," I said.

"Armen, no need to rub anything in. Apologize with respect," she clarified.

I then said something whiney and began again, "Vartan, I apologize for hitting you and yelling at you earlier today."

"And…" my mother pushed.

"And what?" I answered back, losing my patience. "Vartan's right. This is dumb!"

"And that you won't do it again," she added.

"But Vartan didn't have to say that!" I pleaded childishly.

"He will," my mother responded.

"And I won't do it again," I murmured.

"Now, Vartan, will you fight like that again?" she asked, directing her attention to him.

"No," he responded.

"Then say it to your brother," she said.

"I will not fight like that again."

"Good." She smiled.

"Okay, can we leave?" I asked. "This is the last time."

"Not yet," she responded. "I have a few words myself."

We sat, immobilized and silenced.

"Listen, both of you," she opened with a new tone, "I love you two very much, and it breaks my heart to see you two fight. You are men now. Two very handsome men. Since you were young, I've constantly reminded you that we are one family, one team with the same blood. There is no need to go out and destroy that. We all need to support each other because we only *have* each other. If you two can't support the one family, the only brother that each of you has, then what else is left? So please, I don't want to treat you like children, but I will if I need to. Act like you care and don't do that again. Do you promise to always support each other?"

"Yes," we said unanimously.

"All right, good, then we're finished here."

And just like that, my mother stood up and left for the kitchen, and my brother and I followed a few steps behind.

She was right, and I hated it.

With my mother's words in mind, as we walked through the hallway, the door to my parents' room, I noticed, was slightly ajar. From inside, a glow, a momentary sparkle, silently pierced my eye, distracting my thoughts. Thus, I turned and looked through the crack to fulfill my curiosity. A solitary maroon box, open and inviting, sat on a lonely wooden stool. Inside it, the partially unsheathed dagger, the one that Vartan got for his birthday, gleamed brilliantly.

I nudged my brother. "Vartan, look."

He turned to see.

"It's the dagger," I whispered.

Looking around to see if anyone was watching, I slowly pushed open the door. It creaked a little. When there was just enough space for me to fit through, I stepped in and went for it. Vartan followed.

Slowly, I picked up the dark leather sheath and felt its power energize my body. I couldn't explain it, but I felt it.

"Armen, put it back," my brother advised. "Someone's going to see you."

"It's really heavy," I whispered back as I held up the leather casing.

"I know it is. Put it back," he said, pushing it down.

"Hey, stop," I said, aggravated.

Once again, I raised the dagger. I took it fully out of the sheath to expose the double-edged blade. It shone magnificently under the rays of the setting sun as I held it for a little longer. Just then, my grandmother let out a small cough from the living space, and I jumped at the sound and dropped it back into the empty box.

"Armen," whispered Vartan, "stop being so clumsy. Put it back in the case! Let's go!"

Quickly and now nervously, I sheathed the dagger and placed it in the box on the stool, neatly putting the lid back on. Vartan then left the room, and I followed behind, closing the door back to where it used to be. In the kitchen, the ladies were still cooking, and Vartan decided to stop and stare at Nadia, blocking my path. I didn't see him stop, and so I kept moving forward. I quickly put my hands in front of me to push him out of the way.

"Move," I said.

With my nudge, he finally moved, and we walked to the well, passing our father, Ara, and Garo still on the porch along the way. They looked at us as if we had stolen something, but we kept calm.

"Armen, you almost broke the dagger!" my brother warned.

"No, I didn't! It can't break," I said. "You felt how heavy it was."

"You have to be more careful."

I perched myself up on the ledge of the well, admittedly a very dangerous spot, and dangled my legs against the stone. The well wall itself was one and a half meters high, made from the same stone as the church. To my left, I noticed a basket of apricots.

"Wow," I expressed. "That is a perfect stack of apricots."

"It's for Nadia. I want to give that to her before she leaves today."

"Aww, Vartan, that's so special!" I said, mocking him lovingly.

"Be quiet. She loves apricots."

"Well," I shrugged, "when are you going to do it? I guess it's not a bad idea."

"I know, you ape. That is why I'm giving it to her," he responded.

"Are you going to say anything, or are you going to just throw it at her and grunt?"

"Well, I want to say something, but I don't want to scare her away."

"Just say, 'Here, this is for you,'" I said.

"Yeah, that's very creative."

"It doesn't have to be creative, Vartan. What you tell her isn't important. She'll probably forget it anyway because every time she takes an apricot from the basket, she's going to think of you. So it doesn't matter what you say."

Vartan just looked at me.

"Just don't say something dumb," I explained. "Trust me. I know girls."

"You know girls?"

"Of course I do!" I said defensively.

"Since when? I don't even remember the last time you were with a girl!"

"You don't remember Sona?" I asked.

"Ha! Sona? She had a mustache! You can hardly consider her a girl," said Vartan.

"She did not have a mustache!" I defended.

"Let's just ask Tavit," I suggested as Tavit walked towards us from the distance.

"Tavit, did Sona have a mustache?" I asked.

"Sona?" he asked as he stopped and placed his thumbs under his suspenders.

"Yes, that girl by the stables. Last year."

"Oh, Sona!" he said. "Yes, she had a mustache. Sorry, Armen."

Tavit patted my back.

"Ha! Told you," said Vartan.

"Whatever. I never saw it."

"She had really hairy arms, too," Tavit continued.

"Okay! We are done talking about Sona!" I blurted out as I subconsciously scratched the bug bites on my arm.

Vartan laughed.

"Where were you anyway?" I asked Tavit. "I left the house to get Vartan, and when I came back, you were gone."

"Oh, I was out by the cart because my father wanted to show us the broken wheel and needed help unloading the wine kegs," he explained.

"Oh," I said. "Well, anyway, you want to see something amazing?"

My brother looked at me, confused.

"What is it?" asked Tavit.

"Don't worry. Tavit won't say anything," I reassured Vartan. "Tavit, are you going to say anything?" I asked.

"No, I won't. I promise!" he confirmed. "What is it?"

"I think it's better if we showed you instead."

I jumped off the ledge of the well. From behind my pants, I then pulled out the stolen dagger, still in its sheath.

"Armen!" blurted Vartan. "Armen, now they're going to see that it's missing!"

"Oh, wow!" said Tavit.

His eyes were as hungry as mine when I first saw it.

"No, they're not. The box is still there. As long as they don't open the lid, they'll think the dagger is still inside," I clarified.

Tavit grabbed for the dagger, and I pulled it back.

"C'mon, let me hold it."

"All right," I said, "but be careful."

I handed him the dagger, and he held it up. He, too, felt its power. I saw it in his face.

"This knife is huge," he said.

"It's a dagger," said Vartan, "and it's mine."

"It is?" he asked.

"Yes, I got it for my birthday."

"Oh yeah!" snapped Tavit. "Happy birthday, Vartan."

"Thanks," he responded.

"We need to learn how to use this."

"We will," Vartan encouraged.

"Yeah, *Hyreeg* said he would teach us," I pitched in.

"Well, you guys have to teach me how to use it, too."

"Sure, we can practice together," I said.

"But you can't even tell your father about this, Tavit," Vartan said.

"I won't. Don't worry. I'll keep it a secret."

Tavit shifted his eyes to the basket sitting on the edge of the well.

"Wow, that is one perfect stack of apricots," he noted.

"Will everyone stop focusing on that?" said Vartan, annoyed.

"What did I say?" he asked.

"I said the exact same thing before you got here." I smiled.

"Oh," he laughed. "Is it for Nadia?"

Vartan rolled his eyes.

Tavit looked at Vartan and placed his hand on his

shoulder. "We are here to help you, Vartan," he said.

Tavit and I laughed, and Vartan brushed Tavit's hand off his shoulder.

"I don't need your help," he said.

"Yes, you do," disagreed Tavit. "Now, this is what you are going to do," he continued. "Make sure that you give her the basket before she leaves tonight. Otherwise, these perfectly round fruits will rot away just like your relationship with her." He picked up the top apricot from the stack.

"Put that back!" Vartan exclaimed as he grabbed the fruit from Tavit's hands and placed it back on the pile, rotating it until it sat exactly where he wanted.

"You also have to say something to her. Not too long, but not too short. Not too deep, but not too shallow," he explained.

"See, he knows too," I said.

Tavit and I looked at each other and nodded.

"You know," I continued, "something *just* enough so that she's satisfied, but at the same time, not enough so that she wants more—like an apricot. You can't stop after just one; you'll always want just *one* more."

"Well said," Tavit complimented.

"Thank you, Tavit," I threw back.

Vartan frowned.

"We're serious," I continued.

"Yeah, okay, so let's think of some things to say," Tavit said.

"I already know what I'm going to tell her," Vartan explained.

"What is it?"

"I'm going to say, 'Hi, Nadia, before you leave, I want you to have these apricots that I picked for you. They are very delicious.'"

"Hmm, not bad," I said.

"Yeah, it's very basic. Plain. Just enough to show that he cares and yet enough to show that he isn't desperate. Interesting." Tavit nodded. "Well then, I guess we're done here."

"Yup. I told you," said Vartan as he snapped Tavit's suspenders.

"Ayy!" he complained. "That stings!"

Tavit punched Vartan's shoulder.

"Boys!" my father screamed. "Boys, dinner is ready! Wash up *before* you get into the house!"

"You're lucky," Tavit warned.

"Oh yeah?" asked Vartan.

"Yeah," he said.

Tavit and I then splashed our faces with water and briskly began our walk towards the house, but I stopped myself short, remembering a previous offense.

"The dagger!" I blurted out. "Our parents! We have to hide it!"

Vartan, Tavit, and I turned around and collectively moved back to the well. We knew that we couldn't just take it back inside. Everyone would see us. So instead, we looked around the well trying to find a temporary hiding place.

"Here, just put it in the bucket," Tavit advised.

"Yes, good idea, and I'll lower it!" said Vartan.

"Just remind me to get it after dinner," I assigned Vartan.

With a casual thud, I placed the dagger into the empty bucket, and Vartan slowly lowered it so that it hung just above the water. Tavit tied the rope on the old stake in the ground, and we hurried towards the house.

Vartan, Tavit, and I were a team, just like my mother had said. For the longest time, I had considered Tavit as one of my brothers. As much as we argued, fought, cursed, or got angry at each other, we knew that, at the end of the day, we would always guard each other like a fortress of gold, unperturbed by the circumstance. We always knew it, but we never mentioned it. We never had to. It was one of those things that was assumed and for good reason.

Thus, as the sun sat low on the horizon, my two brothers and I ran towards the only home we'd ever known, ready to finish the day with a delicious meal prepared by the best chefs in Armenia.

11

After dinner, we dispersed beyond the dining table, a luxurious gift from Ara, and into the living space. Still at the table, our parents held small porcelain cups in each of their hands, cautiously sipping strong Armenian coffee. Since we had no electricity, my mother set down her cup and strategically began placing candles around the room as the darkness settled in.

The inside of our house wasn't too small, but it wasn't too big, either. We weren't a wealthy family, but we weren't poor. We were considered the upper middle class and our furnishings explained it quite well. Near the central fireplace, simply a large hole in the ground to the left of the front entrance, we had an old corduroy sofa, a luxury at the time, and some floor cushions—the standard seating arrangement for most Armenian households. Near the small kitchen, to the right of the front entrance, was a small, weathered table with one weathered chair. The inside walls were bare and gray in color with a hint of tan. A singular portrait of our family and a small crucifix about the size of a human hand rested on the wall between the dining room table and the fireplace. As my family and friends comfortably talked and laughed in that space we so loved, Tavit and I sat on the porch outside, just after the sun had set over the horizon.

"You know, Armen," started Tavit, "I was thinking about Der Kourken's sermon. About God giving us all the tools we need. You remember that one?"

"Well, I mean," I smirked, "I heard the beginning of it."

Tavit turned and looked at me, unamused.

"You fell asleep again, didn't you?" he accused.

"No, no," I denied. "I remember it. What about it?"

"Well, I was just thinking, do you really think that God has a plan for us?" he asked.

Tavit sparked some new thoughts.

"That's a good question. I'm not sure. I mean, I hope so

because I don't even have a plan for myself," I answered nonchalantly.

"You don't?" asked Tavit. "Why not?"

"I don't know. Maybe because I've never thought about it before or maybe I'm just assuming I'll take over our farm and the business. But right now, all I know is that I'm just enjoying life, living it day by day."

Ignoring my comment, Tavit continued with his train of thought. "But it's up to us to use the tools God has given, right? But what if you don't use them or can't find them? Then what?"

I thought about it, trying to provide useable advice. "Maybe that's how fate is designed. Maybe the tools are just a guide to direct us where we need to go. I have no idea."

"Like the future?" he asked.

"Yeah," I agreed, "like the future."

"Well, where do you see yourself in ten years?" he probed.

"Honestly, Tavit, I can't answer that," I reiterated. "Why are you so interested in this all of a sudden?"

"I don't know. Shouldn't you start thinking about it? Isn't it time?"

"I guess." I paused. "Maybe it doesn't matter what my answer is because you never know where fate will guide you. That's my lazy answer." I laughed a little. "What about you? Where do you see yourself?"

"Well, my answer is sort of similar to yours. I guess my plan is to take over the wine business with my father."

"Hmm… But is that what you *want* to do?" I asked, turning my head to him. "I mean, I'm not sure if I want to take over *our* farm. It's been in our family for generations, and we'd be business partners, but still…"

"Well," he defended, "my father expects me to take over the winery. I agree that it's a good business, and there are lots of things I would do differently, but you're right. I'm not so sure myself."

"What would you do differently?"

"Well, for one, I'd find a way to export the wine out of

our province."

"Do you have anything else in mind?" I asked.

"No, why?"

"Well, I don't think you really want to take over Garo's Best."

Tavit sat, looking into the distance with his hands over his knees. He thought for a moment. "Armen, don't laugh when I say this," he began.

"I won't," I responded.

"But I really want to be a chef."

"*Now* I know why you know so much about cooking! Why would I laugh at that? It suits you!"

"I don't know. It's a woman's job. Women are chefs. My father wouldn't be proud of me. I feel like I'd let him down," he explained as he threw a small rock into the dirt.

"No, why would you let him down for doing what you want? Everyone needs food to survive. You'll just know how to prepare it better than everyone else," I encouraged.

"I guess," he said.

"What will your specialty be?" I asked, probing more.

"My specialty?"

"Yeah, your specialty. Every chef needs their own special dish," I explained.

"Mmm," he thought out loud, licking his lips with a newfound excitement in his face, "my specialty."

"Is there one recipe that stands out more than the others?" I asked.

"Well, I have a couple that I like."

"Which one of those is your favorite? The one that everybody loves."

"Hmm, I've only made small plates here and there, but there is this dish I make with green beans, pieces of lamb, salt, pepper, and garlic. Vartan's had it before."

"It's just green beans and lamb?" I asked.

"Yes, just green beans and lamb. You cook the beans in a pan over the stove until they're almost soft, but not quite. Then you mix in the cooked lamb and serve it with *pilav*," he said.

"That actually sounds good… and simple," I reasoned.

"It sounds like it, but you have to put the exact amount of spice in it so it turns out perfect," he said. "Too much and it's too salty. Too little and it's tasteless."

"I want to try it one day. I'll be your taste tester. If it's not good, I'll tell you 'Tavit, this is not good.' "

"Fine."

"So, now that you have a special dish, what will you name your restaurant?" I asked.

"My restaurant?"

"Yeah, where else will you cook?"

"I'm not sure, probably Tavit's Cuisine," he stated boldly.

"Hmm, I don't like it. Just call it Armen's. It sounds better."

"Yeah, you wish!" he laughed.

I laughed too, but didn't respond, bringing a pause to our conversation. Instead, I leaned back, moved my arms behind me for support, and extended my legs. And, for a few moments, we sat in the silence. I liked those moments, the simple ones, especially when, even at fourteen, I felt like life could easily become overly complex, an unnecessary exaggeration. Thus, I focused my eyes and peered through the darkness. The wind from the east howled, and I faintly heard the farm animals breathing and shuffling their hooves inside the barn as it mixed with all the different voices inside the house, including the one of little Margaret laughing with the girls. And then I thought of Vartan, realizing that I had not yet picked him out from their voices.

"What do you think Vartan is doing?" I asked Tavit.

"Eating is my guess."

"Do you think he'll give that basket to Nadia?"

"He better," said Tavit, "or else *I'll* give it to her and make him regret not doing it."

"I have the same feeling that he's going to get too nervous and back out."

"Then we need a plan," he added.

"What kind of plan?" I asked.

"I think we need to *force* Vartan to talk to her," he elaborated.

"Force?" I asked again, now slightly intrigued. "How?"

"I'm not sure," said Tavit, "but he's sixteen. He needs to make his move already."

For a while, we sat and thought. What could we do? The ideas jumped through my head, but none stood out as one that would actually *work*. At times, I even spoke my mind and blurted out fragments but quickly cut myself short realizing the design had its flaws.

"I've got it!" Tavit blurted a moment later. "Armen, where's the basket Vartan prepared? Did he take it inside, or is it still on the ledge?"

I looked through the darkness towards the well, but the partially risen moon was not enough to light the area so far out. "Um, I think it's still there. Why?"

"I have an idea," he said, leaning forward. "Listen to this. We tell your brother and Nadia that we're all meeting at the well, but we don't show up. Vartan will have no choice but to talk to her!"

I pondered the idea. "That way, we fool the fool!" I finished. "That's what we'll do, then. That's a great plan."

"So, what do you think? Will it work?" asked Tavit.

"I don't see a way that it can't, to be honest with you," I replied. "But what if the basket isn't there?"

"Well, then, at least Vartan will talk to Nadia, right?" said Tavit.

"True," I said.

"Let's try it. C'mon. What else are we going to do? Talk about the future? We're too young for that."

I laughed as Tavit stood up and brushed the dirt off his clothes.

"Help me up," I said, extending my arm.

Tavit grabbed my hand and pulled me up. I also brushed myself off.

"Okay, so where's Nadia?" he asked.

"She's inside. I see her," I replied, as I peered in through the porch window.

"But Vartan isn't," I continued. "I don't see him."

"Well, where is he?"

"I don't know. I don't see him," I repeated, looking around some more. "Okay, I'll go inside and tell Nadia to meet by the well in five minutes."

"All right. I'll find Vartan and tell him the same," said Tavit.

With a quick hop inside, I went to talk to Nadia. A few moments later, the door of the outhouse creaked open, and Vartan walked out.

"Figures," Tavit sighed under his breath. He stepped off the porch and waved his arm. "Vartan!" he yelled with a whisper.

"Tavit?" Vartan asked.

"Yeah, come here."

Vartan walked over.

"Vartan, we're planning to all have a meeting by the well in five minutes. It's very important. Promise me you'll be there?"

"What's it about?"

"You'll find out when you get there," he explained.

"What are you going to do to me? Is this a prank?" continued Vartan.

"No, I promise that we won't do anything to you and that it is not a prank. Just meet us there in five minutes."

"Fine," he replied, "but you promised that it's not a prank."

"I know I did."

"Good," he said.

"Oh, there you are, Vartan," I said as I exited the house.

I looked over at Tavit and gave him a small nod that everything went according to plan. He acknowledged my signal.

"Five minutes," I said. "No more, no less."

"Fine," Vartan agreed.

"Good," I said. "Tavit, let's go."

"What? I'm coming, too!" my brother whined.

"No, this is only for me and Tavit," I clarified. "Trust

me."

Vartan stared at us, confused and understandably skeptical as Tavit and I ran off into the darkness to the west. Vartan then pulled a porch chair for himself and sat, gazing up at the night sky, admiring the stars. Thinking. He always had a passion for the unknown, exemplifying an unreachable knowledge as vast as space itself. Thus, with all he knew about the universe, he took a lot of pride in it.

As he stared up into the heavens, Nadia casually walked out the front door, passing him. Unaware of his presence, she proceeded out into the darkness as Vartan, not knowing what to say, simply watched her leave, striking him deeper into curiosity. He tilted his head to one side, wondering where she was going. To the outhouse, perhaps? He peered to his left where it stood and then back at Nadia. No, that wasn't it; she was walking in the wrong direction, continuing on her path straight out.

"Maybe she's lost," he thought as she disappeared into the darkness.

Looking around, he thus sat patiently, waiting for the time to pass. A minute later, he stood up off the chair. "All right," he muttered to himself.

As he stepped off the porch, he unknowingly followed Nadia's exact same path.

"Look, there he is!" I said with a nudge to Tavit from an apricot tree.

"It's working!" he laughed as he shook my shoulders in excitement.

"Shh… shh… Let's watch," I whispered.

Continuing to indulge in our growing success, we watched as Vartan walked to the well. Just as he approached it, there stood Nadia, standing alone, directly in his line of sight. Seeing this, he quickly slowed his pace but maintained his course, looking straight ahead. Nadia stood as her silhouette marinated elegantly in the warm air of the night. Like a gently flowing river, her dress waved through the calm wind, and her hair shone under the dim moonlight like a gold statue in the bare sun. Next to her, the small woven basket still sat on the ledge of the well. If

Vartan had a paintbrush and a canvas, he could have created a masterpiece that would have lasted through the ages.

Then, as though acting on impulse, Vartan slowed even more, now ready to fully turn around, ready to head back to the house and abandon the mission. Just as he was about to, though, Nadia spoke.

"Vartan?" she asked. "Is that you?"

"What?" he said as he finished his course. "Umm, yes. It's me."

"Where is everyone else?" she asked.

"I'm… uhh… I'm not sure. They'll be here soon," he said as he fumbled with his hands and looked around.

"Do you know what game we're going to play?" she asked.

"Game?" he asked.

"Armen told me that we're going to play a game," she clarified.

Vartan looked at Nadia confusedly and thought for a moment. He then laughed to himself, "Oh, those smartasses."

"Excuse me?" asked Nadia.

"Oh, um, nothing. Tavit told me that we were going to have a meeting."

"You're going to have a meeting?"

"No, no. He told me that we were going to have a meeting here, at this spot, and Armen must have told you that we were going to play a game."

"I don't understand."

"There is no meeting, and there is no game. They didn't tell anyone else to meet here. It's only me and you," he explained. "They did this purposely."

"Oh," she said, shifting her weight uncomfortably.

"Do you want to go back?" he asked. "We can go back if you want."

"No, I think I'll stay here for a while."

"I can walk you back. It's no problem."

"I'm all right, thank you," she said.

"Well, do you mind if I stay with you?" he asked boldly.

"Not at all," she welcomed. "It's a beautiful night."

"Yeah, it is. It's very peaceful," observed Vartan. "I come out here sometimes to relax," he continued. "This is my favorite spot."

"Really?" asked Nadia.

"Yeah, it's this well," he said as he placed his palm on the cold wall. "I've always loved this well. There's something about it. Maybe it's the stone. I'm not sure."

"Maybe you have good memories here," she said, looking at him.

"Well, none that come to mind," he said foolishly. His heart beat rapidly.

"Oh," said Nadia.

Vartan nervously looked around. The conversation seemed to have promise, but it quickly turned as silent as the dead of the night. Neither Nadia nor Vartan knew what to say. Vartan hoped that she would say something to spark a conversation but became impatient and forced himself to speak.

"The dinner was delicious. I really enjoyed it," he complimented.

"Yes, it was so good!" she said with a smile on her face.

"You're all great chefs."

"Thank you, I'm happy it turned out as good as it did. I thought the bread was going to be too sweet."

"No, you can never be too sweet," commented Vartan. "I mean, it came out perfectly. Next time I'll help you."

"Oh, you don't have to."

"I want to. Tavit taught me a few things. He really likes to cook when he's not lazy."

"I didn't know Tavit liked to cook," she said.

"Yup, he's actually pretty good."

"Oh, really?" she said.

"Yup," he responded proudly.

There was another break in the conversation. Vartan thought anxiously of another way to continue the speech.

"You know, I've always loved the night sky," said Nadia, looking up.

"You have?" he asked, shocked, now seeing an opportunity to impress her.

"Yes. It seems so interesting up there."

"Well, it is," said Vartan.

From the house, Ara and his family were getting ready to leave. Vartan and Nadia paused to listen to them speak outside on the porch.

"Nadia!" her father called out a moment later. "Are you ready?"

"I'll be there soon!" she answered back.

"I have to go," she said as she stepped away from the edge of the well and began walking towards the house.

Vartan looked around. "Wait, Nadia!" he yelled.

She turned around. "Yes?"

"You forgot your basket!" he said, carefully running it over to her.

"Oh, this isn't mine," she said.

"Well, you can have them," he said, handing it over.

"No, my father took a whole lot earlier."

"Trust me, Nadia, these are extra, and I want you to have them because I know how much you love apricots."

She recognized his persistence. "You're very nice," she said, accepting the gift. "Thank you." She then leaned in and gave Vartan a kiss on his cheek. "Have a good night."

Vartan stood in his place in shock as Tavit and I looked on from the tree.

"Oh my God, she kissed him," Tavit breathed.

"She kissed him?" I said, turning my attention back to the well.

"Yes, but it was on the cheek."

"Oh, so it was a good-bye kiss." I shrugged nonchalantly.

"No, it was more like a *kiss* kiss."

"What do you mean a *kiss* kiss?" I asked.

"How else do you want me to put it? Do you want me to show you? It was just one kiss on one cheek," he clarified. "And he gave her the basket!"

"It worked!" I laughed with a big smile on my face.

"It worked!" Tavit repeated as he patted my shoulders and did a small celebratory dance with his hands.

"Vartan," I thought out loud, "he's nothing without us."

"I know. Like a fish on land. Useless!"

As Nadia stepped back onto the porch, Garo walked out the door and called for his son.

"Coming!" Tavit responded.

He turned to me in assurance. "Okay Armen, I'll see you soon, my friend."

"Come over anytime you want," I said.

"Okay, thank you," he said as he climbed down the tree. "Do you want to come over tomorrow? I have to chop some firewood in the morning, but I'm free after that."

"Sure, I have nothing to do," I affirmed.

"Good. *Gu desnuveenk*," he finished, saying "we'll see each other later."

In Armenian, it is true that there is no explicit way of saying good-bye; the day always ends with a saying that suggests a reunion, never a solid parting.

"*Gu desnuveenk*," I replied as I stayed perched up in the apricot tree, listening to the leaves rustle in the silence of the wind. Like a bird searching for a worm, I looked at Vartan, who still stood near the well. "Good for him," I thought, happy that my brother finally had faced his only known fear.

After slowly sliding down in his spot, I watched as Vartan backed up to lean against the wall of the well. With a quick touch against the cold of the stone, his back muscles tensed up, causing him to lean forward. Slowly then, he leaned back once more, this time allowing his back to become acquainted to the feel. With a casual swipe, he then picked up an apricot from the ground, one that he missed from earlier, and held it in front of him, thinking how one small piece of fruit could end up writing the unique story of his life.

"Fate," Vartan smiled with a shake of his head, "how mysterious."

12

The sweet aroma of the low-lying fog of the following morning yielded the brand new start of a new day. The early dew had snuck in and settled on the tiny blades of grass, bending them safely out of shape. The rays of the rising sun shone through the tiny droplets of water, making them sparkle like diamonds in the field. There was a small rainbow over the horizon. The animals spoke and welcomed the day to begin again. With my body leaning against the moist bark of the apricot tree, the droplets of water from the leaves rhythmically fell onto my face.

"Get out of that tree, you monkey," I heard a voice call me from below.

"What?" I asked confusedly as I stretched out my arms and yawned, wobbling unsteadily upon the branch. I had forgotten that I had spent the entire night in the tree. It wasn't the first time that I had done so, but I was just too tired and too lazy to climb down the night before.

After carefully finding my balance, I planted my feet on the ground, holding onto my brother for stability.

"So," I began, hazy-eyed.

"So, what?" he asked for clarification.

"Did you have a good time last night?"

Vartan paused. He couldn't hide it anymore.

"You and Tavit are—I don't even know the word for you two," he said with a smile.

"You can say thank you. That works," I replied sarcastically.

"Oh, be quiet," he said. "Thanks."

"You're welcome. How was the kiss?" I asked.

"What kiss?"

"Stop acting stupid! I know she kissed you!"

"She did, but it was just on the cheek. It doesn't mean anything."

"It doesn't mean anything? Has she ever kissed you like that before? No."

"Well, I'm not sure. Maybe she did it just to be nice."

"What do you mean?"

"I think she only kissed me because she felt like she had to."

"But you didn't force her," I reasoned.

"Not like that. She was leaving *and* saying thank you at the same time. You know?" explained Vartan.

"But it was one kiss," I said.

"So what?"

"Everyone here gives *two* kisses when they say hello and *two* more when they say good-bye. *One* kiss means she likes you."

"Really?"

"That's how it works. And *that's* why I think she likes you," I concluded prematurely.

"Really?" repeated Vartan, trying to hold in his excitement.

"Yeah, just hide your face next time."

Vartan frowned.

"Really, though. I see the way she looks at you."

"How so?"

"I'm not sure how to describe it. It's the same way you look at her, except not so creepy. When she's around you, her face lights up like when a farm animal sees food."

"Like a farm animal?"

"Okay, maybe that was a bad analogy, but you get the point."

"Yeah, let's see if you're right."

"Just don't mess it up."

My brother and I had a special relationship, never initially speaking our thoughts or the things on our minds. It always took a little probing on both ends to get inside each other's heads. Like all secrets, though, we initially used them for good and for bad, in support of and against each other. It took a few years and many failed attempts to learn how to use each other's secrets responsibly, but with the development of a trusting relationship, we shared nearly everything and, with the finest of detail, quickly became a powerhouse of each other's knowledge and experiences.

"You two slept outside?" little Margaret asked as she walked out to us.

"Yeah, we were tired," I explained.

"Gross! *Hyreeg* wants your help in the barn," she continued.

"Both of us or just me?" I asked.

"Both of you," she said with her hands on her waist.

After acknowledging her request, we walked into the house where Vartan picked up my brown leather satchel, the one with a floppy top and a rod and loop for the closure, from the floor near the fireplace and put some fruit in it for breakfast. Through the small side window, I then saw my father on the ground near the barn, hammering underneath the plow that the oxen pull.

"Is it broken?" asked Vartan when we met with him.

"No," my father responded. "It seems to be jammed here," he grunted.

My father swung the hammer three more times, and with the third strike, the main support slid back into place, and the whole plow shifted.

"Yup!" he exclaimed. "Now it's ready."

He then slid himself out from underneath and stood up, pulled a handkerchief from his back pocket, and wiped his hands clean, all the while examining my brother and me.

"You two slept outside last night," he stated factually.

"Well, we were tired," explained Vartan.

"Decent human beings sleep inside when given a choice. Let's go to the barn. I want to clean it out today."

My brother and I looked at each other as we followed him to the barn. Cleaning it out was not an easy task. It was dusty, and it was dark with sharp pieces of metal everywhere. To keep the animals inside, a large metal chain hung through the handles of the barn door. Through the thick links was a thick metal rod to prevent the chain from falling loose.

My father slid out the rod and began unwinding the heavy chain. Aside from the clanking of the links, a low scratching sound from inside the door caught my attention. I made no mention of it. My father then slid out the chain and handed it over to me. I leaned my head down as he draped it over my shoulders, letting it rest behind my neck; he then grabbed the handle of the heavy wooden door. With a light tug, a crack appeared between the two doors, and a mixture of hay and dust flew out from inside. My father wrinkled his nose, trying not to breathe it in as I reached for the handle to help him pull it open. In the blink of an eye, however, both doors suddenly and violently flung out. The impact of the doors knocked me to the ground, sending the chain off my shoulders, and threw my father into Vartan behind him. From the ground, I watched as one ox made a mad dash for freedom, and the other followed close behind. My father scrambled on the ground and swore loudly, while I stood up and shook my head, trying to understand what just happened.

"Are you all right?" I asked as I extended my arm for my father.

"*Hyreeg*, your nose is bleeding," stated Vartan from the ground.

Not taking a hold of my hand, my father stood up on his own, beyond infuriated. He took his handkerchief from his pocket and held it over his face.

"Vartan! I told you to tie up the oxen!"

"Sorry, I forgot!" he sympathized. "Is your nose broken?"

"Don't worry about my nose! Get the oxen!"

In the distance, the beasts ran swiftly and rapidly towards the far horizon. Vartan looked at me, and without a moment of hesitation, he ran into the barn, untied our black horse, and hopped on. He ducked his head as he rode out and then stopped to pick me up. I extended my arm, and he leaned over to pull me up.

"Yah!" he screamed as he dug his heels into the horse's side. Its powerful legs kicked the dirt up from the ground and flung it into the air. I adjusted my position on the saddle, and we were off.

As we gained speed, the wind flew threw my dark brown hair as we quickly pushed our horse to his limits. My eyes began to water, but I kept them open to be extra attentive. We passed a few herd of sheep with their shepherds, and they looked on as we passed. Needing a moment to think about the escape route of our oxen, I tapped Vartan to stop for a minute to have a look around the land. He tightened the reins, and the horse came to a halt.

"Do you see them?" he asked.

I rubbed the dust out of my eyes. "No, not yet. I think they ran straight west," I said.

"Okay," agreed Vartan.

"How about by the river?" I suggested. "Maybe they're thirsty."

"Good idea. Let's try there."

Vartan clicked his heels once again, and we continued. I narrowed my eyes and focused them into the distance. After riding for a few minutes, we finally arrived at the banks of the river, a small branch of the Euphrates. The thicket around the shore was dense, so we searched around for an opening for our horse to have a drink. When we found a clearing and the horse had its fill, we patrolled the northern banks for about half a kilometer. We found nothing and thus prowled the southern banks like lions hunting a gazelle. About a third of a kilometer south of the initial clearing in the brush, there stood two humble beasts, drunk on freedom.

"Finally," whispered Vartan.

I jumped off the horse, and Vartan did as well. He tied the reins to a small tree and walked towards the oxen.

"Take off your shirt," he instructed.

"Why?" I asked.

"Just do it."

I took my shirt off, and he did, too.

"Throw it over their eyes," explained Vartan. "Then we can capture them."

"Why don't we just grab the harness?" I asked.

"They won't get scared this way."

"All right," I said.

"Be careful of the horns!" he added.

I nodded my head at his request.

As we crept towards the two oxen, shirts dangling loosely at our sides, one grunted and wiggled its ear, sending the flies scurrying in all directions. We quickly stopped, then began again a moment later. As soon as I got close enough to smell them, I threw my shirt over the ox's eyes. It grunted again and took a step backwards, but I lunged in and grabbed the leather harness. Securely in hand, I exhaled a sigh of relief and relaxed, standing erect, just as Vartan followed suit and successfully grabbed the other.

"Nice job," I commended as we tied the two oxen together and then tied them to the small tree next to the horse.

We then put our shirts back on.

"It's amazing how much happens before breakfast," Vartan said.

"Yeah," I laughed.

For a moment, then, I watched as the river flowed so beautifully and so clearly that it looked like it could be made of glass. The more I looked at it, the thirstier I became. Thus, I leaned in and took the crystal-clear water with the cups of my hands and drank, making a loud sipping sound.

"Ahh," I exhaled with satisfaction.

Vartan looked at me.

"Here, drink some," I offered.

"I'm not thirsty," he responded.

"It's so cold and really sweet," I described. "Just try it."

Vartan crawled up next to me and drank from the river.

"Yeah, that *is* cold," he said. "It's very refreshing."

Vartan opened my satchel. "Here," he said as he reached in and threw an apricot at me.

"Thanks," I replied, "nice satchel."

Vartan laughed, "Thanks."

With the oxen tied up, we sat and rested in the thicket along the small bank to eat our breakfast. I celebrated, apricot in hand, gratified that our mission didn't end in failure. Across the river, where the bank was higher, I noticed a small house made of old, weathered wood. Becoming evermore observant, I noticed the shutters hanging loosely from their hinges and the roof slightly curving inward. I wondered why I had never noticed the house before.

"Who do you think lives there?" asked Vartan.

"I don't know. Maybe nobody. It looks like no one is taking care of it."

"No, I think someone lives there. Look, the land is cultivated around it," he pointed.

"So then why does it look like that?" I asked.

"Who knows, maybe the owner is just lazy."

"Or poor," I offered.

Vartan cocked his head to one side and shrugged his shoulders. "Maybe."

From the northern horizon, I then noticed two fully uniformed, armed men, complete with their red fez hats, galloping on horseback towards the old house.

They were Turkish soldiers.

"Vartan," I pointed, "look."

"I see them," he said. "Just be quiet. Get down."

Quietly, we shifted our positions onto our bellies. We didn't want to be seen. The door of the dilapidated house slowly opened, and an elderly man walked out to greet the soldiers.

"Ha!" exclaimed Vartan. "I knew it!"

"Shh! You told *me* to be quiet," I said accusingly, annoyed that he was correct about someone living inside.

"Yeah, all right, shh," he said, feeding my aggravation.

"Don't walk any closer," the soldiers told the elderly man from atop their horses in Ottoman Turkish.

"Of course," he responded in the same language. "How may I help you today?"

"We are here to collect your taxes," a soldier replied. "The tax collector said you haven't paid."

"Haven't paid? I've already paid them twice this month. There must be a mistake," replied the man.

"Ha, he has paid his taxes already; then let's go!" the

soldier said sarcastically to his partner. They took a small break to laugh then quickly changed their tone. "There is no mistake. You will pay your taxes today."

"If you will allow me, I have the receipts for my payments in my home," offered the elderly man with a casual point to his broken house.

The soldiers didn't say anything, so the elderly man turned around to walk back. In response, one of the two soldiers unholstered his pistol, hanging near his dagger, and pointed it at him.

"Do not move one more centimeter," he ordered.

The man turned around and looked at the soldier holding the weapon. He inhaled and extended his neck, maintaining his composure. Both soldiers then slowly climbed off their horses, pistol still pointed.

"You cannot do this! I have paid my taxes twice already!" he pleaded. "I don't have much left to give!"

The soldiers walked towards him.

"Please, lower your weapon. I mean no harm."

They ignored his plea. The innocent glare on the elderly man's face obviously had no effect, so he changed his tactic.

"We are all equal citizens in this empire!" he demanded. "You cannot do this!"

Keeping his pistol pointed, the soldiers moved closer until the one raised his arm and struck the man's head with the butt of it. The elderly man fell, clutching his bleeding wound. He then turned the pistol back around and pointed the barrel directly at his head. The rays of the morning sun behind us reflected off the metal of the pistol directly into my eyes. I squinted.

"Please," cried the man, "I beg you. My family!"

The soldier cocked his pistol. "Just a disease."

I gasped and closed my eyes as a way to brace myself. With a pull of the trigger, the soldier fired his weapon, and I jumped at the menacing sound. I then opened my eyes in astonishment just as the birds had flown away.

On the ground, the elderly man cried.

He was still alive.

The second soldier had redirected his partner's gun into the sky just before it discharged. Both their hands remained on the pistol, and he turned his head into the direction of my gasp.

"Shh… shh," he whispered, slowly lowering his hand off the weapon.

Vartan put his hands over my mouth and pulled me farther down. He looked into my eyes, and I stared back as the soldiers walked over to the bank and peeked over, trying to find the source of the noise. We were so deep in the brush and so well hidden that they couldn't possibly see us or our animals. We were completely out of sight, and yet, my heart beat irregularly fast. There, the two soldiers stood and searched around for a short time, being limited by their attention span. A few seconds later, they looked at each other, and the one put his pistol back into his holster. They turned around and walked back to the injured man. There, they held his face into the ground and went through his pockets to take whatever they could. They both then climbed back onto their horses and continued back in the direction from which they'd arrived.

As soon as it was long clear, Vartan and I jumped up and rode back as quick as we could with the oxen attached behind our horse. We were more surprised than scared.

"*Mama!*" I screamed as we neared the house, oxen tied. "*Hyreeg!*"

No one responded. I ran inside the house.

"Mama!" I screamed again.

"What is it, Armen? She's milking the cows," guided my grandmother.

Vartan and I ran to the barn to our mother sitting on a small wooden stool.

"*Ayo, ayo*, what is it?" she asked with little Margaret sitting next to her, learning the trade.

"Mama," began Vartan, "you won't believe this, but there was an elderly man and two soldiers, and one soldier was going to kill the man because he didn't pay his taxes, and then the other heard Armen gasp and then he hit him and then—"

Vartan breathed, heavily out of breath.

"Wait, wait. Slow down, Vartan," directed my father, approaching the scene with his swollen nose. "Stop acting like that and speak clearly."

My grandmother sat inside and listened attentively from the open side window.

"Okay. We were sitting on the bank of the river when two soldiers came up to an elderly man to collect his taxes," I said.

"What were you doing by the river?" he interrogated.

"That's where the oxen were," answered Vartan.

"Go on," he said, twirling the tip of his mustache—his signature move.

"And the man said he paid his taxes twice already, but the soldiers didn't care. He even said he had receipts to prove that he paid."

"Uh-huh." My father crossed his arms and lowered his brows.

"The soldiers didn't care that he had receipts, so they hit his head with the pistol and then he fell," I clarified.

"They were going to shoot him, but the other soldier stopped him because they heard a sound," finished Vartan.

My mother turned to my father. "Tevos, this—" she began.

"Hasmig, I know."

"So, what do we do?" I asked.

"Nothing," instructed my father. "Do not tell anyone. Did they see you?"

"No," I said.

"Then we will continue as normal. Margaret, please go inside. Do not come out here for the rest of the day."

Little Margaret ran inside the house and sat next to our grandmother in the living space.

"So what should we do?" I asked.

"Nothing. Do nothing," my father advised.

"What if the soldiers come back? We should at least help that man," I rationalized.

"I'll go with you, Armen," my brother offered.

"No!" exclaimed my father. "Do not involve yourself in someone else's conflict. I don't want you taking any risks. The soldiers are trained," he reasoned. "You are not."

"I agree with your father. Don't be foolish. I don't want you two getting hurt," added my mother.

"So we're going to sit here and do nothing? What if we can save that man's life?" I asked, trying to reason with my parents.

"Absolutely not. The risk is too great. Don't bring this up again," said my father. "Now put the horse and those oxen in the barn—and tie them up this time!"

"Did you clean it already?" asked Vartan.

"Yes."

"How's your nose?" I asked.

"What's with the questions? My nose is fine. Now get moving. Armen, help your brother."

"All right," I said.

I grabbed the reins of the horse, and Vartan grabbed the harness that held the two oxen together. As we walked them over to the barn, the only vision going through my mind was the elderly man, pleading for his life. What if the soldiers went back and killed him? *Why* would they kill him? I thought further. Over taxes?

I couldn't understand the logic.

Inside the barn, as I tied up the horse, I realized just how clean the interior was—a testament to my father's hard work. Vartan followed me in and checked the harness on the post in the wall. My mother and father were talking to each other on the porch, and their faces seemed to tell the story fairly well—concerned and serious, and for good reason.

"Hey, Armen, if you still want to go save that man, I say we do it," whispered Vartan. "I'll go with you."

"Really?" I exclaimed. "Let's go!"

"Just wait. Let's wait until they go back inside first."

I looked around the barn and grabbed a large pickax. "Here, we'll take this with us for protection."

Vartan looked at me as if I gave him a great idea. "No," he snapped with a devious smile. "I've got it."

I waited for his response.

"The dagger," he finished.

"Yes!" I jumped excitedly. "But it's in their room!"

"No, remember we put it in the well," he said excitedly.

"Oh no," I said. "You were supposed to remind me to get it last night. Let's go."

"Wait, wait." He pulled me back. "They're still not inside."

I rested the pickax, and Vartan and I waited a few minutes until our parents walked inside the house. Then, casually, we ran towards the well while cautiously glancing over our shoulders. I then turned the crank as fast as I could, and Vartan took hold of the rope as a guide. When the bucket neared the top, he leaned inside and grabbed it.

"It's not here!" he exclaimed.

"What do you mean?" I asked, dumbfounded.

Vartan tipped the bucket over, and I peeked inside the empty space.

"Look," he affirmed, clearly disappointed, "it's gone!"

"Oh no, it probably fell to the bottom!" I concluded, peering into the darkness.

Vartan's expression became as equally as upset as mine. The mere thought of the dagger now laying on the bottom of a fifteen-meter well defeated me. Only God knew what my father had to do to acquire such a piece of work.

"We have to get it," suggested Vartan.

"Are you crazy?" I blurted out. "How are we going to do that?"

"We need a rope," he answered. "One that's strong enough. This one here won't hold us."

"Are you sure?"

"No, but I don't want to find out."

"And who's going to go down there?" I asked.

"Well, I thought *you* would do that."

"No. No way. This is your dagger, and you should be

responsible for it."

Vartan's blank expression showed that he knew there was nothing else he could do to convince me. So he stood and thought for a while.

"Fine," he said. "But you have to lower me down."

"Obviously."

"Okay then, let's find more rope."

Like small mammals, we scurried back to the barn to search inside, and I curled my face at the smell.

"Armen, what do you feed these oxen?" Vartan asked.

"It smells like your room," I replied.

The inside of the barn was fairly large. It had to house two oxen, a horse, and a lot of other animals. There were individual stables below the top deck, which ran the inside perimeter. As a permanent house for hay and extra equipment, that deck seemed like a good place to start. So, I climbed the ladder and began my search for a rope that would suit our needs.

"We could tie some pieces together," suggested Vartan from across the way. He held up a short piece in one hand.

"What if it comes undone?" I asked.

"Well, we'll tie it really tight."

"You want to risk it?" I asked. "It's your choice. You're the one going down there."

"Okay, maybe not," he decided.

"By the way, Tavit wants us to come over," I said.

"That's great, Armen, but saving that man is a little bit more important."

"Okay, but I meant *after* we save th—"

From the entrance to the barn, a familiar voice quickly cut me off: "Are you boys looking for something?"

I looked down.

It was my father. In his hands, he held the dagger, quickly predetermining the moment into one of bittersweet complexity. On one hand, the joyful relief that we hadn't lost the dagger filled my heart, and on the other, we were now in trouble.

"Where did you find it?" asked Vartan.

"In the well bucket this morning," he said. "Climb down

and go inside."

Turning around, my father walked away. As if looking in a mirror, I exchanged a glance with Vartan, the kind only fools could make. We then did as we were told and made our way back inside the house. My father walked behind us and placed the dagger, in plain view, on the small, weathered table in the kitchen.

"This, boys, is not a toy," he started. "You are not to use it for anything other than what I tell you."

We listened.

"Your grandmother wants a few words with you," he added.

Vartan and I shifted our attention to our grandmother to our left, sitting in her chair.

"Please, sit down," she said with a smile.

Walking over, we quietly sat down on some cushions across from her.

"I want to tell you boys a story that is very important to our family. I will try to keep this as short as I can, but you must promise to always remember it," she began. "God only knows if it will be lost with the others."

I must admit, I was very confused and felt a strange severity fill my head.

"Have you boys heard of the Hamidian Massacres?" she asked.

"I've heard of it, but I'm not sure what it is exactly," answered Vartan.

"Yeah," I said, nodding my head, "same."

"Your grandfather, my husband, died before you could know him. He was very handsome and very strong. Both of you remind me of him very much. As you were told growing up, he worked in the mill. That part is true. The story you know about how he was killed by a mill blade, you would have never known, is not true."

Vartan and I exchanged glances. She had our attention.

"Your grandfather was killed in 1894 by the Turks. He was killed defending my honor inside my home in the village of

Sasun at the beginning of these Hamidian Massacres."

She pointed her finger at us. "Sultan Abdul-Hamid II—have you heard that name before?"

"He was the sultan before, right?" I asked.

"Yes," replied my grandmother, "and you must always remember that name."

"I learned that in school." I poked my brother.

"Armen, pay attention," my father reiterated.

I turned back to my grandmother.

"If evil has a face," she continued, "it is the face of that man. Abdul-Hamid was the mastermind behind what happened to us in Sasun. He ordered the outright slaughter of thousands of innocent civilians, using any excuse he could, all to answer what he called the Armenian question—how are we going to get rid of the Armenians?

"As long as we have been a part of this empire, Armenians have been stripped bare of any hope to share the same liberties and rights as the Turks, leading to the declaration of the sultan's Armenian question as an international problem," she explained.

"The sultan, however, continued, ignoring international reprimand, fixated on his goal of annihilating the Armenian population, and devised a plan. In the early stages, he created a group of Turkish and Kurdish bandits called the Hamidiye Cavalry, meaning 'belonging to Hamid.' They were given uniforms and official status to try to free the empire of all Armenians. And, from 1894 to 1896, the Hamidian Massacres were carried out against us.

"My husband fell at the feet of a heartless group of criminals passing themselves off as soldiers."

My mother came in and sat next to my father against the kitchen table, and little Margaret sat on the floor.

"The morning of your grandfather's death was very cloudy, but it was not yet raining. He was working away on the fields when, without warning or provocation, thousands of those Ottoman Turkish soldiers marched into Sasun. I watched from my window as they torched homes and surrounded the village, strategically blocking all exits. At the hour before noon, they began ravaging and stealing anything and from anyone. Once they had done as they pleased, they began killing, murdering men, women, and children by the masses, without the fear of penalty. By the hour after noon, our village was on fire, and most of the men were dead."

"Why? And why did no one stop them?" Vartan questioned.

"We were unorganized, and more so, we were caught by surprise. The sultan and his government at Constantinople, the capital, ordered this massacre because they felt threatened by our Armenian influence as minorities and devout Christian beliefs. Over the years, they had grown paranoid by our success and the increasing possibility of revolt over simple things like equal rights, even *basic* rights, and an independent state. Eventually, their sickness grew uncontrollably as we became more persistent in demanding these basic freedoms."

Immediately, Vartan and I turned our heads towards each other.

"That man," I whispered.

"Yes, just across the river," my grandmother nodded, quickly finishing her sentence. "That's Bedros. He knows very well what horrors the Turks are capable of."

She covered her mouth with a weakened fist and coughed. It was long and drawn out.

"*Medzmama*, are you all right?" I asked.

"*Ayo*, my dear, I am fine," she replied.

"Here's some bread," said my mother as she broke off a piece from dinner the night before and handed it to her.

"Thank you, dear," she said.

"Turkish soldiers," she continued with bread in hand, "kicked down the door to our home and marched inside with torches. They yelled for everyone to exit. I was alone, and they didn't see me, so I hid under my bed. I didn't know what else to do."

My grandmother looked up at the ceiling.

"They tore the house apart from wall to wall and floor

to ceiling. Eventually, they found me and dragged me out. I tried to fight back, but there were too many of them, and they all supported each other in their crime. With three soldiers standing guard at the front, two held me down on the floor of our house and beat me. One hit after the other, they pounded my body. Afraid that they were going to kill me, I screamed your grandfather's name as loud as I could. By the great miracles of the Lord Himself, your grandfather ran in from the back not one moment too soon, immediately killing the two soldiers that held me down. He then ran to the front door and killed the remaining three. He was so quick. They didn't even have time to react."

She paused for a moment, and her eyes began to swell. My grandmother, however, didn't cry. Her tears, as if too afraid to show themselves, crawled back into her eyes, where they remained. Her feelings, her emotions, then quickly became nonexistent, hardened like rock.

"He killed them," she finished confidently, "with that dagger." She pointed to the table where it lay.

My eyes widened as I sat quietly, not knowing what to say or how to respond. I now had an infinite number of questions racing through my mind. So many detailed questions. I wanted to know more. I wanted to know about her emotions. I wanted to know what she was thinking, what she *saw*, what she *heard*, how she *felt*. I wanted to see my grandfather's footsteps, his actions, the moves he used, the jabs he made. I then wanted to see the soldiers, their faces. I wanted to know what they wore. I wanted to hear their conversations, hear their voices. I wanted details. So many details. I wanted to know because I needed to understand. I needed to be there with her. After a quick thought, however, I bit my tongue.

Did I *really*?

"So what happened to *Medzbaba?*" asked Vartan about our grandfather.

"He then came to me and held me on the floor to calm my nerves. Just as he was helping me, a wounded soldier at the door shot him in the back. Your grandfather, as angry as I've ever seen him, dashed at that soldier and killed him. He, himself, died shortly after, right there in our house. It then burned to the ground with him inside."

She paused.

"Your grandfather," she said, "saved me. And that dagger is all that remains of his memories. You are to defend it and not treat it as a toy. I don't want to see it in the bottom of a well. Do you understand?" she asked.

"Yes," we said unanimously, now understanding the severity of our actions.

"But be forewarned," she added. "What they did to us in Sasun was only the beginning. The end, I am saddened to say, is not near. I feel it. The Turks will keep us satisfied until they find a way to finish what they started."

"Mom, please," interjected my mother.

"Hasmig, they have done it before, and they will try it again. I am sure of it."

With all that my mind craved, my grandmother's words dug themselves deeply and heavily inside my body and engraved themselves into the canyons of my brain. A cold, unnatural pulse ran down the length of my spine and continued through my feet and into the ground.

"How do you know?" I asked, ignoring my mother.

"I feel it," she replied. "I have always felt it in my heart."

Vartan then asked the one question I didn't want to know the answer to.

"When?"

My grandmother locked her eyes with his and then looked away.

"Only God knows. Perhaps tomorrow. Perhaps ten years from now. Whatever the case, I am certain that they *cannot* and *will not* succeed," she responded. "You must therefore always keep a sharp eye. *Always*."

Silence surrounded us.

"So… how…" Vartan began, breaking the silence. "How did you escape?"

"As the house caught fire, I took a pistol and the dagger and escaped from the same door your grandfather entered to save me. I snuck to the perimeter of Sasun and ran east with only the clothes on my back.

"I stopped at a stable at the outskirts and hid there for two weeks. Eventually, I made my way to this house, where your father and mother were living, and stayed here ever since."

"Wow," I whispered under my breath.

"And three years later, you were born," she continued, lightening the mood, pointing to Vartan. "And two years after that, you were born," she said, pointing to me. "And *five* years after that, someone else was born but I forgot who," she said, searching around the room.

"Hey! That was me! I was born!" little Margaret exclaimed from the floor.

"Oh, that's right! It *was* you!" cheered my grandmother.

We all smiled, and I felt a little better.

"Well then, I hope you learned something today, boys," said my father.

"We did," I responded.

"All right, then. You are free," he finished.

"Can I go to Tavit's house?" I asked.

Vartan looked at me as if saying, "Now is not the time."

"Absolutely not," my mother answered. "It's too dangerous."

"But, *Mama*!" I exclaimed. "I'll go straight to his house and straight back!"

"You heard my answer, but I'll pass this one to your father."

She looked at him. He paused for a moment, then spoke.

"Do not stop for anyone or anything. Do you understand? Once you are at Tavit's house, you stay at Tavit's house," he ordered. "And you *will* return before dark."

He turned to my mother. "We will *not* live in fear."

"You heard your father," she said. "You may go. Come give me a kiss before you leave."

Satisfied, Vartan and I got up and kissed her. We then walked out the door.

Outside, I realized there was no quick recovery after my grandmother's story. It was heavy, but it was a story nonetheless that I never forgot. Even at fourteen, I thought about the struggle she must have endured and the scars she must have hidden. I thought about the fears she must have faced, the bravery and courage she must have showed. I then thought about how easy it was to take the things we had for granted, reminding myself how selfish it was to divert the lesson to my own agenda.

Why, I wasn't sure.

"It was your idea to put the dagger in the well," I whispered to Vartan as soon as we were outside and away from hearing distance.

"We're both guilty," he replied, "especially you for asking to go to Tavit's house right after. What was that all about?"

"Well, what else was I supposed to do? I told Tavit I'd come over," I replied, not wanting to admit my faults.

"You could have at least waited to ask," said Vartan, "after things settled down."

"What about Bedros?" I asked. "Let's go check on him."

"Why? You just said you were going to Tavit's house. I'm sure he's all right."

"What? How do you know?" I asked.

"Because I saw the soldiers leave," he explained, trying to justify his want for inaction.

Deep down, however, my guilt took the best of my decisions. I said nothing, and eventually, Vartan's guilt got the best of him, too.

"Fine," he complied a moment later. "Let's take the horse and ride east towards Tavit's house, then double back to the river."

"Yes!" I clapped my hands together. "All right!"

"Because I don't want *Hyreeg* seeing us going to Tavit's house in the *wrong* direction."

"I know, I know. Okay," I said excitedly as we casually walked inside the barn.

To my immediate right, I lifted the saddle that hung on an old nail in the wall and placed it atop our black horse. Then, I hoisted myself up behind Vartan, and we rode out east towards Tavit's house. After a short gallop, we turned south towards the pasture where the Turkish boys herded their sheep and circled back west all the way until we hit the river. We then stationed ourselves in the brush across from Bedros's broken house almost exactly where we were earlier that day. With no way of crossing, we waited low like two toothless tigers stalking their prey.

"Vartan, I don't see him," I whispered, feeling my heartbeat speed up.

"Neither do I," he responded.

"What are we going to do if we see the soldiers?" I asked.

The unanswered question struck Vartan and me a little too hard, and the possibility of our sudden death, for some reason, seemed like a reality. Were we afraid to do something? Or was I just panicking?

"I don't know," admitted Vartan, suddenly on edge. "We run."

Focusing on the mission, we stuck our heads high and used our senses to the best of their abilities, looking for any signs of human existence. The next few minutes seemed to last for an eternity, allowing my one question to soak deeply into my bones. What were we going to do? Anything?

Just then, the front door of the house slowly creaked open. We raised our heads higher to have a better look to see who it could be. It then closed back and nobody came out. Like an owl, I stared at the door, never taking my eyes off it, until once again, it opened. To our immediate relief and satisfaction, Bedros walked out of his house with a tan cloth wrapped around his head.

He seemed all right, and Vartan and I quickly loosened up.

"I told you; he's fine," he said.

"Man," I sighed. "Okay, good."

"C'mon, Armen, do you feel better?" he said as he

clambered up. "Let's go find Tavit."

Despite being likely more nervous than me, Vartan quickly helped ease my anxiety, and all for good reason. As my older brother, he had an unspoken obligation to always have the answers and make the correct decisions in any circumstance. This was his way of being my life-long role model. I admired his self-taught ability, but I feared that sometimes it overshadowed my own qualities, my own strengths. In the end, however, I was more relieved to discover that he had been right all along, even when I sensed that he doubted himself.

As the late-morning sun reached its peak, Vartan helped me up from the brush, then back onto our horse. I felt more at ease knowing there was nothing wrong with what we did, even though we disobeyed my father. I couldn't help it. It was something in me that wanted to fight for what was right, to help those who needed to be helped, with complete disregard of the consequences. Thus, with the powerful rays of the sun bearing down directly overhead, I lowered my chin to block their path as Vartan kicked his heels. With a quick jump ahead, we started our way to Tavit's house in the east.

13

The road to Tavit's house was nearly the same as the road to *Soorp Asdvadzadzin*, our church. However, just before the pasture where the Turkish boys herd their sheep, there was a fork in the road—the right fork continued east to church, and the left turned north to Tavit's house. By horse, it was about a five minutes' gallop, but by foot, it was about a fifty-minute walk.

As we approached his house, Garo, Tavit's father, approached us with a smile on his face and a cigarette hanging from his mouth. He took it out with his left hand to speak.

"Welcome, Vartan! Welcome, Armen!" he delighted as if he hadn't seen us in ten years, even though he had seen us just the day before. The blessing to him was the new day, and he showed it well.

With a swing back to his mouth, he took one last puff of the cigarette and exhaled the smoke into the sky, throwing the unfinished roll onto the ground where he extinguished it with his foot. Even though he smoked too much, Garo tried not to smoke around others, especially his nonsmoking guests. Thus, for the moment, he curbed his addiction.

"*Parev!*" exclaimed Vartan as he jumped off our black horse.

"Hello, hello!" I said, leaning a bit.

Garo grabbed the reins. "I'll tie him up," he said. "Are you boys hungry?"

"Thank you," said Vartan, "but we're fine for now."

"Great, then in that case, I'll feed your horse!" he laughed. "I don't know where Tavit is, but you're welcome to look for him. He told me he was expecting you."

"Okay, thank you. We'll do that," I decided.

Garo then took our horse and led it to his own barn next to the winery, which was much bigger than his house.

"Tavit!" I called out as I meandered around the premises.

No response.

"Tavit!" I called out again.

"Over here!" I heard faintly.

"Where did that came from?" I asked Vartan.

"Not sure," he said.

"Where are you?" I screamed out.

"Over here!" I heard again.

I looked south to the direction of the voice, and we walked to a massive pile of firewood about eighty meters from the front door of their house.

"Where is he?" I asked, scanning my surroundings.

Vartan shrugged as we both searched the land, trying to pinpoint the origin of Tavit's voice. All we saw were the many narrow trees.

"Tavit!" screamed Vartan.

Still, no response.

"That sneaky boy," I said. "He's playing games with us."

Just at that moment, Vartan snapped his fingers, and I noted his gesture. He put his finger in front of his lips, signaling for me to be quiet, and pointed through the woodpile. I closed one eye and peeked through an opening and saw Tavit's white shirt stand out against the brown of the wood. He was slowly creeping towards the edge in an attempt to scare us. He should have been a little more covert.

"I wonder where he is," I said sarcastically as I leaned over and picked up a medium-sized rock.

"I don't know; that's a very good question," responded Vartan, following my lead.

With a casual toss, I lobbed the rock over the woodpile and heard the hollow thump as it hit Tavit square in the head.

"Ow!" he exclaimed as Vartan jumped around the corner to Tavit's side.

"Tavit!" he yelled, causing him to scream and jump.

Instantly, Vartan and I began to laugh as Tavit quickly eased up, defeated.

"Teaches you to not try to scare us," I stated.

Tavit leaned against the woodpile. "I hate you," he said, "but that was good."

"No, you don't," I said as I placed my arm around him. "Let's go inside. We have something to tell you."

The inside of Tavit's home was quaint. He was an only child, and thus his father found no reason to invest time and money into something so big for only three people. I had a particular liking to the intimacy of being inside, though. There was no second floor, like most houses, and the front door led directly into the kitchen, which led to the tiny living space and two small bedrooms. Garo had the house built from plans he drew, and it was obvious that he liked his windows, which he always kept open because it "keeps the ambiance fresh," as he liked to say.

As we pulled chairs around the square dining table, Tavit walked over to the kitchen, where he took out a small frying pan.

"Armen, did you eat already?" he asked.

"No, did you?" I asked back.

"No."

"Do you want some eggs? I'm going to make some for myself."

"Sure," I responded.

"Vartan, you too?" he offered.

"Please."

Tavit peered into a straw basket and picked out six eggs then broke them over the pan that sat over a burning wood fire.

"Last time you wanted to tell me something, you showed me a dagger," he explained, "so what are you going to show me this time?"

"Tavit, be quiet, you don't know who's listening," I warned. "It's just a story this time."

"Okay, so tell me," he retorted.

"Wait until you get over here first," I requested, looking over my shoulder. "I'm not talking to your back."

As the eggs finished cooking, Tavit walked them over with the pan and some wooden spoons and set them in the center of the table. We each took a spoon and divided the portions into thirds, making sure we all took an equal share. It was not a big meal, but for the time being, it suited us.

"So, tell me," he repeated with his eyes set on the food.

As I slid the flat wooden spoon out from between my teeth, I began my story about poor Bedros across the river. I left out no details so as to make sure that Tavit knew nothing less than we did. I wanted my version to be so realistic that he could have convinced himself that he was there with us on the banks. For the most of it, I spoke softly to make sure no one heard me. I didn't know why I did that, or who could have possibly heard, but I realized that this was the beginning of my own, personal paranoia. Listening attentively while he ate, Tavit showed only minor expressions of concern. He finished his meal before I could finish my story, and thus towards the end of it, he gently gnawed at his empty spoon, making an annoying tapping sound against his teeth.

"What's their problem?" he said. "They had no other fight to pick?"

"Well, I guess we can ask them later," said Vartan. "And now that I think about it, I guess it was a good thing that I forgot to tie up the oxen."

"Yeah, breaking *Hyreeg's* nose was a good thing?" I asked.

"You broke your father's nose?!" Tavit laughed loudly.

"No, I didn't. His nose is not broken; it's just bruised," illuminated Vartan.

"Wow, this one is going in the record book," he said. "I can't believe you broke his nose!"

"Be quiet. I told you, I didn't break it."

Tavit laughed more.

"Forget about it," I said reassuringly. "Let's just throw the cards around."

Vartan leaned over and collected the spoons and the pan. He walked them over to the kitchen and then sat back down.

"Wait, but do you think this is serious, or what do you think?" questioned Tavit.

"I'm not sure," I said, "but our parents seemed concerned. They still are."

"Really?"

"I mean, that story *Medzmama* told us makes me wonder, though," I said.

"What do you mean?" asked Tavit.

"She told us this story about the dagger and how it saved her life from Turkish soldiers. It's the way she said it—she spoke with a passion against them. I heard it in her voice."

"Yeah, but Armen, it's understandable; you heard what she went through," said Vartan.

"Why? What happened to her?" asked Tavit.

"Well, the short version is that one day, Turkish soldiers marched in and killed thousands of Armenians in her home of Sasun, including my grandfather. The only reason my grandmother survived was because he used that dagger and killed the soldiers to protect her," summarized Vartan.

"Wait, Vartan, you mean *your* dagger?" exclaimed Tavit.

"The one you got for your birthday?"

"Yes," he replied.

"You mean that dagger has *killed* people?" he asked again.

"I guess so," he said, thinking about it in a new light.

"But that's besides my point," I said. "I'm just wondering if the Young Turks or even the soldiers are *still* like that. I mean, *Medzmama* is an inspiration to me, and we saw what they did to that man across the river, but still."

"Well, I have some Turkish friends from the city," explained Vartan. "They're always nice to me."

"Yeah, those Turkish boys in the pasture? I know them pretty well," Tavit said with a shrug.

"That's true, me too. I always wave to them, and they always wave to me," I explained. "Maybe you're right, Vartan. Maybe *Medzmama's* experiences just *made* her that way."

"Yeah, but, Armen, how would you feel if soldiers casually marched in and killed your family and all your neighbors?" Vartan asked. "Just because the sultan wanted it."

"That's what I just said. I agreed with you. I said that *Medzmama's* feelings are *understandable*, but they have never done anything to me, so how can I share her feelings just for the sake of it?" I said hesitantly, not knowing if Vartan and Tavit would agree with me.

"I know what you mean," nodded Vartan. "We just need to live in peace."

"You know, I hear the same stories from my grandparents," added Tavit. "I also agree with what you're saying, Armen. And, Vartan, I think we're closer to peace than ever before, you know?"

"But she did say one thing that still bothers me," I mentioned.

"What is it?"

"Well, she said that the government will try to kill us again."

Tavit stared at me. "Impossible. My father said the new Young Turks are here to restore things. Just stay positive," Tavit concluded as he took out the pack of old, water-damaged playing cards from his pocket that he'd "borrowed" from his father. We knew we weren't allowed to play, but we did so anyway—we were young and always looking for an adventure. Tavit tossed the deck on the table.

I glanced at them. "Won't your father see us?"

"Don't worry," he reassured. "He's outside."

"What about your mother?" asked Vartan.

"She's sleeping; she still doesn't feel well. If you want, we can play *tavloo*," he offered, suggesting the Armenian version of backgammon.

"No," I said, "that's only for two people. Besides, everyone plays *tavloo*. It's too traditional," I expressed. "These papers are fine."

As adolescents always looking for a better time, our attention quickly diverted from one thing to the next. Thus, after Tavit's reassuring words, he handed the thin stack of cards to Vartan, the only one of us who knew how to shuffle, so we could play the only game we knew how to play—a variation of the game bridge, called *bezique*. Vartan then slid the stack back to Tavit, who passed out our hands and placed the remainder of the stack to the side. Normally designed for two players, we had previously modified *bezique* to accommodate the three of us and the few cards we had. The rules of the game for us were simple—the first person to a thousand points won—but there were tricks and combinations of cards involved, some that we made up and some as actual rules, that could affect your total. Tavit and I weren't very experienced, but at the moment, we were too excited to care.

So, we began to play.

As the late morning passed by, Vartan, Tavit, and I sat on that small kitchen table and gambled in secrecy. Up to this point, Vartan had won most of the points since he was far more experienced, crediting his professor from Great Britain, and Tavit and I had each won very few. The two of us were terrible, and we showed it quite well. We didn't know the tricks like Vartan did, but nonetheless, our competitive side had taken complete control of our decisions. Thus, as we played, we subconsciously and unanimously decided to sit in an unnatural silence, seemingly more focused on our individual winnings rather than helping each other to learn to play the game better. In the end, I felt that we all lost because Tavit and I were becoming increasingly frustrated with Vartan's good fortune.

"Eighty points!" I exclaimed as I threw down my hand in an overdue fit of exhilaration.

"Let me see," said Vartan as he reached his hands and swiped my cards over to his side of the table.

"No, that's not eighty points," he said.

"Yes, it is!" I defended.

"No, it's not," he repeated. "Eighty points would have to be four kings. You have two jacks and two queens. You still won, but not eighty points."

"Ha-ha!" I exclaimed, as I looked to Tavit. "I won!"

He smiled, but not too much.

"Oh no—quick—put the papers away!" he announced as he sat up straight and peered out the side window.

I turned my head just in time to see Garo walking quickly with his short strides towards the side door of the house. Hurriedly, we gathered up the cards, hid them under our shirts, and put our elbows on top of the table, not having enough time to put them neatly into a deck.

"Boys, I see the clouds moving in so you might want to consider the weather before you travel back," he said as he walked in.

"Most definitely. We will take it into consideration. Thank you for letting us know." I nodded.

Garo looked at me, puzzled. That's all I needed to say to raise suspicion. It sounded forced and, quite frankly, strange. Too proper. Garo paused and looked at me, examining our seated positions at an empty table, in now an awkward silence. I held my breath. He knew we were up to no good.

"That reminds me. Vartan, Armen, will your parents be going to the meeting in two weeks?" he said as he placed down the hammer he was holding, not mentioning anything of the sort.

"Which meeting?" asked Vartan.

"The monthly world events meeting at the church, of course!"

"I... am not sure," he answered, "but I will ask them for you."

"Well, if they haven't decided, tell them that Garo is going, and he expects to see them there."

"Of course, I will let them know."

"Excellent!" he laughed. "Then I'll keep my eyes out for them!"

He then turned around and walked out the door and back outside. We glanced at each other and slowly began taking out the cards from under our shirts. Just then, Garo switched directions and came rushing back inside. We scrambled and slid the cards back under our shirts.

"I know what I forgot!" he said.

He reached over on the counter and grabbed his hammer.

"I almost forgot this!" he said with a smile as he held it up to show us.

We laughed forcibly to hide any further suspicion.

Once again, Garo left the house. This time, before we impatiently took the cards out, we waited.

"He knew what we were doing," Tavit admitted.

"Will he tell our parents?" I asked.

"No, he'll be inside the winery for most of the day, but we still have to be more careful."

"So, does that mean you're going to the meeting, too?" I asked.

"Yes," he said with a frown

"But isn't that for old people?" I asked again.

"Yeah, it's so boring," he explained. "My father is forcing me."

Vartan chimed in, "But it's interesting. We need to know what is going on in other parts of the world. We can't sit in ignorance our whole lives, you know. Let's just go."

"You sound like my father," observed Tavit.

I looked at Vartan.

"Really? You really want to go?"

He didn't respond.

"Whatever," I surrendered. "I'll go. Now take the papers back out. Let's throw them around."

With the windows wide open, Tavit dealt the cards once again.

Soon after, a thick set of clouds moved in, darkening the room. With them, a new, cool wind with a sweet aroma found its way into the house, surrounding my slightly slumped body, and wisped into my head. It didn't rain that afternoon, but the fresh wave of seduction overwhelmed the former ambience, eating it away. And so I sat, basking with a newfound mental clarity, and allowed the muscles in my body to enter a perfect state of youthful relaxation.

I thought about how civil it was of Garo to stay silent about our "rebellious" behavior, how he could have easily turned us in. I then thought about the notion of a rule, his rules, how they made me feel lazy and less obligated to actually follow them the harder they were enforced on me, thus allowing the blame to be split between me, the perpetrator, and the enforcer for not properly implementing the rules in the first plac—

"Wait," I thought, stopping my mind from finishing its analysis, "where did that come from? What am I saying?"

I blinked my eyes a few times, still looking at my cards, trying to keep my mind empty for the time being.

Perhaps I'd put too much thought into Garo's actions on that rainless afternoon. For what it was worth, though, the budding intellect of my young mind decided to become more aware of how I carried myself. Tavit was right. I had to be more cautious. Thus, as I carried this long-brewing epiphany with me, I continued on my route of self-discipline, unknowingly initiating a fascination with continuous self-improvement. For the moment, however, as a fourteen-year-old boy, I just wanted to focus on the game of *bezique* with my brother and Tavit, the three outlaws of Armenia, and nothing else.

<u>14</u>

Our home setting was, and always has been, very traditional. So, the next two weeks of my life were more or less the same routine. I would wake up, milk the cows, help my father and brother plow the fields, fix the machinery, feed the animals, and maintain the house. I was relatively new to the game of farming, and so the perpetual work helped my frame build some muscle. Little Margaret, too, would help my mother around the house and help cook meals, and my grandmother would teach us everything she knew. It was only recently that she began to tell us the stories and experiences of her past. Some were happy, some were sad, but all were memorable.

As we loaded ourselves onto the ox-cart, we began our crawl towards our church, *Soorp Asdvadzadzin*, on the same path with the same, pleasantly captivating scenery. We were going to the world events meeting. Along the way, I waved to the same Turkish boys herding their sheep, and they waved back. I tried not to think about how bored I would be, but at fourteen, I knew very little about life outside of Armenia. Perhaps Vartan was right. Maybe it was time already.

Without even seeing him, I knew Garo had arrived solely by his identifiable laugh. As we rode up, I saw him standing with Ana and Tavit, and nearby, Ara stood with his daughter Nadia, having left the younger girls at home with their mother. They had no business at these such events.

"I knew it! I knew it. Here they are!" exclaimed Garo. "Good to see you, Tevos!"

"*Parev*, Garo, it's great to see you as well," my father said as he stepped off the cart. "And, Ana, I'm happy to see that you're feeling better."

"Thank you, Tevos," she responded.

"Now, Garo, what is this hanging from your neck?" asked my father.

As my mother and little Margaret leaped off the ox-cart, I looked over to see what my father was talking about.

"This here, this right here, is what my brother sent me

from America. You will not believe it, but this is a photographic camera!" Garo explained excitedly as Vartan and I jumped down and began helping our grandmother.

He held up a small rectangular box with the word "Kodak" on one side. My father studied the device in a state of confusion.

"Now," said Garo, putting up his pointer finger, "watch this."

With the tip of his finger, he pushed a small black button. In an instant, a flap opened and a pyramid-like piece extended out of the main body like an accordion with a lens attached at the end.

"It's a Kodak pocket folding camera! This is new technology from the West!"

My father smiled and looked at my mother. "Perhaps we should test it," he offered.

"No, we shouldn't," she disagreed. "I'm not ready!"

"You look great. I say we take a photograph," my father pushed as he kissed my mother.

"Yes, exactly!" said Garo, hardly able to keep calm. "Come, everybody, let's get together!"

Extending his arms as if he were going to hug us all, Garo quickly took command of the situation.

"Ara, you stand here with Nadia. Tevos, you stand here with Hasmig and Taqoohi. Margaret, stand next to your father. Tavit, Vartan, and Armen, stand together next to your parents. Ana, stand next to Tavit."

Garo stepped back, put his hand on his mouth, and focused on the logistics of our positions.

"Tavit, make room for me," he said as the ladies complained to each other about their physical appearances while the men stood tall and serious, and, most importantly, quiet.

"Vartan, move to your left. More. Perfect. Okay!"

Garo stopped and looked around while we waited.

"Kevork," he flagged, "quick, come take this photo for us!" he said as he stopped the local baker, who happened to be passing by.

"Can I be in it?" he asked.

"No," he replied. "Otherwise, who will take the photograph? Just press this button."

"Of course," he obliged.

Garo then scrambled into the group and stood next to Tavit.

Vartan turned to me. "Armen, is my hair messed up?" he asked.

At first, I thought he was fooling around, throwing at me a sort of mockery of the ladies, but I soon realized that he was serious.

"It's too long. You look like a mule. Comb it over," I advised bluntly.

Taking my comment to heart, Vartan took the fingers of one hand and combed them through his hair.

"How about now?" he asked again.

"It's all right." I peeked uncomfortably as he shuffled his long hair once more.

As for me, I couldn't have cared less about my appearance.

"Okay great! Now everyone look at the camera!"

As Vartan perfected himself, I put my right arm around him and my left arm around Tavit. Vartan, just as in church, stood nervously. From the corner of my eye, I noticed that his attention kept diverting towards me, and I wasn't quite sure why. Soon, I realized that he was looking *past* me, at Nadia, on the far end of the group. Now he was really beginning to scare me. I don't think Vartan ever looked at the camera or even cared to.

He just wanted to see her smile.

"*Meg... yergoo... yerek*," Kevork counted in Armenian.

Just at that moment, Tavit raised his foot and stepped hard on my toes. I immediately crouched down and grabbed my foot in pain. He tried not to laugh too loud with his father standing next to him.

"All right," said Kevork after he took the photograph.

Detaching himself from the group, Garo then casually ran over to the baker. I took my arm from around Vartan and hit

Tavit's shoulder.

"That wasn't funny," I muttered.

He just laughed more.

"Thank you, Kevork," said Garo.

"My pleasure," he responded with a nod.

Because of prior limitations on the mobility of the camera and the photographer, we rarely took family portraits. Usually, we would need to make an appointment with a professional photography studio days in advance just for one or two prints. The day of the shoot was very important to my parents, and they emphasized the importance and impact only one photograph can have. Therefore, they required us to wear our finest clothes, shave our faces, and appear as respectable as possible. The "new technology" that Garo introduced us to, however, eliminated the superficiality of being inside of a studio with a painted backdrop. Even though this portrait was sporadic, rough, and hastily designed, it felt more natural.

Inside *Soorp Asdvadzadzin*, we took our seats and patiently waited for the meeting to begin. The church was filled with people, so much so that they stood along the inside perimeter like trees in a dense forest. The world events meeting attracted Armenians from many of the different villages of Kharpert. This was the first time I had ever been to one, and all I expected was exactly that—an update on what was going on in the world at the time.

At the head of the church sat the scholars, teachers, historians, and intellectuals of Kharpert. They would be the ones leading the update with their expertise. I recognized one of them from my school and casually waved to him. He nodded, acknowledging my friendly gesture.

"Please, everyone, have a seat and make yourselves comfortable," said Mardiros, the local optometrist, as he stood in front of the altar with his large glasses and casually buttoned the jacket of his oversized suit.

As the crowd quieted, he took a moment to introduce the scholars sitting behind him before he began the announcements.

"Thank you, everybody, for coming to our monthly meeting. As is customary, we will begin our events calendar with the Americas and move our way east towards Europe and then conclude with any local news."

As I heard, through my understanding, that we would be doing a thorough investigation of all the events on Earth for the past month, I sank into my cushion just a little bit lower.

"What has Tavit dragged me into now?" I thought passively.

Next to me, my parents sat attentively—my father with his arms crossed across his chest and my mother with her hands resting atop the purse on her lap. My grandmother and little Margaret, very mature for her age, quietly sat next to my father.

"How am I going to get through this?" I thought again as my eyes wandered. "This *is* for old people."

Mapping out the interior, I saw Tavit sitting with his mother and father in his usual spot and Nadia with her father in her usual seat, and all the other Armenians even sat in *their* usual spots. There was something very eerie about the monotony of it all.

"It seems that this summer has been particularly intense for the United States of America," began Mardiros with the update. "The temperature in the state of California has hit a record high of fifty-seven degrees centigrade in Death Valley."

I heard some gasps and mumblings.

"I have family there!"

"My cousin Paul lives in California!"

"I hope they're safe."

Shrugging off the news, I realized that I needed to do something to save my sanity, so I put my pointer fingers and thumbs on the tops and bottoms of my eyelids and stretched open my eyes. I then flared the rest of my fingers and turned to Vartan.

"Do I look like an owl?" I asked, trying not to laugh.

After doing a double take, Vartan smirked. "No."

He paused.

"Maybe," he answered again.

I dropped my hands down and blinked a couple of times to lubricate my eyes.

"Hey," I whispered, "let's just go outside."

"No, why?" responded Vartan. "Just be quiet. I want to listen to the news."

"Please? This isn't fun."

"Try to imagine that you're there; it makes it more interesting," he advised.

I didn't respond to his comment. Apparently, Vartan was bored as well because of the fact that he had to use his imagination to tolerate the meeting. So, I sat with my drifting mind and stared into the empty space between my nose and the person in front of me. Slowly, as my ears began to shut themselves off, my mind kicked in and reminded them to regain their tolerance and listen.

"Two weeks ago," said the historian, having now taken over after Mardiros, "on June 29th of this year, 1913, we received, through telegraph, notice that the Second Balkan War began when Bulgaria attacked Servia and Greece. This is contrary to the Treaty of London that was signed on May 30th of the same year to end the First Balkan War. As we remember, during that war, the Balkan League ousted the Ottoman Empire's company from her provinces of Europe and..."

"How does this affect us?" interrupted a citizen.

"Well, as you may also know, the Ottoman Empire has lost most of her European territory, which Russia yearns for. To the Turks, this was devastating. Subsequently, their government at Constantinople asked the Empire of Germany for help in reorganizing and modernizing her military. They are currently taking advantage of the war between Bulgaria, Servia, and Greece to try to regain control of their European lands. In essence, it does not yet directly affect us as Ottoman Armenians, but it does affect us because we are part of the Ottoman Empire."

The citizen nodded and raised his hand in thanks.

"Any other questions?" asked the historian.

There was silence.

"We are watching the outcome of this war very closely,"

he continued, "and we are also—"

I tried to listen to the rest of his sentence, but the corruption of my ears had traveled to my eyes. By this point, they felt as if they were bearing the weight of every stone that built the church. I tried to keep them alert but couldn't fight my weakened state anymore. Thus, my eyes fell shut, and before I knew it, I had fallen into a very deep slumber.

I awoke and found myself standing in a large empty room made of a dense, silver metal. At every corner, running the length of the seams, were large, circular bolts. I stood in my corner and carefully observed my present situation. I knew my purpose there, but at the same time, I didn't. From across the room, in the left corner, stood an old, fiercely intimidating man. This man had long, pale white hair, a long, pale white beard, and wore a long, pale white robe; he hadn't even so much as a wrinkle on his face. I stared at him without purpose, and he stared back, studying my existence. Then, with a booming voice, louder than the loudest thunder and deeper than the deepest oceans, he spoke.

"Can you handle the pain?" he asked.

As curious and cynical as the question was, I knew what the old man was asking of me.

"Yes," I responded simply.

With a small inhalation, he studied my answer for a few more moments, then lowered his white, bushy eyebrows and narrowed his powerful eyes. With the extension of his right hand, he then showed me a ball, a small silver ball, a sphere, made of the same dense metal as the walls of the room. I extended my left arm, and the sphere materialized in my palm. I examined the dull metallic surface with a wondrous curiosity. On its right half, a small, circular fire then took shape. The fire, staying close to the surface, quickly began to spread over the entire curvature of the sphere. As it spread, the metal ball grew larger and larger, and hotter and hotter. The intensity of the red-hot fire burned my hand, and its increasing weight tore away every muscle in my arm as I tried to hold it up. Thus, I screamed in pain as loud as I could, sweating tirelessly.

Soon enough, the metallic sphere became too hot to touch and too big to hold until I had no choice but to painfully climb onto its molten surface. Before long, the sphere erupted through the confines of the room and continued to grow at a faster pace until it had become as big as the Earth.

It *was* the Earth.

I stood on the green grass of the churchyard and faced *Soorp Asdvadzadzin*, the very church in which I sat. I was no longer hot, and I was no longer in any pain. Instead, I felt the calming air of the brisk Sunday morning and saw the people of the land casually walking inside.

I felt good.

Just then, the ground began to rumble slightly, followed by a faint whirring sound. I turned around, facing away from the church, and listened as the sound grew louder and the rumbling grew more intense. Then, I saw the chaotic motion of a wall of fire and smoke rushing towards me at an incredible velocity, devouring everything in its path. I screamed to warn the people, but nothing came out. I waved my arms in vain, but nobody saw me. I tried to run, but my legs didn't work. Desperately, I tried screaming again, but to no avail, until the large heavy doors of the church closed after the last person walked inside. As the fire inevitably arrived, I closed my eyes tight and flung my hands up over my head to brace myself for the violent impact. I felt the heat of the wall pass cleanly through my body and out the other side. To my astonishment, I was unharmed, so I opened my eyes. Instantly, I gawked at the hellish aftermath. Every tree, every house, every animal, charred to a blackened coal. And yet, the stone church still stood. As if pulled by a rope, I then ascended into the sky by a force that I didn't understand, originating from a place that I couldn't see. From the vastness of outer space, I saw the true magnitude of the fire's destruction and just how far it spanned, watching even as the unrestricted madness continued around the rest of the globe.

At that exact moment, without even enough time to form a logical thought or try to decipher the message of my eyes, I suddenly appeared back in the room made of metal.

Still in his same spot, the old man stood, now overly irate.

"You've seen enough!" he screamed with his same booming voice. *"You've seen enough!"*

Just then, the sound of a thousand drums filled the chamber, and his terrifying eyes burst into flame. Like a raging windstorm, they shot at me explosively, burning through my skull. Not ever seeing his feet, the old man then flew the distance between us and stood directly in front of me.

"Now get up!" he commanded.

With a raise of his heavy hand, he then slapped me across my face. Instantly, my vision, the room, the Earth, the church, the fire, all turned into the black of night, vanishing forever.

Abruptly, I opened my eyes and awoke, causing my entire body to jolt. My heart throbbed, and my head ached as the blurry crucifix hanging on the wall of the church slowly came back into focus. With my eyes wide open, confusion set in. My parents stared at me in embarrassment.

"What are you doing?" Vartan whispered.

"Huh?" I said. "Nothing. I fell asleep."

"This is no time to sleep. You have to listen to this. We're talking about local events now."

Sitting up straight, I tried rubbing away the headache and the confusion as I listened to my countrymen express their words.

"This is unfair and against all policies for Armenians!"

"They beat my husband so badly that now he can't work and provide us with income!" yelled an elderly woman.

"Our cattle! They killed our cattle!"

"Okay, please, one at a time," said Mardiros, the moderator. "Yes, Armanoush?"

"Three authorities demanded that we pay our taxes," she sobbed. "When I told them that we already paid, they did *not* care but demanded that my son register for the Turkish military as compensation. I tried explaining that he isn't old enough, but they beat me down, stole our money, and left. They said they would return. They cannot do this to us. We have only followed the law."

Peering behind at the scholars, Mardiros waited for their input. They, however, remained silent. Contemplating. In deep thought. Thus, he turned back around to the community members.

"Yes, you there," he pointed.

The lady stood up. "We must protest and demand our rights in this empire. How loud must we shout before they finally hear us? We must fight! We must fight for our freedom, for the freedom of our children!"

The community cheered and roared in applause.

Mardiros put his hands in the air. "Okay, please, settle down!" he said as he stood up. "Do the scholars have anything to say?"

"Yes," answered the lawyer, "it is true. With a loud enough voice, it is imperative for any reasonable government to listen to their people to omit the possibility of an uprising within the empire. As for Armanoush, you must continually voice your concerns, and we will be your backing. They have no choice but to hear them. In order for it to be effective, however, it must be done *collectively*. In the past, it is also notable that our protests and attempts at diplomacy have ended poorly, yielding few results or, unfortunately, ending tragically, but that *cannot* stop us from being diplomatic!"

My father curled his lips, slowly nodding his head in agreement.

"With a show of your raised hands," asked Mardiros, "who has *recently* had trouble with Ottoman Turkish soldiers or other government officials violating their rights?"

"What rights specifically?" shouted a man.

"All rights that were proclaimed as equal by the Young Turkish Revolutionaries who overthrew the sultan," he answered.

About a third of the church raised their hands. At first, I must admit, I sat confused. Why so many hands? Personally, I had never been a victim of mistreatment, and neither had Vartan.

We were merely witnesses. Regardless, though, we raised our hands in support of those who *did* fall at the hands of mistreatment, like poor Bedros across the river.

"Very well," acknowledged Mardiros.

Back and forth, they discussed and deliberated, brainstorming on possible action to take against the mistreatment of Ottoman Armenians. They yelled and quarreled, providing their passionate solutions to an ongoing problem. Some suggested bombing the headquarters at Constantinople, some suggested escape, and some even stubbornly sat in denial, not wanting to believe the tyranny of the government. I knew that we, as Armenians, were trying our best to gain fair representation, but there were so many ideas, so many opinions. This was, after all, our home, our livelihood. Like my father said, no one should have to live their life in fear, at least not in 1913.

After nearly an hour, my attention span had long been exhausted, and I now sat pouting in my seat, fed up with the nonsense. We hadn't accomplished anything nor did anyone come to an agreement. All we'd done was circle back to our past attempts—peaceful protests and demonstrations.

And so, we left it at that.

As we quickly capped the meeting, Mardiros announced a few other events in Kharpert—weddings, funerals, and baptisms and such. We then stood up and quietly walked out. Behind me, Vartan followed us as we met up with Garo and Ara in the churchyard. My father and Ara expressed their concerns, and Garo expressed his denial. Of course, this ignited another argument.

"Boys," my father called, now heated, "boys, come here."

We walked up to him and stood at his attention.

"Boys, unless you absolutely *need* to, your mother and I don't want you two going out at night for the time being. This situation is entirely too unstable," he said. "Do you understand?"

"But you said before that—"

"I changed my mind," my father cut me off. "Do you understand?"

"Yes," I nodded.

"Well, that is completely unnecessary," exclaimed Garo.

My father turned to face him. "Garo, these are my children. Do not say what I can or cannot tell them."

My father turned back around. "Vartan?" he asked.

"Uh-huh," he replied, looking in all directions.

"Good," he said.

My father turned to Garo and Ara, and I looked to Vartan. "Vartan, we—" I started.

Without hesitation or even a moment of warning, Vartan, my own brother, turned away from me and walked directly over to Nadia to complete the rest of an obviously well-thought-out plan. I stood, dumbfounded.

"Hi, Nadia," he opened, "you look very nice today."

"Thank you, Vartan," she responded in Armenian. "As do you."

"Did you like the apricots I gave you?" he continued. "I've been meaning to ask you."

"Yes, they were delicious, thank you so much again!" She smiled warmly.

Vartan returned the smile. "It was nothing. I'm happy you enjoyed them."

The tension between them was dense. I could feel it, and it made me uncomfortable.

"Vartan, the night I was at your house, you mentioned something about the stars in the sky," Nadia said a moment later.

Vartan's face lit up as bright as the very stars she asked about. "Yes?" he asked.

"I want to learn more about them," she continued, "and I want you to teach me."

Nadia spoke confidently, almost sternly. Vartan's face, as alert as a rooster in the wake of the rising sun, remained unchanged. He didn't respond. I could only imagine what was going on inside his head. After a moment's pause, he spoke.

"When?" he asked.

"Tonight," she responded firmly.

"T-tonight?"

"Yes," she repeated. "Are you busy tonight?"

"No!" exclaimed Vartan. "Not at all. Where?"

"The pasture. Where the boys herd their sheep. There's an old tree," she explained.

"Yes, I know that tree," he said, thinking out loud.

"Meet me there one hour after sunset."

"O-Okay," he stuttered again.

Nadia then turned around and walked towards her father, and Vartan stood in his spot as Ana, Tavit's mother, initiated the lengthy process of parting.

"Okay, Hasmig, we'll meet again at church," she said. "It was great to see you!"

"Great to see you too, Ana," replied my mother. "And, Ara, please tell Mary that we miss her!"

"I will bring her the news," reassured Ara.

My mother responded with a look of satisfaction.

"Tevos, good to see you," said Ara as he extended his hand. "We'll stay here for a little longer. I want to hear more about these issues with the government."

"Very well. Let me know what you discover."

Ara nodded his head and began walking back towards the church. As we started walking towards the ox-cart, Vartan casually turned around and whispered to Nadia, "I'll be there."

She smiled softly in response before turning around and walking back with her father in the opposite direction.

During the ride back home, I noticed something different about my brother. There was a subtle glow to his face, one that I'd never seen before. To be honest, he looked intoxicated. His ears were pulled back, and he had a smirk on his face that I felt like pulling off. Wherever his mind was, it was at a place much different, but yet very similar, to the place where he was at church two weeks ago when Nadia walked in late. Yet, all I could do was watch him enjoy his stay in paradise until we got back home.

As we pulled up to our house, my father stopped the cart. I stood up and jumped off to help my grandmother, but my brother still sat in his spot. What was with this kid?

"Vartan," I hinted, *"Medzmama."*

"What? Oh," he responded quietly.

He quickly stood up and helped our grandmother sit on the edge of the cart. Vartan jumped down and stood next to me, and we guided her as she slowly stepped down with one foot. As she put down her second foot, she stumbled for a second, briefly losing her balance. My grip under her arm tightened as Vartan and I prevented our grandmother from falling.

"Thank you, boys," she said quickly.

With a discomforting face, she stood for a moment and inhaled. She then brought her hand up to her mouth and let out a hollow cough, one that emerged from the deepest pits of her lungs. The next few coughs wore the same outfit. We stood by her, and I gently patted her back until she finished.

"Mom, that doesn't sound good. Maybe we need to call the doctor," suggested my mother.

"No dear, it is just the dust," she assured. "Thank you."

"Are you sure? It's been a few weeks now. It sounds worse. I've never heard you cough like that before," she persisted.

"Ayo, ayo, my dear. I am fine. The weather is very dry," she explained.

My grandmother's words, as always, held true; it was mid-July, and it had not rained since June 20th, the day before Vartan's birthday. The dust she complained about didn't bother me but due to her age could have easily bothered her. We helped her inside the house and waited with her until she caught her breath in her chair.

For the rest of that day, we mostly tended to the crops, which, despite the uncharacteristically dry weather, held out surprisingly well. Thus, I wasn't immediately worried about the mild drought. The rich soil where they grew was blessed with an exceptional fertility. Besides, I knew it would rain again soon enough.

I felt it in the air.

15

"I didn't immediately know the extent of Vartan's relationship with Nadia at the time, but I did know that their night under the stars would change everything forever," explained old Armen in the hospital room.

With Vartan lying motionless on the hospital bed, still in a coma, the rhythm of his heart on the EKG began to beat a little faster. As merely just a sound in the background, however, no one immediately noticed.

"Did she like him back?" asked one of his granddaughters.

"Oh yes, of course she liked him," responded Armen, "but not even *she* knew just how much at the time."

His granddaughter smiled.

"Let me continue. This will all make sense to you sooner rather than later."

. . . .

As the sun began to slowly disappear over the horizon, I took my sweat-stained shirt off my back and flung it over my shoulders. I began my way back to the home when Vartan approached me silently from behind.

"Armen," he said as he extended his hand and grabbed my shoulder. "Hey, Armen, slow down."

After hearing his voice, I slowed to a halt and turned around. "What is it?" I asked.

"I need to ask you for a favor."

Vartan rubbed my sweat from his hand onto his pant leg.

"This is the story. I'm going somewhere in one hour, and I need to take the horse."

"And how does this involve me?" I asked, confused.

"If Mama and *Hyreeg* ask where I am, I need you to tell them that I took the horse to go to Tavit's house or something."

"Why don't *you* just tell them?" I said as I took the shirt off my shoulders and began cleaning the dirt off my hands.

"Because I don't want to lie to them," said Vartan, "and I don't know how long I'll be away."

"So you want *me* to lie to them *for* you?"

"Exactly," he said, "but only if they ask."

"But they said we shouldn't go out at night," I reasoned.

"Yes, but *Hyreeg* said we can go only if we need to," responded Vartan, "and I *need* to."

I admired his technical stance on this issue.

"Okay," I agreed, "but you don't have to be so secretive. I know you're meeting Nadia in the pasture."

"Shh… Don't be so loud!" said Vartan as he searched around like a giraffe.

"You couldn't pick a better spot?" I asked. "By that old tree? It's the only one there."

"I know. Nadia picked it, but that doesn't matter right now," he said. "I need you to distract Mama and *Hyreeg* so that I can take the horse."

"Are you going to kiss her?" I asked. "You should kiss her tonight."

"What? You don't know what you're saying. She just wants to learn about the stars. That's it. Will you do this for me or not?"

By the tone of Vartan's voice and the seriousness in his face, I knew he was at my mercy, and to be honest, I wanted to take advantage of the rare situation. For some reason, though, I was happy for him, so I let go of any jokes that I had. Vartan was in no mood to fool around. There was no diverting his attention at this point.

"Yeah, sure, I will," I agreed.

"Thanks. I'm going to wash up and leave soon. Make sure they're away from the barn!" he said as he hurriedly walked away. "Don't forget," he added with a slight turn of his head.

"Fine, but leave quietly!" I instructed, trying to help him out.

He acknowledged, and just like that, we'd planned a covert operation. It was now up to me to ensure a flawless execution, so Vartan wouldn't get caught. Neither my father nor mother worked outside after dark. It was very rare of them to do so, so I felt that I could distract them long enough for Vartan to make his escape.

Inside, Vartan chose a nice pair of pants and a pressed shirt that would surely impress anyone. For the final touch, he sprayed on some of my father's cologne and swiftly left from the back door nearly one hour after the sun had gone, completely averting my parents. From the time that Vartan left to the time that my parents went to bed was another hour. If they were to ask, it would be in that time frame, and I knew that.

From the window inside, I watched as he ran to the barn, took out our horse, and then quietly rode away into the night. As usual, he forgot to close the barn door, so I, too, had to sneak out to close it. Therefore, it didn't take much effort to hide his whereabouts. It was very logical, yet vaguely suspicious, to say that he was sleeping in his room, sick, which is what I eventually said. I never felt good about lying, but in this case, I found it necessary. By the time my parents had gone to bed, and as I lay down in mine, I felt the wave of triumph fill my body with joy. My parents suspected nothing unusual except for, possibly, Vartan's "sickness." Whatever the case, he was in the clear, and most importantly, so was I. For that night, only fate would tell whether or not that same wave of triumph would also fill him with joy.

16

At the dawn of nightfall, Vartan sat atop our black horse, nervously holding the reins as he neared the old, twisted tree. This was the first time that he had come up this close to it, never having a reason to before. For a moment, he sat on its back and contemplated the area. With a swing of his leg, he then jumped off and threw the harness around the wide trunk, catching it on the other side. He fed the end of the leather cord through the other and tugged on it to feel the security of his knot. Gently then, he ran his fingertips over the deep grooves of the thick, darkened bark of the tree. If trees could speak, this one would have a story to tell.

Horse secured, Vartan rested his hands upon his hips and spun his body full circle to scope out the darkness of his surroundings. "Familiar places," he thought, "look vastly different at night." He was, indeed, the lone warrior in a large pasture. Nadia hadn't yet arrived, so he sat, perching himself against the old tree, and waited. The air for the night was crisp and clear, with a light wind blowing in from the west. The heat of the day had not yet dissipated, so it still retained its warmth. In the foreground, hundreds of sheep grazed the pasture without their shepherds. Beyond them, the city lights cast a dim glow under the cloudless night. Without the overpowering strength of the moon, billions of visible stars had seized their opportunity from the especially dark night and twinkled brightly, using the sky as their stage and Vartan as their audience. Feeling the softness of the grass under him, he carefully mapped them out, trying to remember all that he had learned in his astronomy class.

"Betelgeuse..." he whispered, "is there. Orion... okay... Orion's belt."

Periodically, but more often than not, he casually turned his head to see if Nadia was approaching. With each passing minute, he became increasingly more impatient and increasingly more nervous and unknowingly began twisting his fingers through each other. As he once again tried distracting himself with the stars, a faint galloping sound from the shallow distance behind slowly approached the seated dreamer. It was Nadia. Vartan stood up and brushed himself off of any doubts and then casually walked over and grabbed the reins of her horse.

"Hey," he said.

"Hey," she responded from atop. "It's a beautiful night tonight."

"Yeah... I mean, yes," Vartan responded cordially. "There isn't a cloud in the sky."

Nadia jumped off. "I know; isn't this gorgeous? Just look at the stars!" she said, peering above.

Vartan walked to the old tree and tied the rope around its base. Her horse neighed, and Nadia giggled at its unexpectedness. She covered her mouth with her hand.

"She agrees with me," she laughed.

"Yeah," said Vartan as he lightly patted the horse and looked up at its size. "How long have you had her?"

"We've had this one for five years now. She's grown big. We've had her since she was born," she said as she lightly and carefully groomed the horse's mane with her fingers.

Vartan looked at her, but not for long. Like a shy, adolescent child, he stood nervously still, slightly intimidated by her beauty.

"What about yours?" asked Nadia.

"Oh, he's been in the family since I can remember," said Vartan. "He's so powerful."

"Does he have a name?"

"No," he answered. "I could never think of a good one."

"Oh," she shrugged.

"Well, would you like to sit?" he offered.

"Sure. Now you can teach me about the stars."

"Let's sit against this tree. We have a good view of some of the main constellations from here. Trust me, I made sure before you got here."

For the first time all day, Vartan smiled.

"That was kind of you," she said, returning the smile.

Without a rug or a carpet, Nadia sat on the dirt and leaned against the tree.

"Are you comfortable like that?" Vartan asked, taken aback by her ambition.

"Yes, this is perfect," she responded.

Nadia seldom complained. She valued what she had, never asking for anything more. So, feeling a little less tense, Vartan sat down next to her against the same old tree, being careful to keep a reasonable distance.

"So, what would you like to know?" he asked.

"Anything. Teach me everything you know."

"Everything? We might be here all night then," he joked. Nadia laughed. "That's fine by me."

"Well, all right. So if you look up at the sky, all the stars you see, or at least most of them, are part of constellations."

"What are constellations?"

"Umm, constellations are basically groups of stars that form a pattern. It's a way of mapping the sky, so you don't get lost."

"How so?"

"Well, in ancient times, and now, too, I guess, people used the stars as their map, so they would know which direction they were going in. For example, do you see that bright star up there?" Vartan said, pointing.

"No, which one?"

"That one... Look. It's the brightest one," he explained. "Close one eye like me, and follow the point of your finger. You'll find it easier."

Nadia mimicked Vartan's technique and pointed up into the night sky with her forefinger.

"Like this?" she asked.

"Yes. Now close one eye."

Nadia closed one eye, and Vartan glanced at her, wondering how one morning he could wake up only dreaming of this and by evening actually living it.

"Do you see it?"

"I think so," she responded. "Yes, I do."

"Great, so that star is the North Star. The actual name of it is Polaris."

"Polaris?" she repeated.

"Yes, we use that star as a point of reference because that star never moves. It sits there all night, showing you which way north is."

"So you can never get lost," said Nadia.

"Exactly," reaffirmed Vartan, "and all the stars revolve around that one star."

"Interesting."

"Yup, and if you look above that star, there are two

more stars that look like they're in a straight line above it."

"I see them," she said as she pointed her finger again.

"And then above those are four stars that look like they make a square. Do you see those?"

"Umm, yes, I think so."

"So, from Polaris to the end of those four stars, that is called Ursa Minor. It looks like a ladle."

"Ohh! I see it!" cheered Nadia. "That's amazing!" She looked at Vartan.

"Yeah, it's not difficult to remember, either," he responded. "You just have to test yourself sometimes."

"That sounds easy enough."

"Yup, so now you know that Polaris is part of Ursa Minor," said Vartan.

"Yes," Nadia said with a smile. "Now what?"

Upon placing his eyes upon her smile, Vartan immediately became tangled in her net of magnificence. For a moment, he sat speechless. Her green eyes and brown hair reflected the stars perfectly and only made it harder for Vartan to escape from her grasp. He wondered how their relationship had grown into this exact moment so rapidly. It was just one month ago that he couldn't even look at her, and now, there he was, sitting next to her in the middle of a pasture, teaching her about the night sky.

"Umm, what?" he asked.

"So, what about other constellations? Of course, there must be more, right?" she asked.

"Oh," he said, "of course. Yeah, um, so if you look to the left and down some, you can see the big version of Ursa Minor called... Are you ready?"

"Yes," she said.

"Ursa *Major*. Creative, huh?"

"Of course not!" Nadia exclaimed.

For the second time that day, Vartan smiled and even laughed a little. Nadia, still leaning against the tree, braced her arms on the ground and moved forward and lay down to look straight up.

"There," she said, "this is better. *Now* I can see!"

Vartan, curiously intrigued by her ingenuity, followed her lead and slowly eased himself down next to her, still keeping a conservative distance between them.

"Oh, you're right," he responded. "This *is* better."

"So, we have Polaris, Ursa Minor, and Ursa Major," she reiterated, "and we can use Polaris to find our direction."

"Well, technically, we were supposed to begin with the handle of Ursa Major because the last two stars point to Polaris, but if you continue that line *past* Polaris, you will find some stars in the shape of an *ayp*," said Vartan, with *ayp* being the first letter of the Armenian alphabet, shaped like a *w*.

Nadia pointed her finger and closed an eye.

"Do you see it?"

"No, I don't," she said, sounding disappointed.

"It's just to the left of that big cloud."

"Yes, I see it now!"

"That one is Cassiopeia," he said, "the queen."

"The queen," she whispered back, studying the constellation, becoming humbled by the universe beyond.

"Did you know," Vartan stated, "that the stars are millions, if not billions, of years old?"

Nadia turned her head to him lying next to her. "I don't believe you!" she exclaimed. "That's impossible!"

"Nope," he confirmed. "It's true."

"I still don't believe you!" she exclaimed again.

"Believe me."

She turned her head back towards the night sky, still gleaming at the complexity of Vartan's statement.

"But don't you think they're just so... plain?" she asked. "The stars?"

"What do you mean?"

"I mean, all we can do is watch them. That's it. We can't do anything else, right? All the stars. The universe. All we can do is look," she added. "There's too much of it, and that's all we can do. Why?" She looked to Vartan for guidance. "Why is there so much? It just makes life here on Earth seem so... small."

He thought for a moment.

"No," he disagreed respectfully, "not really. Not if you're happy. Not if you're with someone you want to be with."

She glanced at him for an extra moment, rethinking her last comment. Vartan then looked back up at the sky, and a moment later, Nadia did the same.

As the two lay in the grass for over an hour, Vartan continued to teach Nadia everything she wanted to know. Not once did she ever show a sign of dissatisfaction. She enjoyed every moment of it. To Vartan, the entire night was nothing short of a miracle that had transformed itself into a blessing. With the naming of each star, constellation, or planet, the clouds that had stayed away for so long slowly began to move in, until at last, they took full control and shut down the full-stage production the stars had grown so accustomed to love. This bold move by the clouds obstructed their view, and eventually, ended the show.

"Well, there they go," Vartan said with a shrug.

"Yeah," sulked Nadia. "I'm so happy you came out here for me, Vartan. It was so nice of you to do this."

"Oh..." Vartan blushed. "It was my pleasure."

Nadia sat back up and leaned against the tree.

"So, do you want to go back?" he asked.

"I'm not too sure," she said. "I like it out here."

"Me too," agreed Vartan as he also sat back up, this time positioning himself a little closer. "So," he continued.

"Yes?"

"So... What kinds of things do you like to do?" he asked, initiating conversation. "For fun."

"For fun? I like to knit."

"Really? That's interesting. What do you knit?"

"All sorts of things. I also like needlework, and I like to sew dresses. Actually, I wore one to your house after church. Do you remember?"

"Of course I do."

"Well, I made that one," she said proudly.

"Wow," said Vartan. "That's impressive."

"Yeah, it began as a hobby and grew into a passion. I really love it."

"Well, you did a great job. That dress looked very beautiful on you," Vartan said, tensing at his compliment.

"Thank you," she responded shyly.

There was a silence between the two. Vartan knew what he wanted to say but just couldn't get himself to do it, nor find the right time to do so. His nerves began to quiver, and his gut turned in on itself.

"It's getting a bit chilly out here," she noted.

"Yes, it is," he said. "I felt that too."

Driving his knuckles into the ground, Vartan shifted himself a little closer yet.

"Vartan, do you think you'll still be here, in Armenia, when you grow old?"

"Well, I'm not sure," he answered. "I really have no reason to leave, but if I died right now, I'm sure I would die a happy man."

Surprising himself with that comment, Vartan subsequently confused Nadia.

"Well," she said, "why do you say that?"

Like a metastasizing cancer, the nerves inside Vartan grew out of control. His feelings, his love, how he truly felt about Nadia, could no longer be contained. The culmination of it all now burst at the seams of his very existence, and the pressure built more than one man could tolerate, causing him to speak the next words, not as his own, but as a manifestation from his heart.

"Because, Nadia, for my whole life I've been searching for something, but I just didn't know what. Sitting here next to you makes me realize that I've found it. *You* are what I've been searching for."

Taken aback by his sudden comment, she shifted uncomfortably.

"Vartan that means a lot to me, but I—"

Without even a moment's hesitation, with his heart now in complete control of his mind and body, Vartan closed his eyes, leaned in, and planted his lips directly onto hers. He kissed her as passionately as he could for as long as it lasted.

Nadia didn't even have a chance to finish her words.

Instinctively, and without delay, Nadia reacted by pulling herself back. Feeling her disappear from his lips, Vartan flexed his muscles to prevent his body from falling forward. Nadia then raised both hands and quickly moved them through the small gap between them. He felt the blunt force of her palms against his shoulders. As quickly as he was falling forward, he was now falling backward.

Nadia then quickly sprang up.

"Ugh!" she exclaimed. "How dare you?!"

Even as the rocks from the ground painfully pierced his back, Vartan felt the pressure inside easing up. Strangely, he felt better. He perched himself on one elbow and looked at her, dumbfounded, wondering if he'd made a mistake.

"Nadia, I'm…" he tried explaining.

Nadia began untying the reins of her horse from the old tree.

"You brought me here to seduce me?" she screamed. She was furious. "What were you thinking?" she added.

To kiss a girl in old Armenia meant a lot, especially in such a conservative part of the world at such a conservative time. The usually calm, well-mannered girl that Vartan thought he knew was now dancing around like an angry puppy on hot coals.

"What were you *thinking*?" she repeated as she hopped on top of her horse.

"Nadia, please—" tried Vartan again as he stood up to defend his innocence.

"You kissed me! You really kissed me!" she said from atop as she turned her horse around. "And to think you had no false intentions!"

"Nadia, I'm sorry, I just thought that you—"

"I don't care for you or your deceitful games!" she interrupted. "It's time for me to go! Good night, *Vartan*!"

As quickly as she finished her words, Nadia kicked her heels and rode away into the night, leaving Vartan alone with just his horse and the old tree to which it was tied. He took a few steps in pursuit but stopped himself short and regretfully watched as she galloped away.

Perhaps it was best to give her some time alone.

Naturally, Vartan was devastated, his heart crushed. Everything he thought he wanted, he didn't want anymore. He stood by his own horse as everything inside him slowly began to die. Even with no one around, he still couldn't allow his unending frustration to reveal itself. He desperately wanted to fix what he had broken but didn't know how. He looked up at his horse and put his hand on its belly, leaning on it for a moment. The warmth of the animal and the rhythm of its breathing gave strength to whatever life he had left.

Slowly, feeling empowered by the beast, Vartan reached for the reins and untied the knot. With nothing left to do, he thus walked with it to the outskirts of the pasture, not even bothering to get on. There was a lot he wanted to think about on the way back home.

As he walked alone in the dead of the night, with one hand guiding his horse and the other in his shallow pocket, Vartan hung his head low in shame and continually replayed the entire episode in his mind as he usually did, typically analyzing his actions, even remembering the sheep scurrying at the sound of Nadia's voice.

"You are what I've been searching for?" he muttered to himself. "Ugh, how lame. I'm an idiot."

The more he thought about it, the worse he felt about himself. Everything he said suddenly sounded so stupid. As the fireflies glowed all around him, Vartan slowly sunk further into the bottomless pit of misery. Everything that he had worked for had suddenly collapsed with the command of one small, insignificant kiss at apparently the wrong time, and as a result, Vartan had single-handedly redefined the agony of defeat. Yet, as much as he wanted to do so, Vartan reminded himself that there was no changing the past. Everything he said and did was etched in stone forever. All he could do was to learn from his mistakes and carry on.

There was no point to regret.

After a long time but a short wander, a new faint rustling sound from the distance drew Vartan's attention. Not knowing the source, he stopped dead in his tracks and listened, fiercely turning his ear towards it. His senses, now on high alert, felt the noise approaching him, eventually clearing to the sound of a galloping horse. Suddenly remembering his father's warning, he quickly removed his hand from his pocket and grabbed the reins with both hands. In case a unit of bandits came looking for the treasures that Vartan didn't have, he wanted to make a quick getaway.

However, just as the sound grew too loud, a silhouette of one horse and its single rider appeared, thus painting the illusion of safety. As the horse and its rider neared, they slowed just close enough for Vartan to see who it could possibly be.

To his disbelief, beyond his most outrageous guess, it was Nadia.

She had returned.

Stopping her horse directly next to Vartan's, she looked at him without saying a single word. Vartan, unable to determine whether he was happy, sad, or both, kept silent and studied her every move. Was this a trick, or was he dreaming? With his eyes fixed, Nadia then jumped off and walked to him. She stood, facing him. Her toes touched his, but he didn't step back. She stood so close, in fact, that even in the dark, Vartan could see the green of her perfectly shaped eyes. He glared into them as Nadia glared back. With a slow raise of her hand, she ran her finger over the side of his neck, touching the skin softly, and followed it down to his hand. She held it loosely for a moment. Then, with a glamorous lean, she closed her eyes and kissed him.

Her kiss was rich and sensuous and full of great wonder. The passion of the moment, a continuation of before, quickly escalated into a precisely choreographed dance. Like animals searching for food, their bodies became controlled solely by instinct. Vartan, livened by the language, quickly dropped the reins and wrapped his hands around Nadia's small waist, pulling her body closer to his. Their faces interlocked as they fused together into one singular being. Vartan felt her breath on his face and tasted all the delight she had to offer, until, as if the ground began shifting, both birds fell against the horse where they continued their wondrous, forbidden dance.

"I still don't believe you," breathed Nadia.

Vartan smiled and pushed his face deeply into hers once again. As their hands discovered each other's bodies, they continued their kiss until they regained their footing, shuffling the dirt below. And then, from the heavens above, a single drop of rain meticulously carved its own path down to Earth and gently landed onto Nadia's head. As if starting a chain reaction, a second drop mimicked the actions of the first, and then a third, and then a fourth, until before long, there were too many to count.

"It's raining," said Nadia from under the sounds of the new storm.

"It's just rain," Vartan mumbled.

Their session, once again, picked up steam until the rain intensified into a great downpour with drops the size of grapes.

"Vartan!" laughed Nadia as she pulled her face away from his. "Vartan, it's pouring!"

He looked at her, and they both began to laugh.

"I guess it is!"

"C'mon," she laughed again, unlocking the bond, "we need to head back!"

She backed up, soaking wet, with her hair in her face. Her clothes drooped from the weight of the rain, and her dress clung tightly to her body. She took one step forward and extended both her hands, pulling Vartan away from the horse. The water from his clothes flew off him as he jumped forward and kissed her once again.

"Hurry!" she laughed as she held his hand. "We need to get inside!"

"What's the point? We're already soaked!"

Nadia laughed up to the sky. "Why am I *here?*"

Vartan smiled through the rain and leaped onto his horse.

"Hop on," he offered ecstatically.

Nadia ran to her horse and grabbed the reins. She handed them to Vartan. He then pulled her up as the cool rain continued to beat down over their heads. Seated behind him, she wrapped her arms around Vartan's waist. Vartan placed his hand on top of hers to let her know he was there.

"Hold on tight!"

"I will," she responded.

"Yah!" he screamed as the horse jumped.

With the raindrops pounding on Vartan's face, Nadia lowered her head to use his body as a shield from the stinging of the drops. He welcomed the harsh conditions and finally relaxed his nerves with a massive smile inside. Thus, together, they rode through the night as if it were as clear and sunny as the day. To Vartan, there was no greater reward than this.

For some time, the heavy rain that would soon turn the land into a flourishing oasis bombarded them from head to toe unrelentingly. A little while later, the rain slowed into a light drizzle and eventually stopped, cooling the air evermore around them. Vartan pulled the horse to a crawl and wiped the long hair out of his eyes as Nadia rested her head on Vartan's back.

"Vartan," said Nadia after a moment's rest.

"Yes?" he asked.

"You never answered my question."

"Which question?"

"Do you ever think about the future?" she asked, continuing her previous thoughts. "What you would do? Who you'd become?"

"What *I* would do?"

"Yes," she confirmed.

Struck by the odd coincidence, Vartan answered anyway, "I do, actually. A lot."

"Well, what do you see?"

"That's a very good question," he stated. "I've always wanted to change the world, but... I just don't know how I want to do it."

"Why do you want to change it?" asked Nadia.

"There are so many wrongs that I just want to make

right. I don't know. I'm not satisfied with it."

"Even now?"

"No, not now," explained Vartan. "Tonight, Nadia, was the best night of my life."

"Really?" she asked.

"Yes, really," he replied sincerely, "and it's all because of you."

Nadia kissed his back. "Mine too," she whispered.

"What about you?" he asked.

Nadia thought for a moment. "I just want to live a simple life. That's all."

The horse continued its crawl on the short journey back home, and neither Vartan nor Nadia said much. Everything they wanted to say to each other was done through their physical interaction. Nadia, still wet from the rain, rested her chin on Vartan's slightly slumped shoulder. There was something special about the man sitting in front of her. Nadia knew this. She realized that he had no immediate impressive talents. His speech wasn't strong, and he didn't come from a wealthy family, but Vartan did have two characteristics that atoned for all that he lacked—his ambition and undeniable love for her. From this moment forth, Nadia knew that she, too, had found what she was looking for. With that thought in mind, she smiled and tightened her arms around Vartan just a little more.

Vartan, also still wet from the rain, sat in front and loosely held onto the reins of both horses. He felt the reassuring pressure of Nadia's arms and the gentle breathing of her body. Only a few hours from sunrise, he couldn't help but relax his eyes. The evening chill had long set in, but the warmth of their bodies so close to one another made that insignificant detail irrelevant. For once in Vartan's life, everything felt right.

"Nadia…" he whispered. "Nadia, you're home."

Without a response, Vartan realized that she had fallen asleep on his shoulder. The horses gradually came to a stop, and Nadia moved her head to one side.

"Nadia, you're home," he repeated.

She sat up and, as if in a daze, looked around the land

where her house stood.

"Was this a dream?" she asked with her soft, feminine voice, wanting reassurance that the night was now, indeed, forever a part of her beautiful reality.

Vartan jumped off and smiled. "It really happened."

Nadia returned the smile as Vartan reached up and helped her down. With her feet firmly planted on the ground, Nadia leaned in for a long and meaningful hug. Vartan, unprepared for the unexpected, felt the jolt of her body moving forward and took one step behind for balance. The warmth of her body, as before, made him forget about the cold air around him. He wrapped his arms around her torso, and once again, their bodies gracefully intertwined. He kissed the top of her head and looked off to the distant horizon.

"Nadia," he whispered.

"Mmhmm?" she murmured.

"I just want you to know that, tonight, I had the greatest time with you," he finished.

Nadia gently released herself from their tender bond. She replied to Vartan, not with words, but rather with her eyes. What she said could not be written down and thus would be expressed a moment later as one extended and passionate kiss.

"I know," she said. She took a few steps backwards. "Good night, Vartan," she said, rubbing her shoulders for warmth.

Vartan responded from his spot, "Good night, Nadia."

17

The following morning, I hastily awoke to the simultaneous sounds of my brother snoring and my grandmother coughing. The mixture of the two spoiled any chance I had at falling back asleep. Deeply annoyed, I surrendered myself to the kitchen table. In the living space, my mother stood next to my grandmother and lightly rubbed her back as she continued to cough until her face slightly turned red.

"Mom, I'm going to call for the doctor," she said. "This is enough."

On the floor, little Margaret didn't look happy.

"My dear, I told you," my grandmother replied, "there is dust in the air. Please, don't worry."

Her cough now sounded wet and deep. Even I knew that it couldn't have been from the dust. The rain last night should have settled it.

"Yeah, *Medzmama,* I think you should go to the doctor," little Margaret repeated.

"I'll get her a glass of water," I said as I headed for the door.

"And, Armen, please," called my mother, "can you ride to Dr. Thomassian's clinic and ask him to pay us a visit?"

Despite my grandmother's wishes against it, I nodded my head in agreement and went outside. It was for her own good.

At the well, I turned the crank and lowered the bucket. Sooner than usual, the bucket splashed the surface, and the rope went limp. I opened my senses to make myself more aware of the situation and turned the crank up and then down again. And again, the bucket splashed the water too soon. I looked at the spool attached to the wooden support beams above and there was definitely more rope left, so I leaned my head into the well and jiggled the rope.

"That's strange," I thought.

The water level in the well had risen.

After raising the bucket back up, I filled a glass with the water. I grabbed it, and immediately put it down. Not only was the water level higher than normal, but the temperature was as cold as *ice,* instantly surprising my sense of touch. Anticipating the feeling, I picked the glass back up and helped myself to the water. Just as from the river, our well water was crisp and deliciously sweet. I had never tasted water come out of the well with such delight, so I drank the rest before filling the glass again for my grandmother.

"Here you go, *Medzmama,*" I said as I brought the glass

back into the house.

"Thank you, Armen," she responded.

With the help of my mother's hand, my grandmother slowly brought the glass to her mouth. As soon as the water touched her lips, she subtly enamored at its glory. I saw it in her face. Like a frozen waterfall, it traveled down through her body and temporarily numbed her lungs into a state of serenity.

My grandmother closed her eyes.

"Thank you, *dughas*," she said "That feels much better, my son."

"You're welcome." I turned to my mother. "I'm going to get the doctor now."

"Thank you, Armen," she responded.

I left their sight and ran to the barn for the horse. On the way, I passed my father tending to an ox's hoof.

"Where do you think you're going?" he asked.

"I'm going to get the doctor for *Medzmama*."

"Ah," he said. "Good. She finally gave in?"

"No," I said, "not really, but I'm going anyway."

"All right. Hurry back; I want to talk to you and Vartan."

I sighed at the thought of what he could possibly want to talk to us about.

"By the way," he added, "do you know why the horse is so tired today?"

"No idea," I shrugged, secretly smiling inside.

In the barn, I hoisted myself atop the horse as my stomach grumbled. Without eating breakfast again, I left our farm and rode into town to get Dr. Thomassian.

Downtown Kharpert was more or less the same as any ordinary city. To get there, you would follow the main dirt road directly east, well beyond the church. The road eventually cut through two rows of buildings, built at different heights. Some were only one floor and some were two, three, or four floors. All the businesses were on the first floor, and the top floors were small, crowded apartments. The only building that sat alone from the rest was the local police station just before the town square, the center of Kharpert. There, the road turned into an ancient cobblestone field, surrounded by shops and markets of all kinds. Businessmen of all sorts had their wagons and shops set out all around it. They sold sheepskins, vegetables, rugs, farm animals, bread, and just about anything a skilled laborer could sell. Farther east, Dr. Thomassian ran his office in a long white building next to the international post office. Nailed above the door, in black Armenian letters, was the word "Clinic." Anyone who had the unfortunate fate of becoming ill would make their way to this rented space. Inside, Dr. Thomassian had everything he needed to treat each patient accordingly.

After I tied my horse to the post outside, I walked up to the clinic door. I knocked twice and stood, waiting for someone to answer. A few minutes later, without a response, I knocked again, taking a step backwards to check if the clinic was operational that day. It was, so I raised my hand again to knock. Just as I was about to do so, the door opened. A tall, thin man with small glasses stood in the doorway.

"Yes?" the man inquired.

"Dr. Thomassian? Hi, it's me, Armen, Tevos's son."

The doctor thought carefully before each response, even when asked his own name. Looking at me, he studied my face for a moment longer. "Ah, yes, from the west," he reminded himself as he held the door open for me. "Please, come in."

I walked inside, quickly cringing at the sight of a human skull sitting on a desk, complemented beautifully by hand-drawn pictures of different angles of the human body hanging on the walls.

"What can I do for you today?" he asked.

Always being precise with his rhetoric, there was no doubt in my mind that Dr. Thomassian was an exceptionally intelligent man. Had I the patience to become a doctor, I would have wanted to be just like him. As I stood in his presence, I glanced behind at the patients waiting to be treated before my grandmother. Dr. Thomassian's clinic revolved around a first-come, first-served basis, unless there was an emergency, in which case that became an understandable priority.

"Well, my grandmother has had a cough for a long time, and we would like you to make sure she's all right. She's old, so it's hard for her to travel this far. Could you come over and see her today?"

He put his hand on his chin and thought, as if calculating numbers.

"Hmm…" he pondered. "Taqoohi?"

"Yes," I replied, confirming my grandmother's name.

"Yes, I suppose I could. Unfortunately, today I'm busy for the morning, but I will make room later this afternoon, perhaps early evening."

"That works just fine," I agreed. "Thank you."

"All right, Armen, tell your parents I say hello."

"I will," I said, throwing in a smile.

Returning the same, he turned to tend to the rest of his patients as I rode back home to tell my mother about Dr. Thomassian's response. She accepted the short delay and sat with my grandmother until it was time to cook dinner. By this time, but not long before, Vartan finally decided to present himself to the world and taste the aging light of the new day.

"Do you feel better?" my mother asked from the kitchen.

Hearing that question, I raised my head in astonishment, realizing I had forgotten to tell Vartan that I told Mama that he was supposed to be *sick*. Before Vartan could illustrate his confusion, I interjected in an attempt to save the situation.

"Yup!" I blurted out. "He feels a lot better!"

They both looked at me, surprised.

I widened my eyes, signaling Vartan to just go with it.

Replying with a subtle understanding, Vartan finalized our mutual agreement.

"*Ayo,*" he said, smiling, "just like Armen said, I feel a lot better."

"Good," she responded.

Feeling the ease of the situation, I relaxed my posture. Vartan passed me at the dinner table and continued out the front door to the well. I immediately sprang up and followed him there.

"So," I began on the way, "tell me what happened. You've been sleeping all morning!"

Vartan smirked slyly and suspiciously. I will always remember that face, because with that face, he told me everything I needed to know.

"Hold on; I'll say at the well," he said.

After splashing his face with the cold water, Vartan stood and smiled again. Then, he began his story, filling me in with all the details about the night before, even getting as specific as the shove, the sting of the rocks against his back, and the cold of the rain.

Like an uncontainable explosion, my face lit up like a thousand candles.

"*That's* my brother!" I said as I punched his chest and gave him a celebratory kiss on his cheek, the kind only a brother could give. "I knew it! You two were made in heaven!"

Vartan wiped his face and smiled as if trying to brush it off. I was genuinely excited for him. I felt that his struggle with Nadia was also my struggle, and when he won, so did I.

"I *knew* she liked you!" I said excitedly. "I'm telling Tavit. We need to tell Tavit!"

"That's fine," he agreed, "but only Tavit!"

"Okay, relax, no problem," I said, "but this is *amazing* news."

Running back to the house, I yelled at the top of my lungs, "Woo-hoo!" I jumped up, with Vartan casually walking behind me, laughing.

That night, as we sat eating dinner, I could hardly stop looking at Vartan. My excitement hadn't ceased. I wanted to hug him and dance with him as if they were the best days of our lives. I didn't blame myself, though—those *were* the best days of our lives.

Just as I sat high on my pedestal, dancing blissfully with the clouds, my father hesitantly began to speak with a demeanor unlike I'd ever seen.

"Since we are all here together," he began, "your mother

and I would like to share with you some news. It's better sooner rather than later."

As Vartan and I looked at each other, my father prepared himself for what he was about to say.

"Boys," he cleared his throat, "the education system here in Armenia is not as strong as it is in America. I work endlessly to make sure you three receive a proper education."

I listened, confused at the measly introduction.

"Because of this, your mother and I have decided that next year, on January 24th, 1914, so that she receives the best education she can get, Margaret will move to America and live with your uncle Mesrob."

The smile I wore for so long immediately jumped off my face, taking all the exhilaration with it.

"What!" I sprung up in defiance, not understanding my father's words, reacting simply out of instinct rather than by reason.

"Why?" yelled Vartan. "Why?"

My mother, becoming emotional about the issue, did the best she could to explain. "Like your father said, she will receive a much better education in America than she will here."

"Wait, I don't understand. The schools here are just fine!" Vartan objected, raising his voice.

"Let me elaborate, then," said my father. "The schooling is only one part of it. The *opportunities* for her are also *far* greater in America."

"Wha…" I stuttered. "This is—"

"This is what's best for our family," added my grandmother, trying to make us understand.

That was the last thing I wanted to hear. I suddenly had too much on my plate—the first instance that I could remember.

"This is unfair to Margaret!" I defended. "Who asked her?"

"It's not a decision that's up to her," said my father. "We have always wanted the best for you all. Next year, she will begin what they call secondary school, and we have decided that we want her to begin *and* finish her secondary education in

America."

For a moment, I understood what my father said and almost agreed with him but didn't dare to show it. Vartan was at a loss for words. He had nothing to say. I could tell he was grinding his teeth. Instead, he sat and watched as little Margaret put down her head and calmly began to whimper. He extended his arm and gently touched her shoulder. She'd known the news before we did, and now she didn't have to hide it.

"I'm going to miss you guys," she said as the tears rolled down her face. She leaned over and gave Vartan a hug.

As for me, I didn't want little Margaret to disappear from my life. I loved her. And now, I felt like she was already gone. I quickly thought about all the memories we made together, all the happiness, all the arguments. Suddenly, I missed it all. The plan to separate our family like this seemed so much worse than receiving a better education. Everything my mother so carefully taught us about family had suddenly been torn to shreds. With these sudden and agonizing thoughts, my vision had turned into a gloomy tunnel-like state. All the food I had been eating suddenly tasted awful, and I was no longer hungry. What would life be without little Margaret?

Just then, three short knocks at our door reverberated through our house, and, for a second, tore me away from my sorrow.

My father, now unsure about his decision, turned his head towards the sound. "Who could that be?" he asked.

"I'm not sure," said my mother, wiping away her tears. She suddenly looked serious.

Getting up, my father cautiously approached the door. He opened it a little at first and then opened it the rest of the way.

"Dr. Thomassian!" he announced.

"Tevos," said the doctor with a smile, wearing his thin suit. "I hope I'm not disturbing anything."

"No, please come in," my father welcomed as he held the door open and offered him a meal.

"No, thank you," he responded. "I've already eaten."

My mother stood up from the dinner table and quickly composed herself. "Thank you for coming on such short notice, doctor," she said.

"Not an issue at all," he comforted.

"We called you here because my mom has been coughing for one month now, maybe more."

"I heard," he reiterated.

Dr. Thomassian placed his black leather bag on the small kitchen table and took out a stethoscope. He hung it around his neck and walked over to my grandmother.

"Let me see. Taqoohi, if you please, I'd like to listen to your lungs."

"Of course, will I be fine here?" she asked from her seat at the dinner table.

"Without question. Just please, sit forward a bit."

Rushing over to her, my father gently pulled out my grandmother's chair. The doctor then began his examination by feeling at the nodes on her neck. Then, as he leaned over, he put the earpieces of the stethoscope into his ears and listened to her lungs from her back.

"Breathe in," he directed. "Good. Now breathe out. Good. Now cough."

My grandmother inhaled and then coughed. It was very heavy and mucoid. The doctor, undeterred from the sound, listened attentively. He placed the stethoscope on her chest and repeated the process once more on her back.

"Very good, Taqoohi," he said.

Straightening up, he placed the stethoscope back in his bag and closed it up.

"Taqoohi, I'd like to speak to you, Tevos, and Hasmig in private, if I may," he said.

Observing the developing situation, I quickly felt terrible for being annoyed at my grandmother's cough earlier that morning. My father motioned for us to go to the back of the house and shut the door, so they could speak. We obliged and left.

From the crack in the door, however, we listened to

their conversation.

"I listened to your lungs, Taqoohi, to make sure there was no fluid. However, there could be a tiny amount hiding inside your one lung. Sometimes I heard it and sometimes not. It could very well be just a bad cough, but it could also mean the initial stages of pneumonia, a bacterial infection of your lungs. I'm optimistic in the body's ability to heal itself, but you will still need to rest and drink plenty of water."

"Is this serious?" asked my mother.

"My dear, don't pester yourself," my grandmother stated humbly. "What God wants to do, He will do."

"I will be back here in two days' time to see how her cough has developed."

My father placed his hand on top of my mother's. "What should we do?" he asked.

"Nothing now. In the meantime, give her one of these by spoonful, once a day, starting tonight and again tomorrow morning," instructed Dr. Thomassian as he opened his black leather bag and took out three small glass vials filled with a thick, yellow liquid. "This fluid is mold-based to combat any bacteria that may be building. Keep her chest warm, and make sure she spits out anything she coughs up. Wait for my return."

"Great, thank you, doctor," my father said as he stood up and took the three vials.

"Taqoohi, I'll be back soon, all right?" the doctor said.

"Yes, thank you," she replied politely.

"Have a good evening."

Then, he headed out the door.

I looked at my brother and then at my sister, who both sat silently. I didn't even know what pneumonia was at the time, but from the way my parents looked at each other, I knew it wasn't something to be smiling about.

"Boys, Margaret, come here please," said my father.

My father, without cutting corners, moved directly to the point, explaining what we'd already heard.

"But she might not even have it," reasoned little Margaret. "Right?"

"Yes, Margaret, that's true; it just might be a cough," said my mother, "so let's not worry about it anymore than we have to and wait until the doctor returns."

"But until then, we will all help to make sure that *Medzmama* is comfortable and feeling better, all right?" said my father.

My grandmother sat, smiling at us.

"Yes," we replied.

"All right," said my father. "We are done."

That evening, as I lay in bed, I had a lot to think about. Apparently, my mind had reached its threshold of how much news it could bear in one day. As I reminisced, I thought about the day before and how much I yearned for it. My simple life was over. It had suddenly evolved into, as I perceived it, a hastily arranged and complicated mess. I couldn't focus on just one thought—my little sister Margaret, whom I loved dearly, permanently moving to America; my grandmother, with her wisdom, possibly having a disease that I couldn't even spell; and my brother Vartan, who, simply put, was in love. Each person in my family, even with the same blood, I realized, had their own different story.

As we waited for the doctor, the next two days seemed like an eternity. We were anxious to know about my grandmother's condition. By the sound of her cough, however, I wasn't very optimistic.

On the morning of the second day, the doctor made a prompt return to our home. With the stethoscope already around his neck, we welcomed him in to where my grandmother sat.

"How are you feeling today, Taqoohi?" he asked.

"I'm doing better," she responded weakly.

"Have you been eating?"

"I try to, but my appetite is not what it used to be," she replied.

"In order to heal, you must eat. I'd like to listen to your lungs again."

The doctor put the stethoscope into his ears and listened to her lungs, following the same protocol as before.

"Well, Taqoohi, your cough has not improved, so I'm going to prescribe you more vials," said the doctor. "Have you had any chills or unusual sweats?"

She shook her head, and the doctor opened his black leather bag and pulled out a flat, wooden box made of natural wood. With the snap of two small brass latches, he opened the lid and removed another glass vial filled with the same thick, yellow liquid.

"I want you to take two of these a day," he instructed, "one in the morning and one at night, for ten days, until the box is empty, starting tonight. In ten days, I'll return. If anything should arise before then, please do not hesitate to disturb me at my clinic or even at my home."

"Of course," my grandmother nodded with a smile.

Unfazed by the fact that her condition had worsened, she didn't even bother asking why she had a cough, or whether or not she had pneumonia. Regardless of the outcome, it was as if she realized her inability to fight her fate and had already made peace with herself. The doctor took the message quite clearly.

"Do you expect any complications?" my mother asked.

"If I may," he said, "I'd like to speak with you and Tevos."

Dr. Thomassian, my mother, and father then walked to a room in the back.

"From the time that I saw her last, your mother looks noticeably weaker, contrary to what she said to me. Physically, she appears drained, and the fluid in her lungs is now noticeable. I prescribed her some medicine to aid in her healing; studies show the combative effects of mold on bacteria, but, due to her age, there could be, like you mentioned, complications."

"What sort of complications?" asked my father.

"There is a possibility that the medicine might not be effective against her condition."

"Her condition?" asked my mother.

"Yes," said the doctor. "She indeed has pneumonia."

My mother put her hands over her face and began to sob. My father put his arms around her.

"At this point, all we can do is pray for the medicine to take effect," he said. "And like I said, please do not hesitate to bother me at my clinic or at my home."

"Thank you," said my father.

With a nod of his head, the doctor walked out the door, and our parents slowly came out of the back. Judging from their expressions, I knew things had grown worse. Later, they explained the doctor's diagnosis to us. My mother explained the infection and the purpose of the continued medicine. Vartan and I had no trouble understanding the situation because we knew that bacteria were all around us, and it became only a matter of time before someone eventually got sick, and we also understood the possibility that our grandmother would not get rid of the pneumonia. Little Margaret, however, didn't understand it like we did. We took some time to explain to her understandably naïve mind that sometimes bacteria became too strong and needed to be treated aggressively.

"But where did she get it from?" she asked.

"Well, that is a good question," I said.

"We just don't know," chipped in Vartan. "She could have caught it from anywhere. The important thing is that now we have to let her rest so that she can fight it."

"Yeah," I said. "That means we all need to take good care of her until the doctor comes back."

"Uh-huh," said little Margaret. "I can do that."

Ten days later, as promised, the doctor returned. He examined our grandmother and came to the heartbreaking conclusion that her pneumonia had worsened. The doctor, as a result, increased her dosage but kept to his ten-day visitation schedule.

Through the rest of that summer to the beginning of December, despite repeated treatments with the medicine, my grandmother's pneumonia continued to consume her. Some days she felt better and even walked around some, but most other days, she was bedridden. The price for treatments, I remember, came as a hard hit to our family. The vials were expensive, and as a result, we had to ration some luxuries, such as tea, in order to save enough for the rising medical costs. Initially, my father didn't show any signs of the hardship because he didn't want to worry us. However, as autumn crept on us and the leaves turned colors, as the days shortened and the air chilled to a comfortable level, I slowly noticed the anxiety building up. Vartan and I, against my father's wishes, therefore decided to begin school one week into the spring half, February 3rd, 1914, in order to save money, help our grandmother, and spend more time with little Margaret before she left.

Above it all, Vartan, little Margaret, and I continued our duties as much as we could while still helping around the farm. Through the mutual understanding of tending to our priorities, the web that we called a family became tightly knit, and we became even more helpful to each other than before. Therefore, we had successfully put aside any differences we had and resolved any issues quickly and with little or no argument.

With my grandmother's continually weakening state, she eventually stayed in her bedroom, where she spent most, if not all, of her days. There, she continued to weaken and sometimes didn't have enough strength to speak. Her cough had become as common throughout our house as the grapes in our vineyard. All through the night and all through the day, it echoed, sometimes being so bad that she couldn't catch her breath for the next round, making it sound as if she were choking.

News of her unsuccessful treatments then quickly spread throughout Kharpert. Quickly, the influx of gifts and visitations accumulated from neighbors, some of whom we hadn't even spoken to for years. Ara, Garo, and their families tried to stop by every day as it suited our schedule, and thus, the relationship between Nadia and Vartan slowly strengthened with each visitation. My parents and Nadia's parents knew there was something between the two but just didn't know to what extent, and neither one of them came out to fill the other with any viable information. Tavit and I, however, knew otherwise.

We knew what we had created.

As expected, Nadia also grew to know our grandmother. On days that my grandmother felt strong enough, she would continue her stories and provide advice, sharing all that she could, as if Nadia were one of her own. Thus, one day in the afternoon, while strolling with Vartan, my grandmother called for her to come inside.

"Yes, *Medzmama?*" Nadia asked as she slowly walked into my grandmother's room.

"Nadia, my soul, I am weakened. Please, come inside. I want to talk to you."

Fully entering the room, Nadia closed the door behind her, now intrigued.

"Be careful, my dear," my grandmother began weakly. "Love... is very devious. If you let it, it will guide you into the land... of trickery."

"What do you mean?" Nadia asked lightheartedly, trying to liven the mood.

"It's a poison, an addictive poison that can cloud... your mind and alter your judgment. Be careful of it," she explained, eyes nearly closed.

Nadia didn't understand. Was this the infection talking? "But, with respect, why are you telling me this?"

"Because I know," she offered slyly.

"Know... what?" Nadia asked, waiting for my grandmother to clear the ambiguity.

"Nadia, trust me. I've been there, too. I know."

Feeling relieved and embarrassed at the same time, Nadia now felt the lessening of the burden to not have to hold a secret. This was obviously a woman-to-woman conversation, and my grandmother felt the need to pass down her thoughts.

"Have you told anyone?" Nadia asked, concerned.

"Nobody."

"Well, you don't have to worry about me, *Medzmama.* I'll be just fine." She smiled.

My grandmother reached her arm out and grabbed her hand. "I'm happy, Nadia," she said. "But be wise."

With that, Nadia left the room and went back to Vartan.

"So, what did she want?" he asked.

"Nothing, she just wanted to tell me some things," she

replied.

"Oh? What sort of things?"

"You know, just girl things. It was no big deal."

"All right," he shrugged, "if you say so."

That night, directly in the middle of it, well after everyone had left and everything had settled, I woke up to the sound of my grandmother's voice, speaking louder than we'd heard it since before her diagnosis.

"Shoushan!" she cheered happily.

My mother sat on the side of her bed as my father stood and watched over in his nightgown.

Awakened by the same reason, I met Vartan and little Margaret at the doorway of my grandmother's room. We understood what she was saying but just didn't know why.

I studied my grandmother's eyes. They were open, but she was in some kind of semiconscious state, similar to a sleepwalk. She never fully made eye contact with anyone. Her focus shifted all across the room.

"Mom, Shoushan passed away eight years ago," my mother explained to her.

My grandmother repeated herself, "Hi, Avedis! How are you?" This time she spoke a little quieter.

Then, as if she became too tired to continue, my grandmother closed her eyes and relaxed back to an undisturbed sleep. She was in some sort of delusional state. My mother hung her head low and took a moment for herself. She then stood up to leave the room.

For the next twenty-one days, my grandmother repeated the same process and muttered the same words over and over again, clearly speaking to family and close friends who had died long ago as if they were right there in the room with her. We decided to never mention her actions to her out of fear that she wouldn't even remember or possibly deny them. The exhaustion of that lengthy promenade soon took its toll on us, and for those twenty-one days, we seldom slept.

Then, on the cold December day, the 28th of 1913, at the hour before dawn, just after I had finally fallen into a relatively peaceful sleep, I was hastily awakened by my brother.

"Armen, let's go!" he whispered loudly. "We have to get Dr. Thomassian."

"Vartan?" I whispered as my eyes focused onto his face.

"Yes, hurry up, we have no time!"

I speedily jumped out of bed and put on my clothes. From the other room, I heard Der Kourken calmly praying over my grandmother as she frantically gasped for air. Fluid had taken control of her lungs, and she sounded like a drowning man, if I ever heard one. My father stood against the hallway wall and waited.

"Hurry," he whispered.

Immediately, Vartan and I ran out to the barn and pulled out our black horse. We rode him as quickly as we could directly to Dr. Thomassian's house, where we fervently knocked at his door.

"Dr. Thomassian!" I screamed. "Dr. Thomassian, please open the door!"

A moment later, he came out in his nightgown.

"Dr. Thomassian, please," explained Vartan, "it's our grandmother."

Without even changing his clothes, he ran back through his house, grabbed his black leather bag, put on his suit jacket, and ran outside to his horse.

"Lead the way," he said.

Riding close behind, Dr. Thomassian followed us home, and Vartan and I tied the horses to the post upon our arrival. He then ran inside to my grandmother's aid while Der Kourken continued to pray.

"Taqoohi, can you hear me? If you can, please nod your head."

She nodded her head barely.

"We need to put her on her side," said Dr. Thomassian. "Quickly."

Like a chameleon, my grandmother's face changed into a dark-red color as she clawed at the air she so desperately wanted to put back into her lungs. I watched from the doorway as my father helped Dr. Thomassian turn her onto her side. With the shift, a gold chain with a crucifix dangled out from around her neck. Our eyes locked as we made eye contact. She reached for the crucifix and grasped it tightly. I stood, motionless, not knowing what to do.

"Vartan, Armen, leave. Now." My father waved his hand.

We looked at him and remained where we stood. We were petrified.

"Vartan, Armen, leave!" he commanded again.

I glanced at my grandmother just one more time as she lay on her bed, sweating in abundance, fighting for the air.

Thus, we left to the living space and tried sitting on the sofa, but Vartan and I were too anxious, so we paced back and forth. Little Margaret, oblivious to the entire situation, walked out of her room, but I quickly grabbed her before she could see anything.

"Margaret," I said, "come with us here."

"What's happening?" she asked.

Vartan looked at her with glossy eyes. "Nothing," he said. "Just stay here."

He stood and rested his arms around little Margaret. I joined them.

Der Kourken's prayer and the chilling sound of my grandmother's gasps now became plagued by the low-sounding thumps of the doctor's palm aggressively striking her back.

We closed our eyes and silently joined the prayer. I tried to overcome the disturbing conglomerate of sounds, but they seemed to last forever.

Though, as quickly as it began, the sounds ceased, and our house became eerily silent. The commotion had ended. I looked at Vartan with one frighteningly long stare. I didn't blink. Not once.

I will always remember that moment of silence just before the cries that emanated out from that room, out of my mother's body. At that moment, I knew exactly what had happened but quickly rejected it from my thoughts. Before I began to tear myself apart, however, I wanted—I needed—substantial evidence. Regardless, the tears still ran down my face as I stood with my brother and sister. I started towards my grandmother's room, but Vartan swiftly reached out with one arm and held my shoulder. I turned around and faced him.

"Armen"—he shook his head—"no."

I didn't resist and remained where I stood, glad that he stopped me.

As the sun began to rise, the doctor, with his head hung low, slowly emerged and made his way into the living space. Still keeping his composure, he stood in front of us and raised his head.

"I'm sorry," he said, "your grandmother has died."

- END OF PART I -

Part II
January 1914

Chapter 18

Der Kourken stood, wearing his long black robe, facing the congregation. Directly in front of him, my grandmother peacefully lay in a carefully constructed wooden box. Her struggle was now over. My mother stood in my father's arms, accepting his offering of serenity, and I stood with them, expressing sadness the only way I knew how. I couldn't help but look around at the somber faces that filled the church that day, but I needed to know that my feelings weren't alone. Despite the sorrow and mourning, though, an awakened sense of joy filled my heart as I saw beyond my misery and into what made us who we are—a community. Ready, with an undivided support for one another. Everyone knew my grandmother, who she was, what she stood for, what she'd been through. We were her and she was us.

That day, January 1st, 1914, was indeed a terrible day.

"Here lies Taqoohi Abrahamian," intoned Der Kourken, "our dearest messenger from God. She has since returned to His kingdom, taking with her all that she knows, because now, God needs her more than ever. And so I say, let us all bow our heads in prayer in these truly trying times."

Der Kourken extended his arms and motioned for us to bow our heads. He then closed his eyes and humbly lowered his head to begin the prayer.

"Our dearest Father, our protector, our giver of life and taker of life, please watch over Taqoohi Abrahamian, whose body lies here with us today, and let her soul rejoice in your glorious kingdom. Let us all remember the good that she has done and forget that which she has not. May she rest among your saints, among your righteous ones, so she may dwell with those who love you and with Christ our Savior. We pray to you in the name of the Father, the Son, and the Holy Spirit. Amen."

Der Kourken opened his eyes. He paused and looked around the community.

"Now," he continued, "let us all rise and recite the *Hayr Mer.*"

In one accord, we stood and versed the Lord's Prayer in Armenian, which, admittedly, sounds quite the same when expressed through sadness as in happiness. As I breathed through my mouth and struggled to say the last few lines, I opened my eyes and wiped away the tears. In that moment, I felt something. A change. A difference. A warming of my heart. I felt the future and saw the unique road of my life fork and veer in another direction. I didn't know what to make of it or how to describe it, but I felt stronger.

I felt enlightened.

"Please," directed Der Kourken, "have a seat. At this time, we would like to ask for Taqoohi's youngest grandson, Armen Hagopian, to stand here and read a passage from the Bible."

He locked his eyes with mine.

"Armen," he motioned.

I looked at Der Kourken, speechless. No one had told me I was supposed to read a passage, yet alone in front of so many people. I slowly stood at my seat in a silent church and looked at all the eyes directed at me. My heart sped up, beating faster and faster and harder and harder, and the lump in my throat grew bigger. What was I to do now? There was no way I could read, not in that state. I looked at my mother, who continued to whimper; I looked at little Margaret, I looked at Vartan, and then I looked at my father. He nodded his head and motioned at me to get up there as well. Despite the pressure, no matter how hard I tried to get my feet to move from under me, I couldn't do it.

I froze.

"I can't do it," I mouthed to my father.

Quickly understanding, he unwrapped his arms from around my mother. He would take the burden for me on this one. However, before he took a single step, Vartan, my brother, stepped forward. Squeezing by, his eyes briefly met with mine. He looked at me as if he were there to help. I tried to relax my breathing and slumped back down, basking in embarrassment.

"What kind of a coward," I thought, "can't read a

passage from the Bible at their own grandmother's funeral? How could I have let her down?"

I was drowning in my own, deep well of shame.

As Vartan stood facing my countrymen, I listened as he read the short passage, but I didn't understand what he said. My mind remained focused on my mistakes. When he finished, Vartan silently stood back at his spot next to me, bumping my foot with his. At this point, I didn't know what to think of myself. I was disgusted. This much agony for what? Thirty seconds of my life? Despite the fact that I tore myself apart from the inside out, the artful service continued, and the deacons joined Der Kourken in blessing my grandmother's body with fragrant incense, entirely unsympathetic to the issues they didn't know I had.

"Let us now bow our heads now in silent reflection," said Der Kourken.

At least now, I heard what our priest said, so I bowed my head, closed my eyes tightly, and interlocked my fingers. This time, I prayed to my grandmother. I wanted her to hear me. I prayed for her forgiveness of my shameful act. I explained to her how the *Der Hayr* asked me to read the Bible and how I couldn't do it. I explained that I was scared. I explained that I was nervous, too sad to speak. And then I asked her to give me a sign, a mark of some sort, indicating that she understood. I asked for anything—a sneeze, a cough—*anything* that I knew would make me feel better.

I opened my eyes, continually regretting my disrespect. I listened for someone in the church to cough, but no one coughed. I listened for someone to sneeze, but no one sneezed. I then quickly and desolately concluded that my grandmother didn't understand and that she'd never forgive me, forcing me to live my life in regret. Thus, I closed my eyes at the thought and felt the warm tears continue to roll down my face.

With the deacon's help, the *Der Hayr* then closed the lid of the casket. He motioned for my family to come up and begin the procession out of the church and to the cemetery. My father directed me over to the side of the casket opposite from where

Vartan stood. I glared at the rope handle and reached for it with my left hand. However, just before I grabbed it, my mother approached me.

"Armen," she started.

I turned to face her.

"Your grandmother wanted you to have this."

She reached for a gold necklace from around her neck. My eyes swelled, and the lump in my throat hardened. I couldn't respond. It wasn't my place.

"Don't ever forget who you are," she said.

I then bowed my head as my mother wrapped the chain around my neck. As soon as she let go, I felt its new weight grace my body. I reached down and gently held the crucifix with the tips of my fingers as my mother kissed my forehead and turned away.

Respectfully, we then lifted the casket and carried it through the church, passing the community along the way. There was no music and no song, just whimpers. At the large front doors of the church, we waited until two boys, younger than me, opened them to let in the surge of cold winter air. Thus, I held my breath, narrowed my eyes, and marched courageously through the doorway.

Carefully, we loaded the casket onto the ox-cart, and I brushed the dust of the wood from my hands. Vartan and I then helped my mother and little Margaret up onto the cart. As the last ones up, Vartan and I sat on the edge and let our feet hang. We held onto the rope handles to ensure that the casket remained in place as my father grabbed the reigns in front and waited until the community readied themselves on their carts behind us. With a slap of the leather harness, the cart lunged forward, and we began moving to the cemetery. On the way, I remembered every bump, every sight, and every sound.

There was no mistake about my first funeral.

As the cold wind continued to blow, I noted the shovels leaning next to the large pile of dirt that would eventually fill the hole in the ground at my grandmother's ultimate resting spot. We placed the casket near the grave and circled around it with the community. Before lowering her down, Der Kourken read the final verses of the Bible, the psalms, and concluded the funeral with soothing hymns and poetry. He then scooped up some dirt, made a sign of the cross in it, and poured it over the casket. We, too, took our turn and placed branches onto the casket, followed by our own silent prayer. As I lay down my share, I placed my right hand on her casket and closed my eyes.

"Thank you, *Medzmama*," I whispered humbly, "for hearing me."

I then opened my eyes and walked away. With ropes and pulleys, the local boys gently lowered my grandmother into the ground, and each took a shovel to help Vartan, Tavit, and I pitch the dirt back into the hole.

As the wind picked up speed and bit through to my bones, I still couldn't shake the feeling that something was different, a bit off. A change from earlier, something that I couldn't control, and I didn't understand why. I stood tall and breathed in the cold wintery air and gazed at the scene around me, peering far into the distance for answers. I narrowed my eyes. Yes, they were sharper. I then leaned over and scooped up some dirt with my shovel and threw it in. Yes, my body was stronger. I thought about the present, studied the past, and spoke about the future. Yes, my mind was clearer. I then shoveled the final bits of dirt over the grave and patted it down with my shovel, studying my frozen hands after. Yes, I saw the message, read the signs, and thought about it.

It then dawned upon me.

The difference, I realized, was *me*. I had *changed*. I was no longer what I used to be. I was no longer a child. This former self had swiftly vanished and now lived only in my memories. Shockingly, this new wave, this new maturity, came suddenly and with hardly a warning, forcing me to accept and live with a new mentality. A new analysis. I now viewed the world in a new light, with a new set of eyes, and they showed me things—things I never knew existed.

Thus, I took a step back to view our work and rested my body against the shovel, momentarily satisfied with my understanding of myself. I looked at the new mound that time would eventually settle, and with Tavit at my side, remembered my school and how I missed it. I wanted to know how the year had progressed, how our teachers were doing. I wanted to know who sat next to whom and any new stories. I wanted to know everything about it.

So, I asked him.

"Yes, it's great," he responded. "We miss you in class."

"Don't worry," I assured. "I'll be back sooner than you think."

"That would be nice," he said, nodding with a smile.

And that was the end of it.

As happy as I was that we spoke, deep down, however, those few words bothered me. They bothered me not because I didn't get the answers I sought, but because of my best friend's solemn face, his mood, his seriousness. Where was the laughter? Where were the jokes? Tavit was no more the happy kid that I always knew. I wasn't used to seeing him in this light, and I missed what I didn't have.

As the community slowly dispersed, I realized that the ones who remained were the ones closest to us—Garo and his family and Ara and his family. They sympathized with us the entire way, always ready. I couldn't imagine any other time that I felt so deeply intertwined with everyone in such a radically new perspective. It was shame, however, that it had to be at a funeral.

With one hand in his pocket and another around his wife, Garo slowly approached us with Ana.

"Hasmig," he began, "I know I've said this before, but I'd like to express just how terrible I feel for your loss. We all loved Taqoohi and will miss her dearly. May God watch over her soul."

My mother turned and gave him a hug. "Thank you, Garo. Your support will never be forgotten," she said softly.

"It's nothing, really. And you know that if you ever need anything, I will always be there for you and your wonderful family."

"Thank you," she mouthed.

"I will see you when I see you." Garo smiled. "Tavit, come on, my son."

"See you, Armen; see you, Vartan," Tavit said with a wave. He turned to my mother. "I'm so sorry about your loss."

My mother smiled. "This is life, Tavit."

With our walk back to the ox-cart, we slowly turned home. I had a lot to think about on the ride back, especially when I noticed the empty spot where my grandmother used to sit.

Just as on the way to the church, the Turkish boys in the pasture stopped what they were doing and bowed their heads as we passed. I approved of their respect by bowing my head in the same manner.

As we sat in the silence, a faintly familiar squeaking sound caught my attention just at a hearing distance from our home. I focused my eyes and followed my ears to the barn door, which swung wildly like a drunkard in the wind, rusty hinges and all. My father also noticed and immediately turned to Vartan.

"I swear I closed it!" he stated defensively. "I *know* I closed it!"

"Oh yeah?" said my father. "Then *why* is it open?"

"I don't know."

Nobody believed him.

Irritated, my father stopped the ox-cart near the post and hurried to the flailing doors.

"Armen, tie up the oxen," he said.

I jumped off, ready to guide the animals to the post, but watched as my father stopped prematurely at the doorway of the barn and simply stared. He didn't enter or close the doors—he just stood in the doorway… and stared. Vartan ran over to help him.

"Vartan," stated my father as he extended his arm. "Stay there."

"Why? I swear I closed it."

"Vartan!" screamed my father. "I said stay there!"

Vartan stopped dead in his tracks. After hearing the seriousness in his voice, I studied my father from the cart as he looked steadily at something he never wanted to see.

A moment later, Vartan cautiously began moving again, but my father didn't do much else to stop him. I don't think he wanted to anymore. Then, with a casual reach for the first barn door, he cautiously peeked around it and gasped, then quickly let go of the door and backed up.

"I'm so sorry," he said, turning to my father. "I honestly closed the doors."

"What?" I exclaimed. "What is it?"

"Armen," warned my father, "don't be foolish."

"Why? I want to see!" I begged.

Cautiously, I ran over and slowly peeked into the barn. My father did nothing to stop me, either. He already said what he had to say. I then looked at our animals, our cows, and our horse. This time, however, they didn't stare back. It took me a few seconds for my brain to believe what my eyes were telling me, but I soon accepted the fact that they were all dead. Every one of them. Their massive bodies now lay lifeless on the barn floor, surrounded by an infestation of flies, drowning in a pool of their own blood. Instantly, I felt their warm souls slowly exiting the barn as they bombarded my face with steam.

"What!" I screamed. "*What!*" I screamed again. "Vartan, now the wolves got in!"

"No," my father corrected, "these weren't wolves."

"Then what?" I asked.

"Someone did this, and they did it recently," he said.

"Huh?" I questioned in disbelief. "Who would do this? How do you know?"

"The blood is still warm. Go inside."

Not immediately adhering, I only backed up to allow the viscous river of blood and dirt to pass by then stood to the side in horror, looking to my father. Anger couldn't describe his expression, but for our sake, for my sake, I needed—I wanted—inspiration, motivation, consolation, a plan of action. Anything. *Someone* did this, he said. My father, however, simply stood there and ordered me inside once more while he, as usual, analyzed the situation, keeping any results to himself. My mother and little

Margaret, hearing my anxiety, cautiously began to make their way over.

"Vartan," said my father calmly, flaring his nostrils, "don't let your sister see this."

Vartan ran and grabbed little Margaret and walked her to the porch. My mother, however, continued over and eventually peered in. She put her hands over her mouth.

"Tevos!" she screamed.

"Shh…" he said as he closed the barn doors. "Don't worry, we just need to go inside. Now."

As we gazed at this profound cruelty, little Margaret made a frightening discovery.

"Look!" she exclaimed, pointing to the south.

We turned our heads in the direction of her pointed finger. Far up the hill, a few hundred meters away, sat five Ottoman Turkish soldiers on horseback wearing red fez hats, perched in a triangular stance. Each horse and each soldier exhaled, sending their freezing breath into the air. The soldier in the lead had a thick beard and wore a uniform unlike the others. His fierce demeanor overlooked the situation as it unfolded. Without hesitation, my mother turned and began walking rapidly towards the soldiers. She then stopped, and my father pursued to fill the new gap.

"Leave us alone!" she screamed at them.

"Hasmig, *enough*," said my father as he grabbed her wrist.

My mother pulled herself away from his grasp and continued towards them. She picked up some rocks from the frozen ground and threw them in their direction. Like a bottle under intense pressure, she burst, understanding very well the importance of our livestock.

"Leave us *alone!*" she screamed again.

Little Margaret began to whimper.

"Mama, we don't even know if they did it!" I screamed.

"*Leave!*" she screamed in tears.

The soldiers merely sat on their horses and watched. They watched as my mother broke down and knelt to the ground. Then, utilizing the new version of me, I asked myself a series of questions, ones that would never stop. Why didn't the soldiers respond? Did they kill our animals? If so, why? If not, then who did?

Pretty soon, the bearded soldier turned his horse around, and the others followed suit. Just like that, over the hump of the hill, they disappeared. That moment, I uneasily realized, was the *second* time I had ever seen the government. What were they doing on our land? How long had they been watching us?

On the cold ground, my mother knelt and buried her face in her hands. The death of her mother and now the butchering of our livestock was entirely too overwhelming for her. There were, however, more pressing issues at hand, something more to my mother's difficulties. Something more profound. I looked at Vartan, and we ran to her.

"Mama," I said, "it's all right."

"Yeah, Mama, please," said Vartan, "come inside; it will calm you down."

I looked at my father. The toughest, most impervious man that I knew, and will ever know, remained eerily silent. Instead, he knelt down and slowly helped her to her feet.

"*Hyreeg*! Let's do something," said Vartan. "We need to do something."

"No!" he exclaimed. "You listen to me, Vartan. This is not the time. We cannot and *will* not do anything. We have too much to lose. You will understand this!"

And then it hit me.

Even though he didn't speak it, my father always had a plan. He always had a justification for his answers, for his every move. It might have seemed as though he were lost or confused, but in reality, he was so far ahead that he couldn't relate to anyone else. Always think ahead was what he unknowingly taught me. Always plan based on sensical conclusions. He couldn't let anger cloud his logic, and he expressed his philosophy through his answer. He needed to play it safe. It would be foolish to put up arms against trained soldiers, especially since he had women to protect. Thus, I respected my father for his absolute self-control.

Vartan didn't respond and neither did I.

"Margaret," he motioned as he helped my mother towards the house, "open the door."

Little Margaret jumped to the front door and held it open. She wiped the tears from her face as my mother's exhausted body passed through. In the living space, my father gently set his wife onto the sofa and cleared the hair off her face. She put up her feet and extended her legs. My father pulled up a chair and sat next to her, and we sat on the floor. As the pace of her heart slowed, she began to relax. The immediate surge of emotions that had etched its markings on the inner walls of her throat had escaped and, not surprisingly, calmed her down. For the next hour, we came together at my mother's side until she was well enough to walk to her bed. Then, when she did so, we called it a day.

In the wake of the next morning, my mother understandably slept in. We didn't disturb her for any reason. She'd been through a lot. We'd been through a lot. My father issued Vartan and me the daunting task of digging a long ditch in the cold ground to bury the decaying carcasses that once used to be our thriving livestock. With the outside temperatures unusually cold, I doubled up on my wool socks, put on my jacket, and wore a thick pair of gloves.

My father had our shovels ready for us already, so we grabbed them to begin our work. We started by outlining the location of the ditch, between the barn and the vineyard, and continued by hollowing out the inside. At first, it was difficult, but with each passing scoop, the skill seemed more manageable. Within two hours, a majority of the hole had been hollowed out just deep enough to fit the animals inside. Over night, their blood had frozen, so we needed to pry them loose just to move them.

The first was our cow, the heaviest of them, the one that would require the most energy. Next, would be our black horse. Grabbing an old piece of lumber against the wall, my father stuck it under the belly and used it as leverage to detach it from the floorboards. He put on as much of his weight as he could until the lumber looked like it would snap and eased up when one piece didn't suit the job. So, Vartan and I each took our own piece of lumber to try to loosen the beast. The more we tried, the more we heard the thawing ice crack away from the ground, and the easier it got. With each push, my gloves kept sliding off, so I took them off fully for a better grip. Once the cow was pried loose, we put the reddened lumber to the side and tied together the legs with some rope. I leaned over to grab the two front legs when my father showed me a circular wound that had dug through its skull, leaving bone fragments scattered like pieces to a complex puzzle. That's how he knew wolves hadn't killed them.

This was intentional.

Saddened by the sight, I lowered my center of gravity, and with my father's command, we pulled it away from its spot, using an ox to help. Once in the ditch, we took a quick break and moved on to the next.

One by one, we tied each animal to an ox and dragged each one to the frozen hole. Despite the cold, I began to sweat and rolled up my sleeves. Quickly, I noticed that not all the animals had been exterminated in the same manner as our cow. The rest had their throats slit. Even then, I still couldn't contain my disgust in witnessing the aftermath of a cruelty such as this and then having to clean it up afterwards. Whoever did this was not a thief. Nothing was missing. Whoever committed this crime did so with the sole purpose of destroying a family's well-being. That much was clear.

By mid-afternoon, as the sun warmed the air, all twenty-eight of our animals were set in their place. I never realized just how much blood one of those creatures contained until I looked down at my stained arms and couldn't remember the color of my own skin. For the second time in two days, I once again found myself throwing dirt into a grave, and that was the first instance that I remember connecting my life's experiences to each other—a valuable skill that would prove itself useful in the future.

As we threw in the dirt, my father encouraged us to take frequent breaks, despite Vartan's opposition, to help energize our bodies. We just wanted to get it done, but my father said if you're going to do something, do it right. If we worked too quickly, we were bound to hurt ourselves.

So, as I sat on the cold ground, holding onto the handle of my shovel for support, I looked at my hands, crusted with blood and now dirt, like mortar between bricks. I rubbed them together to heat them up, and for some reason, as I did so, I remembered the conversation I'd had with Tavit about Der Kourken's sermon, the future, and the answer I gave. Why didn't I have an answer? Where were the tools God provided me? Was this all *really* part of a plan? What about our livestock? The thought sparked new questions—questions that I had never asked before. Who was I? Who would I be? Why was I here? What was I capable of? And that dream, that disturbing dream I'd had at the world events meeting—I couldn't shake it. What did it mean? Unfortunately, I had no answers, but I did know one thing—I needed consultation, and I knew exactly where to start.

"Armen," said Vartan, "get up; we have to finish."

"Just give me a second. I'm tired," I responded.

"Okay, boys. We've done a lot," said my father.

I smiled at Vartan and held my spot on the ground. My father looked at the both of us and studied our expressions. He sat next to us. I knew him well enough to know that he was about to say something.

Something meaningful.

"Boys," he said, "times are changing."

I listened carefully for him to say more, but he didn't. That was it. Vartan and I sat baffled at his limited speech. Times are changing? Was he talking about our country, Armenia? Or was he talking about me? How did he know *I* was changing? Maybe he meant that *everything* was changing. Whatever the case, it didn't matter. I knew he said just enough for us to understand, but not too much so we would probe at its deeper meaning.

I didn't ask him questions and neither did Vartan. At

that moment, I wasn't ready for the answers. All I knew was that someone killed our livestock, and there were soldiers sitting on the hilltop, on *our* land. Was there a connection? What about that lady at the world events meeting who said the Turkish soldiers killed *her* livestock? It wasn't my place to judge. I couldn't draw any conclusions. Not yet, at least.

A few minutes later, all three of us stood up and finished covering the ditch. Vartan and I then painfully went inside and washed up while my father added logs into the fireplace to keep us warm. As the heat of the fire took effect and the hour of the afternoon struck three, Garo and Ara sneakily rode in on horseback, each with their wives and children, including Nadia. They must have planned it at the funeral.

My father ran outside.

"Garo, Ara," he said, "this is not a good time. Please come back later."

"Tevos, we are here because we are family," Garo firmly answered. "I do *not* want to hear it."

"Garo, show mercy, this is not a good time," my father repeated.

"Tevos, it's okay. Let them in," said my mother, emerging from behind.

My father turned to her. Garo and Ara looked on.

"All right, but please, make this quick."

"Don't worry, we just want to make sure everything is holding out," elaborated Ara. "Mary made some desserts for you, Hasmig."

Mary handed my mother the dessert.

"Thank you, Mary," she said with a dull smile.

My father curled his lips and looked at the dessert.

Garo noticed my father's unclean hands. "Tevos," he asked, "you're working on the fields? In the off-season?"

My father, unable to think of a viable explanation, answered with a variation of the truth.

"Garo, Ara, please," he began. "Come with me. There is something I want to show you."

He looked at my mother, and she accepted his glare.

The three men walked to the well. From inside the house, I watched as Garo and Ara quickly exploded in disbelief. They immediately turned their heads then ran to the barn. Upon seeing the empty stable, they put their hands over their heads and turned to look at the long grave. Garo threw his hat to the ground, and Ara took off his gold-rimmed glasses and rubbed his eyes.

"What is this madness?" he murmured subtly.

"My God," whispered Garo.

"What are we to do?" asked Ara. "We need to do something!"

"What *can* we do?" asked Garo. "These bandits will pay!"

"Garo!" exclaimed Ara. "Bandits? Listen to yourself! There were Turkish soldiers here when it happened. This is *not* the work of bandits!"

"Garo is right. We cannot do anything," said my father. "Who are we to tell? The local police? We have no evidence."

"We need to band together. I will *not* tolerate this!" emphasized Ara, pointing his finger. "I am telling you, the government is too powerful!"

"My God," repeated Garo. "And who will believe us?"

Ara looked at Garo and didn't respond. Instead, he turned to my father. "I am so sorry, Tevos, that this had to happen," he said, lowering his voice.

My father said nothing. The three men stood for a moment longer, staring into the blood-stained floor and then angrily, but slowly, walked back inside the house.

Garo looked at my mother, calmed himself down, and changed his tone to meet the elegance of the new company.

"You know, Hasmig, with everything that has happened, I cannot express my sympathies enough. Here," he said as he opened his brown suit jacket and pulled out an envelope, "I meant to give this to you at the funeral. I know this might not be the best time, but it just might make you feel better." He handed it to my mother. "Please, open it."

My mother hesitated for a moment but curiously began

to tear it open as we stood, watching from behind the sofa. From inside, she pulled out a small white card, perfectly sharp at the corners. Curiously, she flipped it over and revealed a black-and-white photograph, the one Garo had taken at church with his new Kodak camera. Everyone was in it, including my grandmother. My mother admired it, smiled, and even let out a small chuckle.

A second later, she let out another.

And then another.

"Remember that?" he asked, now chuckling like he always did.

"Of course I do," she said as she began to tear up again.

"Let me see it!" little Margaret pushed. "I want to see it!"

With a casual pass, my mother handed it to little Margaret, and we, too, snuck in behind her to grab a peek. At first, I must admit, I was hesitant to laugh because of the circumstances that had surrounded us, but I rationed that if my mother was doing so, then I should, too.

With Vartan to my right, Tavit to my left, and little Margaret between my arms, little Margaret held it so that we could all see it together. I examined the gem for all it was worth. It wasn't long, though, before I realized that that photograph, that exact moment, had captured the true essence of what made us unique—Vartan, with his head turned, stared at Nadia; Tavit, stomping his foot, laughed as I held mine up in pain; my father and Ara stood with straight faces; Garo laughed; the women smiled; and my grandmother oversaw it all.

The perfect moment.

"This is amazing," I whispered.

Tavit laughed. "Ha-ha! Look at your face!" he said, pointing his finger.

I laughed with him. "You're not funny!"

Little Margaret then passed the photo to Nadia. When she saw it, she subtly passed a smiling glance at Vartan, who, of course, returned it.

As the photo continued to circulate, the small chuckles

spread like wildfire and quickly developed into a howling laughter that overflowed our house with joy. It eventually made its way back to my mother, who placed it onto the side table near the fireplace. It was very surreal to witness how the human mood could change so rapidly, how just one right could undo so many wrongs. One moment, we were sulking in deep mourning and anger, and in another, we were laughing. For some reason, I now felt that this wasn't a terrible thing to do. In fact, I believe we all could've used it. As we laughed and joked, I forgot about my difficulties. Were our animals *really* slaughtered? Did my grandmother *really* die? Was little Margaret *really* moving to America? I realized that the people around me were the reason why I counted my blessings and the undiscovered reason why I continued to exist. If there was any explanation as to why God threw these people into my life, this without a doubt, was it.

19

It was 9:15 at night.

Old Armen crossed his legs in the hospital room and casually rested his hands on his knees. Two nurses, on call for the night, periodically came in to check and were now listening. This was the first time that Armen had ever told his story from beginning to end, especially in such vivid detail. At his old age, though, good or bad, some stories were just meant to be told.

"What happened to the animals?" asked Armen's grandson. "Why didn't you just burn them instead?"

"Well," he responded, "they were killed," restating the facts.

"I know, but like, you said that your survival was based on your animals, and now that you didn't have any, how did you guys survive?" he clarified.

Armen subtly smiled at his grandson. After an extended moment, he responded with just one word: "Garo."

"Garo gave us what we needed—two horses, two cows, three donkeys, and twenty chickens, to be exact.

"You can repay me at any time," he told my father sarcastically.

"Thank you, Garo. This is now our debt to you. We are truly grateful and will be sure to repay you," he responded from the porch of our house, bundled in his thick overcoat.

"Nonsense," he said with a wave. "I was only fooling. There is no need to repay me. In fact, I will be insulted if you do. Do you want to insult me?"

My father smiled. "Of course not, my friend."

"Good," he said with a pat on my father's back. "Then we are done."

Garo then turned around and went back home. My father opened the front door and walked inside the house only to stumble over a suitcase on the floor.

"What is this?" he demanded.

"Tevos, relax," said my mother. "It's Margaret's."

"Well, move it. It shouldn't be where we walk. I need to take care of some things."

With an exaggerated step, my father walked clear over it and continued his way out the back. Little Margaret then dragged the suitcase to one side of the room. Earlier in the day, she had begun packing, with my mother's help, of course, in preparation for her voyage to America. So far, one suitcase was all she needed because that's all she had.

My mother knelt. "Margaret," she said, "listen to me."

Margaret stood with a long face. She couldn't even look my mother in her eyes.

"You must remember that we are doing this for *you*. Your *future*. Uncle Mesrob will take very good care of you," she said.

Little Margaret glared at our uncle Mesrob, who sat next to Vartan and me on the sofa. He had newly arrived from Ohio, merely two days prior.

"But America is so far away," said little Margaret.

"Yes, I know, but we will write and hopefully move there ourselves. We just have too much to take care of before we go."

My mother gently rubbed little Margaret's arm.

"Do you understand, *hokis*, my soul?"

"Mmhmm," she responded with a small nod. "Will you visit me?" she added.

"*Hokis*, of course we will! What kind of question is that? You know we love you. Why would we not want to visit someone we love?"

Little Margaret smiled shyly.

"Do you feel better?"

Little Margaret nodded again.

"Good, then let's finish packing."

My mother put her hands on her knees and stood up. With a little less than two weeks to go, she and little Margaret had to ensure that everything had been accounted for, so she walked with her daughter to the back rooms, leaving Vartan and I with my father's brother, our uncle Mesrob.

Uncle Mesrob was a louder, more aggressive version of my father. Every time he laughed, I remember clearly, his massive palm would strike my back with a low-pitched thump, and it didn't matter who he was telling his stories to because his palm would always find *my* back. Rumor has it that he used to be an amateur boxer. At first, I didn't believe it, but with each strike, with each laugh, I became more and more accepting of the thought.

Once my mother and little Margaret left, Uncle Mesrob burst into a thunderous laughter.

"Did you see your father's face?" he said with his incredibly deep voice. "He almost ate it!"

He slapped his knee then hit my back, nudging my upper body, causing me to throw my arms forward.

"Yeah, that was really funny," I responded.

"Well," he said, slowing his laughter, "let's go see where my brother went. You boys behave, you hear me?"

With our agreement, Uncle Mesrob stood up and left, leaving Vartan and me the freedom to finally speak our minds.

"Man," I groaned, reaching for my opposite shoulder.

"Oh, it's not that bad," said Vartan. "It makes you

tough."

"What do you know about being tough? He never hits you!" I defended. "You don't know how to take a hit from him!"

"I can take a hit from anyone." said Vartan, overconfidently.

"Oh right, unless it's from me on the ground after church while wearing a suit."

It was a mouthful, but I said it, and it landed me deep into sensitive territory, since we both still remembered our bloody noses and swollen faces.

"Armen, you clearly lost!" he rebutted. "I was on top of you!"

"Yeah, big deal. It means nothing," I stated. "I want a rematch!"

At first, I didn't realize what I had demanded. With Vartan's punch still fresh in my mind, I wasn't sure if it was the right thing to say or if I'd just spoken impulsively. Perhaps the thought of Uncle Mesrob's boxing background lingering in my head had persuaded me. Whatever the case, I said it and there was no turning back.

"Fine," he replied, "I agree."

"We need to go over some rules first," I said, thinking out loud, solving my own problem. "No throwing punches."

Vartan thought about it for a second and extended his hand. Like a respected warrior of the opposite tribe, I reached out and shook it.

"Let's wait until it warms up outside. We can't wrestle in here," he said, looking around the kitchen and living space.

"Fine. The summer it is."

"Deal," he said.

"Deal."

Vartan stood up, giving me a clear view of the empty chair in the living space where *Medzmama* used to sit. In that moment, I saw her and even pictured her telling us that we shouldn't wrestle anymore. Life took some getting used to without her. My brief reminiscence, however, soon came to an immediate halt when the front door was suddenly flung wide open, and my father stepped clear inside.

"Vartan, Armen," he commanded, "put on your jackets. Follow me."

We looked at each other and stood up. My father went back outside and closed the door behind him. Vartan and I then grabbed our coats and followed him to the barn, where we met with Uncle Mesrob.

With the fewer animals, the barn seemed more spacious. I didn't want to be in the slaughterhouse any more than I had to, especially with dirt still crusted with blood.

"Why did you bring us here?" Vartan asked.

"I want to show you something," my father explained.

He then walked over to the stable where our horse used to be and opened the metal gate. We followed him in onto the wood floor and stood to one side. My father brushed the few strands of hay off the wood and carefully peeled away the blood-crusted burlap underneath. He threw it to one side and peeled away a second burlap covering. Below appeared the outline of a long rectangular panel cut into the floor. My father brushed off the excess dirt and exposed a small circular handle made of metal on one end.

"Stand back."

He then grabbed the handle and pulled it up. For a second, nothing happened, so he let go and stomped his heel into the wood, creating a distinctly hollow thud. He then reached down and pulled harder. The rectangular panel then jumped, but he absorbed the shock with his elbows and fully lifted it out, placing it against the wall thereafter. I stared into darkness of the wood-lined hole, trying to solve the mystery of its contents. As soon as my eyes adjusted to the new darkness, I gawked at what I saw. To my disbelief, inside the secret compartment, lay one Russian Mosin rifle, two pistols, and a strap of ammo.

"*Hyreeg!*" I exclaimed. "We're not allowed to own firearms!"

"That's the government's new law. They only say that to keep us under control," he explained as he reached in and pulled out the rifle. "Don't worry."

Constantinople, the capital of the Ottoman Turkish Empire, denied Armenians the same liberties and freedoms as the Turks and Kurds of the same land. One such restriction forbade any Armenian to own firearms, which in turn, made me question the purpose of the law. Was it to keep us under control like my father said? Or was it to prevent revolt? Perhaps it was a combination of both. If the government wanted to prevent revolt, I thought, it made more sense to give us equal rights instead of taking more away, so that we wouldn't have a *reason* to revolt. As a teenage boy, however, what did I know?

"Here," my father said to Vartan, "hold this."

My father brushed the dirt off the barrel and handed him the rifle. Vartan held it cautiously and measured the device from butt to muzzle.

"I didn't want it to ever come to this, but now we have no choice."

"What... are we going to... do?" I asked hesitantly.

"Nothing," my father answered unconvincingly. "I'm going to teach you two how to shoot a rifle."

I had so many questions to ask. Why was my father showing us this? Where did he get these weapons? Again, I figured it would be best not to know the answers. All I knew for the moment was that I was now seeing a side of him that I never knew existed, and yet, I still trusted his judgment to the fullest.

"But you haven't even taught us how to use the dagger!" rationalized Vartan.

By the look on Uncle Mesrob's face, it was clear that my father hadn't told him about Vartan's gift, and my father readied himself for an explanation.

"A dagger is more dangerous than a firearm. When you have mastered the rifle, you can move to the pistol, and *then* the dagger."

"What?" I said softly. "That doesn't even make sense."

My uncle stepped in. "Of course it does," he said. "The farther you are from the target, the safer you are. The closer you are, the more dangerous."

My father placed the panel back down and put the two

layers of burlap over the seam.

"You are to tell no one about this, do you understand?" he insisted.

"Who will I tell?" I said. "Tavit's at school."

By the look on my father's face, it was apparent that a simple yes was all he wanted to hear, so that's what I reduced my response to. My father took the rifle back from Vartan and blew off the dust one more time.

"Let's go." He motioned to us.

In the cold climate, with the temperature just above freezing, we walked to the northern part of our farm about twenty meters from the base of the smaller hill.

"A rifle," he began, "is a very powerful weapon. You must have complete control over it, or it can be used against you. The first thing you should always check for is the safety."

He turned the rifle to its side and flipped over a small lever so that we could see.

"Make sure it is on. Next, make sure you have bullets in the rifle."

My father looked at Uncle Mesrob, and they laughed.

"To hold a rifle, you put the butt deep into your shoulder socket so that it can absorb the shock of the firing bullet—the recoil. If the butt is not deep into your shoulder, the rifle can kick back and break it. I've seen it happen.

"You hold this with your left hand here and your right hand here. Never keep your finger on the trigger. You might accidentally shoot too soon. Only when you are ready to fire do you put your finger on the trigger. Next, when you're ready to shoot, disable the safety, then cock it back with this lever here. This puts the bullet into the chamber.

"Next, lower your head down, and close one eye to match up your target. Once you have steadied the weapon, hold your breath, and squeeze your finger.

"Watch me and learn," he continued. "Stand back." He motioned with one arm.

My father then got down on one knee and pointed to a rock at the base of the hill.

"Right there." He narrowed his eyes.

In one fluid motion, he brought the rifle up, aimed, then shot, following every one of his steps. The sound of the bullet leaving the chamber exploded and echoed through the farm. Vartan and I covered our ears at the alarming sound. Just like my father predicted, the bullet hit the rock, dead center.

"Wow, my ears!" said Vartan.

"One more thing you forgot to mention, Tevos," my uncle reminded.

"That's right," he affirmed with a sly smile, "a rifle shot is very loud."

Strategically choosing to shoot at the base of the hill, my father didn't want the authorities to hear the shot. He figured the hill would mask the sound, which only seemed to work to an extent. I, on the other hand, thought that, without a doubt, someone would hear us causing a commotion. With the smile on my father's face, however, he obviously felt indifferent, almost careless. He was going to teach his sons how to use a firearm, and he was going to do it on his own time.

Nobody was going to stop him.

As my father readied the rifle for a second shot, from behind us, the back door opened, and out came my mother.

We turned our heads towards her.

"Tevos!" she yelled, visibly upset. "Do you have to do this *right* now?"

My father, still kneeling, rested on the rifle.

"Please, if you must do this, wait until things have settled. At least until Margaret leaves. I don't want to hear any more shots!"

My father rolled his eyes, then stood up and put his arm through the strap.

"Don't you roll your eyes at me!" she exclaimed.

"Well, boys, you heard your mother. We'll do this another day."

"Great," I murmured.

If the government couldn't stop us, my mother definitely could.

She then shook her head and went back inside. We then put the rifle back down into the secret compartment followed by the first layer of burlap and then the second.

"Another thing," added my father, "you are absolutely not to use the rifle or the pistols or firearms of any sort without my direct supervision."

Taking the directive as simply another damper on our adventurous minds, we hesitantly agreed. With nothing left to do in our day, Vartan stayed in the barn with my father and uncle, and I went inside the house. Standing in the kitchen, my mother looked out the window. With no one else around, I felt this was the optimal time to seek some desperately needed answers to the questions I had.

"Mama," I began.

My mother turned around. "*Ayo*, Armen?"

"Can I ask you a question?"

"Of course, what is it?" she welcomed.

This was no time to dance around. I went straight to the point.

"Well, have you ever… or… Did you ever think about who you would be? Or what you would become? When you were my age?"

"Oh, yes, everybody has, I suppose," she explained, "but I wouldn't think too hard about it because you'll never find an answer until it's right in front of you."

"Really? Why not?" I asked.

"Well," she said, "like Der Kourken said, God has given us the tools we need. He has a plan for all of us and only He knows that plan. That's the mystery of life—you just don't know."

"But do you think it's true that you think you will be one thing but end up being another?" I asked again, referring to the future of our farming business.

"Yes, *hokis*, of course," she said, comforting me.

"Is that a bad thing?" I asked cautiously.

"As long as you have God in your life and surround yourself with good people and keep your pace, you will be just fine. I have all my faith in you. Just don't give up and always give it your best."

"What if I give it my best and fail?" I asked.

"Armen, God is always with you. He won't let you fail. Don't worry."

At that time, that wasn't *really* what I wanted to hear, but I ran with it. I tried understanding how God knew how we would use the tools around us, but the more I thought about it, the less it made sense to me. I guess it didn't matter whether or not I knew the future. All that mattered was whether or not I would uphold my morals and use the resources around me to the best of my ability. At least that's what I understood.

From then on, I never gave it more thought.

20

January 16th, 1914.

The morning before our departure to the Port of Mersin was a warmer day. Collectively, we finalized little Margaret's move. Everything in America would be new to her, even the ship that would take her across the Atlantic. She had never seen an automobile, a new method of travel at the time; she wasn't used to electricity, the food would be different, and communicating would be difficult. Despite these seemingly large obstacles, I wasn't worried about her at all. Little Margaret was smart, and she was stubborn, but in a good way. And just like me, she was very observant, so it wouldn't be difficult for her to pick up the American lifestyle.

To aid her in the transition, Vartan and I also tried to teach her anything we knew about American culture, but having never been there ourselves, all we really knew was what we learned in school. We knew that life in America was way faster than in Armenia and that the cities were much larger. We even spoke English fairly well, and in order to give little Margaret a running start before she started her new education, we created a game where we would point to an object, and she, in turn, would have to tell us the name of that object in English.

"Tree," she said.

"Yes," I responded in English. "Good."

I pointed to our home.

"House."

I pointed to the cold ground.

"Grass."

I pointed to my head.

"Ugly!" she laughed.

"Not funny, Margaret!" I said as I playfully chased after her, only stopping to pretend that I was out of breath.

That night, despite having eaten already, we remained seated at the dinner table. My mother initiated the movement to go around and share all of our good memories together. One by one, we began with our childhood and continued to the most recent times. Almost everything we shared was funny, and we each had a good laugh. I must admit, though, I felt uneasy about that bittersweet night because I knew we were doing this for a reason. For little Margaret. And the next morning would mark the commencement of our seven-day journey to the Port of Mersin.

At the crack of dawn, we arose and prepared to venture southwest to the Mediterranean Sea. With an abundance of food and supplies and Garo's promise to periodically watch over our home, we sat on the cart and pushed beyond the boundaries of our everyday life, planning to stay at the various inns along the way. For a while, Vartan and I continued to play the English language game with little Margaret. My mother and father, wanting to help, couldn't since they didn't speak a single word. So, as little Margaret learned with us, my parents did as well. And when we exhausted our English vocabulary, Uncle Mesrob took over and filled her in with cultural details.

"Don't expect to see a lot of trees or open fields or farm animals," he explained in Armenian. "There are many homes very close to each other, and not everybody wants to talk like they do here. Everyone is always in a hurry, and they don't have time for personal encounters or family."

Little Margaret looked at him, petrified.

He noted her reservations. "There are a lot of nice things about America, too," he continued. "You will meet a lot of new friends, much more diverse ones than here, and there is a lot more to do! Have you ever heard of roller skates?"

Little Margaret shook her head. "No."

"Well, roller skates are shoes with one added bonus," he said with one finger in the air. "Can you guess what it is?"

By the look on little Margaret's face, she was thinking about it fairly hard. What else could you add to shoes as a bonus?

"Wheels!" he answered, followed by his deep laugh.

He smacked my back.

"Mesrob, that sounds dangerous!" interjected my mother worriedly.

"Hasmig, I can assure you that it's safe."

He turned to little Margaret. "So, does that sound like fun?"

She smiled from ear to ear and nodded.

"All right, then!" he finished. "Roller skating it is!"

Watching how my uncle communicated with my sister, I noted her reactions, feeling confident that he was the right person to take good care of her, at least until my parents decided to move there themselves.

By the late afternoon of the seventh day, I knew we were approaching the Mediterranean Sea because the temperature had increased. I unbuttoned the collar of my jacket and no longer used my breath to warm up my face. As I looked around, I realized that the rural landscape of our farm had suddenly transformed into a busy metropolis. I remember questioning why I hadn't noticed the change. We had gone from quiet, empty farmland to a place where vendors stood at every corner and sold everything from animal furs to fine European furniture, making it a hectic version of downtown Kharpert. That was the first time I had been so far into such a busy area, and I quickly found it difficult to focus. There were people and things everywhere. Was this what America would be like for little Margaret?

As we turned the bend, still far away, I placed my eyes

upon the largest man-made object I had ever seen. Awestruck, I opened them wide to see a clearer picture. The steamship, with its humbling beauty, gently rocked in the water, close to shore. From bow to stern, it stood, decorated with flags, all waving in the cold wind of the January afternoon. Along its side, wooden planks, acting as bridges, connected the open doors of the ship to the dock where the workers, like ants, hauled luggage and furniture. Lined up on the docks, men, women, and children of all ages, bundled together in their winter outfits, stood near their belongings, waiting to board.

"Okay, Tevos, just ride up to that red flag. Do you see it?"

"No, where?" he asked.

My uncle pointed his finger. "There, just look to the right."

My father turned his head a bit. "Ah, very well."

For another thousand yards or so, the intimidating size of the vessel really became apparent to me, and I continued to gawk at its enormity.

My father stopped the cart next to a post and leaped off, entirely unfazed.

"Well, boys," he said casually. "Here we are."

I stood up, continuously glaring at the massive piece of floating metal. I had seen ships in books before, but never did I imagine their true immensity. I exchanged glances with Vartan. I knew he was thinking the same thing, but it looked as if he were a little less naïve than me.

"Vartan, Armen, one of you grab your sister's suitcase. We'll take it to the ticket office."

"No need, boys! I've got the tickets right here!" my uncle said happily as he pulled out two long cards from his jacket pocket. "We need to move to loading door two," he added.

Taking the lead, my uncle then led us to the end of line, and together, we waited where we stood. I looked around and saw people of all types speaking languages that I didn't understand with faces that I'd never seen, making me come to the realization that the world was, indeed, a very large place filled with many unique people. I figured that trying to make sense of it all would have only ended in complete failure—like a bird with no wings. After half an hour, we finally took a step closer to the loading door. I felt a wave of nervousness hit me as I started to come to terms with the fact that my little sister was moving to the other side of the world. What would she look like next time I saw her? What kinds of friends would she have? Would she remember me?

The minute before boarding, my mother knelt down and faced her daughter.

"Margaret," she said, wiping her hair with her hand, "listen to me. You are a very brave girl. Don't let this ship scare you. Be nice to Uncle Mesrob. I love you." She went in for a hug and held on tight. "We will visit you soon."

"I love you, too," she said, returning the hug.

Leaning in, I hugged them as well, and then Vartan hugged us. My father was the last to move in, and he wrapped his long arms around the entire group, squeezing hard.

"*Hyreeg!*" screamed little Margaret. "You're squishing me!"

We laughed and then hugged her individually, and I gave little Margaret the biggest kiss I'd ever given anyone. My uncle then held her hand and handed the tickets to the clerk. The clerk stamped them both, and they marched up the plank and into the ship. For a moment, we lost sight of them until they appeared second from the top deck and stood along its edge. As soon as all the planks were pulled in, the ship's captain sounded its horn twice, and I felt the tremor of its engines turning on.

"I love you, *Mama!*" screamed little Margaret. "I love you, *Hyreeg!* I love you, Vartan! I love you, Armen!"

At the same time, we all screamed, "I love you!" back to her.

My father was the last to say it.

"I love you more," he said calmly and with a nod of his head.

Perched above with Uncle Mesrob, she unendingly waved to us. The steamship then sounded its massive horn once again, jerked forward, and began its voyage to America. With a swift turn of its bow, it quickly and gracefully pushed to the deep.

And just like that, little Margaret was gone.

21

From the month of October 1913 until January 24th, 1914, in just four months, I had lost our livestock to the unknown, my grandmother to pneumonia, and my sister to America. I had to remind myself, though, that the burden of my empty feelings had been distributed among my family.

I was not in this alone.

As I sat on the ox-cart heading home from the port, I observed my daily surroundings more closely, searching for the moment when the landscape changed back to an open countryside. As a way to gauge the transition, I remember deciding to focus on the buildings. The ones from the port to the main city, I noticed, were taller and closer together, and there weren't as many trees. However, after we passed through and exited by day four, a noticeable change occurred—the number of buildings decreased, and the number of trees increased. And by the sixth day, the buildings became smaller, and the space between them grew. Why had I not noticed this before? With less architecture to admire and engineering to lure my ever-growing curiosity, I began to admire the scenery by day seven. I thought about the trees, the grass, the clouds, and the plants. I thought about their daily lives and how they spent their time. I even thought about the herd of sheep we passed, grazing together in the fields, and tried connecting my life with theirs. If I could question my life, I could surely question theirs. Was that *their* purpose? To eat all day? What did their life mean? Were they on this planet for us? For humans? Did they know about our struggle? Did they know that little Margaret left? What if we never needed sheep? We could surely survive without them. What, then, would be their purpose? To simply exist? If that's the case, then why? And for whom? There *must* be a reason for their existence. There must be a reason for the existence of all the animals! They couldn't simply exist for the sake of existing. That seemed like a waste.

Without any answers to my curious mind's questions, I frowned, unsatisfied at my lack of understanding. I was inexperienced and too young to be thinking about such heavy philosophical contexts. So, for the time being, I placed my questions aside to save them for a day that I'd have an answer.

To my right, I looked at my mother. Across from me, I looked at my brother. Neither one had something to say, so with my free mind spent, I shut my eyes and slightly tilted down my head to rest. However, just a few minutes later, the ox-cart abruptly slowed down, and I awoke.

"What is this?" my father muttered from the front.

"What?" Vartan questioned, turning in the process to face the front.

I turned as well.

At the outskirts of our province stood a hastily arranged post made of old, blackened wood. A short tower with hardly a roof stood to one side. Around the post, eleven Ottoman Turkish soldiers stood, armed, blocking the road into town. They hadn't been there when we'd left.

My mother gasped.

"Nobody say a word," guided my father. "Let me do all the talking. If they ask you a question, answer *only* what they ask. Nothing more."

As we slowly pulled up to the uniformed men, my heart began to pound. One turned around and put his hand up in the air, motioning us to stop. My father then stopped the cart exactly where the soldier wanted.

"Hello," my father greeted in Ottoman Turkish.

"Where are you headed?" the soldier asked.

"We are going home," answered my father.

"How do you know these people?" he continued with a wave of the back of his hand.

The other soldiers took a few steps closer and stood in

front of our cart, resting their hands on the rifles slung over their shoulders. My father noted their positions.

"This is my family," he said.

"Where are your identification certificates?"

"Our papers are at home," replied my father.

The soldier measured us thoroughly with his eyes. He studied us and walked around the ox-cart, probing at its contents. My heart continued its erratic beats from inside my chest. I tried not to make eye contact, but I did.

The situation grew tense.

"Everyone off the cart," he ordered.

My father looked at us, and we all shifted, ready to adhere to the soldier's request. Farther up the road, though, another soldier stood up and moved a few meters towards us.

"Savas," he yelled, "no need. Let them through."

The soldier looked at us for a moment longer.

"All right," he repeated, "let them through."

Slowly moving to one side of the road, the other soldiers made room as we began moving and watched us as we cautiously passed them by. Not one of them smiled, and not one of them spoke.

Why were they stationed there? What business did they have blocking the road to and from Kharpert? I figured not even my parents would have an answer for me. Despite the unexpected startle, we continued our push forward.

By late in the afternoon, we were home. It had been fourteen days since we left, and I never knew how happy I'd be to see our farm again. The soldiers had startled me, and the busyness of the port turned me upside down and had confused my senses. It was too loud, too fast, and simply too much. As I headed off the cart, I turned back around to help my mother. Now that my family had shrunk by a third, I didn't know how to deal with it. I missed my grandmother and little Margaret. It had been a long two weeks, and my mind still wandered in all directions, so I walked over to an apricot tree in the west. I smiled at my surroundings and breathed in the cold air. I closed my eyes, lifted my chin, and exhaled. The blood rushed to my head and through the tips of my fingers, recharging my body and calming my soul. Serenity. Quietness. I opened my eyes and stared directly at the leafless treetop. Inexplicably, I suddenly became fascinated with the twisted limbs of its making. What caused a tree to grow the way it did? Why did it have to be so complex? Even when I tried, I never could turn off my thoughts. For me, it was a gift and also a curse. Why was I even thinking about that? I always questioned whether or not anyone else thought the way I did, the way I analyzed the world. Perhaps, though, it was my mind telling me that I was simply going insane. Whatever the case, I shook my head once again to throw away what I perceived at the time as nonsense. There was no need to waste my time thinking about the branches of a tree or why sheep existed or even if they understood the problems of humanity. For the long moment, though, I needed to focus on the blueprint of my future. My schooling. Life was only moving faster, and I would be starting again in two days. So, before I knew it, it was time to get some rest.

The following morning, on Monday, February 2nd, Vartan and I took Garo's brown horse into town to buy some much-needed supplies for school. Already three weeks into the second half, I knew that I'd have to catch up on my missed work, so I readied myself for a challenging year. I knew that Tavit would offer me his time to explain the material, following the lessons of his teacher who always said that you never really know anything until you can teach it to someone else and have them understand it.

At the store, I picked up a few notebooks, some ink for my father's fountain pen, and an eraser. Vartan, too, bought what he needed. Any textbooks that were required, for me at least, would be provided by the school for free since it was funded mostly by the American missionaries and Great Britain.

Feeling confident with my purchase, Vartan and I rode back home an hour later with supplies in hand. I placed them, still wrapped in brown paper and tightened with twine, under my bed for safekeeping, then prepared for the rest of the day. I helped Vartan pack, and he helped me clean my room and ready it for studying. I thought about how quickly the recent circumstances had begun to flow out of my mind as I focused on myself. It, however, didn't feel right, but I knew I had to be realistic and continue. I didn't have a choice.

On February 3rd, I woke up fresh to begin my first day of school of the year 1914. Hurriedly, I tied on my old leather boots and put on my brown wool gloves and my dark-gray wool jacket. Even after washing it twice, the blood of our livestock still faintly stained it. I kissed my mother and waved to my father and brother, then made a dash out the door to Tavit's house. I, as usual, was late, so I ran. Expectedly, Tavit waited for me, and together, we carelessly began walking the three kilometers to school. I breathed somewhat heavily from my morning rush, but regardless, I smiled. I smiled because I was relieved to finally begin my normal daily routine—wake up, eat, walk to Tavit's house, go to school, come back home, eat, help with the chores, finish my schoolwork, and then go to bed. It was steady, and it was calm, and that morning felt as if I'd never skipped a beat. There was really nothing much to it. I enjoyed it. It was brainless.

Five days later, on February 8th, it was also time for Vartan to depart. He hadn't skipped a day of school since the college had still been on break. I helped him lug his old canvas bags outside, filled with the supplies that he would need, and used the momentum of my body to hoist them up against the horse's side. I then draped them across his back. Nadia had come by as well to offer a helping hand, and she stood in the cold, insisting on her desire to help, but the gentlemen in us didn't allow it. With one swift move, Vartan then climbed onto the horse, and we wished him a prosperous journey. He, too, would have to work hard, and for the same reasons as me. As a thinker far deeper than me, though, I never doubted Vartan's fate as a man of excellence.

As I stood with Nadia and my parents, I waved to my brother as he began his three-day ride to school, and I supposed it was very difficult on them. I felt that they'd had enough waving away their loved ones, and frankly, I had as well.

As Vartan became nothing more than a fading

silhouette, I realized that the excitement of beginning a new journey suddenly seemed dull and not as uplifting or exciting as it once used to be. Slowly, my parents walked back into the warm house and continued to watch from the kitchen window. I approached Nadia and inquired about their relationship. It was the wrong time to probe, but I had nothing else to do. I knew there was more than a friendship; Vartan had filled me in. I just wanted to hear her say it and possibly understand it from a different viewpoint. Nadia persistently denied everything, but eventually, she buckled under my pressure and confessed. I felt out of place, especially after how I saw her blush, and even more for having to listen to her speak about how great Vartan was— the same guy who, up until eight months ago, could have passed for a beggar by his looks alone. She made me promise, however, to keep it a secret from my parents and hers until they thought it would be a good time to tell them. I agreed and held true to my word.

Towards the end of March, nearly two months into my return to school, the routine that had been engraved into my life was suddenly disrupted, causing an unaccounted rift in its design. It also, more significantly, sparked a gradually different perspective of how I viewed our neighbors, slowly drowning my own vision. On March 27th, Mr. Wilkins, our history teacher from London, continued his lecture on the world economic system. As I sat, fighting hard to keep from dozing off, Tavit, who sat to my left, hit me to ensure that I didn't start dreaming. Even though I wasn't at all intrigued by Mr. Wilkins's lecture, I'm surprised at how much I remember that moment.

At 9:26 in the morning, nineteen minutes before the end of the class, the door to our classroom suddenly swung open, slamming into the inner wall. The unpleasant sound of the crash caused the entire class to jump and the girls to shriek. Caught off guard, Mr. Wilkins shifted his attention to it, chalk still in hand. Before he could examine the interruption, however, two Ottoman Turkish soldiers holding rifles, each with fixed bayonets, recklessly marched in, one in front of the other, complemented with the sound of their daggers bouncing against their legs. If I wasn't awake before, I was now.

This was not a dream.

"Out!" they screamed in their language. "Everybody out!"

Some students stood up, adhering to the bold request, but stopped to look to Mr. Wilkins for leadership, who had become as irate as a bull on steroids.

"What did he say?" He pointed to the soldiers. "What did he say!"

"They want us to leave," a student translated.

He placed the chalk back onto the ledge of the board. Mr. Wilkins would not tolerate this. I knew he wouldn't.

"You have no right," he blared with his English accent, "to tell us to leave! This is *my* classroom!"

One soldier, not understanding the spoken language, understood solely from Mr. Wilkins's mannerism. He walked up to him and put his face unnaturally close to his. Standing his ground, Mr. Wilkins beamed back into the soldier's eyes. The situation, unfortunately, was obviously flawed—the soldiers had firearms, and we didn't.

"Mr. Wilkins," a student spoke in English, "it's all right. We… we'll leave."

Standing up, the student then walked out, and those who remained, including Tavit and me, followed thereafter. Like rats escaping a flood, we emptied into the hallway and met with the other students coming out of their respective classrooms. Not one person, be it student, teacher, or administration, even had a chance to grab their belongings, as we moved towards the exit. From each of the classrooms then, the fifty or so soldiers followed behind the surge, having delivered the same message. From then on, the situation escalated quickly, becoming nothing less than chaotic.

As we poured outside, I met with my other schoolmates, and we all stood, facing the building. Some girls even began to cry as a way to express their confusion. Rumors and emotions began circulating through the crowd, and it was difficult to establish anything certain. Nobody seemed to know anything, not even our teachers, who stood at our side. After realizing the seriousness of the matter and establishing that this was not a drill, I noted my surroundings, the army, all on horseback, strategically positioned around the perimeter of the school. Why were they doing this? What purpose did they have to disrupt our education? I, like my classmates, my teachers, and my friends, had withered down to a series of unanswered questions.

Just after the last of the students exited, two soldiers jumped off their horses and ran inside to scope out the school. The doors closed behind them after they ran inside, and two other soldiers stood guard in front of it and watched us. A moment later, the door behind them flung open, and the first two soldiers came out, holding a man under his arms. They struggled to restrain him as he kicked and screamed for them to let go. It was Dr. Pratt, our principal. He was putting up a good fight, so they loosened their grip and threw him down the concrete steps that led up to the entrance. He tumbled on his back and arms until he hit the thawing ground below. One soldier then shot his pistol at the ground near his feet, sending the dirt jumping at the spot and the students jumping at the unnecessary show of power. With that shot, I wanted to run, to escape, but I held back because at that moment I was scared that the soldiers would open fire on us if we did. Dr. Pratt, weakened by the struggle, now bloodied, struggled to stand but eventually did so as some brave students cautiously approached and helped dust off the leader of their school. The two soldiers who'd thrown him down then slammed the front doors shut and tied a chain through the handles and locked it with a large metal lock. They then jumped back onto their horses and positioned themselves to join the semicircle around the building. With everyone out, a third soldier marched up and guarded the entrance with the standing two.

"By order of the Ottoman Turkish government at Constantinople," he screamed, "this school is officially shut down!"

He held up a paper for us to see and threw it carelessly into the air. I followed its path as it gently floated to the ground.

"Everybody to your homes!"

Nobody moved simply because we were perpetually afraid of being shot and, now, because we didn't understand the developing ordeal. Was he serious? If we were confused before, we were more confused now. The soldier looked around at the cavalry sitting on horseback and nodded his head. The soldiers immediately unholstered their small pistols and moved their horses a full body's length forward. They pointed their weapons at us, and a lot of the students began running.

"I said everybody go to your homes!" he screamed again.

The soldier then unhooked his pistol from its leather holster and cocked it back. He then pointed it to the sky and fired the weapon.

"Now!"

Immediately, we scattered in every direction, completely unorganized and with one agenda—to go home. The adrenaline in my system pumped through my veins as I fled. Somehow, I managed to stay with Tavit as we ran west.

"What the hell! What the hell!" he said as we ran. "What is going on? Why did they do that?"

"I don't know, Tavit. I don't know! Let's just please get home first!"

Just as with everyone else, there was a lot racing through my mind, but to be honest, Tavit asked the only question I wanted answered. Why did the soldiers shut down our school? For the next ten minutes, we ran. I wasn't used to running in the spring, so I was terribly out of breath. Eventually, we calmed to a jog and then a walk as I put my hands on my hips and panted.

"I'm going... straight to my house," I said at Tavit's house. "I have to make sure they're safe."

"Of course, okay Armen," he said, "but are the soldiers coming here? I didn't see them following us."

Tavit raised a valid point. Did the soldiers follow us? Did they plan on following us? If they did, they would have been here by now. They had horses, after all. I looked to the east, the direction we just came from, searching for them. Was I afraid of the government?

"I'm not sure, Tavit, but I feel that I should still warn them."

"Sure, of course," he agreed, "I'll do the same."

I shook his hand then gave him a hug.

"Are they home?" I asked.

Tavit turned his head and looked through the windows of his house.

"They should be," he responded.

"Okay, be safe," I advised.

"You too."

Thus, continuing my path, I ran the rest of the way home, constantly glancing over my shoulder. For the first instance of my life, it was true; I was now living in my own hometown in paranoia, perhaps even in fear—exactly what my father didn't want.

As I swiftly ran inside, I let the door slam behind me. By the look on my mother's face, she knew something was wrong.

"Armen!" she exclaimed. "What happened? Why are you out of breath?"

I leaned over onto my knees and put up my index finger to allow me a moment. I eventually pulled a chair and sat down on the kitchen table with my arms rested in front of me.

"They shut down the school," I panted.

My mother listened attentively. "Who shut down the school?"

My father walked in from the back room. "What's all the commotion? Armen, why aren't you in school?" he asked.

"Uff, Tevos!" said my mother. "Shh!"

He looked at her and expressed his confusion with his hands.

"The government. Soldiers came in and told everybody to leave. They said the school would be closed until further notice."

"Excuse me?" my father exclaimed. "For what? How can they just shut down the school?"

"*Hyreeg*, I don't know. They marched in with rifles and

told everybody to leave. Students. Teachers. Everybody," I responded.

"They took their rifles into the school?" questioned my mother.

I looked at her. "Yeah, they were in full uniform. When I went outside, they were surrounding the school... at least one half."

My mother rubbed her eyes with her hands and then casually went over the corners of her mouth. "Are you all right?" she asked. "Did they hurt you?"

"What do you mean?" I asked. "Yes, I'm fine."

My mother's tone changed. "Did they hurt *anyone*? Did they use their weapons?"

I thought about it for a moment. "I mean, they yelled and screamed, but they didn't hurt anyone that I saw. I just ran, Mama. I turned around and ran. I didn't even look back."

"Those sons of asses," swore my father. "I work all day and all night to put my children through school, and this is how the government repays me!"

The truth is, I wanted to tell my parents about the one soldier who shot his pistol at Dr. Pratt and then into the air, but I couldn't bear to see my parents more worried than they already were. This brought a new question to mind. *Would* they have hurt the students? I still hadn't the slightest idea as to why the school had been shut down. I did, however, make some guesses, none of which ended up being correct. At this point, my thoughts and feelings, like I mentioned before, were yielding a gradually different perspective on my unfulfilled decisions about the new young regime, solely based on my experience with their decisions and their actions. I knew which direction I was heading but still couldn't muster an admission.

Over the course of the next few days, my parents discussed the matters of a certain importance. As merely a young boy, I, as usual, was left out of the path, completely uninformed. I knew they cared deeply about my education, so I assumed it to be the issue. My father had no formal education past the elementary level and insisted that we didn't follow suit, working endlessly, as he put it, to put us through school so that we wouldn't have to struggle like he did. He always tried to cover it from us, though, but the burden of providing for a family on a farm in the Ottoman Empire as an Armenian overcame his best attempts. It was too much work for too little pay. He wanted us to become doctors or teachers, leaders in a time when we desperately needed them. What was to become of our future now that we couldn't even get a proper education? Knowing the answer, I wanted to tell my parents that I would be all right. I wanted to tell them that I accepted my fate as a farmer, like most other boys in our province, and that I enjoyed the labor. It didn't matter what I'd told Tavit before. I, however, never mentioned it. I was hesitant because I wasn't sure if that's what they were arguing about, but at the time, that's all I could imagine. Therefore, I quietly worked like my father and acquired my farming skills so that one day I could provide my *own* family with a passable standard of living.

As I roamed aimlessly through our farm, examining the methodology my father used to take care of it, I thought of ways to do things even better, more efficiently. I planned ahead so that when the time came for me to take over, I would already have an established strategy—a better one.

With all that time to think, I thought about Vartan and his future. He seemed to be moving forward, but what was *his* plan? Did he even have one? Just as I thought about him, I watched again as he rode in from the east. What a coincidence, I thought.

I ran to notify my parents about his early comeback, and my mother stood on the porch to greet him. As with his departure, his arrival was no happier. In fact, it was almost depressing.

My father also stood to greet him.

"Vartan," he started, "what are you doing back so soon?"

"They shut down the college," he replied simply.

Everything I had thought of about myself, the uncertainty, seeped into Vartan's life like a contagious disease, thus immediately merging what seemed to be two separate paths. There were so many educational institutions in Kharpert. We had kindergartens, primary schools, high schools, and colleges led by different countries. Were those shut down, too? As she stood in our presence, my mother, seemingly thinking the same thing, began to weep. I felt sorry for her; I really did. She knew who shut down the college. There was no need to elaborate. Not at that moment, at least.

For dinner that night, we sat quietly and listened as Vartan explained how the Turkish soldiers used the *exact* same method to shut down his school. By the looks of it, my father had had enough. He barely spoke. However, by this time in my adolescent life, I understood how he operated—he chose his words very carefully, making sure they were short and meaningful. Still, I wanted to hear his thoughts, even before he spoke and even how he processed them. It was a lot to ask, but my unrelenting curiosity drove me.

As for Vartan and me, there was always work to finish, especially after the abundant rain that spring season. I couldn't shake the feeling, however, that the air, the vibrancy of my home, of my family, had completely changed. The uplifting spirit that once used to follow us had lost its way. I thought it would never come back, and perhaps I was right.

When things settled deep within the next two weeks, Garo, his wife, Ana, and Ara and his wife, Mary, found it reasonable to spend most of their time in the good company of my parents. With our home as theirs, their time spent together, unfortunately, was not solely for leisure. Whatever my parents had been discussing seemed to spill over to the other two families. Not only that, but they discussed it all, including things much more important.

With the company, of course, came Nadia, who spent most of her time with my brother. Tavit and I were happy about their relationship. We still joked, knowing what we'd created, but we knew it was serious. We knew what it meant for them. As it had been so deeply engraved into my skull, this was apparently all part of God's plan, but I had to ask myself, why were Vartan and Nadia the only ones laughing and smiling? Was this the work of love? Did it not bother Vartan that his college was shut down for no obvious reason? Did he not see that this would postpone his future indefinitely? If he had a plan, what was it now? To be a farmer with me? As Tavit and I sat in the field south of our home, I expressed my concern for my brother's careless behavior, and Tavit eventually understood my analysis, but only after I spelled it out for him. Even then, he casually shrugged it off. Before that day, I hadn't seen Tavit for almost one week and a half. We hadn't spoken much, not since our school was shut down. It seemed that since that day, he, too, had changed. Perhaps his views were changing as well. I sat and let my thoughts take control again. What would my grandmother have said about all this?

"You know, Tavit," I said, playing with the necklace she gave me, "I miss *Medzmama*."

Tavit looked at me then to the ground. "Yeah," he responded, "we all miss her."

Right there, the conversation paused. Tavit didn't respond and I figured it was best to leave it there. So, I looked around the scene and focused on our parents inside our house.

"What do you think they're talking about?" I asked him, changing the subject.

"Who?" asked Tavit.

"What do you mean who?" I asked, annoyed at his ignorance. "My parents. Your parents. Nadia's parents. *Our* parents. They're always in there… discussing."

"Yeah, but, Armen, they're friends like us. Do you think they're asking each other what *we're* talking about?"

I quickly searched for a more precise explanation. "Why are you being so difficult? Doesn't it look and feel different, though? They look more serious."

Tavit raised his head and looked inside the house from the far distance. "No," he answered.

"You can't even see them from here!" I retorted.

"What, okay, you wanted my opinion, and I gave it! What more do you want?"

"Listen, I need to know what they're talking about. It's making me anxious." I stood up and brushed myself off. "I'm going to listen."

"What?" said Tavit. "You can't do that! That's spying!"

"I know," I shrugged, "but I need to know."

I started walking towards the house and stopped a few paces in. "Are you coming or not?" I asked.

"No," he said. "I will have no part in it."

To be truthful, I had no intention of spying on our parents. I agreed with Tavit and felt that it was the wrong thing to do. Therefore, halfway to the house, I changed my plan, never telling him.

Before I carried it out, however, I stood on the porch of my house for a moment and composed myself. I knew Tavit was watching me, so I took in a deep breath and walked in. They all stopped talking and looked at me.

"Hi, Armen," said my mother.

"Hello," I said.

"Did you need something?"

"No, not really." I paused. "So, what are you guys talking about?" I asked, getting straight to the point. I was nervous, and I didn't know why.

"Armen, please, make sure the oxen have been fed," said my father.

I looked at him and nodded. "Okay, sure," I said, lightly clapping my hands in front of me. I then turned around and left. "Well, there goes the honest approach," I muttered to myself.

As I walked to the side of the house to make it seem as if I was going to the barn, my father watched me through the window until I passed. When I moved out of sight, instead of continuing, however, I quickly pressed myself against the eastern wall of the house and covertly slid to the open window. I turned my ear and listened carefully as my parents talked over coffee.

Through my investigation, I discovered that my father and Ara were seriously considering the possibility of escaping the mistreatment, of moving, especially in wake of the schools being shut down and our animals being slaughtered. However, they considered the many factors that outweighed any justification, and I heard two of them. First, neither my father nor Ara, collectively or individually, had nearly enough money for relocation, stemming from the heavy, unfair taxation. The monetary risk for them was too great. Second, as we found on the way home from the Port of Mersin, the main roads to and from Kharpert were now checkpoints. If, hypothetically, they *did* have enough money to relocate and they *could* get beyond the checkpoints, who's to say that life would be better on the other side? It was very difficult, if not impossible, to leave behind an entire family's established living. My father and Ara, with their farming and furniture businesses, respectively, knew that very well. Garo, on the other hand, wasn't convinced that relocation was absolutely necessary. He sat, continually hoping for better times ahead.

Then, after a while, I heard something beyond comprehension, something that I knew I had to keep a secret with the ones I already had. I stopped myself short and moved away from the window. Why was I so oblivious to these problems? Did Vartan know this? Did Nadia? Did Tavit? I suddenly wished that I hadn't heard the rest of it. I guess it's true what they say: ignorance is bliss. As I sat against the wall of the house, I realized there was a lot that I didn't know and, more importantly, a lot I needed to learn. I thought about Vartan and Nadia and how I wished I were them, prancing mindlessly. I slapped my palm to my forehead in hopes of trying to organize the mess upstairs. To no avail, I shook my head and stood up. Hopefully, it would get better.

Little did I know, however, this was only the beginning.

22

It was a clear spring day.

April 1914.

The warm spring air blew peacefully, alluding to an exceptionally hot summer. The grasses of the new season had already sprouted, draping the ground lusciously like a soft carpet. Vartan, with his fingers linked with Nadia's, raised his hand and kissed hers as they walked thoughtlessly through paradise. Their physical reassurance replaced the need to speak, and their only purpose was to be with each other. They knew what they were saying; no words were required. He was there for her and she for him, and that's all the comfort they needed.

It was harmony.

With the hills to the north and the western meadows directly ahead, Vartan smiled blissfully as he absorbed the beauty of the landscape, his mind lost in heaven and his heart filled with peace. There was no reason to worry. Neither Vartan nor Nadia had anywhere to go or anyone to please. They would get to her house when they got there.

Time moved leisurely for the two who'd newly discovered love.

With a keen smile, Vartan slowed and briefly stopped his pace. Nadia, unaware, continued forward and gently outstretched his arm. When she realized he had stopped, she turned around only to feel the gentle tug from Vartan's powerful arms. He brought her close to his body, just enough so that their chests touched. He looked into her pale green eyes and kissed her like a king with his queen. She smiled and unwound from his arms, smiling at the dream she was living.

Nadia, too, was in harmony. Her bond with his and his with hers destroyed all confines and cast down all bounds. This was their freedom, and Nadia basked in it.

A butterfly, in a seemingly random path from the meadow, flapped its brittle wings and glided near the two. When it became too tired from its long journey, it found a landing on the tip of Nadia's nose. She stopped her footing and carefully began laughing so as to not scare away the most fragile of insects.

"Vartan," she called, "look!"

Noting the passive traveler, Vartan joined her in laughter. "It's so pretty," he commented.

Then, another butterfly, flying in its own random path,

flapped its wings nearby.

"Look, look, another one!" Vartan pointed.

Nadia shifted her eyes, being careful not to move her head. The butterfly flapped its wings closer and nudged the one resting on her nose. Together, they lifted off and playfully danced away.

"That was so cute!" she said joyously.

Vartan smiled, and Nadia weaved her arm through Vartan's and leaned her head onto his shoulder. They pressed forward.

"Vartan," she said.

"Yes?"

"Tell me a story."

Vartan paused for a moment. "A story? All right."

For a few more paces, he thought of the one our mother frequently read to us from a book of fables when we were children.

"One day," he started, "there was a crane. This crane, unlike his brothers and sisters, often flew the skies alone. The eldest crane of the flock made note of his uncharacteristic behavior and confronted him.

" 'We are cranes,' " Vartan said as he lowered his voice, "said the eldest."

Nadia giggled.

" 'We are not like other birds. We take flight together and caw to give way to each other. You do neither.'

"The crane, being stubborn, took no lesson from the eldest and continued his rebellious and stubborn ways. On the second day, the rebellious crane took flight alone and became lost near a family of eagles, who hunted cranes. The eagles chased the crane until he became too tired to fly. Out of desperation, he cawed out to his flock. They heard his cries, and immediately, they all took flight. They chased away the eagles in unison, using their collective power, and rescued their one in need. The rebellious crane was very grateful for their noble and forgiving act and made an oath, a promise.

" 'I will fly with you from now on,' he said.

"The eldest crane accepted his words, and the eagles didn't bother them anymore. Since then, cranes are the only birds that continuously safeguard each other."

"Is that a true story?" asked Nadia.

"I don't know. Probably not," said Vartan. "I'm really not sure."

Nadia nuzzled herself closer to him. "It was still very beautiful."

A few meters away, an old rocking bench hung from the sturdy branches of two nearby trees. It displayed itself boldly as the combination of two benches that faced each other and swung in unison. It was purely of magnificent design. The old weathered coat of paint stood as a testament to the environment; chipped in many spots, it revealed the golden-brown color of the natural wood beneath. Surrounding the bench and around the trees, a garden of fragrant spring flowers bloomed. Each year, they multiplied and grew until they became so thick that the garden felt just like a rainforest. Once at the oasis, Vartan quickly took inspiration from this new universe. He'd been there before, but each time seemed like the first, and Nadia knew of Vartan's passion for the majesty of the garden. Taking a simple step up, Vartan wrapped his hand around the moistened wood, then sat on one bench. Nadia sat on the one opposite. They faced each other as they used their momentum to rock back and forth, being careful not to snap the green vines that had twisted around the support beams.

"Vartan," Nadia said, motioning subtly, "come sit next to me."

With the bench still swinging, Vartan cautiously moved across the connective landing and sat down. Nadia slid and closed the small gap between them and then wrapped her arms around his chest. She curled her legs up, and Vartan rested his arm around her torso. With the chirps of the birds and the humming of the insects, he still couldn't fully comprehend why he deserved such peace, such happiness. Even the squeaking of the hinges couldn't deter him from his serenity. The guilt, however, seemed much stronger before. Perhaps it had started to fade with time as he undoubtedly accepted his fate.

"Vartan, answer me one question." Vartan listened. "Why do you love me?"

After quickly landing back into his body, Vartan heard the question plain and simply but wasn't ready to answer it. The truth was, he didn't exactly know why he loved her. He just knew it *felt* right. He then clambered into the attic of his mind in search of the perfect answer. Was it because she was beautiful? Yes, he thought, but that couldn't be the only reason. Vartan tried not to panic or wait too long to respond, so he spoke, once again, not from his mouth or his mind, but from the guide of it all—his heart.

"Because everything that I've ever done in my life that has ever had a meaning, I did with you."

Nadia stared blankly into the garden. She had come to a realization, an epiphany, and her face showed it. She raised her head and turned her eyes towards him. Was that the wrong answer? Why did she suddenly seem so surprised?

She slid her legs off the bench, just enough so she could turn her face to his. Vartan remained uncertain of her reaction until she tenderly leaned in and kissed him on the lips.

She then stood up and extended her hand. "Come with me."

Vartan hesitated to grab it. His heart beat wildly, understandably so. Unable to resist the devilish lure of temptation, he stood up and grabbed her hand, which she guided to the inside of her house, then into her bedroom.

They stood, facing each other, and lightly played with the fingers of their hands. They closed their eyes and delicately found each other's lips, after which the rules had been broken and quickly overturned.

Their bond quickly strengthened at an unfathomable rate, and neither dared to slow down. They knowingly and purposefully jumped into restricted territory and charted the contentious map. They groped each other and soared through the flowers and the trees and into the heavens beyond the known universe. They twisted and circled as their energy collapsed the walls and vigorously shook the ground. Nothing could interfere as they created marvel from nothing.

Vartan's strong chest rubbed against Nadia's soft, naked breasts as they danced to the song of the garden. She felt every muscle in his body twitch and flex as their bodies warmed from the roaring fire they created. They glistened, they glowed, they tasted each other's bodies, and the ground still shook. They breathed heavily, and their voices echoed through the house as smoothly as honey. Her petite and innocent appearance was deceiving.

She was in control.

When the steam took peak and the energy soon faded, the walls recomposed, and the two gently floated back to lie together in a newfound unison. Nadia casually rested her head, barely peering out from under her sheets, on Vartan's handsome chest. She listened to the gentle sound of his breathing and enamored at their creation. Vartan, perplexed at his own composure, protected her until she spoke the three words that have caused so much wonder and so much strife in the times before and the times yet to come.

"Vartan," she whispered, "I love you."

Vartan, not taken aback, returned what he'd been meaning to say from the start. "I... love you," he responded before kissing her head.

For a moment longer, they lay on the woolen mattress together. Upon their brisk return back to Vartan's house, however, they realized that they hadn't been exempt from the course of time, yet they hadn't missed a thing. Their parents' conversation persisted but seemed as though it would expire. They would be leaving soon. Vartan and Nadia smiled at their impeccable timing and gingerly strolled through the apricot orchard and sat on the chairs of the porch, as if nothing was the matter.

"They're back," said Tavit from his exact spot away from the house.

"Who?" I asked as I lay, looking at the fading clouds traveling by.

"Who else?"

I sat up with my elbows and narrowed my vision on my brother and Nadia. A few seconds later, the door to our house opened, and out came her parents and Tavit's.

"Finally," he whispered. Tavit stood up and began walking to the house.

"Help me up!" I called.

He turned around, grabbed my arm, and lifted me up. I brushed myself off, and then we walked over. Everyone said their closing words and departed their separate ways, including Vartan, who simply hugged Nadia. My mother and father stood in the doorway and watched everyone leave.

"What a day," exhaled my father. "Armen, did you feed the oxen like I asked?"

"I did," I responded.

"Good, now fix the panels on the barn."

"What? Why?" I complained.

"Because one day," explained my father, "I will not be here, and it will be up to you to work the fields and watch over the women."

"What about Vartan?"

"And, Vartan, help your brother."

Vartan looked at me and smiled. He seemed unusually happy that I'd called him out.

Three months later, on the scorching 15th of July, our assumptions for unrealistically high temperatures turned out to be correct. With the heat, of course, came gratuitous amounts of rain, even more than the spring. It rained so much that, for once in a long while, we produced a surplus of crops, which we eventually sold in the market to pay off the maintenance fees for our livestock.

On that day, as we tended to business as usual, I particularly remember my father excitedly riding back from a morning into town. In the air, he eagerly shook a small, discolored envelope. He shook it all the way into the house, luring us in with curiosity. This was, for once in a long while, a time that I remember even a hint of joy.

"Hasmig!" he yelled happily. "Hasmig, come quick!"

My mother emerged shortly after and stood next to my father.

"It's a letter from Margaret!" he said. "She wrote to us!"

My eyes beamed with curiosity. I looked down at the tattered, weather-yellowed envelope that had traveled across the ocean. With his pocket knife, he turned the envelope around and carefully cut through the top. He then pushed the blade's spine onto his leg and snapped it shut. Carefully, he pinched the ends of the envelope to separate the freshly cut edges. From inside, he pulled out one, singular piece of paper. As nimbly as he could, he unfolded it to reveal the letter, handwritten in Armenian. As unique as the language, the beautiful letters from the fifteen-hundred-year-old alphabet shone out of the page like rays from the sun and were best exemplified through a young girl's handwritten letter.

"My dearest family," my father read aloud,

I miss you so much. I want to let you know that my travel across the ocean was peaceful. The ship rocked, but the water was calm. Uncle Mesrob is very nice to me and takes very good care of me every day. He even lets me eat as much ice cream as I want! How is everything there? Every day, I am learning to speak English, and I have made many friends here at school. I also teach them Armenian. They think I am very interesting. I think about you all the time and the farm, and I always pray that we can be together again. Please write back to me so that I know you received my letter, and tell Vartan and Armen that they smell bad.

Love,
Margaret

I looked at my mother. She wiped the tears of happiness

away from her eyes. I, too, smiled at the fact that little Margaret was smiling. I couldn't believe it had been six months since she had left.

"Well," said my father, "that was a very nice letter."

"We're going to write back to her," added my mother.

"Let's do it now," suggested Vartan.

"Yes, we will. Armen, go find your father's pen and some paper."

I walked to my room, opened my unused notebook, and tore out a page. I dug around some more, pulled out a fountain pen, and returned with the bundle.

"Here," I said, handing the pen to my mother, who pulled out a chair and sat down. She flattened the paper, perfected the edges, and began writing.

"Our dearest Margaret," she said,

> We are so happy that you wrote to us! We miss you and love you very much. We, too, are counting down the days until we see each other again. Here, everything is fine. Vartan and Armen are taking good care of us. The weather is very hot and very rainy. The storm just the other day blew off part of the roof on the barn! What is the weather like in Ohio? Be nice to your new friends, and don't eat too much ice cream. Please tell Uncle Mesrob we say hello. Study hard and be nice to him as well. We miss you and we love you! Please write back.
>
> Love,

"Boys, come here and sign your names. And, Tevos, you as well."

My mother handed me the fountain pen and I signed my name. Vartan, my mother, and my father did so as well. My mother then waited for the ink to dry, then carefully folded the letter and placed it into a new envelope. She then glued and sealed it shut.

"I'll run this to the post office right now," volunteered my father.

She handed the letter over to him, and he jumped onto the horse to ride into town.

To be honest, I thought about little Margaret more often than not, even when I never spoke it, and that single letter made my week. She always filled my life with an innocence and naïvety that, as I grew older, made me realize that it was all a part of what made life so beautiful.

Just about two weeks later, at the minutes before sunset on July 28th, 1914, as we sat in the living space, a single muffled thud at the door caught our attention. My mother had begun preparing for the night by placing the candles around, and Garo, Ana, Ara, and Mary, their daughters and Tavit, who were all over, stopped their words mid-sentence. My father stood up and peered through the window just as a delivery boy rode away. He casually opened the front door and walked onto the porch cautiously, where he picked up a rolled copy of the evening press—a newspaper only issued for special news and big events. By that alone, I quickly knew the contents were important. Paper in hand, my father walked back inside and unwound the thin twine to unravel the sheets. He held it up high and immediately announced to us all the inevitably disturbing news.

My father called me to his attention.

"Armen," he ordered, "Armen, go find your brother and Nadia. Right now."

With his calm yet intimidating voice, I took his threatening undertone seriously and ran outside to the barn looking for the two. They weren't there. I then ran through the vineyard. I searched as thoroughly as I could but still couldn't locate their whereabouts. The significance of his rhetoric weighed down upon me and threw me into a shallow panic. I even considered running to Nadia's house to fulfill my father's simple request but held myself short and kept it open for my last option. It didn't even strike me, however, to look at the one place where I should have started.

. . . .

Vartan and Nadia, not completely unaware, wandered through the apricot orchard to the slow beat of an untailored promenade. As they held hands, Vartan's heart beat irregularly, and his stomach slowly turned in on itself. He thought a lot the night before about what he would say and what he would do.

It would, after all, change his life forever.

"Nadia," he began, "I've been meaning to tell you something."

"Oh?" she asked.

Just as the sun had completely hidden under the horizon and twilight found its place, Vartan stopped to face Nadia and placed his other hand on top of hers.

"For my entire life, I've always wanted to be someone. I've always wanted to be successful. I would stay awake at night, thinking and worrying, about how I would be the person who I wanted to be. It drove me insane because I just didn't know how... And that's when I fell for you. At that moment, I realized that I had accomplished what I've been trying to accomplish my whole life because it was at that moment that I became successful... because you, Nadia, are my greatest success. I've finished trying to understand life, and I'm done wasting my time doing so. I just want to be with you forever."

Vartan removed his right hand off hers and reached into the back pocket of his old wool pants. From inside, he pulled out a thin, silver band. With the unexpectedness of his actions, she gasped slightly under her breath and cupped both hands over her mouth, letting go of his. Vartan then humbly lowered himself on one knee.

"With this ring, I promise to uphold myself to you in this life and the next. You're all I've ever wanted. Will you, Nadia, marry me?"

Nadia stood completely overwhelmed as the tears rolled down her face. She could not, and did not, immediately respond.

"Vartan!" I screamed as I finally found him. "There you are!"

With my brother on one knee and Nadia standing in tears with her hands over her mouth, they both turned their heads and faced me.

"Vartan—quick!" I screamed again. "The war! The war has begun!"

23

Nadia wiped the tears from her eyes, and Vartan stood up. He took her hand and followed me the short distance back to our house. Along the way, he placed the ring snugly into his back pocket for safekeeping. By the time I fell through the front door, the twilight had left, and the darkness had set in. The sound of my interruption caused my father to pause from his reading. Strewn around the living space and kitchen were my mother's candles, shimmering radiantly and turning the ambiance a golden yellow. The wine, too, was also in abundance. The news of this war, to me, came as a surprise. I wasn't quite sure if, in the instance that I knew more, whether or not I could have predicted this.

Quietly finding a spot next to each other, Vartan and Nadia sat on the floor while my father, newspaper in hand, resumed:

> Austria-Hungary, in response to Servia's role in the assassination of Archduke Ferdinand, has declared war on this day, July the 28th, 1914 upon the nation. Austria-Hungary has issued a statement regarding a note of resolution written by Servia on July the 23rd as showing an ill spirit and has regarded it as unsatisfactory, citing the circumstance. They are recounting that, prior to the deadline for response, the Servian Army had already begun mobilizing her troops, ending all claims at resolution.

The small room became littered with voices of disapproval. My father continued:

> The European countries, over the years, have formed mutual defense alliances—oaths to defend each other in times of battle. The Empire of Germany has an alliance to Austria-Hungary, and Russia with Servia. Vague reports indicate that Russia has begun a partial mobilization of her troops as a precaution, as have other neighboring countries. Going to war or staying at peace is largely the decision of the German Kaiser, who will uphold Germany's alliance to Austria-Hungary should war begin—

"This is outrageous," commented my father as he continued to read.

> In the event that Russia invades Germany, subsequent other countries will be included in this conflict. The big powers—England, France, and Russia—do not want to fight. They are not anxious for war, but are preparing.

"This is childish! It's going to spread!" Ara boomed dramatically, wine in hand. "Each country is mobilizing troops in response to the other countries mobilizing troops! How does that make any sense?"

" 'Italy will not accept any action, including intervention,' " my father finished. "And the article keeps going."

He lowered the newspaper and neatly folded it along its crease, resting it atop the table. He raised his wine glass and took a sip.

"And what about us?" asked Garo. "Who knows how this will affect us!"

"I'll tell you, Garo," responded my father as he set down his glass, "if the Kaiser decides to get involved, Germany will drag in the Ottoman Empire."

"How do you know this?" he asked.

"During the First Balkan War," my father explained, "Constantinople asked the Germans to help restructure and update their military after they lost a majority of their land in Europe. There are German soldiers stationed all over this empire. The Turks even wear new uniforms! Constantinople will stand at Germany's side without question."

"Ah," Ara expressed as he adjusted his gold-rimmed glasses, "he's right."

My mother worriedly glanced at the young girls, at my brother, and at me.

"And yet, Ara," interjected Mary, "there is a chance for peace. There's *always* a chance for peace. The article mentioned that the big powers have no desire for war. The conflict might be localized between Austria-Hungary and Servia."

"She's also right," said my mother, relieved. "Peace is always a possibility."

I listened to their opinions, heard their pure thoughts, the women in our family. I looked at their faces, as they spoke, one by one. I studied their expressions and the plain clothes they wore. For a moment, I saw the same innocence I saw in little Margaret. Were they being realists or idealists? Or were they merely reassuring themselves for the sake of their families? I couldn't tell. I didn't know. At that moment, for the first time in my life, I understood the power these women had, the capabilities they possessed to transform an idea, a principle. Their opinions, as serene as their voices, came as a relief—an angelic and hopeful answer to an otherwise unforgiving problem.

I needed that.

My father paced from one side of the weakly lit room to the other as he twirled the tip of his mustache. He didn't need to hear both sides of the story to make a logical conclusion. My understanding of him had become scholarly.

"Of course," he said, pointing his finger in the air while looking at the ground, "we have time. This all cannot happen overnight. We will follow the events that unfold hereafter." He stopped at the table and rubbed his eyes. "For tonight, however, I think that we can retire. It is late. Garo, Ara, you should also have this newspaper at your homes."

Garo put down his empty glass of wine and took out his gold pocket watch to note the time.

"A great idea," he agreed as he stuck the watch back into his front pocket and pulled out a pack of cigarettes from inside his suit jacket.

Ara stood up. "By the way, did you hear of Raffi's fate?"

"Azatian?" asked Garo as he put a fresh cigarette in his mouth. "The dentist?"

"Yes, the dentist. I went to his home to deliver some furniture and nailed to his door was a sign that read 'Arrested for Conspiracy and Deported.' Nobody was there. I couldn't even get in. The door was bolted shut."

"Arrested for conspiracy? Raffi was deported for conspiracy? By whom?"

"Garo," said Ara, "listen to yourself. Who do you think? His house was empty. His entire family is gone!"

"They were not conspirators," added my father.

"Then why would the government deport him for conspiracy?" asked Garo.

"That's my point!" Ara continued. "The government is too powerful! They've become tyrannical! They're trying to silence us with fear! Anyone who dares to speak against them is arrested or killed. And who remembers them? What Abdul-Hamid did before, the Young Turks are doing again!"

"They wouldn't!" Garo persisted.

My father shook his head from side to side, knowing the conversation would only continue in circles. He was well past-due for the evening.

"Tavit, let's go," said Garo, now visibly upset.

Getting up off the chair, Tavit walked with his mother outside. Ara then commanded his three girls, who also left with their mother. Garo and Ara remained inside. Just as they were about to leave, however, my father stopped them.

"Garo, Ara," he whispered, "if you do anything, please,

spend more time with your families."

Like men of the same cause, even as they remained bothered, they set aside their differences and nodded in approval, understanding their duties. With no reasons left unsaid, they walked nobly to their waiting families outside. Gently closing the door, my father then sank deep into the sofa.

In that moment, I thought this war might, in fact, affect us somehow. Could it be possible? Could the war in Europe spread to the Ottoman Empire? What about Armenia? Then what?

Obviously fatigued, now mentally exhausted, my father looked at my brother and me for an extended period of time.

"Armen, Vartan," he started with his eyes half closed, "do good... Do good in life. Just promise me that."

I hesitated to respond and so did Vartan.

"We... we will," I agreed. "I promise."

My father smiled, then looked up at the ceiling and closed his eyes. For a moment, it seemed as though he were praying. His lips moved as if he were speaking, but no sound came out. My heart began to beat a little faster because of his uncharacteristic behavior. He then turned his chin down and moved his hands over his face and then onto his knees. Using his arms for support, he stood up and grabbed his glass of wine off the table. With one gulping swig, he downed the rest of it.

"I love you, boys," he said, pointing the empty wine glass at us. "Remember that." He then placed the glass on the kitchen counter. "I'm going to bed. *Kisher paree.*"

"*L-looys paree,*" stuttered Vartan, as a response to my father saying "good night" in Armenian.

My father then wobbled to our mother, kissed her, and disappeared into his bedroom. Vartan and I sat and moved only to shift to a more comfortable position. My mother leaned over the kitchen counter. She, too, was visibly drained.

"Boys, come give me a kiss. I'm going to bed as well," she said.

"Uff," I said, sarcastically showing how annoyed I was.

Vartan quickly stood up, and I sprawled across the floor.

"Come on, get up, you ape," he said as he extended his hand. I grabbed it and he pulled me up. I then joined him, and we kissed our mother good night.

She pinched my cheeks.

"Mama," I stated, "I'm too old for that!"

"You are never too old for your mama's love," she responded. "*Kisher paree.*"

From time to time, I found it therapeutic to take a moment of my day and think about all the blessings I had. In those aging times, especially as the war slowly tore away my faith in the future, I figured it could only help. As I sat quietly on the bed in my room, I thought about my family, my friends—Garo, Ana, Tavit, Ara, Mary, Nadia, her sisters—and their endless support for us, our endless support for each other. I especially thought about the time when Garo donated his own livestock to us when we couldn't afford it, when we needed it most. Vowing to one day repay the man, my father not once overlooked this gracious act that saved our family. He never mentioned it outright, but I knew his intentions. Fatefully, though, that day came to my father sooner than he thought, when, two days later, on the morning of July 30th, Tavit's voice echoed through the farm, shaken and in a state of dread.

"Armen!" he screamed as he ran towards me. "Armen, quick!"

Luckily, I was nearby and ran out to him.

"Armen, they tried to kill us!"

I reached out to stop him and looked at him, even as he bent over to catch his breath.

"Slow down, Tavit. Who tried to kill you?" I asked.

"Please get your father! The winery is on fire!"

He then stood upright, and for the first time ever, I knew he'd seen evil as the fear that engulfed his eyes transferred to mine.

I immediately turned around and called out for my father.

"*Hyreeg,*" I shouted anxiously, "Garo needs your help!"

Not a moment too soon, he ran over from the orchard

to hear what I had to say. Never explaining why, my father, without pause, ran to the barn and took out our brown horse, pulling Tavit and me up with him.

When we arrived on his land, Garo was kneeling on the grass in front of a heated storm, crying like a newborn baby and hyperventilating like a balloon. On the ground in between his knees lay one single pistol and ahead of him, an uncontrolled, raging fire engulfed his winery.

My father quickly scanned the scene directly ahead of him and swore to himself. He then jumped off and ran to his friend, noticing the pistol soon after. He needed to calm Garo down, especially after Dr. Thomassian had diagnosed him with an anxiety problem as a result of his smoking habit and heavy weight. Refusing to change his lifestyle and claiming that his cigarettes were actually a cure to his anxiety, Garo's panic attack had debilitated his ability to respond and thus needed to be controlled; we weren't sure how much his heart could handle. Standing next to him, his wife, Ana, also played her role, but she, too, had been touched by the hand of terror.

"Garo, Ana," said my father, "Garo, please calm down. It's all right. Everything is all right. Tell me, Garo, what happened?"

Through his tears, he spoke, keeping his head down: "I killed them."

"Who, Garo? Who did you kill?"

He cried and pointed his finger towards the burning winery next to the barn. Fifty yards down, the bodies of two Ottoman Turkish soldiers lay dead on the grass. Out the chest of one, the single handle of a pitchfork used to bail hay stood upright. Next to them, their unharmed horses.

"My God," whispered my father.

"They tried to rape her," he whispered, diverting our attention back to him. "They tried... to... rape... *her!*" he screamed angrily as he pointed to his wife, using any energy he had left before burying his face into the ground. "What have I done? My God, what have I done?" he murmured.

My father shook his head. There was nothing he could

say.

"Are you all right, Ana?" he asked.

The fabric of her dress fell loose from her waist, and she held it up. "Yes," she answered, nodding her head, finally letting her experiences settle to an ugly realization.

My father knelt next to his friend. "Garo, listen to me. Did anyone see you? Were there others?"

He shook his head. "No."

Garo was the last man I would think of as capable of killing another man, much less two. Push a man into a corner hard enough, I figured, the outcome would surprise many.

"Tavit, Armen, let's go," called my father.

"What? Where?" I said uncertainly.

My father paced towards the barn right next to the burning winery, answering my question. And we, without a choice, followed him. We passed the soldiers, and I glimpsed at their bleeding bodies on the ground. The adrenaline in my body had corrupted my emotions, and I was left untouched by the sight. The shock of the situation felt almost nonexistent and thus inspired me to question their transparency.

As we stopped behind the barn door, I felt the heat of the fire from the winery against the side of my face. Just as we were about to enter, my father extended his arm and motioned for us to be still. The fire twirled and roared like a freight train being lifted by the wind as I curled my face away from the heat. My father put up a finger to his lips and pointed inside. The door was slightly ajar, so he peeked through the cracks in the hinge. He looked for a few seconds then slightly opened it and put his head fully inside. Even though Garo stated that there was no one else, my father took the possibility as a serious precaution.

"Okay," he said out loud. "We need to get the animals out of here."

Unsympathetic to our personal danger, and with the high probability of the fire next door engulfing the very building in which we took refuge, we fully opened both barn doors and stepped inside. To my utter dismay, and now, with a fiery anger as hot as the flame that consumed the winery, I saw the animals, dead on the ground. In the back of the barn, however, some goats and four pigs still stood alive in their stables. The job was left undone. Sensing the danger next door, they screamed in agony for our rescue.

Tavit swore at the sight.

Wasting no time, my father carefully walked over the carcasses towards the animals in the back, and we followed to aid him in the rescue. As I stepped over the dead livestock, I noticed the same pattern, gunshot wounds to the heads of each animal and sliced throats, killed in cold blood. With my emotions growing harder, I remained, once again, unperturbed at the sight. The goats, feeling the heat of the fire, yelled at us to move faster. They pulled at the ropes that tied them to their posts, trying to break free. As quickly as we could, we unwound the reigns and led ten animals safely outside, even rescuing the two horses that stood next to the soldiers' bodies. My father then drove a metal stake in the ground away from the fire and temporarily tied them to it.

In a few minutes, the wind carried the fire up into the air and pushed it onto the barn, starting with the hay roof. That, too, was consumed by its fury.

"Tavit, go to your parents," said my father. "Armen, go with Tavit."

"But what about them?" I exclaimed. "The soldiers!" I pointed as I began walking towards them.

My father grabbed my arm.

"You will *not* touch them!" he advised sternly. "I will take care of it."

"But you can't lif—" I started.

"Go!" he yelled, interrupting my offer.

Thus, turning around, I ran back. With Garo still in agony, I put my hand reassuringly on Ana's shoulder and held it there while I watched my father pull the pitchfork out and drag the bodies into the fire. He then ran to their horses and unhitched the saddles and any gear, including their weapons, and threw those into the fire as well. Then, with a glowing timber, he burned the grass to eliminate the blood that stained it.

After dealing with the issue, my father ran back to us. Moving a human corpse could not have been easy, but my father wasn't terribly out of breath and was, remarkably, blood free.

"Listen to me, Ana. Breathe in, deep," he instructed as he leaned down. "Slowly."

Her eyes met with my father's, and she took in a staggered breath.

"Good. Now please, Garo, you do the same. Can you stand up?"

He nodded his head and slowly followed my father's lead. He put one knee out in front of him and supported himself on it. My father put his hand under Garo's arm and spotted him the rest of the way up.

"Easy," he said.

Like us and most other Armenian families of the time, Garo depended on his livestock and his business to make a living and support his family. This, however, landed as an overwhelming shock to him particularly because of his strong faith in the new Young Turkish regime and their Committee of Union and Progress that promised equal rights for all Ottoman citizens.

He'd been betrayed.

"I saw them," he murmured. "I saw them take Ana. Like an animal. They took her to the barn like she was some sort of beast!"

"Garo, my love," she whimpered, "we will be all right."

He turned to my father. "They shot at us, Tevos. They shot! At! Us!" he said, banging his chest with his fist.

"Are you hurt?" asked my father.

He shook his head in defeat. "No. They came searching for firearms and other weapons," he continued. "They searched only minutes before they placed their eyes on Ana and took her to the barn while the other set fire to the winery."

I kept my distance from the situation.

"What would have been my fate had I given them my pistol? How would I have defended myself?"

Tavit, who remained next to me, turned his head.

"Thanks," he said before replacing my father to help his own.

With Garo as a witness, I had now established that the Turkish soldiers were, indeed, the perpetrators, which again raised a series of questions. What was the meaning to all of this? Was this just another attempt to destroy business? To kill prosperity? What was my role in all this? What was *I* supposed to do? I simply stood like a useless log, wishing that I understood. All I knew at this point was that I wanted to help, but without my father's guidance, I didn't know how.

"Armen," my father said, pulling me to one side, "I need you to go home and bring me two cows, two goats, and one bull. He needs the cows to live and the bull to make wine. He will keep both horses."

"But their winery is destroyed, and the barn is on fire."

"We will rebuild them. Go. Now."

Happy to have a larger role in aiding Garo's family, I ran to our brown horse as quickly as possible. In one swift leap, I jumped on and galloped home. I explained to Vartan the currently unfolding situation as quick as I could while rounding up the animals. He helped me organize the livestock, and in an instant's time, all five requested animals were accounted for, and for once, they weren't stubborn, as if they knew they were needed for a greater cause. As I leaped back onto our horse, I waited for my brother, who still lingered inside the barn.

"C'mon!" I yelled.

"Wait just one second. I'll be out quick!"

My horse neighed, expressing his impatience, and I rode him in a circle until Vartan finally emerged atop the second horse. With the animals tied to each other, I safely guided the fleet to Garo's house, using Vartan as my lead.

Before we came to a halt, Vartan swung one leg over the other and jumped off his animal. He brushed the dark hair out of his eyes and searched the landscape full circle, looking high in the hills and into the distance as I galloped a few more meters ahead. I, too, jumped down, reigns in hand, and searched with Vartan, trying to see what he saw, but only noted my father, Garo, Ana, and Tavit slowly mustering their way back to their home.

At the porch, they waited for a moment as Garo inhaled and exhaled until he felt calm enough to step inside. He had already calmed significantly since I had left, but not nearly to where he needed to be. The interior, as Garo already knew, had been ruined. The floor cushions were torn open, the furniture was strewn, and the dishes were broken, all scattered in pieces like seeds in a field. My father examined the new setting and righted a small, overturned table and some chairs for his friends. They both sat as Garo continued to control his breathing.

"Garo, listen. You were benevolent enough to provide me with, in times of great need, your livestock. As a man of my word, I am returning the favor."

He pointed through the window to the new animals.

Smiling wide, Garo opened his mouth to say something, but my father cut him off before he could even begin.

"I don't even want to hear it," he said. "Please accept."

Garo took a moment to fill his lungs with air.

"Just… please. Just give me a cigarette."

Often, I reminisced about the tragedy that day. I wasn't terribly distraught by what my senses presented to me—the sight of the dead soldiers, the dead livestock, the sound of a grown man's whimper, the roaring fire, the smell of blood, and the desperate feeling of understanding. I tried to make sense of what I'd witnessed and sought an explanation for my desensitization, questioning why I'd been impervious to those things. Was it because it no longer surprised me? Or had I transformed into some sort of coldhearted man, careless to other's sorrows? Perhaps the happiness of its end overshadowed the sadness of its beginning. I tried hard not to beat myself down in order to find the answer about myself. I knew my mind was clouded by so much, including the war that I knew nothing about. But, the more I thought, the more I realized that one thing stood greater and more bothersome than the rest—the attempt to harm Ana. Like earlier, I felt the need to do something, to repair what had been damaged. How would I even begin with something that great? The fact that she had to endure such sorrow and continue with her life right after took an immense amount of courage—

courage that, at this point, I wasn't sure I'd ever have.

As I stood with Garo's family that day, I thought of those things and realized that my thoughts were rendering me useless. I therefore stopped momentarily and did what I could to help, by accompanying Garo, Ana, and Tavit, until we decided that it was time for us to leave them alone.

As my father, Vartan, and I left, I reassured Tavit that we'd check on them from time to time. It only felt right.

Back at our house, my father then rode our brown horse away, while Vartan and I walked the other back into the barn. With a swift pull, Vartan opened the metal gate, and I walked her in. I then threw the reigns to my brother, and he tied it to the post inside. I walked out of the stable and held the metal gate open until Vartan finished tying the knot. Just as I was about to close it, however, he switched directions.

"Oh wait," he said.

"What?" I responded impatiently.

He seemed embarrassed.

"Umm, we need to take the horse back out."

"Why?" I asked.

Vartan then reached behind his back and pulled out my father's pistol. I gasped at his rebellious behavior.

"Don't tell *Hyreeg*," he said. "I just wanted to make sure there weren't more soldiers."

Just at that moment, all my previous assumptions about Vartan seemed irrelevant. Maybe he *was* aware of his surroundings. Maybe his head *wasn't* in the clouds.

"But you don't even know how to use it!" I exclaimed.

"What's the difference? You pull this back, aim, and shoot."

"Well, hurry up and put it back. It's dangerous."

Quickly untying the knot, I moved the horse to lift up the burlap coverings and put the pistol back in its place. Before we closed the trap door, I couldn't help but lean in and grab hold of the other pistol, simply to feel the weight of it in my hand. Before I became greedy, I put it down and covered it once again with the two layers of burlap.

Over the next few days, we followed the events for the newly developing war, specifically listening for any news concerning the Ottoman Empire. The involvement of other countries, however, soon became inevitable, just as my father and Ara predicted. Russia continued mobilizing over a million troops, and Germany, who wanted Servia punished, threatened Russia with war if their mobilization didn't cease. The Czar of Russia declared that they would back Servia, who defended their stance of innocence. In the midst of it all, bridges were blown and ships were destroyed, all in response to each other's aggression. In the end, however, despite their efforts, the German Kaiser declared war on Russia on August 1st, 1914, after not adhering to her requests, and subsequently began her invasion of France and the invasion of Germany exactly one day after. On August 3rd, 1914, Germany sent two armies across the border to Luxemburg, breaking the neutrality, claiming Luxemburg as a strategic access point to France. In response, Great Britain considered declaring war to support the triple entente consisting of Russia, France, and Great Britain. At the time, I remember imagining the countries of Europe being pushed together like lumps of clay to create nothing more than an ugly mess, and to be truthful, that's what it became. All the countries seemed to be invading each other. If this war had unfolded one year ago, though, I'm not so sure I would have cared.

To paint a lighter picture of the developing war and persuade its citizens, including Armenians, in support of a possible decision to support Germany, the government at Constantinople seized strict control and issued extreme censorship of influential newspapers throughout the empire. This was the first instance, in my life, that I realized the severity and devastating effects of a media controlled and filtered by the government—propaganda. We subsequently believed that supporting a possible war for Germany was best for the empire and a necessity for her citizens. Whether or not it was true made me question, still, the Ottoman Empire's stance on neutrality. Did she want to become involved? If not, why would her government spread propaganda about supporting Germany if her intention was to avoid conflict? Was this merely the first step in a well-planned, carefully thought-out series of events?

For the next three weeks, I heard little to no news about Turkey or the Ottoman Empire and their involvement or noninvolvement in the War in Europe, as it was now called. At the time, it didn't bother me because no news was good news. And, as each day of those three weeks passed, I felt increasingly optimistic that my father's prediction of Turkey being "dragged in" was, simply put, wrong. Let's face it—nobody wanted war.

On August 26th, though, like all good things, any confidence I had in my own optimism came to an abrupt end. The German ambassador believed that, in order to prevent a Russian invasion, the Ottoman Empire should mobilize troops. Like my father, others also believed that Turkey would be drawn in to aid Germany and her many war fronts. Now, as an old man who's had enough experience to analyze the facts, I should have, at the time, questioned the three-week silence between August 2nd and August 26th. Within that period, a document called the "Turco-German Alliance" was signed *in secret* by Baron von Wangenheim, for Germany, and Said Halim, for the Ottoman Empire, thus changing the outcome entirely. With the signing, the empire's involvement in the war became as secure as Germany's, but only a select few knew about it.

Just three months after the secret alliance was confirmed, in the late afternoon of October 29th, with the War in Europe still in its infancy and the Ottoman Empire still not officially involved, the revelation of our times indeed found its beginning. As we sat near and around the circular fireplace, a familiar thud reverberated through the house. I sharpened my senses, hoping to understand more about the war as my father, annoyed that he had to get up, did so anyway after losing the fight with himself to always be in control. With a casual tug, he opened the door and picked up the newspaper. Hastily, he rolled away the thin twine and placed it on the table, then tapped it so that it would take shape. He didn't hold it up for long because upon first glance at the headlines, he gently let it sag and blankly

247

stared into the floor of our house, penetrating deep into the floorboards. My mother looked at him from the hallway, curiously, as he smiled a weak and pathetic smile.

"It has begun," he whispered.

24

As the vine grew and inevitably spread throughout the Ottoman Empire, an emergency meeting was issued in our church that we all were required to attend immediately.

It was two hours past mid-day.

October 31st, 1914.

By the demand of my father, my brother and I climbed onto the ox-cart with my mother, and we began our ride towards *Soorp Asdvadzadzin*. On the way, Vartan sat emotionless, making it difficult to distinguish what he was thinking about. I, on the other hand, wondered whether or not to be worried about the news, the outcome of my future *even* as a farmer, or even its implications on our country. Who was involved now? Why did this happen?

As we approached the pasture, I glanced over at the Turkish boys that I always saw herding their sheep from atop their donkeys. Each one now had rifles, almost as long as their bodies were tall, hanging from the straps over their shoulders.

"That's strange," I thought. "Why do shepherds need rifles?"

Despite the mystery, I, as usual, waved to them from my seat. Only two of the six, however, waved back. The rest turned around and away from us. One boy even partially raised his hand, but another pulled it down before he could fully extend it. They exchanged glances as I lowered my brows in disappointment. What was that all about? Did I do something to them? I thought we were friends.

When we pulled up, the churchyard just outside the entrance was crowded with fellow citizens. I took some time getting off the cart just to soak in what I was seeing: the commotion, the arguments, the anger—all entirely overwhelming. I had never seen our church so busy in my life. I began to worry a bit, thinking that the news really *could* affect our lives, but decided to keep my composure. It's true that my father didn't tell us why we were required to go to the church, but now, I had a vague idea. Unfortunately, though, this wasn't enough. I needed more.

As I moved through the maze of people, I listened intently as my countrymen spoke. I tried to hear anything that could possibly answer my questions by picking key words in hopes of learning something, *anything*, new.

"How dare they!" I heard someone say, shaking a leaflet in his hand, entirely different than the newspaper.

"This is unruly!" I heard another as he held the same leaflet.

All I heard was reaction, but no substantial talk of factual information. I searched around and noticed that most of the crowd held the same peculiar leaflets in their hands, and not one of them seemed happy. Curiosity then lured me into its trap, and I looked for the person distributing them so that I could have my own piece of knowledge. Unfortunately, I never found that person, so I turned to the ground and found one that was partially torn. Happy with it, I leaned over to pick it up and held its two hanging pieces together. In basic black lettering, with a red outline around the page, it read:

Turkey threatened! Disloyal Christian Armenians to blame! Armenians conspiring and in league with the enemy!

"Conspiring and in… what?" I muttered to myself.

At first, I didn't understand what I read or why I was reading it, so I read it again. "*Armenians… conspiring… and… in… league… with… the… enemy.*" In league with the enemy? I was conspiring with the enemy? Who's the enemy? France? Russia? We aren't even allowed to own firearms!

Angrily, I folded the leaflet and stuffed it into the small pocket of my gray wool pants. Things had gotten serious, and I now felt comfortable with my concerns. By this time, the rest of my family had surely read the same material littered throughout the area. Seemingly frantic, my father walked speedily into the church, and we followed, bumping into everyone along the way.

With no floor space available, we stood against the back wall so close to everyone else that I thought I could jump into their clothes. I leaned back and felt the cold of the stone wall against my palms. Mardiros, the moderator for the world events meetings, stood at the head of the church. Behind him, on the slightly raised altar, sat the scholars—the historians, lawyers, and professors—in a row of neatly arranged chairs. They each wore their clean, tailored suits with their hats on their laps and their worn leather briefcases next to their chairs, each as unique as the men who carried them, filled with papers and books. Directly facing Mardiros sat Der Kourken, our priest, with his long dark beard now sprinkled with subtle streaks of gray. Mardiros, with his oversized glasses, clapped his hands to win the attention of the crowd. Der Kourken, realizing that the clapping was nearly useless, placed his hands on the back of his chair and twisted his body around to display his disapproval of the crowd that wouldn't stop talking. When that also didn't work, the men standing around him also turned their bodies and whistled with their pointer finger and thumb. A few minutes later, the sound of the crowd dissipated into a few certain voices.

"I'd like to have everybody's attention, *please!*" said Mardiros as the last few voices were spent. "I understand everybody's concern and would like to note that all of your questions will be answered to the best of our abilities and expertise."

He stood and waited until the church became eerily quiet. Only then did he continue, using a quieter and more relaxed tone of voice.

"As you are well aware, July 28th marked the day of the commencement of the War in Europe. Initially, the implications of this war were not immediately known, but many premature theories from the time have officially been put to rest. Two days ago, on October 29th, the Ottoman Empire, for reasons soon to be discussed, has decided to side with Germany and the Central Powers, guaranteeing her a position in this war.

"The leaflets scattered around, of origins we can only speculate, have been spread over the empire and other provinces of Armenia. Before we continue with these issues, however, I'd like to introduce Professor Goshgarian behind me, who will entertain the immediate causes of this war."

Mardiros turned around and held out his hand as a way to allow passage of the historian. The man stood up to a short, impatient set of claps. In his left hand, he held a couple of pages of notes for himself.

"Good afternoon. My name is Harut Goshgarian, and I am a professor at the college here in Kharpert. As Mardiros factually stated, war has erupted in Europe. On the 28th of July, the country of Servia was invaded by Austria-Hungary following the assassination of Archduke Franz Ferdinand of Austria on the 28th of June. Over the years, as the evening press illustrated, the countries of Europe have formed what we refer to as 'mutual defense alliances.' The German Empire, for example, is allied with Austria-Hungary, and the empire of Russia is allied with Servia.

"As of the morning of July 29th, we received news that the German minister at Belgrade, the capital of Servia, was *also* assassinated. We predicted that this action would sanction Germany's involvement in the war, which it did. However, we also predicted that the conflict between Austria-Hungary and Servia might not spread beyond the two countries involved because of peace talks that were currently taking place at the time between the diplomats of each representing country. The talks failed. We were wrong."

"What about us?" a man screamed. "Why are we involved?"

"As Armenians, we are not involved in the war. As citizens of the Ottoman Empire, the answer is entirely different, and I will answer that soon. Let me first finish what I was saying."

The man in the crowd folded his arms and listened.

"As a defense, we correctly believed that Russia had intentions of invading Germany, which they did. We concluded that if that happened, the Ottoman Turkish Empire would most likely side with Germany and her allies, the Central Powers. As of two days ago, with the delivery of the evening press, those predictions were also proved correct."

He adjusted his wiry glasses and looked at his notes.

"This is where we are currently. I'd like to defer the reasoning behind the empire's involvement in this war to economic analyst Dr. Alan Khacherian. Doctor?"

The doctor stood up, and the crowd clapped slightly. Professor Goshgarian took his seat, crossed his legs, and rested his arms over his knees, watching, paying attention. It was very interesting to see that, even as a scholar, he was still willing to learn.

"Thank you, professor," said Dr. Khacherian as he brushed his brown suit free of wrinkles.

Dr. Khacherian was a very precise and soft-spoken man. This, I believe, was the result of the type of work he did. Every bit of information he analyzed resulted from a meticulous set of details. Not a single fact could be overlooked.

He continued.

"As someone just asked, there are many reasons for the Ottoman Empire to join the War in Europe. The most fundamental and most basic I will discuss here. The world economy, in simplest terms, is connected. Nearly every country's economy is dependent on every other country. Recent European industrialization has, in effect, weakened the Ottoman Empire's economy by enabling the production of high-volume, high-quality goods at a lower price. The empire has been unable to match the falling prices. Coupled with problems in authority, agriculture, and domestic and international trade, among other issues, the slow process of decline has gotten the new Young Turkish Regime and their Committee of Union and Progress increasingly worried about a possible total collapse. And— remember—it is this current regime that effectively ousted the sultan in 1908. To aid in a reform and possibly prevent their demise, the government, your government, at Constantinople has borrowed money from European financiers. Currently, they are incapable of repayment and are now severely in debt."

He turned the page.

"The Minister of War, Ismail Enver Pasha, who was trained in Berlin, considering the empire's debt and the imminent decline of a seven-hundred-year-old empire, has made the decision to enter this war partially based on monetary promise by Turkey's allies, if their side wins… *if.*"

"What do you mean by 'partially'?" yelled a man. "We're going to war over money and what else?"

Dr. Khacherian immediately became uncomfortable. He glanced behind him at the rest of the scholars and deferred the question.

"Well, first I'd like to explain the reasons that the Ottoman Empire has decided to join Germany and the Central Powers. I will… get to your question later."

He cleared his throat.

"It has become apparent that Germany's goal is to coerce the Turks into war, therefore putting an excessive amount of pressure on Constantinople to avoid neutrality. You must not forget that Germany's influence in the Ottoman Empire is very powerful. They have helped, and are currently helping, the Turks reorganize and update their military. To Enver Pasha, this has become his opportunity, like I said, to what he believes is an easy victory in war and an opportunity to crawl out from the graves of debt."

He paused and started again.

"Two days ago, on October 29th, amid a previous and escalating tension, the Turkish naval fleet, under the command of Admiral Wilhelm Souchon of Germany, bombed the Black Sea's Port of Odessa held by the Russian navy, causing significant damage. This action blatantly eliminated any claims by the empire of wanting peace, and we believe they always carried the intention of joining the war from the start."

"What? Why? What are the other reasons for going to war?" the same man repeated.

"For that, I'd like to give the floor to Dr. Nerses Kouyoumdjian."

The crowd didn't applaud.

The third scholar stood up and smiled as a way of thanking Dr. Khacherian.

"Good afternoon, my name is Dr. Nerses Kouyoumdjian, and I am a historical analyst at the College of Kharpert. I'd like to discuss the future of this war and where we think it is headed. Dr. Khacherian explained that on October 29th, the Turkish Naval fleet bombed the Port of Odessa, held by the Russians. We predict that this instance will cause Russia to declare war on the Ottoman Turkish Empire, and in essence, cause the Allied Powers to *also* declare war on them.

"In my profession, one lesson that stands far more important than the rest is that history has taught us everything we need to know about the future," he continued. "It is up to us, however, to learn from its teachings so that we do not fall into her cyclical trap. The Ottoman Turkish government has a terrible history of mass murder against the Armenians under Sultan Abdul-Hamid II. Many instances over the past twenty years or so, including the aforementioned, undeniably prove, as evidence, a deeply rooted plan to eliminate the Armenians. These instances have grown faster than we would like to believe, one recently being the massacre at Adana where twenty-five thousand Armenians were killed *after* the revolution brought hope nearly six years ago. Be forewarned and understand that this was the result of the sultan's influence on the Young Turks. His voice still lingers, and it is still strong, contrary to what you may believe. The leaflets that many of you hold in your hands, the propaganda, are Constantinople's way of spreading falsities against Armenians so that their policy spreads beyond their realm and across the empire like a mutated virus for which there is no cure. We are well aware of Abdul-Hamid and his age-old Armenian question—how are we going to rid the empire of the Armenians? With my colleagues, I have discussed this matter in depth. The Young Turks who comprise the forty members of the Committee of Union and Progress, the CUP; Mehmet Talaat

Pasha, Minister of the Interior and Posts; Ahmed Jemal Pasha, Minister of the Marine; and Ismail Enver Pasha, Minister of War, have been secretly manipulating and ruling the government without the public's knowledge to fulfill their own insane vision of radical Turkish fanaticism by means of total empire domination. They've taken complete control of the now militarized government and all her interests, including, of course, the military and all her future affairs. Their rule has ultimately withered from a promise of democracy to a violently deceptive and secretive government in a decaying and divided empire, which has surprisingly shown an exponential growth in Turkish patriotism.

"The CUP blames the Armenians for the demise of their empire and the failure of the Ottoman Turkish people. It acts as an ineffective bond, a fraudulent contract, to keep Armenians in the empire satisfied until they find what they are looking for. This new war, my fellow Armenians, is the answer… to the sultan's question."

The crowd boomed over Dr. Kouyoumdjian, showing their disapproval. He looked around uncomfortably, nervously.

"We believe," he announced with a louder voice to overcome that of the crowd, "that the underlying purpose—the intentions from the start—for the involvement of Turkey, is to use this growing war as a cover to increase and justify violent action against Armenians."

The church's chamber erupted with a sudden onslaught of screams.

"Impossible!" yelled a man.

"That's preposterous!" screamed another. "The sultan has been overthrown!"

"They promised to protect us!" a woman defended.

"It won't happen!"

By dismissing the warning, the crowd displayed a coarse unacceptance of the facts. Noting it, the scholars exchanged worrisome glances.

Increase violent action? Was my grandmother right? Was this the revelation of our times? Dr. Kouyoumdjian's warning made my stomach churn. I, like my fellow citizens, didn't believe a word of it. I couldn't! Why would I be so willing to accept their dismal prediction? There was no way something like this could happen. We wouldn't let it!

Seemingly on an imbalanced scale, I thought it through, looking at both sides of the argument. Then, I suddenly realized why the soldiers killed our animals and not us. I suddenly knew why they didn't kill poor old Bedros across the river. I understood why they didn't kill Garo and his family!

They wouldn't have been able to justify it!

My God. Was it true? Were the scholars right?

Again, I doubted my own logic and further realized that I needed advice. I needed guidance. I needed someone to help me make a decision. I felt that I didn't know enough to pull any conclusions. Who would I turn to? As I looked around the church for Tavit, I only spotted Ara and his family, who squeezed their way over to where we stood. In truth, I was worried about my best friend and the safety of his family, but soon figured they needed as much time as possible to rebuild their barn and winery. Besides, I needed to check on him like I promised I would.

"I'd like to also express that," continued Dr. Kouyoumdjian, "we have made these predictions based on what the past has taught us about the future."

....

"Wait," said old Armen's granddaughter in the hospital room, "so who spread the leaflets? Were any of the predictions true?"

"Yes. All of them. The Turkish ambassador in France, Rifat Pasha, did not want to go to war. In fact, he warned that both sides of the war would willingly tear the Ottoman Empire apart. Becoming evermore indecisive between restoring an empire and joining the conflict, the government, with pressure from Germany to prevent them from siding with the enemy and the heavy pressure from the Minister of War, Enver Pasha—they decided their fate. To Enver Pasha and the Young Turks, siding with a strong ally like Germany was simply an opportunity for an easy and essential victory. They wanted to solve all their empire's problems with one war. And so, during this time, the secret Turco-German alliance was signed to create the alliance of what was later named World War One."

"So did the violence against Armenians escalate?" asked his grandson.

"Yes. The violence escalated very quickly. There were more soldiers across the empire than ever before, both Turkish and German. And yet, we continued to build churches, adding to the ones already there for hundreds of years, and we continued our businesses, our trades, and daily routines while persistently demanding our rights. We, after all, still needed to make a living. With the change in regime, growing population, and increasing prosperity, the Armenians had little reason to leave. It would've been too risky. Thus, with the empire on the brink of collapse, Constantinople felt increasingly threatened by the success of the Christian minority in their Moslem-dominated empire. They needed a way to suppress what they viewed as the 'causes' of their troubles.

"The sultan's Hamidian Massacres of the 1890's diverted the world's eyes to the Ottoman Empire. They were watching. Any abuse or violations of human rights would be condemned by the West and deemed intolerable, especially in times of peace. Therefore, Constantinople waited for a distraction. By 1914, their opportunity arose. The Young Turks knew that as the world focused on the trenches in Europe's new war, they could hide their true intentions behind this curtain.

"The Ottoman government at Constantinople then spread false propaganda to make *us* the enemy. They stopped at nothing to get what they wanted, even resorting to fooling and manipulating the minds of their own people. They violated the Turkish public, using their own society who had entrusted them with right, to turn against us for crimes that we did not commit, and we were defenseless in its presence. From the days after the empire joined the war on October 29th, like you asked, hostility against Armenians intensified. Turks of all sorts—soldiers, policemen, citizens—consisting of mobs and individuals, vandalized our businesses, desecrated our churches, raped our girls, and killed or deported our men for 'conspiring' and 'plotting' against Constantinople, each one of them grossly tricked into supporting and carrying out the work of evil. This immense effort was the government's immediate implementation of a long-overdue solution to their fear, and they acted out of paranoia."

"How much of what Dr. Khacherian said was correct?" old Armen's granddaughter asked again.

"Every prediction those scholars made turned out true. All but one."

"Which one?"

Armen didn't answer.

"On November 1st, 1914, the day after the meeting with the scholars, Russia declared war on the Ottoman Empire. Three days later, on November 4th, the Allied Powers *also* declared war on the Ottoman Empire, just as predicted. Almost immediately, that's when the soldiers increased their presence even more and surrounded our province. They set up posts and stood guard on the streets downtown, in front of every store and every business. They shut down the banks and even stopped the postal service, but only for Armenians. It was a shame because we never received another letter from little Margaret, or for that matter, from anyone else. If leaving or even resistance was a slight possibility before, it was now an utter impossibility. They had cut us off completely."

"Did they still have Kharpert surrounded?"

"Yes, they still maintained the checkpoints just like the one we passed through after we sent little Margaret to America."

Old Armen curled his lips.

"It was all a terribly well-thought-out agenda. Through and through, this false war against us proved to become an increasingly heavier burden, especially, against my best guess, on the relationship between my brother and his love…"

....

Vartan and Nadia sat next to each other on the old wooden bench at her house. They rocked minimally, listening to the short creaking sounds of the hinges holding them up. With Vartan's arm around her shoulders, Nadia peered blankly into the open air as her mind wandered in all directions and something deep inside, something terribly bothersome, tore her apart. Containing it for too long, at last she couldn't tolerate it any further. She had something to say. It was time to tell him. As she played with her fingers nervously, she breathed in and began.

"Vartan," she said, "I need to tell you something."

"Yes?" he asked.

"I can't go home anymore."

"Huh?" he laughed, not understanding the confusing joke. "Why not? You *are* home."

"No, not like that. This is my last night here. The meetings our parents were having… Do you remember those?"

"Yes, of course."

"Well, they were… They were about us."

"Me and you?" he asked, removing his arm from over her shoulders.

"No. My family. My parents… decided to give me and my sisters away… to a Turkish family, a couple. Your parents pushed for it. They've been talking about it for a while."

"*What?*"

She paused to let a tear fall.

"*Why?*"

"Other Armenian families are doing it, too. They say it's safer for us," she said as she held onto his arm, "because of the war."

Vartan straightened his posture. "So, where? Where is this other couple?"

"They're family friends just north of us, half an hour by horse. It's a small tan house with double front doors. They promised to protect us. Vartan, it's only temporary until things get better."

"But how will I ever see you now?"

"Vartan, it's for our protection! Every day, every… single… day, the violence against us, especially against women, is growing. It's just not safe anymore. Don't you see?" she cried subtly.

"I do, but, Nadia, my God, I don't know what to say."

"Don't say anything, please. Just pray."

Staring deeply into her glossy and innocent eyes, Vartan immediately understood how much of what she was saying came from her heart and quickly gave up any of his own selfish claims.

"I will," he promised.

"And, Vartan, please, I haven't forgotten about us. I think about it every day. It's just… this war, your proposal… Everything is happening all at once. We'll still see each other, just not as often. I'll need time to think."

Vartan edged himself forward on the bench, worried and confused, still unsure as to why it had taken her so long to give him a response. Did she doubt their relationship? Was it nearing the end?

"Sure," he responded. "Anything. Just let me know when you're ready."

Through the expression on his face, Nadia saw into his doubtful thinking and thus spoke her unique words of comfort.

"We have the rest of our lives, Vartan. We're still young. There's no need to rush things just yet."

"Yes," he said, smiling unconvincingly, "of course. We're still… young."

25

By mid-December, a little more than a month after the Ottoman Empire joined the war, Vartan, with his new somber attitude, and I patrolled our vineyard behind the house, ensuring that it had been adequately prepared for the coming brutal winter. The summer yielded a successful harvest, but preparations were understandably late. The empire's involvement had depressed most aspects of our lives, but nonetheless, we did our part, carrying on the best we could. We had already collected ample firewood and had nothing more to do but wait for the cow dung to dry, a more common source of valuable fuel.

I felt that I should have been paying more attention that day because it seemed to spark off my list of life-long regrets, or blessings, as I often saw it.

I could have at least warned them. We could have been more prepared.

From the vineyard, a faint but steady squeaking sound caught my attention. I turned my head towards it, but the house obstructed my line of sight, so I found a viewing from the back windows through to the front. Casually perched outside the front door, on horseback, sat five armed Turkish soldiers. Where they came from, I didn't know. Two carried German Mauser rifles with bayonets attached at the ends, and the others had their pistols and daggers at their waists. Each wore their army uniforms with two rows of buttons, a leather belt tied at their waists, and red fez hats. Behind them was a shallow cart, being pulled by two donkeys, filled to the top with firearms.

I jumped at the sight.

"Vartan," I breathed. "Shh."

My brother looked up and grabbed my arm to pull down my body. We hid low.

The two soldiers nearest the house then jumped off their horses. From inside his jacket, one pulled out a piece of rolled paper. He unrolled it and silently read it to himself, then proceeded to pound angrily at our door.

"Open up!" he yelled in Ottoman Turkish.

There was no answer.

"By order of the Ottoman Turkish government at Constantinople, open this door!"

I knew my father was in the barn, but my mother, however, was alone inside. She lifted her head and peered around like a ferret in the desert, hesitating to stand up, while I hoped to God that she wouldn't answer.

He knocked again.

"Open this door, or we'll break it down!" he screamed.

My legs and feet grew restless. I felt every muscle in my body recoil like a spring, ready to snap at any moment. I wanted to move. I needed to move. I needed to do something. I couldn't just sit and hope that everything would be all right.

"C'mon," I breathed impatiently, "where's *Hyreeg?*"

"I'm going," decided Vartan, thinking like me. "She needs us."

I acknowledged his decision, and we carefully stood up, trying not to bring attention to ourselves. Silently, we moved towards the back door of the house. Once again, the soldier lifted his fist to hit the door, but before he could feel the wood, it opened.

Standing in front of him was my father.

"Yes, good afternoon," he spoke in Ottoman Turkish. "How may I help you?"

"We are here as ordered by the government at Constantinople to collect firearms for the war effort. You are also notified that any ownership of firearms by Armenians is illegal."

"I am aware. We do not own any such weapons." My father smiled with his palms in front of him. "We are of the law."

The soldier returned my father's smile with an ominous glare as he stood relaxed and fearlessly held his smile. My mother stood behind him in a half-seated, half-standing position. From behind her, Vartan and I entered the house as quietly as we could, but the soldiers noticed. From behind the two standing ones, two more stepped off their horses and stood guard at the entrance.

"Search the house," ordered the soldier in back.

With those three words, my father's demeanor suddenly changed. He rid his smile and put his large, burly arm across the doorway, blocking the soldier's path.

"You will not," he commanded lowly, not making eye contact. "You are *not* welcome here," he added softly but firmly.

"Really," the soldier said sarcastically.

He then stepped to one side.

Immediately from behind him, a subordinate stepped forward, pulled out a fixed knife and with one swift move, thrust the blade into my father's side. My mother screamed as the hole began bleeding instantaneously, staining his shirt brightly. My father, however, did not fall. He clutched the bleeding wound and took a step back with a ravenous stare. Just then, a bearded soldier, the one delivering the commands, emerged from behind and stepped into our house. He raised his heavy leather boot and kicked my father to the floor. Horrified, I looked down at him. He put two fingers in his mouth and looked at it. Vartan and I immediately jumped to his aid.

"You're not welcome here!" I screamed from my father's side, feeling the blood in my heart mix vigorously and heat up.

"Armen," calmed my father, who had now crawled to a seated position against a leg of the small kitchen table.

The other four soldiers then followed suit and stormed into our house with their rifles, leaving trails of mud, turning our once spacious living space into an overcrowded zoo, each one smelling as rancid as the next. They stood at ease, studying the walls, the furniture—our home.

The bearded soldier then unhitched the buckle from his holster and pulled out his pistol. He cocked it and pointed it down, square into my face. I felt the heat from the barrel radiate between my eyes and onto my cheeks. He had recently used it. I glanced at the tan leather bandolier of bullets across the chest of his new uniform, blackened with use. A third of them were missing. Undisturbed, unrightfully so, I stood up and took a step closer to him, studying his barbaric, hairy face. It was at that moment that I realized that I had seen him before. I had seen this man. Yes, he was the one on the hilltop the day our cattle were killed. I recognized him!

"Are we welcome now?" he asked cockily.

My father pulled on my pant leg, and I sat back down with him.

"Foolish boy," mocked the bearded soldier.

He turned and faced his men. "Let's go!"

The four soldiers then dispersed, each taking a section of our home. For a short couple of minutes, we watched from the floor as they tore the house apart, searching up and down for weapons. They turned over tables and broke dishes, ruining everything they could in every room of the house, even the ones in the back. One soldier even ripped down the small crucifix on the wall as he passed by and another tore pages out of books.

"*Miralai* Barçin," he said, "look what I found. This book has the word *Armenia* written in it."

"And look at these," another said, stepping forward, "I found these weapons, and here are religious books." They both held out an almanac, kitchen knives, and two Bibles, one of which belonged to my grandmother.

The bearded soldier snickered, "Books of faith. Destroy them all."

The soldiers left the house with their newly found bundle and threw the items into the cart while the others searched through and through, frantically looking for our firearms. When they didn't find what they were looking for, they became desperate and tore the walls apart, riddling them with holes.

"Where are your firearms?" screamed one.

"We have none," said my father calmly, still bleeding.

Angrily, the bearded soldier clambered over to my mother and grabbed her by the hair. He was obviously tactical about his targets, knowing how to hit where he knew it would hurt the most—killing another man would've been too easy. He held onto her hair tightly, pulling on it with a solid, clenched fist. She screamed and grabbed onto his wrist to prevent her hair from being pulled out. She clawed at the floor with her feet as he dragged her and put her within my father's sight.

"There are other ways," he whispered to my father, "to find the truth. I will not ask you again," he continued, slowly escalating his voice. "Where are your firearms!"

My father looked at him and then to his wife.

"Tevos," she cried.

"In the cushion," he sulked, "the middle cushion. There

is a pistol. That's all I have. I swear it."

One soldier quickly upturned the sofa and tore open the fabric. Inside, he took out one small pistol—one that I'd never seen before.

"I found it!" he rejoiced.

With one arm still holding onto my mother's hair, the bearded soldier dragged her over to the sofa and grabbed the pistol with his free hand. He then dragged her back and leaned over to my father.

"You said you had none!" he screamed as he shook the pistol in my father's face. "What is this then? *What is this?*"

The other soldiers pointed their rifles at us.

"You let go of her!" my father yelled into the soldier's face, being careful to not beg, a clear sign of weakness for the circumstance. "You let go of her this instant!" he yelled louder, undaunted by the pointed weapons.

"Tevos," she cried again, still holding onto the soldier's wrist.

The soldier then stood up and raised the very pistol they found in our sofa into the air. With a hard swinging arm, he hit my mother, directly on the head, with the butt of it.

She fell to the floor.

The soldier then smiled at my mother's limp body, showing no remorse and no emotion, and turned back to my father. "We will be back for you," he said scornfully through his long, untrimmed beard.

The soldiers then turned around and exited, and the bearded soldier threw my father's pistol into the cart with the others.

"Baran," he ordered, motioning to the cart, "photograph this. Photograph it and send it to Constantinople as evidence of a violent uprising by Armenians."

"Yes, sir," the soldier agreed.

The soldier then took out a camera and photographed the cart of firearms, pistols and rifles of all sorts, all collected from other Armenian homes. Only God knew what fate had delivered to them.

The soldiers then mounted their horses and left, pulling the cart behind them. From the floor, Vartan kicked the door closed and spit at it.

"Armen, help your mother," my father said. "Vartan, help me up."

Still on the floor, I crawled over to my mother and repositioned her slouched, unconscious body against the overturned sofa.

"Will she be all right?" I asked.

"Yes," assured my father, out of breath. "Put pressure on her head, and bring her water. Wipe the blood off her face. She'll wake up."

I stood by the window, waiting for the soldiers to leave entirely.

"Boys—Armen, Vartan," he said as he stood up. "I'm proud of you."

He looked down at his blood-crusted clothes.

"But, *Hyreeg*, your wound," reminded Vartan as he tended to it.

"I'll be fine," he consoled. "They didn't pierce my lung."

"How do you know?" I asked.

"They are poorly trained and inexperienced. Look," he explained as he put his fingers in his mouth and showed us the result, "no blood. No blood means my lungs have not been pierced. Amateurs," he snickered as he limped to the back.

With the soldiers out of sight, I ran out to the well to get some water, thinking along the way. Where did that pistol come from? It wasn't there before.

Bucket in hand, I ran back and grabbed a towel and a wooden cup from the kitchen. I dunked the cup, filling it with the cold water, then dipped in the towel. Placing the items on the floor, I sat down next to my mother and gently repositioned her head. Carefully, I wiped the blood off her face then picked up the cup and tipped it to let the water wash over her. With the first few droplets finding their path, my mother quickly regained consciousness.

"It's okay," I reassured. "You're all right."

Dazed, my mother raised a hand and placed it atop her head. My father came out of the back room wrapping a white cloth around his torso and stood over us. He tried leaning over, but straightened back up at the pain.

"Armen, Vartan," he said unrelentingly, "clean up this house. I'll take care of her."

"That pistol," I confronted from the floor, "was not always there. Where did it come from?"

"I put it there," my father explained as he finished tying the knot. "I put it there because I knew that if soldiers ever came looking for weapons, like they did at Garo's, they'd kill us if they didn't find any. It's old and doesn't work."

"And where's the dagger?" asked Vartan. "Why didn't we use it? Why didn't we kill them!"

My father turned to him, surprised. "Since when are you in the mood to kill? Have you ever killed a man? Have you ever had another man's blood on your hands? Have you ever heard their bones break? Do you know what it's like?"

Vartan defended his stance. "I would have killed them!" he blurted.

"Killing is the last desperate move. You *always* negotiate first! You have no experience with that dagger. As inexperienced as those soldiers were, that dagger would have been turned on you *instantly*!"

"Yeah?" screamed Vartan. "Well, whose fault is that? You promised you would teach me, but you never did!"

My father limped over to him with his hand over his wound. "You will learn when you are ready," he said firmly, pointing to the floor.

"What kind of answer is that?" Vartan retorted. "You're just afraid!"

Instantly, like prey sensing imminent danger, I raised my head, knowing full well that Vartan should not have said that. With those three words, he unintentionally opened a box with contents he couldn't handle.

"You listen to me, boy!" my father screamed. "Fear is in your mind! It is only as real and as strong as you let it to be!"

"What is that supposed to mean? How do you even know?"

"Because you can overcome your fear of anything! *Anything!* And if I ever—"

"Tevos," my mother wearily interrupted from the floor, "Tevos, please. Enough. We need to take care of ourselves."

With my mother's soothing and feminine voice, in a room dominated by screams and testosterone, my father and Vartan rested their primal instincts and quickly understood the real issues at hand. Quickly limping over to her, my father and I helped her sit up. I then made my way over to Vartan, whose nerves were still numb.

"Armen," continued my mother, "thank you, *dughas*, my son."

Leaning slightly forward, she hung her head between her arms. She tried hard to look up at me, but did so only barely. A subtle glimmer from around my neck, however, shone into her sensitive eyes and gave her the strength to continue. She then became adamant about her next words.

"Armen," she began firmly, "it's a miracle they didn't see that. It's a miracle they didn't kill us. Take off that necklace," she demanded. "Take it off immediately and hide it."

"What?" I asked confusedly. "Why?"

I didn't fully understand the purpose of her strange request. Was my mother panicking? Was she delusional?

"Hide it, so they can't take it," she repeated, "so they won't find it."

Still baffled, I reached up to my neck and touched my grandmother's gold chain, gently rolling my fingertips over the links, each one only as strong as the next.

I then looked at Vartan. He shrugged.

"O-okay," I hesitated, "but... where?"

"A place where you know. Not in here. Please, just do it."

I took the necklace fully out from under my shirt and loosely held onto the hanging crucifix with my thumb. Since it was big enough that I didn't have to unclip it, I thus lowered my chin and took it off from around my neck. In an instant, I had it balled up in my hand. Despite the assumption that my mother wasn't thinking straight, I thought of possible places to hide it and dropped the necklace into my pocket.

I then looked around at the unjustified mess. "Vartan," I suggested, "let's just clean up this house."

....

If you haven't noticed by now, lately, I've been a thinker. I wasn't always like this, but much was left to be explained by people who didn't have any answers. So, I asked myself; I looked to myself for direction, becoming increasingly more observant. I always thought that guidance and explanation came from the external—from family, friends, teachers, doctors—but with a lot still sitting in the unknown, my theory only proved partially correct. They can only take us so far. Ultimately, it would be up to me to become my greatest teacher and uphold the foundation laid out by those around me, a foundation sturdy enough to support a building that would stand the test of time.

I, Armen Hagopian, have thus far learned from every lesson in my life—some were easy, some were hard, but all came eventually. By the time the year 1914 had wound itself down and I had turned fifteen, I thought of myself prior to my initiation into the muddle of life. I had grown tremendously, faster than I would have ever imagined. Perhaps too fast. From time to time, I think about the man I would have become if the next set of events had not taken place. I think about my views. Would they be different? Would I accept myself? If not, what would I do about it? Is it possible that I was always destined to be the same man that I am now regardless of the circumstances that surrounded me? Or would other experiences shape me into someone different?

I'll never know.

If you haven't noticed by now, lately, I've been a thinker. I wasn't always like this. I must admit, I was naïve about the world around me. I accepted things as I saw them from the outside. I never saw behind the curtain, the thoughts, the framework of society, as I do now. I never analyzed my surroundings—people, situations, events—like I do now. I never probed for a deeper understanding, like I do now. With my new set of eyes, it's become difficult to stop analyzing and impossible to stop questioning. The more I knew, it seemed, the deeper I fell into the hole of confusion. Perhaps this was the result of looking to others for what I was searching for—*my* purpose, *my* place. And yet, through the analysis and the questioning, a new force, a new insane power, pounded at me from the inside out. It pulsated from deep within my heart, growing and weakening, and then growing some more, becoming ever more powerful. Too powerful. Slowly, it seeped through the stitching of my soul, trying to show itself. With each passing experience, it clawed and roared like a caged lion trying to set itself free. Something, however, held it back. It was too great for me. It was a force that I didn't know how to control. A force that I didn't yet understand.

I had a lot of faith in the Young Turkish government, and so did a lot of others, including Garo. We all hoped that we could have lived together in peace, discovering a way to set aside our differences. At this point, I could hardly say that to be true. I tried to keep an open mind, but my judgments came to me from my own experiences, not from my grandmother's, not from my father's, but from my own. Were we Armenians *really* the cause of the demise of the Ottoman Empire? Were we *really* a direct threat to the future of Turkey? Is it true that we were in league with the enemy? Like I said, the more I knew, the less I understood. The thought alone and the inability to find what I sought was enough to make sane men go mad, and these were merely the thoughts and experiences of only one person.

On the 20th of December of the year 1914, like I promised Tavit months before, I routinely checked on him and his family. They were, after all, rebuilding their barn and winery in hopes of not missing a beat before the spring season began again. As with all our winter days, it was bitterly cold. Initially, my father, Vartan, and I volunteered to help with the construction since our business depended on theirs, but as a direct result of the attack by the Turkish soldiers, my mother suffered from excruciating headaches. At times, they would be so intense that for her to leave bed would have been impossible. Thus, in order to tend to her, my father worked less around the farm or even to help Garo, leaving most of the construction duties to Vartan, Garo, Tavit, me, and occasionally Ara, who guided us with his expertise in carpentry. With the increased physical labor, Vartan, Tavit, and I became very muscular. Our frames grew and our shoulders broadened to the point that people began to notice.

My father's wound slowly healed, thanks to Dr. Thomassian, who had also helped my grandmother when she was sick. Through it all, we acted together, helping each other in times of peace, and now, in times of war.

On that 20th of December, I remember riding with Vartan to Tavit's house, carrying a basket of *choreg*, sweet Armenian bread that my mother freshly baked as a gift, before we began the rebuilding process. As we entered their land, I noted the pile of singed timbers of what was left of their barn and winery. In neat piles next to the coals lay the large pieces of fresh lumber that Vartan, Tavit, and I had carried by hand. They lay exactly as they had the days before, outlined in the shape of the new northern wall in hopes that, one day, they would be transformed back into a thriving business. That day, however, they remained untouched. A strange observation. Figuring that Garo and Tavit would be working by this time of the late morning, I made no mention of it as we rode past the pile directly to their house. Near the door, I jumped off from behind Vartan and looked around. No one was in sight.

From atop our horse, Vartan pointed.

"Armen," he said, "look."

I turned my head to see.

Nailed to the door, a regular, plain piece of paper gently swayed in the wind. I swiftly paced to it to get a better look. Resting one hand against the wall, I leaned in. In bold, dark-red letters, it read:

Arrested for Conspiracy and Deported:
By Order of the Ottoman Turkish Government at Constantinople

Like an anvil, my heart fell through my body, and my pupils dilated. I ripped the posting and threw it to the ground, sickened by the sight.

"What's it say?" asked Vartan.

I didn't answer. Was Garo a conspirator? I knocked on the door ferociously in hopes that someone would open it.

Nothing.

Like a panicked madman, I tried again.

Nothing.

I looked at Vartan, who sat on his horse to watch guard, his breath crystallizing in the brisk air. He shrugged.

I then took a step backwards and moved to the frosted window to the left. Like a turtle going back into its shell, I slid my hand into my sleeve and rubbed away the ice to peer inside. As I looked through the circular clearing, I felt the hairs down my spine stand on end one by one from my neck to my legs, sending a jolt as if I were struck by lightning. My legs quivered, and my throat swelled to the point that I couldn't swallow my own saliva. I closed my dilated eyes, hoping that when I opened them, I would realize that this was merely a dreadful nightmare. However, after another look, I realized that what my eyes were showing me stood eerily true. Even God couldn't help me now, because hanging from the rafters, gently rocking from side to side, was the naked, beaten body of Tavit's mother, Ana, with her hands tied behind her back.

26

"Vartan!" I screamed. "Oh my God, Vartan!"

I quickly moved to the door and stood in front of it. Raising my brown leather boot, I drove my thick heel into it as hard as I could. The door, however, was bolted shut. Panicked, Vartan jumped off his horse and looked inside the window.

"Oh my God," he whispered.

I took a step back and drove my heel once again. The hinges rocked and clanked, and the wood began to split. And again, it remained shut. Despite the cold, I began to sweat. I kicked again and again, each time becoming more and more angry. I kicked ragingly because I thought Ana could still be alive. Vartan jumped next to me, and he, too, drove his heel into the door, staggered from my attempts.

It wasn't working.

"The window," exhaled Vartan, out of breath, "break the window."

"No," I disagreed. "Together. On the count of three. We throw our shoulders."

Vartan nodded, and we took a step back.

"*Meg… yergoo… yerek!*" I yelled, bracing myself.

With the thrust of our bodies, the door finally gave way, and we fell through the doorway and into the house, landing just under Ana's body. From the floor, I glanced up at her—her blue face, her bloodied wrists. I tried to regain my bearings and stand up, but my muscles tensed as my eyes held true. I stared at the unimaginable sight, not knowing how to react. Were my emotions re-sensitized? Had I returned from my time as a coldhearted, careless man? No, I thought. It had nothing to do with that. This time was different. These weren't two dead soldiers or slaughtered cattle. This was my friend. I *knew* her.

"Armen!" yelled my brother. "Armen, don't look at her!" he ordered as he stood up without hesitation. "Tavit!" he yelled. "Garo!"

Quickly strolling through the house, he disappeared into the back, opening doors and frantically searching in the bedroom closets. A few moments later, he came back.

"They're not here," he concluded, still looking around.

With my eyes still fixed on her body, I gently placed my palms on the wooden floor. It creaked as I leaned my weight and slowly clambered up. It was at that moment that I completely lost what was left of my faith in the human race. I had let go of every last bit of it through that one experience. I now questioned everything, even more than before, the things I thought I knew about humanity. It was at that moment that all my knowledge of it meshed together into a foggy confusion that I rationally deemed irrelevant, and yet it lingered in my mind, uninvited. I questioned what it stood for and where it was going. I questioned its intentions, its goals, and more so, I wanted to know why.

Vartan grabbed a stool and placed it near Ana's body.

"Hold this," he commanded.

I didn't react.

"Hey," he pushed, "I said don't look at her! Now hold this steady."

"They were deported," I whispered.

"Who was?"

"Tavit and Garo. The sign… on the door… for conspiracy."

Vartan didn't respond. He stared blankly, hesitating for a moment, and simply blinked as his head raced with thoughts. He then climbed on top of the stool. It rocked a few times from the uneven legs, but he quickly found its balance. From his back pocket, he pulled out a dull, muddied pocketknife and extended his arms up high to begin cutting through the dress that hanged her. As he cut, the stool wobbled, so he stopped just as quickly as he began.

"Hey," he said, "Armen, hold the stool."

I did what Vartan told me to do and held the stool while staring down at the floor, trying not to look up. Whether or not Vartan was disturbed by the situation didn't make me wonder. What I really wanted to know was whether or not he was acting brave as an example to his little brother. That really would have taken a lot to admit.

After a few more seconds, Vartan stopped again.

"Armen," his voice cracked, "you need… You need you to hold her legs… so she won't fall."

My eyes widened at the unthinkable request.

"I need you to do this. You need to."

Slowly, I let go of the stool. My brother didn't move, so

his balance wouldn't be offset. I looked at Ana's bare legs and took one small step closer to her. Slowly extending my arms, I felt the joints in my fingers creak like an old door as I felt her body radiate to me like a block of ice. Preparing to take hold of her, my hands neared her solid body. Just as I was about to steady her, however, the sound of reigns clanking, horses neighing, and men talking caught my attention. I pulled my hands back in surprise. Vartan heard it too. Like an eagle, he widened his eyes, and like a bat, he moved his ears. They were speaking Turkish.

Too far away from the house to hear a distinct conversation, the voices clearly said the words "horse" and "door," and we knew immediately they were talking about us.

Without even finishing his task, Vartan jumped down onto me, tipping the stool, and threw us both against the wall. The back of my head impacted just below the windowsill, and I raised my hand to rub the pain away. Vartan then leaned up and looked outside. Sure enough, about a hundred meters away, sat eleven Turkish soldiers on horseback moving towards the house, some with rifles hanging from their shoulders, others with swords.

"Armen, listen to me. We have one chance to get out of here, and we have to do it right now. Are you ready?"

His heart beat rapidly. He was scared. I heard it in his voice. I nodded my head.

Immediately, Vartan sprung up and so did I. I sprung up so fast, in fact, that my foot slipped and I lost traction. I threw my arms out and tried to catch myself but fell backwards and hit my forearm on the windowsill. The adrenaline in my body was too great for me to care, so I pushed myself off and plowed through the door after my brother. It flung open, making a hollow woody sound and quickly rocked back to equilibrium. I then jumped off the porch and onto the frosty ground. Everything about our escape was rough; it was loud, hastily arranged, and anything but covert. Upon seeing us, the soldiers snapped their reigns high and whistled. They kicked their heels into their horses and started a swift gallop towards us. With one leap from behind, Vartan mounted the horse, and I grabbed his hand from the side. With a swinging motion, he pulled me up, and we began our escape.

Lowering his chin to the back of the horse's neck, Vartan reached behind him and pointed to the ground.

"Keep your head down!" he exclaimed. "We'll go faster!"

As I lowered my head as close to the horse as I could, we increased our speed, and I felt the hair of the horse cut through the cold wind as the steady beat of her breath froze in the air. My eyes quickly began to water, and I blinked hard to get rid of the tears just so I could see. I then turned to look behind us, and the soldiers in the lead took out their pistols and aimed them at us.

"Gun!" I screamed. "Vartan! Gun!"

At that moment, a blast went off, and I felt a bullet whiz by so close to my head that I felt it inside my ear. The horse neighed at the disruption as the bullet struck the ground in front of us. Waking up to the realization that all this was, indeed, my living reality, I immediately raised my hand and touched the side of my head to see if I'd been struck. Vartan, too, turned and checked.

"I'm fine!" I screamed. "Go!"

One after the other, and sometimes two at a time, the bullets screamed past us as we rode away. The dirt around us jumped up as my body twisted and turned with the horse as we followed a curved path. The only thing on my mind was to escape. I had no time to think about anything else. Vartan had done a great job of making a getaway, and thus far, it was working.

Looking back, I realized that one of the soldiers had stopped. He sat on his horse and steadied a long rifle level with his one eye. Methodically, he followed our movements with it. Vartan turned the horse left, and out of instinct, I reached over with my right hand and grabbed the reigns to quickly pull us right, feeling my arm throb painfully in the process. The jolt of the sudden switch of direction caused Vartan to lean over too far to the left, and I caught him with my free arm. Just then, the soldier with the steadied rifle shot his weapon. The powerful sound that stood more distinct than the others echoed through the landscape, and the bullet hit the ground exactly where we would have been had I not switched our direction.

We had enough starting distance between us and a powerful enough horse that after eleven or twelve shots, the soldiers slowed down. Eventually, they stopped and shot once or twice more with their pistols, then turned back around as we rode away. Perhaps they had more important things to deal with than two unarmed Armenian brothers. Relaxing my posture, I rested my head down and wiped the cold tears from my eyes. Miraculously, not a single bullet pierced us or our horse. Vartan turned his head and looked behind him. Realizing the same, he eased up his stance and rode a little higher. Not once, however, did we slow down.

Riding still, I peered at my bloodied shirt and realized that a large splinter the size of a pencil had lodged itself through my wool sleeve and into the outer part of my forearm. I reached with my left hand and pulled it out. Immediately, a trail of blood spit out from the hole and onto my pants, quickly turning into a slow trickle. I looked at the path of blood and closed my eyes. My forearm wasn't in pain, and there was nothing I could do for the moment, so I lowered it and let the blood drip, one drop at a time, onto our horse. For the rest of the ride home, I realized what I'd just been through, and the warm tears fell onto my face. I didn't cry, but my eyes watered like a rain cloud, most likely as a relief that it was over.

As we neared our house, the pain in my forearm slowly began to punch through me, making me realize again about the events that just passed. I thought about Ana. I thought about Garo. I thought about Tavit, my best friend. I hadn't tried hard enough to save them. What had they done to deserve this? The more I thought about it, the worse I felt. How had things escalated so quickly? What was I to do now? More importantly, why did I always feel like *I* had to do something?

Soon enough, Vartan and I were at our farm. We rode

our horse straight into the barn, not stopping for anything or for any reason. I jumped off immediately, happy to be in the safety of my home, and fell to the ground; my legs were too weak to carry me.

Vartan took his time and eventually climbed down after me.

"C'mon," he said as he put his arm on my shoulder, "get up, Armen."

Clambering on all fours, I held my head low. I took a free moment and inhaled. From my position, it was hard to ignore my red-soaked sleeve and bloodied hand. I shifted my eyes to it and dropped my head down farther. I then quickly weighed the odds and realized that I needed to clean it up before an infection set in. Unwillingly, I put one leg up towards my chest and shifted my weight onto it. Slowly, with my injured arm across my chest, I stood up. I touched the back of my head and felt the lump where I'd hit my head on the windowsill. It was painful. I then slid my good hand up into my clean sleeve and went over my entire face with it. I stretched my neck, widened my eyes, and took in a deep breath. Vartan, with his dirtied face, waited for me at the entrance. As soon as I began walking, he did, too, but slowly, so I could catch up. He put his arm around my shoulder, and together, we walked towards the house, forcibly accepting the life we were living.

By the end of 1914, everything about my life bothered me. I was deeply distraught by the fact that the only living thing that had ever tried to kill me was my own species. Vartan and I didn't tell anyone, even our parents, about Garo's family—my mother would have died from the thought alone. Her headaches were enough suffering for her. So, we convinced my father and Ara that the process of rebuilding the winery, the one that we never completed, was going well and hoped our tale would hold them off for the time being. And as a result of the unwarranted intrusion of Turkish authorities into our home, they instead spent time patching the walls.

To care for my wound, I washed it deeply with cognac and garlic. I bit down onto the collar of my shirt until the muscles in my jaw hurt. Garlic, as a natural healer, would fight the infection—something my grandmother taught me. When my forearm became numb, I grabbed an old linen cloth and tore it to length. I then wrapped it tightly to let it heal.

That evening, Vartan suggested that it was only right to give Ana a proper burial. She deserved it. Thus, the next day, we decided to do just that. I, however, despite my agreement, couldn't amass enough courage to join him. Seemingly ready at the start, I couldn't understand how Vartan had collected enough strength or stamina to finish what we started, and so early on. Two days later, however, I awoke to the realization that I needed to do it for Tavit. It had to be done. Inspired, I grabbed a shovel, as did my brother. We then, unquestionably and unanimously, decided to take the weapons my father told us not to use. It would be nonsense to return unarmed. Cautiously, we rode back to the scene. Upon our arrival, a new devastation filled my corrupted mind. The fire of the winery and barn from weeks ago had been purposely reawakened to finish what it started. It had consumed the fresh lumber, the grass, and taken its last meal at their house, with Ana inside. The place where a quaint house once stood had been reduced to nothing more than a hill of ash. From that time forth, it seemed impossible to look at that land the same again. We were too late. Upon seeing the smoky aftermath, Vartan and I took a moment and lowered ourselves down onto one knee to say a small prayer for her. We said what we knew, remembering what we could. Solemnly then, we returned home.

We didn't know what else to do.

By that time, Ara and Mary had come over, which didn't occur as frequently as before. Traveling had become only for the stronghearted. The chaos of the empire had torn everyone apart—families, friends, lovers—and the absence of Nadia and her sisters, since they had been given to a Turkish family, had taken a toll on their parents. Mary constantly worried about everything. What if the Turks found out that her daughters were Christian? What if they knew they were Armenian? It was too much for her to think about. Why should any parent have to do what they did?

Listening to the slow and shallow conversations and seeing the solemn faces, I envisioned our times before. I remembered the days when we sang. I remembered the days when we danced, when we ate, when we drank, when we laughed. I remembered the days when sitting on our porch with good friends and good company was commonplace—a time when things were fine. I remembered the days when my mind was sharp, my lungs were never empty—the days when my body was filled with energy. I remembered how those days weren't too long ago, barely a year, and yet they were so far out of reach. I remembered speaking with Tavit about anything without the fear of being judged. I remembered seeing my mother smile, my father work, little Margaret play. I smelled the food we used to eat, the freshness of the water. I tasted the apricots, the grapes, and the vegetables we used to grow. I even saw my grandmother. Now, it seemed, it had all spoiled, gone to waste, sent away to the land of sour. Nothing seemed right, nothing felt right, and what was worse was that I couldn't escape it. I felt too weak, too small, and too powerless to change it to the way it used to be.

I couldn't ask for Ana to come back. Doing so would've been useless. I didn't know where Tavit went, where Garo went. I didn't know why they were sent to the unknown. They were not conspirators. They were not planning a revolution or an uprising. I didn't know anything anymore except that something had to be done. I couldn't sit and accept these things into my life. So, I desperately searched inside for the answers and only felt the power within my heart, with pressure only a bomb could produce, intensify. Still within its confines, it gave me only the strength to move forward. And even then, it wasn't enough.

I paced, looking at the world from the outside, and saw Armenia. I saw our men being tortured, our women being raped. I saw our children starving. The inequality. I saw the thriving businesses intentionally being burned to the ground and our churches being destroyed. All for what purpose? I saw it all, and the force inside my heart grew stronger. I saw the Turkish soldiers, the officers, their countrymen, all being fed the same poison from the same source. I saw them stealing our gold. I saw them killing our livestock and taking our land. I saw them forcing us out for the mistakes we never made. I saw it, and my heart beat erratically.

And then I saw the old man, the fierce-looking one from my dream over a year ago. He looked at me and asked me what the bother was. I told him there was too much for a straight answer. Understanding, he clapped his hands once, and in that exact instance, I felt a spark and an explosion as the flame from his eyes ignited the force into an everlasting flame, one that I couldn't extinguish, one that I didn't *want* to extinguish. It warmed me and awakened my mind, placing my soul on a guided path. It gave me the new markings of strength, of courage, and more importantly, of wisdom.

A new awakening.

If change was what I wanted, then I had to go and change it myself. Nobody would do it for me. I realized through all the odds that I needed to *choose* to be the change. I had no choice. I had to choose to taste the good food, drink the good drink. I had to choose to be happy; I had to choose to laugh, choose to dance. I had to choose to think clearly, more so than before. I had to choose to use the tools around me. I had to choose to shape my life the way *I* wanted it. Relying on others would've been ridiculous. If I was scared, I had to become fearless. If I was small, I had to be big. If I was powerless, I had to become powerful. I was no longer a child. This had to be my choice, and I needed to choose it because I wanted to, because I *could*. And yet, I persistently asked myself, was it in me? Was this greatness I imagined really in me? Or was it just a temporary illusion of a twisted reality that would melt away like snow in the spring? If it was, then I, too, would melt away into the land of the forgotten. If not, if I really were destined for greatness, if I were to be remembered, I knew that all this would take time, because it takes time to sculpt a man to the exact specifications of the artist.

I loved Tavit, I really did. I loved Garo. I loved Ana. They were a beautiful family with a beautiful set of morals. They had a future, a business. Garo was funny. Ana was pretty. They had friends and they had each other. I already knew how fragile life was and its importance, so I didn't need to focus on that. It's true when they say that a devastating event takes time to settle in before the mind accepts it. I'm sure this is what happened to me, because it took me a few days to fully grasp that my best friend, my second brother, had left my life. Who knew how many others had been living, or had lived, the exact same fate as me right now. How many other families were destroyed by similar events? It wore me down both mentally and physically, but like I said, I found the strength to carry on—the new everlasting flame inside lit my life and shone exuberantly in a time of darkness. It gave me a tiny hint of hope, of possibility, that Tavit could still be alive, and so could Garo. They could be in another country, another province, another city, waiting for fate to unite us again. I didn't know that, but I had to believe it because accepting the opposite would've been an admittance of defeat, something I couldn't do.

Something I hadn't been taught.

I then prayed to God to give me the courage to walk my path. I couldn't do it alone. I prayed for Tavit and Garo and to take care of Ana. I prayed for Ara and Mary and for the safety of their three daughters. I knew it wasn't easy for them. I prayed for my grandmother, I prayed for my parents, I prayed for little Margaret. I'm sure her life was better now. I prayed for Vartan. I prayed for Nadia. I couldn't imagine how love could prevail in a time like this. I prayed for Armenia, our state, Kharpert, our province, and even our village. I then prayed for all the other villages and for everyone inside, for their protection. I prayed for the violence to end—the senseless violence by a tyrannical and oppressive regime against a peaceful people.

The violence, however, continued to escalate.

I then began to pray for God to simply *listen* to my prayers. I didn't know what else to do. With each passing day and each passing night with no answers, I began to think that my prayers were useless. An ineffective waste of time. Did God not hear me? Did I have to pray louder? What if God needed my help? If so, I would help Him. I wanted to. He knew that. Nothing would make me happier than to know the purpose of all this, to know *my* purpose, so that all this would have a meaning—the meaning I never searched for in the past. There had to be a reason for it. There always is. Would I find it? Would I be ready? If so, I knew it would be a challenge—a challenge that would prepare me to endure the life to come.

- END OF PART II -

Part III
February 1915

Chapter 27

It was a quarter before ten at night. The two nurses who had been listening slowly made their way out the door. The hospital was very quiet. Vartan, as far as they knew, was only one of three admitted patients.

"Okay," old Armen stated as he lightly slapped his knees with his palms, "this seems like a good place for a recess."

His grandchildren sat, unsure of what to say. The seemingly infinite aspects of life had been condensed down to the words of one night, and they weren't sure what to do with it or how to absorb it.

"It is good for you, I know," he said with a smile.

Slowly, the boys rubbed their eyes, then stood up with their lanky legs and left the room. Their sister, who'd been wiping the tears from her eyes, also stood up as her parents helped Anahid, Armen's wife, off her chair.

"Come with us, Dad. Let's get some food," they said.

"I'm fine, trust me," Armen responded. "Go on. I'll be here when you get back."

"We'll bring something back for you."

"No, no, please. I'll be fine. I can't eat this late."

So, one by one, they, too, left the room.

The story of old Armen's youth was emotionally charged. It wasn't yet happy but proved to be invaluable, even to his granddaughter and two grandsons. It was a story about love and power, lies, deceit, and adventure—something each found fascinating. His style, however, had thus far proved to be more than just a story.

It was a lesson.

Old Armen knew what he was saying. He had a purpose to every part and an answer to every question, every question except for one. Why did he wait so long to tell it? All throughout, he pestered himself with this simple understanding. He could have at least written it down so that he wouldn't have to speak it. He could have *at least* done that much. Whatever the case, in his old age, he realized that it was too late for a biography. Too much time had passed in his life. Hopefully, he thought, someone else would mark his place in time. People needed to know. They needed to know the truth.

With the hospital room now empty, the sounds of the background came forward—Vartan's slow breathing, water traveling through pipes, a distant hissing, and the maddening beeps of the EKG. Armen glanced over at his brother and then back down to the floor in front of him. Slowly, he extended his legs, one at a time, to loosen his knees. Sitting for a long while made them stiff. As he locked them out, he pointed his toes up, stretching his calves, then slowly brought his feet back in. He then placed his thick palms onto his thighs and with the support of his arms, leaned forward, bent his elbows, and stood up, reaffirming his intimidating height. A scar on his forearm reflected with a subtle glow in the dim lighting. He rubbed it and watched the skin around it redden. He then outstretched his arms, lengthened his torso, and inhaled a deep whirlwind of air. More alert than before, he peered at his aged brother on the hospital bed one more time before stepping outside into the hallway.

There, he stood for a moment and looked to his left—a long, light-green corridor leading to two swinging doors. He looked to his right—a much shorter and more inviting path. At his own pace, Armen walked the shorter path of the low-lit hallway, looking down at the tile floor, thinking. At the end, he turned back around and walked back to the hospital room door. He didn't pull it back open but instead waited until his family returned. He wasn't hungry. He didn't need to join them. His body was accustomed to not eating for long periods of time. The few minutes to himself would allow him to collect his thoughts and decide how he wanted to word the rest of the story. Up until this point, he was amazed at the amount of detail he remembered and with such clarity, perhaps another gift from his grandmother. With his thoughts carefully organized, Armen soon heard the familiar voices approaching. His daughter, her husband, his grandchildren, and his wife slowly passed through the revolving doors at the end of the hallway, walking only as fast as the slowest walker. He stood plainly and smiled at the small army. One by one, they passed him by and walked back inside the room, acknowledging his presence with a respectful "hello." His youngest granddaughter, a teenager, held the door open for her grandmother.

"I'll be inside soon, honey," said Anahid as she placed her bony hand gently upon her head.

The girl smiled as she disappeared into the room, letting the door close behind her. Armen stood alert as Anahid turned to face him.

"How do you feel?" she asked.

"Old," he said. "How do you feel?"

Anahid smiled. "That's not your fault."

Armen shrugged.

"Armen," she continued, "my love, listen to me. I don't know what happened. I don't know where this is going, but promise me one thing."

Armen listened attentively to his wife.

"Promise me you'll be easy on them. Please, they're just kids."

Looking at Anahid's wrinkled face, her white hair and sagging cheeks, old Armen remembered when they'd first met, when they'd first fallen in love. It was hard to believe that it had all happened fifty-six years ago. He envisioned the exact moment in time when he saw her, sitting alone on an old crate, wearing a head-wrap. He remembered the first time they made eye contact, the first words they said to each other. He remembered their first dance, their first kiss. He remembered because she was the only beacon of light, the only evidence that love had not died and life would carry on. He reminisced wholeheartedly as she patiently waited for a response.

"We, too, were just kids," he answered finally.

Anahid closed her eyes. That wasn't the answer she wanted to hear. She leaned her head against his chest, and he wrapped his arms around her. They stood in the hallway for a moment.

"Let's go." Old Armen motioned with a kiss on her

head. "I have a story to finish."

And together, they walked inside.

<u>28</u>

By mid-February of the year 1915, almost seven months after the start of World War One and nearly four months after the Ottoman Empire had joined the Central Powers, life, it seemed, had found another beginning. The sun was strong that day, easing my mother's headache. Standing outside on the porch, she breathed in the fresh, cold air and watched as Ara came by with his wife, Mary. My father and Ara, growing increasingly more skeptical about Garo and his family, together decided to pay them a visit. Despite all that Vartan and I pleaded, to no avail, they had made their decision.

"Vartan, Armen, let's go," my father commanded. "We're going."

As he stepped into the barn, he removed the two coverings of burlap and unlatched the door. He reached inside and grabbed his Mosin rifle and let the door drop, making a loud echoing clank. Like a soldier restricted by no law, he laid the weapon across his horse.

For a moment, I closed my eyes and held them shut; it had been a long while since my father had last seen Garo. Thus, he had understandably grown restless. Vartan and I had used every excuse, but I figured it was only a matter of time before they found out. I only had the power to postpone the future, not change it. If this had to happen, I figured it would be better to just get it over with.

Staying behind, Mary kept my mother company. My father and Ara each jumped onto their horses, and Vartan and I jumped onto another. Then, like a free militia, we journeyed east. My mind raced, trying to grasp what just started, and I rode my horse as slow as possible to delay. My father, as usual, had none of it and, in his persuasive voice, edged me to move faster.

Eventually, we arrived at the field where the Turkish

boys herded their sheep. I looked around for them, but they weren't there.

"*Hyreeg*," I started, "maybe we shouldn't leave the women alone."

"Yeah," sprang Vartan, "it's dangerous."

"Nonsense," he replied. "They'll be fine."

Reluctantly we continued on our way.

Before long, we arrived at the land where Garo's life used to be. As the scent of smoke overwhelmed their sense of smell, my father and Ara sat atop, high and strong. They showed no expression. Ara rode a few meters and stopped short of a small burned piece of paper on the ground. He dismounted and brushed the small coals off the surface, revealing it as the one that had been nailed to the front door. He read what he could and neatly folded the paper into his pocket. He then walked over to the pile of ash where the house once was and squatted down on one leg. Cupping his hand, he scooped up the blackened past and squeezed it hard between his fingers. He then hurled the contents into the pile and walked angrily back to his horse. My father turned to Vartan and me.

"Where are they?" he asked softly.

"*Hyreeg*, listen—" Vartan started nervously.

"Where are they?" my father screamed.

His horse neighed.

"Tevos," said Ara with a tilt of his head and an extension of his palm, trying to calm my father.

Taken aback by his sudden outburst of anger, I yelled back, "They were deported!"

My father studied me as he calmed his horse.

"They killed Ana!" I cried. "Garo and Tavit are—I don't know where Tavit and Garo are!"

Closing his eyes, Ara clenched his teeth. His gold-rimmed glasses moved with the muscles on his face as he massaged his temples with the thumb and forefinger of his right hand. I tried desperately not to burst out with emotion. Doing so in front of my father would have meant the end of my existence. Even if I did, though, I didn't know what I would've said or what I would've done. I didn't even know if I would express anger or sadness or an intoxicating mixture of both.

My father turned his horse around and moved in the opposite direction.

"Where are you going?" I asked.

"We're going home," he said. "Let's go."

I peered over at Vartan, dumbfounded.

"Home?" burst Vartan. "Why are we still here? We need to leave! We need to escape! It's senseless to risk our lives!"

My father turned back around. "What did you say?" he asked for clarification.

"I said we need to *leave*!"

Poised with a premeditated response, he long anticipated the question and answered immediately, pointing his finger down to the ground with each of his statements.

"Leave?" he questioned. "Why would we leave? This is *our* life!" he boomed. "This is *our* land! This is *our* family. We are *not* like sheep! We will not be led to the unknown and *give* our land to the enemy. The Turks did this. *They* killed Ana. *They* burned down their house. *They* are responsible, and we will *not* let them intimidate us. If we do, we have unquestionably accepted the destruction of our livelihood. You will never, *ever* accept that. And you will never, *ever,* in my presence or anyone else's, speak those cowardly words or take that cowardly stance ever again. Stand up for your rights! Stand up for who you are and defend it. We are Armenian, and this is Armenia! Do you understand?"

Vartan didn't respond.

"Do you understand?" my father repeated.

"Yes," he muttered finally.

"Excuse me?"

"Yes, I understand!" my brother screamed. "I said I understand!"

"Good." My father smiled in satisfaction. "*Now* let's go."

With each of my father's statements, the flame inside me strengthened, absorbing and feeding from his words. I now saw my father's thoughts. I began to feel as he felt. I began to see the world as he saw it. I saw it, I felt it, and I believed it, bringing with it what most people yearn for, what they wish for—a belonging, a community. As a result, it gave me the vision of many men, a power unlike any that, if used unjustly, would yield dangerous consequences.

My father meant what he said, and he said it with a hardened zeal. It was short and went directly to the point. There was no sympathy in it—just fact. Even the horse was frightened. I admired the passion and the depth to which he carried it. Vartan, I must admit, took my father's words truthfully. He faced him and listened without interruption. He didn't look away. He didn't look down. He didn't blink. He simply maintained eye contact and sat upright. It was very intimidating to respond to a man sitting atop a horse emptying the words of his soul with such craze and such intensity, and it was especially intimidating if that man had a mustache like my father's. And yet, despite it all, I still couldn't shake the new series of questions. Were my father's words logical? Or were they stubborn? Did Vartan admit a defeatist attitude? Did he expose a weakness? Who was right? Who was wrong? Should we escape or shouldn't we? If my questions had answers, no one spoke of them. Perhaps, though, the answers didn't matter because the truth, as it usually is, was simple, and I had yet again made it overly complex.

Ara said nothing. I knew he agreed with my father. Ultimately, neither did Vartan, nor did I. What could I have said? I was only fifteen.

My father then simply turned his horse around and continued on his way, rifle still within reach. In silence, we rode back to our home. Once there, my father jumped down and guided his horse with Ara back into the barn. Built from the ground up with their bare hands, that was the only place where they felt they could speak freely.

"Tevos, listen," Ara started, "what is happening here is unlike anything I've ever seen, unlike anything we've *all* seen for six hundred years. It's happening on a massive scale all over the empire and to the other villages. The villages are even banding together in defense and response to this… this *lunacy*. We can join them so that we can protect who we are, so that we can fight for our rights just as you said."

"Ara," responded my father, "I am a man of my words and of my people, but before that, I am a man of my family. As are you. My duties to them have not been—"

"Tevos, they looted my shop. In front of my own eyes, they took it over and dumped all my furniture out onto the street. I made each piece by hand! These hands! They then destroyed my machinery. I have nothing left."

"Good Lord," my father said, shaking his head.

"The government is taking control of our lives, and their corruption has spread to the people. I've seen it. I sent my daughters to the Turks in order to save them. I sent them to the enemy. That's something I would have never, *ever* even *considered* doing before. I know very well the sacrifices I need to make in order to protect my family. To protect my religion. My culture. Garo was our friend, God rest his soul, but he, unfortunately, was naïve and impartial to the truth. Joining your brothers is one step towards the freedom of an entire race of people. Your race of people. Your family. It's the only way."

My father crossed his arms and raised one hand to twirl the tip of his mustache. "We all want freedom, and we must be extra vigilant, but what happens if you are killed? What happens if I am killed? Who will take care of your daughters then? What about their future? Who will take care of Mary?"

Ara adjusted his glasses. "In this case, the benefit of freedom outweighs the risk of death. That's all it comes down to. I am ready. Besides," he added, "you know how stubborn our women can be. They're tough; they're resilient, especially if they have to deal with men like you." Ara smiled, adding some light to a darkened matter.

"Yes," said my father, returning the smile, "you are true. They are as stubborn as they are wise, which makes me wonder, what does Mary say about your decision?"

"I haven't told her yet."

"When do you figure?"

"Only time will tell. Some things need to be settled first," he responded. "I plan on joining the resistance by the first week of May."

"My God, Ara, you are as good a friend as any, but I cannot join you. I can, however, pray for your comfort."

"Thank you, but pray not only for me, pray for my family, your family, and the safety of all the other Armenian families."

Ara extended his hand, and my father shook it.

"It is done. Thank you, Ara. And please, be safe."

<u>29</u>

By the third week of March 1915, five weeks after my father and Ara discovered Garo's burned land, everything about Vartan's life bothered him. It had been almost eight months since he had proposed to Nadia, and he still couldn't understand why she couldn't give him a definitive answer. Everything about her actions said yes, but her words became increasingly more uncertain. Vartan even carried the small silver band with him wherever he went, hoping that he would get an answer to his question. He needed to let her know how he felt but didn't want to jeopardize their relationship. He had worked too hard to get to this point. Thus, he spent his days and nights thinking and planning a meticulous course of action that would push her resolve. He, of course, understood the burden of conflict and the toll it played. The empire's involvement in the war had been difficult, especially since traveling, even in broad daylight, could now become dangerous for Vartan, nonetheless for an Armenian girl with such splendor and beauty as Nadia.

As the spring season fought its way through and began its pleasant invasion by warming the land, it was refreshing to see the small layer of water atop the thin overnight snow echoing with such brilliance. On that particularly glorious day, the most refreshing in a long while, Vartan, the gentleman that he is, took it upon himself to live through the illusion of freedom to overcome the certainty of submission.

Stopping his horse short of the Turkish home where

Nadia and her sisters now lived, a forty-five-minute gallop away, he slowly slid off. Feeling the moist ground under his feet, he cautiously approached her bedroom window, facing the south, reigns in hand.

"Nadia," he whispered aloud.

He heard a rustling inside.

"Hey, Nadia," he whispered again.

Nadia approached the window and wrenched loose the heavy wooden frame. "What are you doing here?" she asked, looking down at Vartan.

"C'mon," he said with a smile, "let's go for a ride."

"Vartan, please. It's cold. It's not safe."

"Sure it is. I'll protect you."

Nadia frowned.

"And I'll keep you warm," he winked.

"I'm not sure, Vartan."

"Nadia, please, I haven't seen you. I just want to talk."

She rested on her arms, thinking.

"All right. I'll tell my sisters."

Inside the house, a woman spoke. "Nadia," she said in Ottoman Turkish, "who are you speaking to?"

"Nobody," she answered into the room.

Vartan smiled.

"Give me a moment," she said as she disappeared into the house.

With her steps, every floorboard creaked under her petite frame. Much like all the others, it was an old house. A minute later, she returned with her two younger sisters, who looked older than the last time Vartan had seen them. After they leaned through the window to say hello, Vartan sent his best wishes from his family, and they smiled in return. Carefully then, Nadia raised one leg onto the sill as Vartan raised his arms to hold her steady. Using him for support, she jumped down to the soft earth, and her sisters stood inside and watched, dreaming about the days when they, too, would be swept off their feet.

With a casual gallop, they started away from the house until they arrived at the river across from Bedros's home. There, they sat in the brush atop some blankets.

"See, nobody is going to see us here," Vartan said, trying to ease the mood.

He could tell she wasn't as excited as she used to be. There was something different about her, and it wasn't new. He sensed it months ago but made no motion to address it. In his attempt to lighten her up, he joked, brought up past memories, and laughed, but she simply shrugged it all off. Her mind was somewhere else. When Vartan's attempts ended in failure, when he couldn't manage to find the old Nadia, he approached the problem directly.

"Nadia, listen," he began, "I love you. You know I do. I know you said you need time before our marriage, but I need to know that you haven't forgotten about it."

She looked at Vartan, perturbed. "Vartan—"

"I mean, you've been acting very strange, and it's bothering me. Please tell me what's wrong," he pleaded, trying to get something out of her.

There was something she wanted to say but didn't. "I told you. The killings, the war, the deportations. I haven't been home in months—"

"I understand," Vartan interrupted, "but this couple— they treat you well, don't they? They feed you well, give you nice clothes, right?"

"Yes," she answered.

"Then what's the problem? I know you. There's something more. That can't be all of it. Look at me, Nadia. I want the truth."

Nadia turned her head to face Vartan. "The truth?" she replied, obviously angrier. "How dare you accuse me of hiding something from you?"

"I'm not accusing you of anything. I'm just saying I know there's something you're not telling me. You haven't been the same and—"

Nadia stood up, and Vartan watched her from the ground.

"This day is over," she affirmed. "I'll see you when you

grow up! *If* you do!"

She then stormed away, and Vartan simply watched her do so.

"What did my grandmother say to you?" he screamed. "What did she tell you before she died?" He stood up.

Nadia stopped in her tracks and turned around, stomping back to Vartan. "What she said is none of your business! She said it to me and no one else! You are *not* who I thought you were!" She stormed away again.

Vartan knew he'd hit the nail on the head. It bothered him that he had dedicated himself to this relationship and still had no idea what was going on. "What did my grandmother tell you before she died?" he repeated. "It was about us, wasn't it?"

She continued to walk away.

"So you're just going to walk home? It's too far! I have the horse!"

Nadia continued, still on her way, holding onto the bottom of her dress to keep it from dragging on the wet ground.

"Just tell me what she said. If it concerns us, I have a right to know."

She kept to her pace.

"Nadia, please, it's dangerous out there!"

"I don't care!" she screamed back.

Vartan climbed onto his horse and walked it next to Nadia, searching around the landscape at the same time. "Nadia, you're acting ridiculous. It's too far to walk home. Just get on with me. Nadia..." He jumped down. "Nadia, listen. I'm sorry I brought it up, but I care about you. We need to talk about these things if we're going to be together. We can't hold secrets like this!"

She slowed her pace, and Vartan noted it.

"Nadia, just listen. I jus—"

"She told me that love is a poison," she cried. "She told me to be careful because it's dangerous."

"What?"

"She said love will consume my thoughts and alter my judgments."

The tears rolled down her face, and she wiped them away to clear her vision.

"But why would she—"

"Vartan, and she's right. All I think about is you. All my decisions, all my steps. Love is maddening. In a world maddening enough, I can't do this."

Vartan stood, unsure of what he had withdrawn. "But, Nadia, you can't think of it that way."

"Oh yeah? Then tell me why she's right. Why would she say that to me if it wasn't true?"

"I'm not sure. I love my grandmother, but please, don't listen to that. For me, you have no idea. Love is my driving force. It's my motivation. You're my motivation to want to be better. If you use it wisely, I think it can be beautiful."

"I just—I don't know what to do," she cried. "I need you."

Unexpectedly, she dove into Vartan's inviting arms. Her burden had been lifted. Her heart relaxed. Unknowing of what he'd done wrong, what he'd done right, or even how he'd gotten to this point, Vartan held her, feeling relieved that she felt better. He closed his eyes and gently rubbed her back as Nadia rested her head firmly into his chest. As one, they once again held onto each other for all it was worth.

A moment later, she let go and faced him.

"Yes," she cried, wiping the tears from her eyes, "I will."

Her response took some thought to register, but soon enough, Vartan's emotions began to swell, and he stared into her glossy eyes. He pulled her in again, and for the first time ever, a tear rolled down his face.

A tear of joy.

"It's going to be magnificent," he whispered.

He reached into his back pocket and pulled out the silver band and delicately slid it onto her finger. She laughed a joyous laugh as she looked at it glistening in the sun.

Together, they climbed back onto his horse and galloped in the direction of the Turkish couple's home. Before long, however, they decided upon a much-needed detour. They decided that it was time to take the next step. Vartan would be the one to do it.

Things like this couldn't wait.

....

Two wine glasses sat upon a small table on the porch. Ara sat on one end and my father on the other. The third chair sat empty. My mother and Mary strolled together through the apricot orchard, and I sat inside. Despite the interior of our house still not being back to where it used to be, it was, like I mentioned, a glorious day. Up until that point, however, I had never in my life experienced such emptiness as I did sitting in the kitchen by myself.

As my mother and Mary walked close by under the shade, Vartan and Nadia rode in from the west, bearing the best news we would receive in years. The two mothers stopped mid-stride and stood, waiting to see who was approaching.

"Nadia!" exclaimed Mary in disbelief when she saw her eldest daughter.

Casually jumping down, Nadia kissed her.

"Where were you?" my mother asked Vartan.

"C'mon," he said with a smile after giving her a kiss, hardly able to contain himself, "we've got some news for you."

My mother and Mary looked at each other and followed them to the house, staying close behind, as Vartan peeked his head inside. "Armen," he said, "get out here. I have something to say."

My father and Ara put down their wine glasses and waited. Ara clearly wasn't happy that Nadia had left the Turkish couple's home.

"Well, get it out already," my father stated impatiently.

"I'll wait until everyone's here," my brother responded.

My mother and Mary stood near Vartan and Nadia.

"Well," began my mother, "what is it?"

"Okay," he began. "I... If you didn't know, Nadia and I have been seeing each other for some time now."

Nobody seemed surprised.

"And we're happy to say that... we're engaged!"

The two birds smiled from ear to ear. For a moment, though, nobody said a word. Vartan's heart beat like a drum in the silence, and a moment later, my father sprang up.

"*Ha!*" he laughed to Ara. "We're going to be fathers-in-law."

"*Ha-ha!* Congratulations, my old friend." Ara jumped up and kissed my father's cheek.

My father kissed him back. "The blessing is to you."

My mother covered her mouth with her hands, and Mary shrieked then wrapped her arms around her daughter. They, too, celebrated with smiles and tears of joy as my father took Vartan's hand.

"Congratulations, my boy," he said with a vigorous shake, followed by a pat on his back.

"My son, may God bless the both of you for all time," my mother stated as she took Vartan's head with her hands and kissed both cheeks. "She's a very nice girl. You should be proud."

With cheers and smiles in abundance, it had been a long overdue round of happiness. I, too, celebrated with a long overdue smile and laughed a long overdue laugh, and we all drank it to the last drop.

"Armen, find us two ducks!" my father directed. "We will feast well tonight in light of this excellent news!"

I responded with a triumphant smile. Duck was my absolute favorite dish and a highly regarded delicacy. Without hesitation, I ran to the southern field, chased down two nicely rounded birds, then brought them back to my father who took care of the rest.

My father sat at the head of the table, across from my mother. Vartan sat next to Nadia, across from me, who sat next to Mary and Ara. The two cooked ducks, baked with asparagus and carrots, sat in the middle. Next to the ducks was the *lavash*, thin Armenian bread. In a separate bowl, the aroma of sweet baked potatoes, sprinkled lightly with pepper, quickly filled our senses. Vartan smiled. I couldn't resist as I rested my eyes upon the greatest dinner I'd ever seen, and it couldn't come at a better time. Walking around the table, my father set down wine glasses at each of our places. He then popped a bottle of Garo's Best and poured each of us our share and sat down for himself.

"Vartan, Nadia," he said as he raised his wine glass, initiating a toast. We all picked up our glasses as well. "May the Lord's greatest wishes smile upon you in this time and the time to come. I am happier than ever and cannot wait to be here for the both of you."

"Yes," continued Ara, "may you work together, smile together, laugh, and cry together. I couldn't be more proud. I wish, Nadia, your sisters could be here. I wish little Margaret could be here. I wish, God bless their souls, that your grandmother, Ana, Tavit, and Garo could be here. I know they're looking down at us, smiling, especially Garo, for watching us drink his wine. Thank you, Garo."

My father chuckled, and Ara raised his glass higher.

"God bless you both. God bless this meal. God bless all there is, all there was, and all there is to come. Amen."

"Amen," we said.

My father then began the celebratory meal with the *Hayr Mer*. We bowed our heads, recited it together, and then, of course, ate like kings.

It was only a matter of about fifteen minutes after our meal that my father casually excused himself to the back. We weren't initially sure why he'd left so suddenly and so silently, but our simple question was answered when he returned with a drum, a *dumbek* as we called it. With a single thump and a deep, but elongated, vocal note, he started a tune, thus directing all the attention to him.

It was time to celebrate.

We all laughed and covered our heads in embarrassment. He then extended the note to a single word and thumped the drum twice to continue the song. It started out slow, with a few more thumps between the beats, and then sped up with each passing verse. Nadia, on one hand, enjoyed every moment of it, but Vartan and I, on the other, sat in our seats unable to comprehend what was being presented to us. Despite being on key, any act of musical talent should have been prohibited if it were coming from my father, and for good reason—his voice was just too loud for the space. Ara, being the good friend that he was, then stood up and joined him, and together, they sang their song, letting their low-pitched voices reverberate throughout the house and out the open door. What seemed loud before was now even louder. I shouldn't have expected anything different; Garo's Best brought the musician out in all of us.

"All together!" my father yelled, with his mustache following the curves of his face.

Vartan and I looked at each other, allowing our minds to process this surprising act.

"Let's go, boys!" Ara invited.

My mother, Mary, and Nadia then began clapping their hands and harmoniously smoothed out the tune with their voices.

Before we knew it, our parents were singing their hearts out, and in between verses, they took turns drinking more wine. The more they sang, the more they drank, and the more they drank, the more they sang. It was an entertaining mix. Eventually, with too much pressure, my brother and I joined the chorus. Why not, I figured. Vartan was getting married.

After the song ended, we laughed. A part of me, contrarily, hoped that they wouldn't begin again, but despite my inner wishes, my father started a new song, using the same beat on the *dumbek*—the only beat he knew. Quickly, he sped it up to match the speed of the new tune, filling our house with a remarkable power. Just as quickly as it started, though, the song ended, just in time to begin another.

And another.

By the third or fourth song, we were all singing our hearts out. I even threw my hands up into the air to accentuate the notes. I'll admit it; I was having a lot of fun.

After the final verse of the final song, my father, unfortunately, placed the *dumbek* down and sat next to it, wiping the gratuitous amount of sweat from his forehead. He reached for his glass and exhaled.

My mother, Ara, and Mary, chuckling their last few chuckles, also, in turn, sat for a breather.

"Uff, that was good," my father said satisfactorily. "Remember those days, Ara?" He gave his friend a light pat on his shoulder, reminiscing.

"Yes," he said with a smile, "they seem so long ago."

"Brings back memories, doesn't it, Hasmig?" he asked my mother.

My mother smiled and patted his knee. "Of course it does, Tevos."

After that, they simply sat in their seats, satisfied with their fill. To be honest, I never really thought about what my parents were like in their youth. Any ambiguity, however, was summed up by the last few lines between my father, my mother, and Ara as they painted their times just enough so that my imagination could fill the gaps. Nothing I envisioned seemed much different than mine. We were all the same, I figured.

Quickly drifting away, my father then closed his eyes, and Ara followed suit. They were drained. In the kitchen, my mother and Mary continued a soft conversation, and Vartan and Nadia sat next to me doing what Vartan and Nadia did best. Not nearly as tired as my parents, but surrounded by so much exhaustion, I, too, let out a big yawn as I stretched out my arms and extended my legs, letting the tears fill my eyes, even closing them momentarily.

Just then, a faint voice called my name.

"Armen."

I opened my eyes and turned to Vartan. "What?" I said, bothered by the disturbance.

He looked at me strangely. "What? I didn't say anything."

"You said my name," I responded.

"No, I didn't," he defended.

I knew I was a dreamer, but this wasn't a dream. I knew for certain that I heard someone say my name. Vartan must have been playing with me, I thought.

So, once again, I closed my eyes.

Then I heard again, "Armen."

"Seriously, Vartan, stop fooling around. I know it was you," I accused.

"I'm not fooling! It wasn't me!"

Figuring I would catch him in the act, I fixed my eyes on my brother. Not soon after, I heard my name again. Vartan was telling the truth.

Like a ferret, I raised my head and looked around the room. My mother and Mary didn't say it. They wouldn't do something like that. My father and Ara didn't say it, either. They were asleep.

Then I heard it once more, now louder, "Armen."

Vartan looked around the room. He heard it, too.

I stood up. The voice sounded familiar.

"Armen, please!" the voice pleaded.

It was in distress.

I ran to the open doorway and peered into the darkness of the rising moon. Just to the point where my eyes couldn't see any farther, the moonlight expanded my limits, barely illuminating the image of a single, slouched and limping body moving towards our house.

"Armen!"

I narrowed my eyes, unable to believe my ears, and ran out a few meters. Vartan and Nadia stood by, listening attentively.

I stopped short and focused my eyes once again.

"Oh my God," I whispered.

It was Tavit.

Sprinting as fast as I could into the wet night, I slid to his aid. Immediately, I noticed how thin he was. His clothes, badly torn, were draped over him like a tablecloth. His eyes bulged out of his head, his cheekbones protruded sharply, and he wore rags around his feet in place of his boots. As soon as he saw me, he fell into my arms and began to cry.

"Relax, relax," I soothed. "Vartan!" I yelled out,

awakening my father. "Quick! Bring water!"

Not a minute too soon, Vartan ran over with the detached bucket from the well, letting it splash over the edges and onto his pants. I helped Tavit sit up, and Vartan slowly tipped the bucket into his mouth. He was too weak to drink on his own.

"Tavit, we need to get you inside. It's too dark out here. Can you walk?" I asked.

With his eyes closed, he weakly shook his head. "No."

"Vartan, what is it?" Nadia asked.

"Vartan, Nadia needs to help us. Go get her."

"Nadia," he yelled, "hurry, we need you!"

With a quick dash, Nadia ran out to us. Immediately, she shrieked upon seeing Tavit's transformed body.

"Nadia, we'll get under his arms, and you'll carry his legs," I instructed.

"Okay," she said, nodding her head.

With a deep squat, Vartan and I placed our shoulders under each of his arms and lifted Tavit's torso while holding onto his wrists.

"Okay, grab him by the ankles," I said.

Nadia then leaned over and grabbed both swollen appendages. She carried them at her waist to the house and powerfully kicked the door open with the sole of her foot. My mother and Mary jumped at the sound, and my father rubbed his eyes.

"What the hell is this?" he said, jumping up. "Good Lord."

"*Hyreeg*, quick," I stammered.

My mother turned and shrieked.

"Tavit!" yelled Mary.

Newly opening his eyes, Ara watched as we carried Tavit into the living space and carefully placed him on the torn sofa. In the new light, he barely looked alive.

My father ran onto the porch and looked out into the night. He stood in the darkness. Studying. Watching.

"Get some water and blankets," he said as he slowly

shut the door.

"Here, I have the water," Vartan mentioned while I ran to the back and brought two blankets.

With the bucket on the floor, I covered Tavit's body up to his shoulders. Mary dipped in a rag and placed it across his dirt-crusted forehead. Slowly, he became more alert, so I grabbed some bread from the table.

"Here," I offered, placing the bread near his mouth, "eat this."

Barely opening it, Tavit tried taking the small piece.

"Now bite down," I instructed.

He bit down but was unable to tear it off.

"That won't work," said my father. "Break off a smaller piece by hand, and put it inside his cheek. Even if he doesn't chew it, it'll dissolve."

I pulled the bread from between his teeth and did as my father instructed as he looked down at the cloth around Tavit's feet. Squatting down, my father carefully began unwrapping it. It cracked and tore as each layer, stuck to the one above it, unraveled from itself. Not much later, my father tossed the maroon-colored cloth to the side and exposed a disfigured set of feet, blackened with dirt and reddened with bruises, severely gashed like canyons across the soles. We all wanted to look away but couldn't stop staring.

"Armen, get Dr. Thomassian," my father called.

"No," I disagreed, shaking my head. "I'm staying here with him."

"Fine, then. Vartan, get Dr. Thomassian."

I looked at Vartan.

"Okay, sure."

He then ran out the door.

Kneeling down, my mother placed a shallow bowl underneath Tavit's feet. His eyes were still closed. She then poured the water from the bucket over the thickly crusted skin causing Tavit to abruptly scream in pain. Instantly, the water turned red and swirled in the path of the current in the bowl.

"Shh... shh..." said Mary as she held the towel over his

forehead.

Nadia rubbed his shoulder in consolation.

The cold sting of the water made Tavit more alert. He squirmed in his seat, causing the blanket to partially slide off. Nadia then pulled it back and tucked it behind his shoulders.

"Tavit, tell us what happened," said Ara.

"Ara, are we going to do this *now*?" questioned Mary hypothetically. "He just got here. On his own time."

Ara threw his arms up in defeat and walked away.

Instead of pouring the water again, my mother soaked a new rag and wiped his feet instead, seemingly making it more tolerable.

With each dab, with each swipe, more surface blood and more surface dirt was cleared away, slowly exposing his wounds underneath. Quickly, I realized just how severe they actually were. All of them were on his soles—gashes from every angle and bruises covering every centimeter. I was horrified by the sight. Nadia looked away before finding the muscle to look again.

"Tavit," I tried, "Tavit, can you speak?"

He shook his head a little more stoutly than before.

"Tavit, eat this," I said as I broke off another piece of bread.

He opened his mouth a little wider than before. I placed the piece inside his cheek. He let it sit there, then chewed it slowly. He then swallowed and nodded his head for another.

And again, I fed him.

Minutes later, after about four or five pieces, Tavit opened his eyes. He shifted his eyeballs around the room, and all I could do was smile. He smiled back, but weakly.

"Can you speak now?" I asked.

Tavit cleared his throat. "My feet," he whispered as he lifted his head to look down at them.

"No, no, no," my father said as he covered the view, preventing Tavit from seeing them.

Resting his head back against the sofa, Tavit closed his eyes once again, trying to regain more of his strength. We relaxed until he spoke again.

"They lied," he whispered.

Ara raised his awareness and walked over. "What did you say?"

"They lied to us," he whispered again. "They said we would... be free."

"Who lied to you?" Ara asked.

"They took us to a camp to work the roads. The Turks did. Thousands of us. From all over Armenia. They made us... their slaves." He inhaled and closed his eyes. "He's dead." A tear rolled down his face.

"They beat my father... with a hammer. They starved us and killed the rest with axes by the hillside. I tried to escape, but they found me."

We sat, listening.

"They arrested me and beat my soles... with a cane... until I fainted."

"Good lord, they tortured him!" Ara swung his arms up as he walked away. "Now he could lose his feet!"

"For three days... and starved me. They thought I was dead, but I escaped... I ran here... My house is gone."

He began to shiver, and his eyes watered more as if it were a blustery winter morning. "What's happening? Please don't cut off my feet. I don't know what to do. I don't want to be here anymore."

"We won't amputate them, don't worry," my father stated.

My mother put her arms around his shoulders as she cried softly.

"Mary, I swear to God," Ara raised his voice, "with the great Lord as my witness, I—"

Before he could finish, the door suddenly swung open, interrupting Ara. Vartan was severely out of breath.

"Dr. Thomassian is gone. His clinic destroyed. Turkish, German soldiers... are everywhere. Every corner. Every intersection. The Turkish soldiers... are shooting, killing Armenians. The mobs... are attacking the Armenian shops, stealing, looting. It's chaos there. I had to turn back. I barely made it. Quick… blow out the candles." He pointed. "They're moving to the villages."

My father swore loudly.

Hurrying around the house, we blew out all the candles, filling the air with darkness. The moonlight shone powerfully through the windows illuminating the thin strings of silver smoke rising away from the extinguished wicks.

"These Turks! We've been on this land for over two thousand years, trying to preserve our culture, and all these *peasants* want to do is destroy it all!"

"Tevos," my mother warned, "lower your voice! There's no need for that. It doesn't help."

My father turned to Tavit, "Tavit, listen," he began again, "we can't find the doctor, but I have to make sure your feet are cleaned, so they won't get infected. This is going to hurt, so please bite down on this."

He picked up a small, thicker stick from the fireplace and brushed it clean with his hands. He then handed it to Tavit, but Tavit couldn't grab it on his own, so my father placed it in his hand. He followed my father with his eyes.

My father then took the bowl of bloodied water and dumped it outside; he then filled it again with clean water.

"Armen, get the salt," he said.

At that moment, I hesitated, not knowing if it was a good idea, but my father knew what he was doing, so I brought it to him.

After unscrewing the cap, my father dissolved half the shaker into the clean water. He stirred it up with his fingers and placed the bowl beside Tavit's feet to let it settle.

"Get the cognac," he ordered.

I brought that too, and he placed it on the floor.

"Now hold his ankles," he directed me.

With a firm yet careful grip, I took hold of Tavit's ankles with my hands.

"No," my father said, shaking his finger, "put them under your arms. Hold them tight, like this."

I watched my father's animated instructions and

rearranged my body to put Tavit's legs snugly under my one armpit.

"Please, Tavit," my father warned, "stay quiet."

Tavit's eyes widened. He looked scared. My father then knelt next to his feet and rolled up his sleeves.

"Pour some on my hands," he said, pointing to the bottle of cognac.

Vartan popped the cork and liberally poured it over my father's hands, letting it dribble down into the bowl. My father then deeply rubbed his hands together and waved them through the air to let the alcohol evaporate as Vartan put the cork back into the unlabeled bottle and set the bottle on the floor. With two fingers of his left hand, my father then opened one of the wounds on the sole of Tavit's left foot. Tavit cringed and tried to pull his legs back.

I held them tight.

"I know, I know. Put the stick between your teeth. Sideways."

Barely with enough energy, Tavit put the stick in his mouth.

My father took his other hand and dipped it into the bowl of salt water. He tightened it into a fist, sending a quick jet of water directly into the wound. Fragments of dirt and rocks flew out along with a profuse amount of blood.

Tavit bit down on the stick and opened his eyes wide, groaning loudly. He held his breath as he grabbed the torn cushions of the sofa. When the stream stopped, he began a relaxed yet heavy breathing. The rag over his forehead fell, and Nadia picked it up and held onto it.

"The poor kid," I thought. "As if he hadn't been through enough."

Again, my father opened the wound with one hand and squirted salt water into it with the other. Tavit grunted and bit down hard onto the stick. The tears rolled down his face and glistened in the moonlight. As the pain thrust his body into a more alert state, he fought harder and more violently, squirming and twisting his body. This began to irritate my father.

"Hold him down," he said.

Nobody moved.

"I said hold him. Let's go!" he demanded adamantly.

Mary and Nadia both positioned themselves by his shoulders and held them firmly.

Without hesitation, my father squirted more salt water into the wounds, waiting less and less between squirts, and each time, more debris fell out, splashing his clothes. Only once all the debris was cleared did he move onto the next gash, and then to the next foot, repeating the process of clearing out all the excess. In between, my mother refilled the bowl with clean water and new salt.

Once his right foot had been cleaned, my father then took the bottle of cognac and pulled the cork out with his teeth and spit it onto the floor. He then partially covered the bottle's opening with his thumb, and without even a warning, dribbled the alcohol into the wounds of Tavit's left foot. Tavit screamed out loud, and the stick fell out.

Nadia quickly placed her hand over his mouth to muffle his voice. We couldn't risk being heard.

At his discretion, my father stopped pouring, and I loosened my grip and sat back. Nadia removed her hand.

"Please," cried Tavit, "no more. No more."

Mary loosened her grip from his shoulders and made the sign of the cross. "Jesus, please, watch over this boy."

"Tevos, it's enough," my mother said. "It's enough."

My father made no mention of it.

"Tavit," explained my father, "the pain will be far worse if I don't clean your wounds. I need to clean these. I'll break until you can tolerate it, and we'll begin again."

Tavit nodded his head in agreement, and my father stood up, being careful not to touch anything with his hands.

We relaxed for a minute until Tavit gave the clear.

"All right," he granted, breathing nervously. "I'm ready."

"Atta boy," congratulated my father. "After this, nobody can say you're not a man. Nobody." He pointed his finger at him to make sure he got the message. "Armen, his legs."

Again, I put Tavit's legs deep into my pit like before and wrapped my arms around his ankles. Nadia handed the stick to Tavit.

"No," he urged, shaking his head, "I don't need it."

Grabbing the bottle once more, my father angled it above his foot and let it drip over the entire sole. Then, one by one, he poured it into each individual wound. Tavit squirmed. He cringed and he fought, jolting my body like a wild bull. His knuckles turned white and his face turned red, and what's more, he didn't make a single sound. After an excruciating lap, all the wounds were disinfected, and the alcohol was allowed to soak in. My father sat back.

"Tell me when it gets numb," he instructed.

By the color of his face, we knew when the burning in his feet had ceased. Tavit's color came back, and he closed his eyes. With a nod of his head, my father emptied the rest of the cool, clean water from the bucket over his feet, washing away the alcohol. Instantly, Tavit soothed to a relaxed posture and closed his eyes. My mother then brought over a wrap and tightly bound both feet individually and placed them atop a pillow.

"You're a brave kid, Tavit. Now get some rest."

My father then stood up and turned to Ara. "Ara, I think it would be best if you and Mary stayed here tonight. Don't take any unnecessary risks."

"You're right," he agreed. "And, Nadia, that includes you. You're not going anywhere. You should have *never* left the house. We'll leave tomorrow."

"I'll get some blankets," offered my mother.

With the house full of people, I tried to sleep that night but couldn't. There was a lot that I needed to accomplish, a lot that I needed to conclude. It would be a fool's game to go through life and not learn from the world and experiences around me. Every day, like I promised myself ages ago, would be my attempt into sculpting a better version of me, a strict following of my plan of continuous self-improvement, until one day, I would create exactly what I wanted. Exactly what I dreamed. This became my life goal, and I planned on stopping at nothing to make sure I met it. I hoped that, by this point, I had done a good job or at least displayed a solid attempt while trying not to ruthlessly judge myself. But, as my toughest critic, if I wanted to be the best, I had to be honest with myself.

I took a lot of inspiration from Tavit that evening. He taught me that no matter the circumstance, no matter how hard the struggle, the day will continue as long as you allow it to. Tavit could have very well found a quiet place near a boulder or a tree to relax and eventually die, but he didn't. He mustered the courage and the strength, even after witnessing his father's death, to continue. Only God knew over what roads and over what terrain he'd traveled, and for how long, on what barely qualified for feet, just to survive. From his gift, I now saw the satisfaction of a beautiful triumph after a perilous struggle, and I refused to be blind to it. I wanted it. Through his unrelenting will and his unshakable strength, Tavit, I realized, survived not for only himself but for us. He came to us as a warning. He came to warn us of the danger. To prepare us. To prepare me. What, if not that, would otherwise have been his purpose? If we were going to survive, if *I* were going to survive, I needed to defy all the odds, and Tavit lived to plant that seed into my mind, so when it grew into a full and blossoming tree, it would teach me the meaning of this undying power of will. And when the time came, I would be ready to use it.

That night, however, was not my time. The soldiers never came, and we grew evermore thankful.

Within the week, the last week of March, Tavit had regained some of his energy and a bit of his weight. He, however, still couldn't walk without help. Despite my father's efforts, an infection had unfortunately set in, and my mother spent every day thoroughly cleaning the wounds to encourage the healing process. During the nights, however, Tavit's reality settled in. At times, he would awake from a nightmarish sweat, reliving the torture that he'd been subjected to. It was a shame. My mother, being the best at consolation, therefore expanded the healing to include the mental. I was never worried about Tavit, though. I knew him well enough to know he wouldn't allow that weakness to linger in his head.

The week after, by the first week of April, after avoiding the topic for long, we finally mustered enough stamina to tell Tavit about his mother, but we dared not say anything about the details. We never did. He never knew. Tavit took the news like the man that he now was, already assuming his mother's fate long in advance. It was not easy, but it had to be done.

It became very rare to see anyone besides our own family, even more rare than before. We were, after all, isolated on a farm. Most everyone stayed to themselves from then on, except for the Sundays that we went to church. Even then, the congregation fluctuated in numbers—some days there would be more, most days there would be less.

As often as he could, Vartan still saw Nadia, but I never thought of him as someone who was good at acknowledging, or perhaps admitting, danger. As an acquired trait from my father, it seemed to have spilled over to her. So, by the second week of April, as my brother escorted Nadia over to our house, they began their plans for the wedding. I thought it to be too risky to freely prance the farm as they did, so I, on that hand, considered all the outcomes and all the possibilities that they could encounter with their behavior, frequently playing out the scenarios of the many paths that would result from the different decisions. I thought of this strategy as a defense mechanism, one on high alert, assuming Vartan had returned to his one-track mind.

"Nadia," called my mother, "Nadia, could you come here, please?"

With her quiet footsteps, Nadia found my mother in the back of the house seated near her sewing machine.

"Nadia, it's going to be a wonderful time ahead for you. Nothing would make me happier than to see you become a new light shining in our family. Congratulations, again. This is from our house to yours."

She handed her a gift.

"Please. Open it."

Trying to hold back her grandiose smile, Nadia peeled

away the thin paper wrapping and unveiled a folded cloth of striking colors. She let it fall down the length of her body—a long, fitted dress. She held it away to examine its intricate details, then placed it against her body to absorb the full effect.

"I don't know what to say. This is so beautiful." She leaned over and gave my mother a hug. "Thank you so much."

"You're worth it," she responded. "Welcome home."

<u>30</u>

It was a pleasant day. The sun was shining, and the birds were singing in celebration of another victory over the brutal winter. Even the curious spring flowers found their way to gaze at the surface of their new world. What a beautiful day in Armenia.

The calm spring breeze blew gently through the open window of my room. In the field, the apricot trees waved in the wind, and the grape vines swung freely in the air. Their scent carried far across, marinating the landscape. The oxen stood outside as defenders of our land while my father found something to fix. The scene was picturesque, and to us, this was home.

As I lay in my room, I took a moment from the world to myself and rolled over on my woolen mattress. This day was going to be a long one. I felt it. With a small swing, I took the blanket off and sat upright, rubbing my eyes with the palm of my hand, then stretched my body like a lion in the wake of the new day. The blood rushed through me like a river of molten lava.

This felt better.

I felt more awake.

Leaning forward from my bed, I peered outside my window, as if I, too, were celebrating with the birds. I narrowed my eyes from the strong sun beating through the window and thought to myself, "What a gorgeous day."

I blinked a few times to let the tears lubricate my eyes. Soon, the walls of my room came back into focus. I looked around, revealing the emptiness of the space. I looked at the small end table where my Bible used to be. I thought about my life up to this point. I thought about my friends, my family. I was a smart man, a well-respected man, a logical man. Yet, I needed refining, a well-accepted challenge. I sat, reflecting on my life, the beauty of it all.

Such a peaceful thought.

With my still sensitive eyes, I peered outside once more, and once again, I thought, "What a beautiful world God has created—the green of the trees, the rich blue of the skies, and the sweet song of the birds. How was it possible to put so much beauty into one world?"

I stood up using the bed as my support. My hands were thick and strong. I had working hands. I had callused hands. I turned my head towards the lonely chair against the wall, then reached over and grabbed my wool pants and work shirt.

Time for the new day.

From all the years of use, the wood floor creaked under my bare feet as I shifted my weight over each foot. I stood, shirtless, and let out a long sigh.

"Armen! Vartan! Are you both serious?" I heard through the hallway.

In a momentary shock, I didn't know what we'd done.

"What?" I retorted.

"You're both late!" My father opened the door to my brother's room. "Get up!" he demanded.

Vartan groaned.

The door to my room was already open so my father walked clear inside. "We agreed to this last week!" He pointed at me. "I want you out in one minute."

"For what?" I retorted.

"Church!"

"All right, you don't have to be so bossy," I answered. "You're not even ready!"

"Put on a shirt—let's go!"

He then stormed out. Quickly, I became quite irritated with my father, especially for ruining my beautiful morning. He demanded too much, and I was tired. After not going to church for several weeks, I fell out of the routine and forgot about the agreement with him. Personally, I didn't think it was a big deal. I just wanted to relax. So, taking my time in rebellion, I took off my work pants and put on my nice church pants. I was in no mood for it.

As I walked out of my room, I combed my fingers through my long, black, wavy hair, just as Vartan walked out of his, wearing his new suit. He didn't look too happy, either. We mumbled some stuff to each other and walked into the living space.

"*Paree looys*," welcomed Tavit, saying "good morning."

"Ehh, *paree looys*," I mumbled.

"What's the matter with you?" he asked.

"Nothing," I said, "I'm just hungry. How's your infection?"

"Not good," he responded. "We can't get the treatment I need, and no one knows where Dr. Thomassian is. I think it's better than before, though. I think the garlic is helping."

"Well, that's good at least. Can you walk?"

"I can, but it burns. There are boiled eggs on the counter."

I reached over and took two eggs, handed one to Vartan, and casually began peeling mine.

My father stuck his head through the window. "Let's get going, boys!"

"He is so annoying," Vartan mentioned.

"See you when we get back," I told Tavit.

"Yeah, see you," repeated Vartan.

Nonchalantly then, we walked outside, purposefully feeding into my father's anger. It was very entertaining.

"You're not going?" Vartan asked.

"No," my father answered, "your mother has another headache, and Tavit can't walk, so I'm going to stay back with them. Hurry up. You can still catch the sermon."

"Of all the days to have a headache," I thought, "it had to be on the most beautiful day of the year." I felt bad for her. I really did.

Then, after a casual walk to the barn, we made our way out and began our deliberately slow journey.

....

Der Kourken stood at the head of the church in front of the altar, facing the congregation. He looked at the faces of his community, the boys, the girls, the men, the women, their brothers, their sisters, sons, and daughters. Their family. His family. Our family. He looked at them as they sat in their sanctuary. They had come to him for answers. They had come to him for safety, for shelter in a time when they didn't have it. They came to him to escape the brutality and to ask for forgiveness, but not for themselves.

They came to him, and he was ready.

"Jesus Christ, our Lord and savior," he announced, "today, the good day of our Lord, Sunday, April 24th, 1915."

Der Kourken opened his small brown Bible and began reading.

> Jesus left that place and entered their synagogue; a man was there with a withered hand, and they asked him, "Is it lawful to cure on the Sabbath?" so that they might accuse him. He said to them, "Suppose one of you has only one sheep and it falls into a pit on the Sabbath; will you not lay hold of it and lift it out? How much more valuable is a human being than a sheep! So it is lawful—"

Abruptly then, the heavy wooden doors flung open, filling the church with a reverberating and hollow sound. Five Turkish soldiers entered on horseback, rifles in their holsters and daggers at their sides. In the front, leading them, was the bearded soldier.

Miralai Barçin.

Colonel Barçin.

The colonel.

The congregation turned to look and shrieked.

"Please," Der Kourken urged as he raised his voice to speak over the sounds of the crowd, "stay calm!"

To an extent, they listened, especially when the soldiers simply sat in the back and waited. Colonel Barçin, with a terrifyingly calm demeanor, then motioned for Der Kourken to carry on with his sermon. Uneasily, as his people sat in discomfort, he continued:

> "So it is lawful to do good on the Sabbath." Then he said to the man, "Stretch out your hand." He stretched it out, and it was restored, as sound as the other. But the Pharisees went out and conspired against him, how to destroy him.

"Amen," he finished, "Matthew chapter 12, verses nine to fourteen." He then closed his Bible and held it at his side for a moment.

Speaking still nervously, he began, "In our time on this planet, this world,"—he cleared his throat—"we must make many decisions. Not all will be good, not all will be bad, but all will be made. Should that man from the passage save his sheep, even if it means breaking the law of the Sabbath? Jesus answers yes. He says that by not saving the sheep, by not doing good when it is in your power to do so, it is the same as doing evil, even if it falls on the Sabbath."

Still atop their large horses, the soldiers now began moving down the center aisle, the same aisle where many brides and their grooms had walked down before, where many of the deceased had made their final exit, calmly studying each person they passed.

Two soldiers stayed behind.

The congregation began talking among themselves, and their different voices filled the chamber.

"Please stay calm!" Der Kourken yelled in Armenian. "Stay calm and forgive. Do not make any judgments. Let us see what they want!"

A few individuals, however, rushed in an attempt to leave, but were stopped by the two soldiers guarding the exit. Even if they'd tried to fight, it would've been useless against cavalry.

The three soldiers atop their horses, still being led by Colonel Barçin, slowly carried on. The steady sound of the horses' hooves partly on the stone floor echoed an unfamiliar sound for the setting as the soldiers sneered bitterly at the people they passed. Stopping short just in front of our priest, the colonel then dismounted and stepped up onto the altar.

"You are hereby under arrest by orders from Constantinople," he announced in Ottoman Turkish.

"Under what terms?" Der Kourken asked as if a wave of confidence had struck him over.

"For operating and running a center of sedition," he replied, "and treason."

The chamber boomed with disbelief and aggravation as the community rose to their feet. Throwing their fists up in despair, they yelled and swore at the soldiers but were forced back to their spots after the soldiers drew their weapons. The colonel then grabbed Der Kourken's tunic by the sleeve, but he stood firm and pulled it back.

"I can manage," he cooperated, despite the fabrication of the useless charges against him.

The colonel stood back to let Der Kourken step down. He slightly lifted his tunic and stepped off the altar, walking past the other soldiers. Firmly clutching his Bible, he began his way down the aisle. The soldiers walked closely behind and pushed him to move faster as the congregation watched in vain. Stopping at the closed doors of the exit, they waited as Der Kourken placed his palms against the wood, one on each side. Looking down to the floor, he said a word to himself, then, using his weight, he leaned in, revealing first a sliver of light, then the full barrage of the sun's rays. Without regret, he took his first step outside, letting his pupils adjust to the intensity. The soldiers pushed him forward once more. After taking a few balancing steps, he glared at the scene—the prefect of police, his squad, and over fifty Ottoman troops in front of him, the full cavalry, sitting at arms on horseback. With the doors now wide open, the congregation scrambled out, squeezing past the guards and bumping into Der Kourken along the way. Some slipped and fell as they all unknowingly ran directly into the lion's den. One by one, the soldiers raised their arms and systematically shot at the unarmed civilians like wild deer. To his left and to his right, they fell, completely indiscriminate of age or gender. Der Kourken cupped his hands over his ears at the deafening sound of the rifle shots, and he yelled and begged them to stop. In a few short minutes, what used to be a green and fertile land now became spotted and scattered with lifeless bodies. The soldiers nearest our priest then dismounted from their horses and lowered their shoulders to push the doors shut, even as the last brave ones squeezed themselves through the shrinking gap.

From inside, the congregation pounded and screamed as the soldiers used the full weight of their bodies to keep them in. The policeman then carried over a heavy chain, spun it through the handles of the doors, and locked it solid with an iron padlock.

Doors secured, the soldiers stepped away and kicked Der Kourken to the ground. The policemen tied one end of a thinly braided rope around his waist and the other end to a horse. A soldier on top then kicked his heels against the horse's side and dragged him through the dirt and between the bodies to a distance away from the church as if putting on a show. There, they stopped only after the rope snapped over a sharp rock. The soldier then dismounted, and four more soldiers rode in around him, including the colonel. They gave him a few seconds, so he could catch his breath. Wiping the dirt from his face and combing it out of his beard, Der Kourken then stood up, Bible still firmly in his hands. Casually, he brushed the dirt and clumps of mud off his black tunic and shifted his bare feet to admire the world around him. He noted the soldiers' positions: two standing at his sides, one behind him, the colonel in front, a fifth outlier, and the rest surrounding his church. He watched them as they sat, waiting patiently for orders.

"Kneel," Colonel Barçin commanded.

Der Kourken stood and faced forward. His face burned and stung from the scrapes over the rocks. He heard the instructions clearly but didn't obey.

"Kneel!"

Still, he did not kneel.

Exchanging a glance with the one in back, the colonel casually signaled an order with a slight tilt of his chin. They had no intention of keeping this man alive. The soldier then unsheathed his sword and, as if cutting through rope, sliced through Der Kourken's tunic, completely severing the tendons behind his knees. He screamed in pain and fell forward, kneeling, using his knuckles for support. He clenched his fingers tighter around his small brown Bible and closed his eyes.

"Christ, my Lord," he whispered, "forgive these men for—"

The colonel began laughing. "Christ? Where is your Christ?" he asked, looking in all directions. "Where is he? I don't see him."

His men joined him in laughter.

"Look at your people! Look at them!" he yelled as he pointed to the church, where the doors clanged and the people desperately pounded for their freedom. "Tell your Lord to save them—save you! Have him *strike* me down. Strike us *all* down!"

"Please," Der Kourken cried as he pushed himself up, "they have done nothing wrong."

Without response, Colonel Barçin then reached for the Bible and tried to pry it out of Der Kourken's hands. Der Kourken, however, tightened his grip, using his body as a shield, and pulled it closer to his body. When Colonel Barçin struggled, the soldier in back thrust a dagger fully into Der Kourken's kidney so hard that it could have emerged out from the front. Der Kourken opened his eyes wide and screamed. He arched his back and reached for the wound, instantly unraveling his fingers and dropping the book. On the ground, the Bible lay open, revealing the Armenian letters to the sky. Colonel Barçin looked at the pages, at the letters, then leaned over to pick it up. He measured the weight of it with his hands and thumbed through it as Der Kourken cried in pain.

"Give that back," he begged. "Please."

The colonel curled his lips, causing his nostrils to flare, and nodded his head. The soldiers at his sides then grabbed Der Kourken's arms and pulled them out wide. The soldier in back grabbed Der Kourken's shoulders and pushed his knee into the open wound. The blood dripped down the soldier's leg, staining it red. Der Kourken grinded his teeth and flared his nostrils in agony.

"Open his mouth," he commanded, "this slave."

With his arms stretched wide, the soldier in back grabbed hold of Der Kourken's hair and pulled it straight back. The fifth soldier standing to the side then walked into the mix and pulled his long beard straight down. They pulled his head so far back and his beard so far down that the whiskers broke free from his chin, forcing the soldier to let go and readjust his grip. It took four men, and yet, Der Kourken didn't open his mouth. The soldiers at his sides then pulled his arms wider, making it seem as if they could be ripped out of their sockets at any moment. Using his body's full momentum, Colonel Barçin then thrust his fist into Der Kourken's abdomen, just under the ribs. Der Kourken coughed a spurt of blood onto the ground and onto the colonel's tall, black boots. He tried falling but was caught by the soldiers extending his arms. Thus, he sagged his head down onto his chest, letting the blood from his mouth drip onto his tunic. The colonel then took a step back and commanded them to try once more as he calmly tore a page out of Der Kourken's Bible, balled it up, and let it fall to the earth. The soldier behind then pulled his hair back once again, and the soldier in front twisted the beard around his fingers and pulled his beard straight down. There was not much fight left for such a peaceful man, and so the soldiers managed to finish what they started. With a ravaging glare only a madman could make, the colonel then reached deep into Der Kourken's mouth, pulled out his tongue, sandwiching it between the Bible and his thumb, and cut it off. The colonel then thrust the Bible into Der Kourken's face and walked away.

The soldiers at his sides then let go of Der Kourken's arms, and the one in back kicked him forward. He barely caught himself as he fell on all fours and tried wiping the blood with his shaking hands. The soldier to his right side then unsheathed his sword, raised it into the air, and swung it down ruthlessly. It sliced cleanly through to the other side and became stuck in the nearly dry mud, forcing him to twist it loose. Immediately, Der Kourken's shoulders sagged and his body fell forward as his elbows buckled under the dead weight.

And Vartan and I got there just in time to watch it happen.

From behind a tree, we watched as the soldiers laughed pitilessly at the headless body. We watched as Colonel Barçin leaned over and picked up Der Kourken's head by the beard and held it upside down. With the pages of the Bible still littered on the ground, he finally mounted his head on an old branch and stuck the branch into the ground on display in front of the church.

Then, forming a thick perimeter around the church, the soldiers doused the walls and grass with kerosene as the congregation continued to push and pry at the doors. It rattled and clanked as they tried to escape their new prison. With the drop of ten or eleven lit branches, the soldiers then ignited the fluid. Instantly, the kerosene burst into flames as tall as the trees, forming a wall of fire around the stone structure. In seconds, what used to be a calm sanctuary for prayer and reflection became a heated oven from which there was no escape.

Not a moment later, a brass candlestick flew through the top window, glimmering brightly in the sun as it turned and rolled and spun in the air, sending shards of glass in all directions, and landed on the fiery ground just outside. The thick smoke quickly hurled out from the new opening and carried with it the screams of the hundreds of men, women, and children, each crying and begging for their lives. Deaf to the suffering and the anguish, the soldiers, however, ignored their pleas. It was a horror unlike I'd ever heard, followed by a horror unlike I'd ever seen. A horror that I could never describe with words. A horror that I wished to forget.

I remember that day, the day the world caught fire.

Not realizing the significance of my next move, I sprung up from the ground and tried running to the church to free those who were still alive, unsure as to how, but Vartan pulled me back with all he had, clinging to me like an anchor on a ship.

"What are you doing?" he screamed. "Don't go!"

"Those people," I cried. "We need to open the doors! Let go of me!"

I kicked and squirmed, but Vartan had a solid grip on both my legs. Eventually, I fell, and we scurried on the ground.

"We're defenseless!" he cried. "Don't do it. You'll die!"

Just as Vartan finished his last few words, two or three soldiers turned their horses towards our location. Peering over, they found us and called upon each other. It was now a race to the death.

"Dammit! Look what you did!" he screamed.

Dashing to our horse, we sprung up onto it and quickly galloped west towards home. Just as quickly as we started, however, Vartan changed his mind.

"We can't go home! We'll lead them there!"

And thus, we changed our heading north.

Putting my head down, I tried erasing my memories. I tried erasing the screams, the roaring of the fire. The sound of death.

I tried and I failed.

After the bloody and undignified beheading of our priest followed by a massacre of my people, Vartan and I lost our bearing and rode chaotically without direction, desperately trying to escape, desperately trying to survive, until we arrived at the outskirts of the main city, Kharpert. As the horse slowed, we jumped off, and Vartan turned it around and hit its back end, scaring it off in the opposite direction.

"Why did you do that?" I criticized.

"In case they're still following us, we need a diversion."

"We don't have a horse now!"

"We'll find another one," he replied. "Don't worry. Let's go."

Casually, we hurried into the city streets to blend in with the crowds. In case any soldiers recognized us as witnesses, we grabbed two blankets hanging on a banister and draped them over our heads. A few soldiers on horseback galloped in and spoke to each other. I couldn't hear what they said, but one pointed in our direction. My heart skipped a beat as he walked towards us to the loaves of bread behind me.

As calmly as we could, we walked past many people, none of whom said a word. They walked with their heads low and mouths shut. Sad and depressed, they looked as if they were walking the streets of a city taken over by an enemy. A very unnerving and eerie feeling encircled us, and I hated it. It was nothing like before. No one spoke. No one laughed. No one waved hello.

They all seemed… afraid.

Following the main road east, we kept our heads low the entire way. We never once looked to our right. We never looked to our left, and we never once looked up. Like the rest of them, we kept our heads down and walked. I didn't know where we were going or why. I didn't care. All I knew was that we were being chased by an army that killed unarmed women and children. I didn't know what else the soldiers were capable of, and I didn't want to find out. Eventually, as the road turned to cobblestone, I knew we had gotten to the town square—the center of town. We walked through it to the other side until a pair of black leather boots stepped into my path.

I raised my head slightly to look. The sun, not yet at its peak, shone from behind him—a Turkish soldier, not much taller than me. The sun's rays glared into my eyes as I saw his face—a kid, not much older than me.

"Drop the head shawls," he ordered. "Women wear shawls."

We slipped the blankets down onto our shoulders.

"Where are you going?" he asked me in Ottoman Turkish.

I shivered with fear.

"Where are you going?" he asked again.

"We're looking for our grandmother," replied Vartan.

The soldier looked at my brother.

"I did not ask you," he said. "I asked him." He pointed the butt of his rifle and quickly shifted his eyes back onto me.

I tried not to look back.

"For a third time, where are you going?" he repeated.

"We're l-looking for our grandm-m-other," I answered.

He paused. "How old are you boys?"

"I'm seventeen and he's fifteen," replied Vartan.

We held our breath.

"Well, your grandmother is not here; turn around and go back."

He pointed behind us and stood firmly at his position, ensuring that we would obey his orders.

"Yes, sir," I said.

Nervousness had taken over my mind, but I also felt more at ease knowing that Vartan and I weren't recognized. As the soldier kindly asked, we kept the head shawls off, turned around, and started walking back in the other direction.

After a few steps, however, we stopped.

I couldn't bear to continue through the cobblestone square. It wasn't fair. It wasn't believable—the hastily arranged wooden support beams, triangular at the ends. I followed my eyes up them, the old tree trunks, stripped bare of their bark. I then focused my eyes on their feet, then to their knees, to their legs, their torsos, then to their heads. I looked at their faces. I recognized most of them. The professors—my professors—the lawyers, the doctors, the leaders of our community. Anyone with an influence. Anyone who could make a difference. The scholars. The intellectuals. The ones who had warned us of the increased violence but failed to predict to what coordinated scale—all hanging along the same crossbeam, next to one another in the center of their own community, high above the cobblestone square.

We had unknowingly walked right past them.

"Oh God, please," I said to myself, "this is not happening. This *can't* be happening."

I closed my eyes and opened them back, and the sights, as usual, had not changed.

"Get moving," the soldier pushed.

My heart raced, and the flame inside my heart, sparked from the old man's clapping hands, burned molten hot and spilled over, coating my organs, saturating them with boiling conflict. I began to hyperventilate, unable to control the power. My hands turned to fists as it fed into my veins. It muffled my ears and narrowed my eyes. My muscles tensed and coiled, much like before. I couldn't stand still any longer. I wanted to move, but I didn't. Just as new to this world that had changed so suddenly, the flame remained still young. It needed to be fed, to be adjusted. To mature. It needed to grow and develop before I could use it to its fullest potential, and I knew that. For that exact moment, however, it sufficed until Vartan grabbed hold of my arm. The touch of his hand immediately brought me back to reality, forcing the flame into a short-lived dormancy, a temporary remission. My eyes relaxed and my fists loosened.

"Armen, let's go." He pulled me forward.

Keeping a steady face, I walked past the Ottoman Turkish soldiers standing at arms near the wooden support beams and next to them, the Germans. Their emotionless expressions. Their heartless demeanors. The Turks stood as if protecting their trophies—the bodies of our leaders, of all the people who had something good to say. Their drooping heads now stared down at me in silence. Dr. Thomassian among them. All killed that same morning. Their bodies tormented. Tortured. The sickening display curled my stomach, and I felt a tear roll down my cheek, and then two, and then a steady stream as I pushed past the unimaginable. What had these people done? What possible debt had they had on society to warrant such a cruel end?

For that instant, I felt guilty for my existence. I felt guilty for being who I was and afraid to be myself. There were so many people against me, there were so many people against *my* people, that I almost had no choice but to imagine that I, that we, had done something so terribly wrong. I thought long and hard as my mind raced at an abysmal speed. I thought about our collective history, our contributions, and our intellect. I focused on every dent, every scratch, that Armenians could have made on the Ottoman Empire but failed to find one shred of evidence, one bit of falsehood, to merit such a humiliating end, such a humiliating feeling of defeat.

And then, it suddenly made sense.

There was nothing to understand about the seemingly sudden escalation. It was all very simple. These people had done nothing wrong. They were innocent. Every reason for their death was simply a lie, a grossly forged version of the truth, generated by the government and fed to their people who mindlessly accepted it. The framework of society, as I thought I knew, was weak. It took so much effort to build and so little to destroy. In a few hours, with the destruction of our voice, the Young Turks toppled everything our society stood for, collapsing it in its entirety. Armenians weren't the cause of the demise of the Ottoman Empire. We never were. We weren't a direct threat to the future of Turkey. We weren't in league with the enemy. We weren't conspiring against the government. This wasn't even about taxes. We were being killed; we were being tortured; this was happening to us, to our future, *because we were Armenian.* There was no other reason for this gruesome endeavor, this government-sponsored, systematic execution of an entire race of people. This genocide. Our genocide. The Armenian Genocide, a heinous ploy, derived entirely from an unprovoked situation.

I tried wrapping my mind around it, but no other explanation was believable as I walked down the road, past the burned shops and destroyed businesses with broken windows and looted merchandise—the piles of furniture, sewing machines, beds, and clothes, the upturned traders' carts, and the rotting food, scattered over the city streets. The livelihood of the craftsmen, the skill and expertise of our people, the carpenters, the bakers, tailors. The middle class. The post office, the restaurants, all boarded up and shut down "By Order of the Ottoman Turkish Government at Constantinople" as I read so many times.

There was not one good soldier there that day. Not Turkish, not German. None that I saw. Not one at our church, not one in the city. Not one had the courage to stand against this atrocity, this crime against humanity and civilization. Not one had the courage to stop it. Not one had the audacity to speak out against something so terrible that a word describing it hadn't even been created yet.

Once at the western edge of town and out of sight from the soldiers, Vartan and I ran. We ran for our lives; we ran for ourselves, for the lives of all who had been lost. We ran together, slowing down only to let the other catch up. We ran and ran the entire way home, the only place we had left to go—the only place where innocence hadn't lost its meaning.

. . . .

My mother sat on the porch. It was early afternoon. She closed her eyes and breathed in the crisp air in an attempt to soothe her terrible headache. The nerves traveled up her neck and into her head. Her eyelids grew heavier as the pressure in her forehead eased, and the flow of blood carried the headache away. She exhaled and opened her eyes.

Next to my mother, Nadia stood majestically. Her long brown hair flowed gently in the wind, and her pale green eyes sparkled softly under the sun. Her long fitted dress waved as gracefully as ripples in a pond.

"That dress looks so good on you," my mother complimented.

Nadia smiled.

Just then, Vartan and I burst into their sight, out of breath and still in our church clothes.

"They're all dead!" Vartan screamed in a crying panic.

"Oh my God, they're all dead! I don't care what you say! We're going to leave!"

Not too far away, my father ran to us to understand the nonsense he heard. Suddenly then, in the distance, the haunting sound of machine gun fire echoed through the air. My father stopped dead in his tracks and listened. Still seated in her chair, my mother jumped, shocked by the surprise. She looked towards the origin of the gunshots. The west. Soon after, a woman's deafening scream spread over the land, followed by two more gunshots. With each shot, my mother blinked and jumped a little more. Nadia did the same. My father ran a few more steps, then stopped again. He gazed at the direction of the sound. Even the remaining farm animals scurried out in different directions, sensing that something wasn't right.

We stood, trying to catch our breath, and listened.

My mother looked around and eventually focused on the hill to the south. "Tevos!" she yelled to my father. "Soldiers!"

A few hundred meters out, two soldiers sat on horseback, and five stood on foot, all of them in full uniform, complete with their red fez hats, and armed with pistols and daggers hanging at their waists. The five foot soldiers marched towards our house, and the ones on horseback stayed behind. My father narrowed his eyes and examined the situation. He was quick to make judgments, but he usually ended up being correct.

"Hasmig, Vartan, Armen, go inside, now!" he yelled.

He turned to Nadia. "You should go inside, too. We don't know what these soldiers want."

"I need to go home and warn my family," she responded.

"It's not safe. Please, Nadia, just go inside," my father repeated with his stern voice.

He was serious and we knew it.

"I need to warn them," repeated Nadia. "I'm sorry."

Then, as the soldiers marched closer and moved only faster, Nadia picked up the bottom of her dress and started running west towards her house, which was only a thirty-minute walk from ours. Seeing her do so, one soldier pointed to her direction, signaling to the others. He unholstered his pistol and cocked it back.

"Nadia!" my father screamed. "Nadia, run!"

Without hesitation, the soldier shot his weapon and missed.

Two soldiers then quickly broke away from the formation, including the one who shot, and began pursuit after her. My father saw this and so did Vartan. Nadia turned to look and gasped, then ran faster than she'd ever run, as if God had given her wings to fly. My father quickly ran inside the house and emerged immediately after. He ran towards the soldiers to try to intercept them and give Nadia a head start. I've never seen him run as fast as he did. He moved like the wind, like a bird in the sky. Vartan, realizing my father's plan, also ran towards the soldiers. I, on the other hand, simply stood, frozen with indecision.

After managing to catch up with Nadia, the soldiers knocked her to the ground. She kicked and screamed, trying to escape, but they held her down and forcefully lifted her dress, smiling perversely.

Just then, like an eagle picking out a fish from the sea, Vartan, surpassing my father's glide, lowered his shoulder and dug it firmly into the soldier's gut, sweeping him clear off of Nadia's body. His red fez hat flew off his head as his face smashed into Vartan's upper back. The soldier flew through the air and landed on his back with a hollow thud, temporarily knocking the wind out of him. And, like a wrecking ball against a building, my father crashed into the second soldier shortly after, driving him to the ground next to Vartan. They collided into each other as they rolled and swore. They grappled and punched as their noses bloodied and their shirts tore. This wasn't just a wrestling match anymore.

Someone was going to die.

Through the mess, Nadia managed to stand but hesitated to continue her way, seeming as though she wanted to help but didn't know how.

"Just run!" my father yelled from the ground.

Now as her decision maker, Nadia listened and continued her escape.

With a subtle snap, one soldier pulled his pistol out of the holster. Before he had a chance to use it, however, Vartan used his strength and flung it out of the soldier's hand. It fired in the air and spun in circles before landing on the ground a few meters away. The soldier lunged for it, but Vartan held him back by his legs, much like how he held me back before.

Then, reaching behind to his lower back, my father pulled out a dagger—Vartan's dagger. He grasped it tightly by the ivory-colored handle and kicked the soldier off him. He then sprung up, following his motion, and shoved it into the soldier's chest, straight through the heart. Without hesitation, he then jumped over Vartan, who still pulled upon the soldier's legs, and stuck the blade into his back. The soldier grumbled and wheezed as my father got up on one leg and steadied his knee onto the soldier's spine. He then placed his palm on the man's forehead, pulled back his head, and sliced his throat, letting the body slump down right after. In seconds, both soldiers were dead.

My father wiped the dagger onto the grass and sheathed it. He extended his arm so that he could help Vartan to his feet just as three muffled shots vibrated powerfully, one after the next. Like a rock thrown off a cliff, my father fell to the ground next to Vartan. He patted and searched his torso to see if he'd been shot. He hadn't. Vartan then patted and searched his own body as well, mimicking his father's actions. He hadn't been shot, either. Keeping his head down, my father searched the land for the source of the shots only to discover the three other soldiers dead on the grass, barely ten meters away. He then traced the path of the bullets to the barn, where my mother stood in the doorway with the rifle in her hand. He smiled at the relieving sight and clambered up with his son. He then ran towards her, and Vartan, with his new suit encrusted with dirt, ran after Nadia.

Before my father slid onto the dusty barn floor, he kissed his savior in passing. That's the only gratitude there was time for. With the two layers of burlap already removed, he lifted the trap door and took out the two pistols and hung the bandolier from his one shoulder and across his chest. He put one pistol in the back seam of his pants and stood by the edge of the barn with the other.

"Get down, Armen!" he screamed out.

I ran out south, following the edge of the barn and laid flat. My father scoped our land, focusing on the two soldiers on horseback, still sitting on the top of the southern hill. They turned around and marched back in the other direction. My father watched them do so and grabbed my mother's hand and ran with her inside the house. He took the rifle from her and slung it over his shoulder, placing the second pistol next to the first.

"Let's go!" he demanded before he leaned over and picked up Tavit from off the sofa to make his way towards the door.

"Hasmig, let's go."

Just as he was about to step outside, with Tavit in his arms, a new score of soldiers appeared over the horizon. Over thirty of them on foot and on horseback. All of them armed.

"*Hyreeg!*" I screamed from the ground.

Just as he took one step onto the porch, a bullet raced past my father's face and dug deeply into my mother's head, knocking her back inside. She fell immediately at the doorstep, dropping everything she had in her hands.

I screamed for my mother and sprung up towards her. My father, however, roared harder and louder than I've ever heard.

"*Armen!*" he cried. "*Stay there!*"

I slid to a halt and fell down as a bullet hit the ground near me. I laid back, flat on my stomach, and covered my head with my hands. Pinned, I didn't even bother getting up.

In that instant, my father threw Tavit back onto the sofa and stooped over to his wife. He placed his two fingers on her neck and felt for a pulse.

Nothing.

He then glared up at the sight ahead of him. His heart

pure. His mind ready. He studied the line of soldiers marching towards him. He stood up and straightened his body. The nerves in his neck electrified his reflexes. The blood in his veins boiled, and his heart slowed to an impossible speed. This was *his* family, in *his* house, on *his* land, and he would defend it at all costs. It was no longer just a plan. He now knew what he had to do. He had found his meaning.

One calm bullet at a time, my father loaded his rifle. Then, with a steady arm, he raised it eye level, held his breath, sharpening his instinct, and made the sign of the cross. Finally, he stepped off the porch.

Before his boot even hit the ground, my father had already fired a shot. Completely out of sync with each successive step, he continued firing at a remarkable rate. With spot-on accuracy, he fired that weapon in ways I didn't know a rifle could be fired. He shot to his left. He shot to his right, and, like clockwork, the Turkish soldiers fell to the ground. Some from their horses, some from their feet. The sound echoed loudly as they returned fire. Just three or four meters in, a bullet found its way into my father's upper abdomen. Blood spurt out through his shirt, and he cringed. My father, however, didn't fall. Instead, he kept the rifle steady and smiled a gregarious and insane smile, revealing his bloody teeth.

One after the other, the casings flew out of the chamber, landing on the green grass below him, leaving none to go to waste. He stepped to his right as the empty casings continued to fly out, until he finally ran out of ammunition. Throwing himself onto his stomach, he picked at the bandolier across his chest to try to reload. In the process, however, a second bullet grazed his left shoulder, sending fragments of his shirt out like a puff of smoke. He did nothing to acknowledge it. Neither in the form of a single word nor in the form of a single twitch on his face. He simply finished reloading and fired again at the soldiers from his now prone position. Before long, his weapon drew blanks once again. The soldiers, too, reloaded as they moved closer. Once they started again, they now aimed in a different location, a place too close for comfort, to a teenage boy hiding in the grass. And, from the ground, my father saw them do it.

The soldiers had found me.

Thus, my father ditched the unloaded rifle and thrust himself up with his arms and reached behind his pants. He took out one pistol and pointed it at them, swearing as strategically as the bullets he fired. They fell just meters from where I lay as my father distracted them, diverting them away. To protect me. As they continued firing back, the bullets shattered the windows of our house behind, turning the walls into dust. Just then, a third bullet grazed my father's leg, and a fourth pierced through his right shoulder. My father, yet, didn't fall. He continued his pace until a fifth passed through the wrist of his right hand, shattering the bone on impact and ejecting the pistol. With his good left hand, he reached behind him, grabbed the second pistol, and continued firing without ever skipping a beat, leading them farther away from where I lay. A sixth bullet then swiftly pierced his upper leg, then a seventh through his shin and out the calf of the other. Alas, after seven attempts, my father finally fell to the ground. His body bubbled out with a copious amount of blood as each of his many wounds pulsated with fury. Despite the immense danger, I ran out to him. I needed to.

He was still alive.

"My son, my son," he mumbled.

"You knew this would happen, didn't you?" I screamed in vain. "*Didn't you*?!"

"Look at me, Armen, please," he whispered. "I'm dying."

"That's why you sent little Margaret to America! That's why you were arguing with Mama! You wanted her to go, too!"

"I didn't think—I didn't imagine this. Never like this. Not to this extent. This, Armen, is a mass… extermination… but not for you. You will survive."

My father reached behind him and pulled out the dagger.

"I know… who you are. I know what you can do. You need to find it in you. Take it." He pushed the dagger towards me.

"But I can't—I don—"

I tried to speak but couldn't. I didn't even know which words to put together in a time like this.

"You already know how to use it. Please, Armen, find your brother. There's no time."

Peering over my shoulder, I saw the soldiers.

"Never hesitate," he breathed. "Save—"

With one last exertion of the energy he had left, my father extended his burly arm and grabbed my collar with his bloodied hand, the good one. Wanting to make sure I heard him, he pulled me towards him as hard as he could. I glared into his blood-ridden eyes, barely able to see past my own tears. Leaning his head up one last centimeter towards my ear, he said good-bye in the only way he knew how.

Thus, with his final breath, he whispered to me.

"Save us."

Then his arm went limp, and he closed his eyes for the last time.

Thinking I could revive him, I shook him and pulled him aggressively, unaccepting of the sacrifice, but the circumstance wouldn't allow for it, so I knelt in my spot and screamed out loud, louder than I've ever screamed as I cried harder than I've ever cried. I wanted to give up, to let go entirely. I wanted to die, just like my father, just like my mother, but I couldn't.

Something wouldn't let me.

In that instant, amid my primitive bawl, the flame inside me erupted, drying my tears and clearing my vision. It had returned from its dormancy. It rekindled my courage and tested my boundaries with a reach far greater than before, with a longer, continuing effect. It worked through my head, my hands, and my feet. As powerful as ever, it changed me into a man of principle, transforming me into one who needed to face the truth. It then forced my body into a great bound as I removed the bandolier from around my father's chest and leaped towards the rifle that rested between the blades of grass. It was beginning to control me. Slinging it over my shoulder, I sprinted towards the house as the bullets raced past my ears. I ran to the west side of it, nearest the apricot trees, passing my fallen mother along the way. I tried not look at her, but I did. Her golden face, now painted with blood. All I wanted to do was give her one last kiss, and I couldn't even do that.

"Tavit!" I screamed as I ran through the back door. "Tavit, let's go!" I yelled again.

I ran to the living space to Tavit, to poor Tavit who couldn't walk, the kid who'd been tortured, who sat comfortably on the sofa. Seeing only the back of his head, I yelled his name again. Yet, he sat quietly, entirely unresponsive. So I ran in front to face him and took one good look.

One last look.

The last few minutes of my life were so shocking, so shamefully appalling, so disgraceful, that I didn't even know what other emotions I had left to express, so I took hold of the small wooden table by the front door, picked it up over my head, and smashed it down onto the floor. I did the same with the chair. I did it again and again until there were no more pieces left to break, until a bullet kicked the last unbreakable piece spinning out of my raised hand. Tavit wanted to be a chef. He liked to play cards. Now, he became the youngest person I ever knew to die... and alone. He was only fifteen. I tried refuting it all, wishing that I were sleeping solely so my dreams would set me free from this nightmare. Why was I spared? Why did he die? Why did *anyone* die? Trying to convince myself that everything was fine, I even tried to imagine Tavit's jokes and his laughs that followed. I tried to imagine my mother's voice and my father's demands. All that, however, was deemed as an impossibility as I now glared at my best friend, sitting on the blood-soaked sofa with his pale skin and slumped posture.

With the rifle over my shoulder and the dagger in the waist of my church pants, I wandered around in rage, knowing that I could only save myself now. Then, as if a miraculous sign, a sent message, the black-and-white photograph, delicately balancing on the edge of the fireplace, caught my eye. Remembering what my father told me, I reached for it, but a bullet denting the floor told me otherwise, so I left it there and jumped to my room. There, I grabbed my leather satchel, the floppy brown one held shut by a rod and loop. I needed to find my brother. He needed my help. Thus, with only the satchel draped across my chest, I hurled myself through the back door, commencing my sprint towards Nadia's house.

From about fifty yards away, I stopped and watched from the grassy plain as Vartan struggled to keep her outside. She fought and kicked just to get past him, but he held her back, so she wouldn't go in. He tried desperately to hold her, but there was only so much he could do. Eventually, Nadia twisted free and wrenched through the door of her house to the sight, first of gold-rimmed glasses on the floor, then of something no person should ever see—her hanged parents, bodies riddled with bullets. Whether they were hanged then shot or shot then hanged didn't prevent Nadia from the bellowing screams and cries that spread across the land like a fog. Following her in, Vartan grabbed hold of her with one arm and carried her back outside over his shoulder, closing the door with another. Trying to escape it all, she threw a fanatical tantrum and flung herself all over him. With both arms firmly around her, he closed his eyes to focus on his one task. Nadia, however, cried and cried and cried like I've never seen anyone cry before. She cried so hard that I thought her lungs would give out, until her legs gave out, until Vartan let her slide to the ground where she cried some more.

"Nadia, please, you have to stop," he told her consolingly.

Wiping my face free of the sweat and tears out of my blood-ridden eyes, I prepared myself and ran down to them.

"Nadia, you have to stand up," I advised, setting the rifle against the far wall of the house. "There's no time."

I peered over my shoulder.

Slowly, she began to calm down. Tears still streaming, she crept up to her feet and wiped the ocean from her eyes. They were so red. So painfully swollen.

She tried to speak, to say something, but there remained nothing to expel. It took every ounce of energy to cry the way she cried, and thus Vartan and I formed a wall around her to let her know we were there, so she wouldn't have to go through this alone.

"It's all right," I said, still trembling.

We put our heads together and composed ourselves in the security of each other's arms. Vartan glanced at me, asking the one question he didn't want to know the answer to. I shook my head no. Understanding, he ground his teeth and pulled Nadia's head firmly into his shoulder.

Just then, a familiar hollow thud caught my attention—the kind only a boot could make over a wooden floor. I steadied my ears to it as it slowly crept towards us and eased my grip from the pack. Sure enough, someone was inside the house.

Vartan, now attuned to the amounting danger, tiptoed just out and to the side of the front door and waited.

"The rifle," he mouthed nervously as he pointed to it leaning against the same wall, farther down from him.

I took a few short steps towards it when, abruptly, the front door swung wide open followed by a man's yell. Pointing a pistol, a Turkish soldier jumped out at Nadia. She shrieked. Vartan, with his unbelievable reflexes, then hit the soldier's wrist, knocking the pistol clear out of it. He then used his own weight and pulled the soldier to the ground.

I looked at Vartan. I looked at the soldier. I looked at the rifle. Then I remembered the dagger—the closest weapon to me. With a nervous reach behind my back, I grabbed it and unsheathed it from the leather. My hands shook so much, however, that I dropped it on the ground. I wasn't ready for this. It wasn't my time. Vartan, seeing it fall, grabbed it without hesitation and thrust it into the soldier's gut, slicing the wound larger as he pulled it out. Immediately, blood spewed over his hands and black pants. So much, in fact, that there seemed to be more on Vartan than in the soldier. Grasping the lesion in disbelief, the soldier fell to the ground. Vartan then stepped over him, knocked away his red fez hat, and killed him just as my father had. Like paint, the blood smeared his new suit jacket and white button-down shirt. Not a moment after, three additional soldiers ran out the same front door. In a thirsty rage, Vartan lunged at them and killed them equally the same where they stood.

With his new suit dirtied and drenched in blood, Vartan stood in his spot, petrified. He huffed and panted, clearly out of breath. Nadia and I stared at him in disbelief. We had no idea he was capable of this, and by the looks of it, neither did he. Trying to keep his eyes up, he briefly studied the result of his fury. He looked at each of them, the fallen soldiers lying around him, appendages bent in on themselves in impossible ways, faces to the dirt, uniforms undone, boots untied, and blood, so much blood, everywhere. He then peered down at his hands, covered with the same red liquid. They shook uncontrollably. None of us knew what to say. None of us knew what to do.

As if a wave of guilt struck him, Vartan then unwound his fingers and dropped the dagger to the ground, seemingly as though he hated himself, as if the sound of his own name sickened him for what he did. He then knelt in his place, and for the second time in his life, he wept. He wept for himself, he wept for our parents, for Nadia's parents, and he wept for the soldiers. He then cried to God in anger and in sadness for throwing him into a situation like this.

Vartan was seventeen years old, almost eighteen, when he first killed a man.

I put my hand on his shoulder, on his blood-saturated suit jacket, and knelt with him. Nadia did, too.

"It's enough," I spoke softly. "We need to keep moving."

Brushing the crusty long hair out of his eyes, he stood up on his own. Nadia ran and grabbed the rifle as I remained balanced on one knee to wipe the dagger against the blades of grass. I sheathed it and dropped it into my satchel, securing the flap with the rod and loop and draping it across my torso soon after. Together then, we ran. We didn't know why. We didn't know where. We had nowhere to go and nowhere to be.

We were now orphans.

We didn't have to be home for dinner; we had no curfew, no rules to follow or laws to break. We had nothing. We simply needed to get away, leave it all behind, and escape in hopes of finding something better.

Something liberating.

We were, unfortunately, so very mistaken.

No words were capable of describing the things that I saw along our directionless course. No words of any of the human languages were capable of describing a time like that. Aided by the Kurds, the Turkish soldiers and dangerous prisoners, officially released from their cells, ran and rode in all directions, chasing after Armenians, shooting, stabbing, torturing, hanging, raping, and eventually killing men and women of all ages, purely for the sport of it. They dragged them behind their horses over rocky terrain and strung them up, playing competitively with each other, collecting Armenian heads, turning women into slaves, and hunting children, not ever abiding by a single law of humanity.

I watched as my countrymen dropped to their knees to meet their final moments. I watched as each father and each son fell in front of their homes, protecting each mother and each daughter, and with them, the destruction of their unique visions, their unique plans, and their unique dreams. We were in a single-sided war zone. Each person, taken, judged, and destroyed by people who had no right to do so. By pitiless soldiers and men alike who, like machines, blindly served an evil purpose. What happened to us was happening to all other Armenian families, and it was happening everywhere.

I couldn't help but question everything that I thought I knew and everything that I'd been taught. Where was God now? Why was He doing this? Would He be back for my final day? When would that be? Today or tomorrow? Without His protection, I couldn't see myself getting through this. I couldn't see myself living to seventeen. I couldn't see myself as an old man with grandchildren. I couldn't see myself married with *any* children of my own. I couldn't see myself living beyond the day after next or simply through the night. I just couldn't see it. It was blocked and corrupted by a thick blanket of iniquity, until Nadia, beautiful Nadia, the girl more courageous, more brave than I, spoke the four words that granted a partial glimpse beyond the blanket and revealed a small glimmer of hope. The *only* glimmer of hope.

"The Turkish couple's home!" she screamed.

The possibility of survival was not in our favor. Initially, I hated the idea, but I quickly realized the insignificance of my opinion. It didn't matter if the couple would meet us well. It didn't matter if we could trust them or not. It didn't matter if they were Turks. It was the only choice we had, and we clung to it like driftwood in the middle of the ocean. If Nadia's sisters were all right, I thought, then maybe we would be, too. And thus, with it floating in our minds, we changed our bearing northwest to their home.

Out of breath, we ran up to the small tan house with the double front doors. Nadia knocked ferociously, rattling the tile shingles on the roof. Quickly, the door pulled open but was held slightly ajar, only enough to barely see a man's face, his thick brows, defining nose, and part of his hand.

"Özkan, please, you need to let us in," Nadia begged.

Peering at us cautiously, the Turkish man held the door firm. "Who are they?" he asked about Vartan and me through the gap.

"They're…" She paused. "My family."

"Why is he so bloody?" He eyed Vartan.

"He fell in blood," she answered, "after a slaughter."

Quickly remembering my father's blood upon my collar, I spun around, flipped it in on itself, and then faced forward once again.

"They are Armenian?"

"Yes," she confirmed.

"I'm sorry," he said, "but I promised only for you and your two sisters. I cannot let them in."

"Özkan!" a female voice yelled from inside

A thinner lady in her mid-thirties with a plump yet pretty face then squeezed between the man and the frame of the door. She wore a head wrap and a beige dress, covered by a white apron.

"How dare you," she accused. "Look what our government is doing. They've turned to evil. With God as my witness, I am ashamed to be a Turk!" she continued. "Let them in right now."

"If we let them in, others will follow. We can't risk it! We'll pay heavily for harboring Armenians. They'll *kill* us!"

"You listen here. I have six uncles. I'll leave you, then have them break your limbs and feed you to the wolves if you don't," she threatened as she pulled open the door.

Özkan took a step back. "Damned if I do, damned if I don't," he muttered under his breath.

"What did you say?" she asked with attitude.

"Nothing."

"That's what I thought. Now, please," she greeted in Ottoman Turkish, "come in."

"Thank you, Güler," Nadia said as we passed through.

Immediately inside, the space seemed very comfortable. Straight ahead was the kitchen, to the left, a narrow, dark-brown staircase that ran up to the bedrooms. Against the wall under the staircase was a single brown chair. The wall on the right consisted entirely of shelving, from the ceiling to the floor. On each shelf sat pottery of various sizes. They each had their own unique flavor. Some were big, some were small, some were fat, and some were skinny. Some had color, some didn't. One even quickly erased any feeling of comfort I had because on it was the crescent moon and star, the Turkish flag, painted in red, making me truly realize exactly where we were.

To the left of the wall of shelves was an entryway without a door that I didn't initially see because of the shelving. It led to a small pantry that I never fully explored. From there, Nadia's two younger sisters ran to her for a joyful reunion. The strap of the rifle dropped from her shoulder into the pit of her elbow as she leaned over. I slid it off her arm and slung it over my own shoulder. Her sisters had no clue what we'd been through, but there was no need to tell them. They didn't need to know.

Güler then closed the door and stood against it. She

pointed to Vartan. "We need to clean you up," she declared. "Otherwise, they *will* get suspicious. Özkan, get water."

Walking through the doorway near the shelving, Özkan left the house from the side door. Returning moments later with a bucket of water, he stretched out his arm and offered it to Vartan. Vartan, looking at the wooden bucket swinging from the tips of his fingers, didn't take it.

"Go on," he offered, "get yourself clean."

Still, he didn't take it.

"Vartan," I spoke in Armenian, "you need to wash the blood off."

Without emotion, he took it hesitantly and headed outside to a grassy patch in the back. Taking off his shirt and pants, he tipped the bucket slowly over his head. The blood, now pasted over his skin like dried putty, didn't immediately wash away, so Vartan used his free hand to scrub his face and hair. On the way down, the water carved its way over his body and rinsed away the color. By the time it reached his toes, what used to be a clear and refreshing source of life was now a stained and putrid juice that soaked into the ground.

"That's better," Güler said satisfactorily as Vartan walked back inside.

She handed him a towel and looked at Vartan's muscular frame as he stood and dried himself.

"Özkan, he will need clothes. Get your big shirt and those pants that don't fit. They'll fit... um..."

"Vartan," I quietly finished for her. "And I'm Armen."

"Vartan. They'll fit Vartan."

Özkan then climbed the steep staircase, which creaked only once, and disappeared into the second floor.

"And you. You also need a new shirt." She pointed to me.

Just as Özkan began his descent, just as he placed his foot on the top stair, Güler began again, "Özkan," she yelled, "make that two shirts!"

Stopping in his tracks, Özkan let out a long sigh and turned back around for his wife's second request. A moment later he returned, clothes in hand. Vartan put on the pants and the shirt over his fluffy long hair and sat down on the unstable chair under the staircase. He stared quietly into the empty void, stagnantly thinking the same things I was. It was impossible not to. I leaned the rifle next to him and set my satchel next to it, then changed my shirt as well.

"That'll do for now," she said.

Suddenly, a knock reverberated throughout the house and awakened Vartan's mind.

"Shh!" Güler sounded. "Take them inside!"

Directing Vartan, Nadia, her sisters, and me, Özkan took us to the far room of the house. Again, a knock on the door echoed inside. Just before the third knock, Güler opened it to a young Turkish soldier standing in the doorway. Nadia's sisters began to whimper, and my heart sank to the pit of my stomach as I watched the tears roll down their faces. I thought for sure that we would be dragged out and killed. My head raced with thoughts and visions of all the things those poor girls wanted to accomplish, but now would never have the chance to do so. I felt pity and blamed myself for living so selfishly all these years. Alas, the moment had come. How could I have taken each day for granted? Who was I to think that time was on my side? Even when I believed the opposite, I eased my mind by assuring her sisters that everything would be all right. Even when I feared everything, I told them that there was nothing to fear, and even when I couldn't remember them, I told them to think of all the funny things in life.

It worked.

Güler cleared her throat and greeted the soldier, "Good evening, sir."

"Good evening," he responded. "How are things tonight?"

"They are just fine, thank you. How can I help you?"

"We are searching the villages for Armenians. We will need to search your home to make sure there are none inside. They are dangerous."

The soldier took a step inside.

"How dare you!" interrupted Güler.

The soldier stopped, stunned, and took a step back.

"Does our house smell of pigs and dung? There are no Armenians here. We are Turks, pure and pure! As are you!"

"It's for your safety. Please, move aside."

The soldier took one more step forward.

"How dare you insult a fellow Turk? There are no Armenians here!"

He looked past Güler into the home.

"Whose rifle is that?" he pointed. "And why is there blood on that shirt?"

Turning her head, Güler looked at the rifle peacefully leaning against the staircase and my bloody shirt on the floor next to it.

"It is my husband's! He went hunting earlier today. Do you want to know whose dress this is too?" she asked as she lifted the cloth from her apron.

"I'd like to see you and your husband's identification certificates, please. Is he here?"

"Yes, he is. He must be in the back."

"Go get him."

With a closing of the door, Güler casually walked inside to where we sat perched, huddled together. Reaching over our heads, she opened a low-lying cabinet. She knew, as well as we did, that whether or not we lived or died was in her hands. As she pulled out the papers, she called for Özkan, who stood only a meter away.

"Özkan!" she called. "The government is here to see you!"

"Coming!" he responded to her game.

Casually, Güler walked back and opened the front door once again. As she handed the soldier her papers, Özkan, too, came in. Fiddling around with them, the soldier examined the certificates.

"Thank you for your time," he said a moment later. He then handed them back. "Have a nice day."

Güler closed the door behind him.

I tried breathing easier but still found it difficult. I didn't want to talk to anyone. I didn't want to look at anyone. I couldn't live my life as a refugee. I just wanted this to be over.

Well after the soldiers had gone and we no longer felt threatened for the moment, we returned hesitantly.

"Thank you," I stated humbly, before finding a place on the floor against the wall.

Güler could have easily turned us in to rid herself and her husband of the responsibility. She could have easily turned to the wickedness of her people and accepted the greed and corruption that so easily poisoned her society. She could have, but didn't. Even though she was Turkish and we were Armenian, she risked all that she had, even possibly her life, to help the people her country viewed as dangerous and inferior. By doing so, she chose to see through the thick veil of deception that controlled and blinded an entire empire. She saw truth where there were lies, happiness where there was misery, kindness where there was violence, beauty where there was bloodshed, love where there was hate, and she shared her sights with those she loved. It didn't matter if they were Moslem and we were Christian. It didn't matter if they were wealthy and we were poor. Güler and Özkan petitioned to overcome it all, including the differences we may have expressed, and they won. They protected us, and without them, we would have died, meeting an untimely and gruesome death like so many Armenians before us.

Güler and Özkan, that day, restored an infinitesimal bit of my faith in the human race, even after it had been torn completely from my mind only months prior. It was a small amount and wouldn't last, but at least I knew that I was capable of believing again, and that was good enough for me.

It was a pleasant day, April 24th, 1915, the day we lost everyone we ever knew. Everyone we ever cared about. Everyone we ever loved. The day I needed to remember but wanted to forget.

31

By the first week of May 1915, thousands of scholars and intellectuals had been killed or deported all over the Ottoman Empire. Without their minds, without their leading voice, it became effortless for the Young Turks to manipulate and control the Armenian community and keep their own people uninformed. That first week of May made me remember the problems I used to have and made me realize that they weren't really problems. It made me remember the little things Vartan and I used to argue about and how they blurred the line between what was important and what wasn't. It also made me wonder if the others had done the same.

Per the advice of Özkan and Güler, Vartan, Nadia, her sisters, and I stayed with them, adopting their Turkish family name in case anyone dared to ask. With a radically new daily routine, time for us had blurred. We didn't go to church, we didn't milk the cows, we didn't chop firewood, and we didn't feed the oxen. The days and the weeks moved faster than I cared to count, and thus, with no tasks to accomplish and no routine to follow, we made with what we had. All in all, Özkan and Güler treated us as family. They fed us, they clothed us, they washed us, and they took care of us. They had no debt to us in any way, and yet their actions spoke solely from the kindness of their human hearts.

After living with them for over a month, Vartan, at sunset, suspiciously patrolled east with the rifle slung over his shoulder, as though he were on a mission. From inside, I observed his every step, his every move, wondering what he was up to. He moved nervously, erratically, and seemed highly distressed. When he had ventured out much farther than usual, I realized there was more to his movements than just a protected stroll. So, with the diminishing rays behind me, I left my spot and ran out to him.

"Vartan!" I yelled out, quickly lowering my voice soon after. "Vartan," I repeated sternly.

Looking around to see if anyone had heard me, Vartan

turned to me.

"Where are you going?" I asked.

Nearly certain that he wasn't going to respond after weeks of silence, he, however, finally decided to speak.

"I can't stay here any more," he muttered angrily. "Look at us, speaking Turkish, eating Turkish food. We're becoming Turks!" he finished.

"Well, what do you want us to do?" I confronted. "Do we have a choice?"

"I need to go back," he continued. "I need to lay them to rest. We've been here for way too long. I won't let their bodies rot away any more. They each deserve a burial, just as Ana did."

Like a cast reeling in a fish, Ana's name alone brought back the hauntingly chilling recollection. I immediately envisioned my last memory of her, something that I could never unsee, and replayed all the events that followed. Except this time, I faced the culmination of the experiences with a hardened and emotionless poise. Before I judged myself again as a coldhearted man incapable of feeling, though, I realized that now wasn't the same as then. Of course I knew my parents. Of course I knew Tavit. Of course I loved them. Of course I was enraged by their brutish murders, but why had I felt less inclined to show it? I fixated on this degrading thought until I learned from the deepest tears of my soul that this was different because I could now *control* it. Ana paved the way for that. I had taken those experiences, mixed it with the flame inside, and channeled the potent mixture from my head through each vein of my body and down to my toes, so that together, it would continue to feed the strength, the courage, and the wisdom my mind craved and push the fear and the sorrow to starvation so that it would wither away like petals in the fall. My father was right. Fear was in my mind, and it was up to me to rid myself of it. Quietly then, with the quick acceptance of this calling, I took the stand and agreed to put myself through the ultimate test. And thus, I smiled, knowing that I was now a better person than I was the day before.

"Well, you were just going to leave without me?" I questioned. "I'm going with you," I finished, standing my ground.

"Are you up to it?" he responded, finally. "It's going to be dangerous."

"Yes," I said confidently, lowering my brows.

"All right then, let's go."

Without a horse, as the darkness slowly settled over the land, we thus moved through the late dusk like escaped convicts, frequently stopping to hide when the slightest suspicion arose. Solely telling Nadia about our undertaking, Vartan promised her a return before the morning. In reality, however, as we neared our house, I knew he wasn't sure. With the familiar sight in view, I readied myself to meet the test that I accepted to put myself through.

At first, I looked for my mother, fallen at the doorstep. To my confusion, she wasn't there. I then noticed the front door, slightly ajar. Turning to the field, I looked for my father. He wasn't there. Quietly then, we hopped onto the porch and put our backs against the clay brick wall filled with dusty bullet holes. Carefully listening for any sounds that could indicate soldiers on the premises, Vartan slid on his back to peek through the small, shattered window near the front door. He closed his eyes for a lengthy time and I, too, peeked inside. Tavit wasn't there, and neither was anything else. Our furniture was gone. Our table. Everything. The house stood barren except for shards of glass and a few small items sprinkled lightly over the dirty, carpetless wood floor. The wood paneling had even been torn from the walls. It was simply a void—an empty wooden box.

Slowly, Vartan nudged open the door with the muzzle of the rifle and stepped cautiously inside. I followed. Without character, without life, it looked entirely different. I barely recognized it.

Stepping around the glass to not make any sounds, I walked through the living space and entered my room, searching for clues, anything that could point us in the right direction. That, too, had been stripped of its contents. Everything from my bed down to my clothes was taken, including my school books, leaving solely an old woolen sock. I leaned over and picked it up.

"Where are they?" Vartan asked as he entered behind me.

I turned to face him, sock still in hand. "I don't know," I responded.

"What do you mean you don't know?"

"I said I don't know. How would I? Look around you. Everything was stolen."

"Listen," Vartan began, "we need to find them. That's the priority."

"All right. That's why we're here. Where should we look?"

There was too much on Vartan's mind. I could tell.

"They dedicated their lives to us, and they at least deserve the respect. Wouldn't you want your children to do the same for you? We still have to dig th—we don't know where the soldiers are or if they'll be back. We have to move quickly and efficiently. I suggest that you sweep the field while I check the bar—"

"No," I cut him off. "We are *not* splitting up."

"We won't be that far from each other."

"That's not the point."

"Then what is? We have no choice. You need to stop being so afraid!" he accused.

"Afraid?" I slightly raised my voice. "The entire Turkish Army is trying to kill us. All of us. We have one rifle, and all we have left is each other. I am not risking splitting up! This has nothing to do with being afraid!"

Vartan stepped closer to me. "If this has nothing to do with being afraid, then why did you just *stand* there while *Hyreeg* and I fought those soldiers? Why did you just *stand* there when they tried to *kill* us? Why did you just *stand* there when I killed those men? Where were *you*? You just watched it happen. You did *nothing*! Absolutely nothing!" he screamed.

Not knowing how to respond, I knew only that I needed to defend myself. "Where was *I*? Where were *you*?" I yelled back. "Where were *you* when Mama died? Where were you when *Hyreeg* died, huh? I'll tell you where you were. You were too busy chasing Nadia like a blind goat! *You* did nothing. *You* let our parents die! You—"

Vartan threw down the rifle, cutting me off.

He then raised his hand, tightened his fist, and closed the gap between his knuckles and my left eye. The impact rattled my brain and jolted my senses, but I didn't let it defeat me. I was different now. Stumbling backwards, I dropped my sock and from the power of my legs, thrust my body forward directly into Vartan's abdomen. I was bigger now. Tightly wrapping my arms around his torso, I took him to the floor. Without a moment's pause, we punched each other mercilessly, letting our fists crush our bodies like jackhammers. I was stronger now. We rolled and screamed and hit each other with every opportunity, even as the shards of glass embedded themselves into our clothes and under our skin. Not even that stopped us. We were livid. Pulling my collar tight to keep me within arm's length, Vartan hammered my body as I aimed for his gut. I struck multiple blows, knocking the wind out of him as he returned a strike to my jaw, nearly cracking a tooth. For a seeming eternity, we attacked each other with every appendage, trying to inflict as much damage as possible. I felt the blood boil through my veins and into my hands. I felt the rage intensify to an insane level. Something about it, however, didn't feel right. Something was off.

What were we doing?

Grabbing Vartan's thumb, still firmly wrapped around my collar, I twisted it out to evade his grip and blocked his other incoming punch. I then thrust both his hands down from the wrists and pushed his chest to free myself. Vartan fell backwards, and I jumped up, backing away with my hands in front of me.

"Stop!" I yelled. "Stop! This is enough!"

There was a crying rancor in his eyes, and I saw it.

Slowly, though, he stood up.

"Vartan, please, listen to me!" I cried. "You're not thinking straight. I'm just as angry as you are, but for God's sake, Vartan, just listen to me!"

Stationary in his spot, he panted like a wolf.

"Look around this room. Look around this house.

We've lost everything! The *last* thing we should do is go off in our own separate directions. We can't do that. We just can't. I am not letting you go out there alone. What if something happens to one of us? Then what would you have left? What would I have left?"

I wiped the blood from my upper lip with the back of my hand and took in a deep breath, my emotions running rampantly.

"Remember that story about the cranes? The one Mama used to tell us?"

"That's just a story," he retorted. "It's fake!"

"Do you remember?" I repeated.

"I do," he answered.

"Well, what happened to the crane that always went off on his own? What happened to him, Vartan? There's a reason Mama kept telling us that story! It's because she *knew!* She knew that one day we would learn from it. That's why she kept telling us! We need to look out for each other, and that's the way it has to be!"

I breathed a bit easier.

"We loved our parents. There's no question. And I want to give them the respect they deserve just as much as you do, but if we're going to get through this, we can't blame or take it out on each other. That's exactly what the Turks want. We need to stick together because all we have *left* is each other. Mama and *Hyreeg* would have wanted that. We're so much stronger that way, and *that's* the respect they want from us."

I felt my left eye pulsate, drumming at the rapid pace of my heart.

"Promise me that we're going to stay together until this is over," I said, "no matter what it takes."

Vartan continued his now slower pant.

"Promise me," I repeated, almost desperately.

There was nothing left to say. This was my final attempt. My only plea.

"I promise," he exhaled.

After we sealed that eternal oath to each other, Vartan

now viewed me with a newfound respect. I felt it. Far greater than that, though, I had managed to convey how I truly felt, who I truly was—a man of other men, learning from their mistakes through observation and relentless criticism and using those faults for the better, just as I did to my own self.

Vartan then leaned over and picked the rifle back up and held it by the barrel at his side. He brushed the hair out of his eyes, combing it with the tips of his fingers as I massaged the skin around my eye, feeling for the bruise.

"Sorry," he apologized, "for—"

"I'm through," I replied. "First, let's get some water. Then, let's try the barn. There could still be weapons there."

Thus, I staggered out of my room and led the way for Vartan to follow. I turned left into the short hallway and stepped into the living space, taking one good look at the emptiness we would leave behind. Finally, we walked to the well.

If I had known that that would've been the last time I ever saw my house, I would have looked for a little while longer.

Grabbing hold of the wooden handle, Vartan tried to turn the crank for the bucket to ascend, but it was snagged on something below. Before he could investigate, however, I diverted his attention to my hand tapping his shoulder.

"Wha—" he began as I quickly cupped my hand over his mouth and pointed through the window to the back of the house to a team of soldiers, walking freshly to where we stood just moments ago, searching with their torches, looking for anything of value.

Immediately, Vartan let go of the crank handle, and we cautiously slid to the other side of the well. Keeping low, we ran in that direction, south, towards the hills. Just as quickly as we began, though, the silhouette of more soldiers stopped us dead in our tracks. Like baseball players between bases, we juggled directions and changed our heading west, the direction of the Turkish couple's home. From the apricot trees, however, foot soldiers scouring the area prevented our escape. With only one direction left to go, we ran east, passing the well once more. Yet again, though, we stopped at the sight of the Turkish army marching down the main road, also carrying torches. They moved towards us atop their horses, pulling wooden carts with large, wooden wheels that squeaked with every turn. Completely surrounded, Vartan and I ran back to the well and sat down on the grass against the cold stones of its wall. We brought our knees to our chests and waited, terrified. Vartan held the rifle firmly across his waist and checked for its function as I placed my hands over my mouth to keep silent.

With nothing left to do, we sat helplessly and waited. Soon enough, the front door of our house opened, and the soldiers nonchalantly stepped onto the porch. Only thirty meters away, they were so painfully close that I could see their armed figures glimmer faintly under the torchlight. For Vartan, that was too close, so he pointed to the well behind us, and I nodded my head in agreement. One foot after the other, we thus climbed inside, keeping our bodies molded against its shape, and hung with only the tips of our fingers visible from the outside while resting the tips of our toes against some protruding stones on the inside.

As the soldiers from the north met with the soldiers from the west, they exchanged information on our porch.

"This one's empty," one said.

"The others beat us to it!" another laughed in response.

From the east, the slow squeaking sound of the wooden wheels turning under the wooden carts, and the sound of the shifting blades of grass compressing under the weight of horses and men from the south, all amplified intensely in the stone well. Inside, I trembled uncontrollably. My heart thumped, and the sweat dripped down my forehead. I closed my eyes to sharpen my hearing and listened for a few minutes until the squeaking of the wheels and all the other sounds grew louder and louder until they all stopped.

They were here.

"All right, gentlemen," the one in charge announced in Ottoman Turkish, "welcome to your new home! We'll rest here for the night."

Letting out a sigh of relief, the soldiers began to unwind.

Immediately, the sound of unbuckling gear and dropping rifles from every direction unlocked my darkest and most uncomfortable imagination. We were surrounded. Suddenly, I felt a burning heat sear past my knuckles as a single, lighted torch silently flew over our heads, glowing vibrantly. It sparked as it impacted the inner wall behind us then sizzled when it extinguished at the bottom of the well. With each passing moment through this inconceivable threat, my fingers ached until the tips became numb, and I wasn't sure how much longer I could hold on.

"Sir, and what about these carts? They're slowing us down. We can't keep pulling them," a soldier complained.

"We were specifically ordered to bury them," their superior explained, "and we'll do as we're told."

"But, sir, they're going to rot and attract bugs. I hate bugs."

"Fine then," the one in charge responded a few seconds later, changing his mind, "dump them in that well."

Immediately, my heart beat faster to an absurd speed and pounded at the inner wall of my chest like a blacksmith's hammer, ready to burst through my ribs. At that moment, I desperately wished it would stop just so the soldiers wouldn't hear it. Looking around our tight spot, Vartan busily calculated an escape plan. He searched all around and envisioned every scenario, using every option. He looked at the rope, up at the night sky, then down at the bottom. In seconds, he had made a decision. He pointed at me, then at the hanging rope, and then down towards the bottom of the well. I shook my head in disagreement. There was no way I was doing that. There was no way I was letting go. Widening his eyes in anger and realizing that time was against us, he let go of one hand and grabbed the taut rope himself. He then let his other hand free and signaled for me to watch him as he clung freely and entirely by a rope only meant to support a small bucket and water. The wooden support above creaked from the immense amount of weight but, thus far, proved sturdy. One after the other, Vartan carefully moved his hands down, twisting his feet around the bottom for support, and descended into the darkness. In a few seconds, a pebble flew up from below and hit my leg, followed by another. Unwilling to let go, I held my position on the ledge only to feel the pain move from my fingers to my arms.

Just then, the familiar squeaking started up again and stopped only as the cart tapped the well wall.

Terrified of the other option, I grabbed the rope with one hand, followed by the other and swung freely in a small, circular motion as the support creaked again from above. Just like my brother, I placed one hand over the other and descended at a heroic pace into the freezing cold water below. Not letting go of the rope, I felt for the bottom with my feet, but the water level had risen so high that, even as my chin touched the surface, I still couldn't feel it. Noting this, Vartan grabbed hold of me and pulled me to some more protruding stones. We stood against them for support making me realize that I was in the exact same position as before, only now fifteen meters down. Shivering from the cold, I wiped the water from my face and jiggled the rope under the surface, trying to find the bucket, but it was snagged on something below. I lowered myself, trying to free it, but Vartan raised his fingers over his lips, telling me to be quiet and stay still. Just then, a hollowed voice caused me to look up, and the faint silhouette of a red fez hat appeared into my sight.

And then another.

"One… two… three," the voice counted.

And then a grunt.

Like a kite, a darkened figure blocked the light of the stars and drifted down from above, turning and twisting. It scraped the inner stones of the well wall, using the rope as a directive guide. Pushing me out of the way, Vartan pinned me against the inside wall just as the figure landed behind us with a terrible splash and rose to the surface, bobbing face down.

A body. Naked. Newly killed.

"One… two… three," they counted again.

And again, another fell, headless, and landed with another great splash.

"One… two… three."

And another.

We moved to dodge it.

"One… two… three."

And another. Still warm. Mutilated.

And another.

Soon enough, it was raining bodies.

Inevitably, one became twisted in the rope and the speed of its descent combined with its weight broke the support beam, causing it to come crashing down altogether. The soldiers at the top laughed and joked as I realized that our only method of escape was now gone. With no way left to get to the surface, I thought for sure that I was going to die at the bottom of a well.

Underestimating the number of bodies the soldiers had brought with them, the continuous rhythm persisted, one after the other, almost endlessly, quickly tightening the space where we remained hidden. With each body, the well became warmer and increasingly shallower. Thus, as each one began suffocating our air supply and twisting our beaten limbs, and as the water soon became only as visible as the blue of the night sky, Vartan and I had no further choice but to stand on our newfound support, to climb up above them, one terrifying meter at a time.

Nearing the top, we let the bodies cover us to retain our mask until the well had reached its capacity. Even then, we waited for the wheels to begin turning again, until it had become so noiseless that I could hear the beat of my rampaged heart. After we were convinced that the soldiers had left, Vartan and I dug ourselves out from underneath and back into the night. Just as I inhaled my first deep breath of fresh air, however, the moment caused my burdening heart to drop through my feet like a rock, and I became dizzy from the shocking sight, because peering down, waiting for us, was the score of Turkish soldiers and the local Turkish police.

We were caught.

32

The Turkish policeman, with his black, rounded hat

slightly pointed at the top and long, dark coat, reached out and forcefully pulled the weapon out of Vartan's hands.

"What is this?" he said with a smile. "An Armenian boy with a rifle."

As he walked away with it, two other policemen grabbed us by our shirts and belt loops and pulled us fully out of the well. They threw us down at the feet of the soldiers waiting behind them, where they beat us, kicking and punching, only adding to the bruises, cuts, and scrapes already upon us. Up to this point, I thought I knew how to fight or at least how to endure a beating, but not like this. This was unfair.

With our noses bloodied and bodies battered, the soldiers then bound our hands together at the wrists and tethered us to each other with a thick, wiry rope about five meters in length. Under the cover of the night, they attached us to one horse with distinct orders not to speak to one another on grounds that we would be executed for collaboration if we did. The rider then began moving, roughly edging us forward. After a few paces, though, he purposefully sped up until we lost our footing and dragged us over the dirt road, just as they had done to our priest. I held onto the rope to keep my shoulders in their sockets and felt the individual stones scrape across my belly and back. As the soldiers laughed at us in ridicule, the rider then slowed down to give us a breathing chance to stand, only to speed up again before we could do so. Again, the rocks scraped across our bodies, and I tried keeping my face away from the ground. After a mesmerizing distance, the rider stopped a final time to allow the soldiers the opportunity to pound us with stones.

"Get up! You're walking the rest," they screamed before shooting the ground near our heads.

Crouched on the ground, I spit the pebbles out of my mouth and coughed, feeling the pain from my damaged ribs curse my senses. With short, shallow breaths, I blinked a few times to let the tears clear the dirt out of my eyes, then blew the dirt out of my nose. Together, with the knuckles of my bound hands, I pushed myself to a seated position, then, one scraped leg at a time, stood back on my feet. Vartan did the same. Pasted with dirt and mud, we then resumed our torturous journey on foot until something ahead made me instantly forget my own struggle, depressing my body to an unreasonable trance. The stench, like rotting garbage, soaked my cleared nostrils and turned my stomach, putting me in an internal state of revolt, forcing another agitated cough. The crows and vultures circled the sky above, picking at them uncontrollably, not even fighting. There was plenty to go around. Thousands of them. Naked and unrecognizable corpses, butchered, lying wasted by the wayside, collectively thrown into heaping stacks, forming a range of their own. Illuminated only by the starlight, the grotesque sight of the men, women, and even children, mangled and disfigured, stripped entirely in every way possible, now rested without discrimination upon the dirt of the ground. What I once knew as a thriving and lively community now lay as a pitiful excuse for a graveyard, merely a month's worth of work.

If death had a name, it was Armenia.

As I stared at the vile outrage, my hands jerked forward, burning through my wrists, quickly reminding me that Vartan had been tied to me.

"Get moving!" the policeman yelled harshly, entirely unperturbed, as if he'd been walking on a different road, instead made of daisies. Like cattle, they herded us forward, forcing us to walk between the blood-soaked remains of the deceased. I held my breath for as long as I could at the unbearable scent until our arrival at the police station—a beat-down, scary-looking place. There, we met with hundreds of other Armenian men from all aspects of society. With the tip of their swords, the soldiers then cut Vartan and me loose. As I rubbed the swelling redness around my wrists, I questioned, once again, all that humanity stood for.

"Take off your boots and socks," they screamed. "And keep your eyes down!"

Keeping their rifles pointed at us, we stood in a group, lined up outside the prison. I leaned over to begin untying my boots when a soldier, as angry as I've ever seen, ran up to the man next to me and struck his face with the butt of his rifle, cracking his nose. The man fell and painfully held his hands over his bloodied face.

"I said keep your eyes down!" he restated.

Not fully understanding my instinctual actions, I then leaned over to help that man.

"C'mon," I said as I grabbed him by his underarm, "you need to listen to them."

Slowly, he clambered up, shaking his head, and noticed the scrapes across my arms and face. He limply stood next to me, holding his bloody nose, as we worked off our boots and shoes. We held them at our sides, waiting for the next step.

"Into the station! Now," they commanded.

Thus, we did as they said.

Immediately inside, to the right of the door, was a chipped, low-lying counter. On top of it sat a small wooden crate filled with gold jewelry, and behind it, a pile of clothes.

"In the pile," they ordered us. "Let's go!"

Passively, we threw our boots and socks behind the counter and into the pile. Now barefoot, we turned and stood facing the row of thirty or so cells down the narrow hallway and the closed, metal door at the end. We then followed the soldiers and policemen over the golden-brown stained tile floor to a cell halfway down. Sweaty and filthy, we stood in line against the wall until they cut it every fifteen or so men and sent each group to a different cell. Vartan and I, sandwiched between the others, were the last of one group of fifteen and thus remained where we stood. With a long key, the policemen then unlocked the door to our cell and frisked each of us before shoving us inside to join the other Armenian men who'd come before us. They then slid the bars closed and locked us in.

We were now prisoners.

As I lightly held the warm metal bars, I watched as the soldiers led the rest of the men each to their respective cells. As they marched away, the noises from the hall faded, and the sound of coughs, moans, and whispering prayers behind me found its way forward. Hesitantly, I turned to the sight of the pathetic statures of the diseased and starving men crammed into the same overheated quarters, barren of their hope to survive or even fight. There they were, merely as bearded skeletons, barefoot and barely clad. Some stood, but most sat hunched over on the cold, concrete floor. Only God knew how long they'd been there prior to our arrival.

"Don't tell them a single thing," Vartan advised me in Armenian.

"It makes no matter," an old man warned with his old and fatigued voice. "Innocent or not, we are all here to die."

"Wh-what was your crime?" I asked, feeling the burning of my cut lip.

The man shrugged. "Same is the story for us all."

Before I could probe further, Vartan tugged on my shirt. "Let's go."

So, letting the poor man be, we passed through the small spaces between the prisoners and found a spot towards the back on the right wall. We stood against it. There, I began peeling the clay off my body when two policemen returned and unlocked the door of our cell. They didn't open it. Instead, they stood, guarding the entrance for the two soldiers behind them, dressed in full uniform, to finish the task. Stepping barely inside, they chose four men, including the old one whom I had just spoken to, and tied them together with the same thick rope they'd used to tie Vartan and me. Without even a final deserving defense, they freely left the cell, dragging their deprived and ruined bodies with them.

"Where are they going?" I yelled from behind the other prisoners.

It was another instinctual burst, but I wanted answers.

"Who said that?" the policeman screamed out angrily.

Nobody said a word.

"Who said that?" he screamed again.

Again, the cell fell silent.

"The next Armenian to speak will have their throat slit! You are prisoners now! This is not a place for conversation!"

Dejectedly, Vartan and I sat down at our spot and

listened as the short tapping of prisoners' bare feet against the tile floor faded to a stop. They had arrived at the room at the end of the hall. Heavily, the door then creaked open, carrying its sound throughout the prison. The shuffling of feet then scurried inside, and the metallic door closed behind them.

"What are you plotting against the government?" the soldier began immediately, rattling the metal around us.

"I-noth—"

"Where are you hiding the weapons?" the policeman screamed fanatically, disallowing of an answer. "We know about the stockpile! Where is it? Where's the stockpile?"

"We... we have none," finally answered the old man with his raspy voice. "We are bare."

"You're lying," he accused. "Tell me where they are!"

"I turned them in properly, my rifles," another prisoner answered, trembling, "as soon as it was posted by the government."

Being asked the same questions in different ways, the two remaining prisoners also denounced their ownership of arms and begged for release on grounds of truth and mercy. I heard it. We all heard it. With their honesty, however, came an asylum for the pain standing in front of them.

"You are a liar and a conspirator against the government," they judged. "A plague upon the Turks!"

Not even bothering to ask for their names, not ever obtaining a shred of evidence, allowing for a jury, or even expressing a simple upholding of the justice the badges on their uniforms represented, they continued their process of submission by fear.

For an unbearable amount of time, I then sat and listened as the sound of lashes and the banging of various metals turned man into demon, nourished only by the utmost agonizing screams of their prisoners. This was the extent of their trial. Vibrating through the walls of the stone building, the crying voices penetrated deep into our eardrums, followed by the unchanged, useless questions, derived as a ploy. Where are your men hiding? How many Turks have you killed? Who is the assassin? Where is the ammunition? Where are the bombs? When is the next rebellion? Thus, after not hearing the answers they wanted to hear, the screams, the yells, the cries, and the questions ceased only after the casual sound of gunfire exploded throughout the prison. For that beautiful moment of silence, we relished in its short existence and collected its luxury, absorbing as much as we could. Then, shortly after, the door of the room opened, and the soldiers returned, out of breath and stained red. At their side, they carried their newfound shirts and pants alongside their hammers and casually tossed them into the pile of clothes, adding to their collection. They then dropped rings and gold teeth into the wooden crate on top of the counter, exposing their wretched and filthy palms with jagged fingernails as black as their hearts and smiled as if someone had told them a joke. After turning to face our cell, they again selected a new set of men, thus starting afresh the same, twisted process.

All through the night, I sat in judgment in that dimly lit cell and listened to the sickening screams. I watched as each soldier and each policeman passed by, taking turns, leaving boot prints along their chosen path, quickly turning the jail into a slaughterhouse. In order to not waste bullets, the sound of pistol fire was heedlessly and eventually replaced by the swishing sound of lashes, the muffled sound of clubs, then of a sword slicing the air, followed by a low thud and the cracking of ceramic tile. All through the night, I watched the regretful and hollowed faces of the men who had been successfully reduced to a submissive state of terror. All through the night, I waited for my turn to die while fighting exhaustion and the sudden onslaught of cold, not even daring to close my eyes. All through the night, I prayed for the silence, and all through the night, I prayed for deliverance from this place, this death row.

I prayed, but my words remained unanswered.

At the sun's rise, Vartan and I were physically still alive, but our minds had been numbed to the sound of brutality. Thirsty from the overbearing heat, my bruised and cut-up body, my sweat-stained shirt and torn pants, both caked in dirt, now illuminated by the new light, told the same tale. Thirty-six men from our cell alone had been taken to the room down the hall, all of their fates ending the same. Vartan and I were two of only sixteen survivors in our cell. Then, by that morning, without even a questioning, without even a second guess, a fresh set of policemen slid open the door to our cell for the fresh set of soldiers behind them. They stepped inside.

It was our turn to die. I was sure of it.

I readied myself for the impending execution.

"Gather your belongings," they said to us. "We're sending you out."

With my bloodshot eyes, starving body, and empty thoughts, I sat, hunched over like the rest, momentarily shocked, and didn't even bother to move. The other prisoners didn't move either. They, like me, took their words carefully. With the best of our understanding, we sat dumbfounded, unbelieving of the ease of liberty. Only after the second call did I realize that my mind hadn't turned on me.

"Gather your belongings and get out!" they yelled once more.

"We're free?" I thought passively through my weakness. "Just like that? Perhaps these are the righteous ones."

"Where are we going?" a man asked.

"Stand up. We're relocating you to a temporary safe zone!"

The sounds of murmurs throughout the cell echoed the same confusion.

"Where is it?" the man asked again.

"Gomidas, be quiet. We're being freed," the man's friend whispered as he passed him and walked out the cell to the place beyond the guards.

"Gather your belongings. Let's go," they ordered the rest of us.

Hesitantly, Vartan stood up, extending his hand to help me. I grabbed it, but instead of pulling myself up, I unintentionally pulled him down. We were both tired. Thus, using the wall that I sat against for support, Vartan finally managed to get me to my feet.

As we staggered out of our concrete box, we met the other men staggering out of theirs. Most simply walked past the armed soldiers and left the building barefoot, while the few rest of us, including Vartan and me, dug through the immense pile of clothes behind the counter. It was a horrid task, especially now that we knew where it came from. Halfway through, we found our boots and slipped them on, laces loose. We then stepped out into the scorching rays of the sun and joined the remaining weakened men, our possessions being limited to the clothes on our backs.

"Sir," another man requested, noticeably thinner and malnourished under the day's light, "we haven't eaten for days. We need food."

"We'll feed you on the way to the military zone," a soldier reassured, answering in a new tone.

"And water?"

"Sure, water will also be provided."

After that, he left to help with the organization of our relocation as the rest completely liquidated the prison. Then, we began our trek. Under armed guard, we walked through the unpaved roads of a ravaged city with no citizens, soaking our thoughts with freedom. What would the safe zone look like? Who else would be there? What kind of food would they have? What would the water taste like? Through my prevailing hunger and thirst, and the assurance of nourishment, I felt momentarily quenched until I felt ashamed at my naïvety. First, the soldiers tortured and killed us, destroying all morale, and now they're going to free us and provide us with food and water? After all that we'd been through, *now* they want to take *care* of us? No way. It wasn't right. Something was off. Trying to keep as much optimism as I convinced myself that I had, however, I carried on.

At the last turn of the final bend, perhaps a kilometer or two later, the sheer immensity and precise organization of the relocation became immediately apparent. I finally saw where the soldiers were guiding us. For as far as the eye could see, thousands of Armenians filled the length of a single road, marching out of the main city, moving under their own weight and sometimes under others. I wasn't ready for this. Clad in the clothes of the working day, they brought only what they could. No two families and no two individuals carried the same things. Some had chickens, still in their coops. Some pulled donkeys and horses, sometimes for the crippled and old. Some drove ox-carts filled with fine European furniture. Some even carried plants in ornate pottery. The majority, however, walked on foot, carrying their bundles of clothes, rolls of bread, carpets, and bedding. There were so many random items, so much variation in this caravan. This mass deportation. The children, oblivious to the situation, played games with each other, dancing carefree. The boys wore their caps, and the girls wore their dresses. They threw around balls, kicking them and laughing cheerily. Many, now orphaned, chased and ran with each other with their raggedy clothes, hiding behind the adults in their juvenile ventures, completely worriless. Their mothers, however, told a completely different story—a story of a forced action against their will. They moved somberly, weeping and moaning, dragging their belongings, some with heavy bundles in one arm and infants in the other. Their useless cries, attributing to the slow depletion under the burning rays, mixed with the youthful laughter and painted a confusing picture for a confusing time. What seemed like a carefree dance soon became the unsightly truth of a shared history.

On both sides of the caravan, the policemen stood at attention, guarding the piles of furniture, clothes, beds, and sewing machines, all taken from Armenian households and emptied onto the street. With a few ineffective German troops scattered throughout, an unreasonably few number of Turkish soldiers, perhaps less than a hundred, walked alongside with whips latched at their waists and rifles with attached bayonets at their arms.

As we neared, a group of westerners, with their brown leather backpacks and professional suits, complete even to the tie, caught my attention. They were the missionaries. Bunched together between the soldiers, they walked, slowly following the pace of the deportees, desperately trying to gain access in any way possible. Some photographed, some wrote in their journals, and the rest watched, soaking in everything they could, solely to be a witness as the Armenians begged for deliverance. The soldiers, contrarily, using their methods of intimidation, worked hard to prevent direct contact, not from the outside in, but from the inside out.

It, however, seldom worked.

A woman I saw from the caravan, wearing a long, brown skirt, a baggy purple top, and a shallow head wrap, mustered enough courage to throw herself beyond the soldiers, directly at the mercy of one of the missionary's feet. Those nearby immediately pointed their rifles, some at the woman and some at the people.

"Back up!" they yelled to the portion of the caravan that stopped to focus on the commotion.

The caravan obeyed.

"Please, help us," the woman begged the missionary. "They took everything! They took our homes. They killed our men. Now they're going to kill us!"

Quickly stooping over, the male missionary picked her up. He stared into her face as she clung to his body. Not immediately knowing what to do, he reached into his canvas bag and handed over some bread and whatever currency he had in his pockets.

"Here," he said, "take this."

Like a starving child, the woman took the bread and bit into it. She then took the money and slid it into a small pocket of her dress.

"Thank you," she cried. "You are from the West. You have a powerful voice. Please," she begged with her broken English, "remember us."

Growing restless with the woman, the soldiers all converged to her location.

"Get her away from that man!" a man commanded his troops.

Something about that voice, however, something about it, didn't sit well with me. It didn't sit well at all. It was a voice that I recognized, a voice that I'd heard before, and it didn't make me smile. Disconnecting all my senses, I thought hard about its origins but couldn't put my finger on it. Before probing deeper, my intuition proved correct, and my question was quickly answered. Seemingly out of nowhere, the one in charge, the bearded one, Colonel Barçin, emerged.

My heart mixed with my stomach, tearing away all hope from what was left of my soul as I stared at him atop his horse. He had been reassigned, now in charge of our freedom.

Like a fig on a tree, five or six of them, heeding their command, quickly pulled the woman off the missionary. She kicked and screamed as they threw her back into the dusty caravan, where she cried on the ground, barely calming, even as the other Armenians helped her to her feet.

"You must leave," the colonel ordered the missionaries as he dismounted. "This is a lawful military intervention. No journalists are allowed."

Being missionaries, however, they didn't do so without answers.

"What was that woman saying? Where are the men?" the male missionary demanded adamantly, looking into the caravan. "Where are their husbands?"

"They are here," the colonel answered. "Those who are not were enemies of the empire. Now leave or you will be arrested."

Without acknowledging his threat, he stayed true to his course. "And what happened to the enemies you speak of? Why are they not here? And what of these people?" he added, pointing to the caravan. "What have they done? Why are *they* being relocated?"

"These people are threats to Turkish national security. They are dangerous. They are accused of plotting against the state and thus are subject to deportation on grounds of treason," the colonel explained with his unconvincing tone. "This is a lawful intervention."

"They're just women and children, for Christ's sake! How can they possibly be dangerous? Have they any water? Any food? This must be stopped! Put an end to this right now. Send them home!"

"I can't," he answered. "Orders from Constantinople."

"You can't? You mean you don't want to! I see the sick and the crippled. The old and the young. There are starving, crying babies among them. Babies! And you're accusing *them* of conspiracy?" The missionary had lost his temper.

"Don't worry," the colonel said, smiling reassuringly, "they are in good hands. We will protect them all the way to the safe zone. They will not be harmed. Now please, you will leave."

"That is a lie! I've seen the death camps. I've seen the massacres. I've seen the bodies. This backward state! Now I understand why this empire is a century behind!" the missionary shouted. "This is an atrocity and a clear violation of international human rights, and I—"

"You will what?" Colonel Barçin interrupted, now formally sharing his anger.

"I am going to publish a book documenting *everything* that I've witnessed! You, and all others like you, will be convicted of crimes against humanity."

"Go ahead," he dared, pointing at the man. "Write it! And tell me… Who will believe you?"

"The civilized world," the missionary stated. "Those who seek and stand with the truth."

The colonel measured the missionary with his callous eyes. "We are in war, and in every war, there are casualties. You will leave right now or face severe prosecution."

The colonel then took a step back and mounted his horse, making room for the new round of soldiers who forced their way between the missionaries and the caravan, consequently increasing the density of the blockade. They stood at arms with their rifles and fixed bayonets and pushed the missionaries out. Without any remaining options, they turned around and subsequently left.

With the commotion over, the soldiers then ordered the caravan to continue its outward flow. Taking a moment to gaze at the sight ahead, I soon realized that the woman was correct.

Most of the convoy *was* comprised of women and children. As one of just a few hundred men, Vartan and I, along with the prisoners, were thus pushed to where a pregnant woman walked with her mother and newly bearded husband, their arms around each other. Deciding to continue the missionaries' work, Vartan, too, probed for answers.

"What's happening here?" he asked in an erratic, almost panicked, tone. "Where's the safe zone?"

"We're being relocated," the woman replied. "They say it's for our protection."

"But where is it? Where's the safe zone?" he asked again.

The lady shrugged. "They haven't told us."

"Well, it's temporary, right? Do you know for how long?"

"Listen," the lady's husband intervened, visibly agitated, "Sara's eight months pregnant. She's very tired and can't deal with any more stress. The soldiers gave us one day to ready our things. *One day!* We packed what we could and sold the rest so that these thieves can send us away and *steal* our possessions. And to answer your questions, I don't know where we're going, I don't know how long we'll be there, and I don't know when we'll be back. All I know is that we're walking south with every other Armenian, and we'll return only once it's safe for us to come back. That was their *only* promise to us. Now stop asking so many questions and just walk… like everybody else."

Disregarding the justified outburst, I thought it through for a minute. Safe for us to come back? What were we trying to evade?

I was so confused. As Armenians, we had no outside enemies at the time. Not Russia, not France, not Great Britain. The only threat to us, our only enemy, was leading our caravan… to freedom of all places!

Wanting to voice my many observations aloud but not wanting to further upset Sara's husband, I ultimately kept silent. He had probably been through just as much as everyone else solely to get him to this convergence. Besides, I figured, he must have seen it the way I did.

"C'mon, Vartan," I suggested, "let's leave them alone."

And with that, we stopped cold to let the three gain some distance. Immediately, though, the unruly commands of the soldiers edged us forward. With thousands of people to collectively move at once, it was a monstrous effort, and thus we continued out of the city at the unbearably slow pace of the caravan, never being allowed a break without permission. Often, I glanced behind me as the racing set of unanswered questions loomed in my mind, including that of an unsure return. But by the end, as the entire city was vacated of Armenians, Kharpert, our home, vanished from sight.

Through the unrelenting mid-June heat, we thus marched into the ridges of the mountainous wilderness that our province was known for. The deep valleys and towering hills filled the landscape with awe and surprise. It was a treacherous, inaccessible place and certainly not a setting for the ill-equipped. Nearing the end of the early afternoon, we were completely surrounded by this new desolation. At this point, well beyond the outskirts and completely out of sight of the missionaries or any semblance of civilization, the demeanor of the soldiers quickly changed. What seemed like a hopeful answer to an impending question of violence now became the source. Quickly, they unlatched their whips and began lashing all who couldn't keep the pace, including another woman that I remember, perhaps seventy years old, lying atop a mule. Just a few hours of exposure under the burning sun was evidently too stressful for her and her aging animal. Through their nonstop orders and intense yells, three or four soldiers pushed and pulled the animal, trying to get it to move.

The mule, however, refused.

"Please, Marnos," one of her two friends yelled, "you must get off and move yourself!"

Unable to speak, the woman took to her friends' advice and slid to the dusty ground.

"Walk!" a soldier yelled, sending her a cracking lash.

"Enough!" her friend interfered.

Wheezing and breathing heavily, the two women helped

her to her feet, but the soldiers, disallowing of the amity, pulled them from under her arms, threatening them with death if they offered their services further. Consequently, after a few small steps on her own, the woman, once again, fell.

At the sound of a horse's gallop, Colonel Barçin joined in from the front. He stopped his horse over the woman and watched as his men deliberated over her fate. It didn't take long, however, before he dismounted, planting his tall leather boots on the ground, and, with the help of the other soldiers, dragged her to a cliff nearby, creating a thin cloud of dark-orange mist along the path. It was a quick, predetermined judgment as we watched in perilous wonder. Just short of the edge, the soldiers dropped her, and the colonel gave her a choice.

"If you swear to Islam," he offered, "we will let you live."

Staying true to her Christian faith, however, she shook her head in defiance. The colonel then unclipped a braided rope at his belt and tied one end around the woman's ankles and the other end around the trunk of a fruitless tree.

"Go ahead," he said to the younger soldier.

With a slight brush of his foot, the younger soldier rolled her over the edge. Immediately, the rope went taught as she swayed freely, suspended upside down.

The caravan shrieked.

"Convert," he repeated from above, "and the freedom will be yours to keep."

Unable to see the woman or hear a response, he then shrugged his shoulders a few moments later.

"Do it," he instructed to those at his side. "For the future."

Approving of his command, the soldiers unsheathed their scimitars, their long, Arabian swords curved at the tip, and sliced into the rope, tearing the individual fibers at first, then sending it fully recoiling back. Without even as much as a single sound, the woman plummeted to her death into the valley. The caravan screamed and cried as they covered the eyes of their children. Trying to escape, some, as if driven by a premature insanity, even attempted a desperate flee. Unprotected and slowed by fatigue, they didn't get far as the soldiers easily chased them down and hacked them to death, cutting them to pieces. Others who managed to run an extra distance were simply shot, and their bodies remained exactly as they fell.

Not even showing the slightest attempt in hiding his next words, the colonel then continued unremorsefully.

"Tell the rest," he commanded his troops, "and collect their animals."

As they spread the word to the others, the soldiers, as free as could be, immediately combed through the caravan. Forcefully pulling them away, they took the chickens, the donkeys, the horses, the oxen, and any other animals there might have been. Upturning carts and dumping their contents, they knocked away all that rested atop their sturdy bodies, including the people. With nothing to pull their belongings, the plethora of items, including food, was quickly left abandoned, creating a distinct path of discard for the soldiers to rummage through and take what they desired. Callous to the all pleas and indifferent to the need they served and to whom, the lack of help now forced everyone to walk, including the old, the sick, and the crippled, giving them an invitation only for a more creative death, including one foreseeable by exhaustion and exposure. Thus, with the sound of more pistol fire and prayer, many more perished as the soldiers fell to the feet of temptation and placed their new items atop their new animals.

Leaving the dead behind, we were pushed to march for the latter quarter of that day until we set our sights on a local Arab mountain village. Immediately, after the loss of their items, my people begged to stop for food and water. Impertinently, however, the soldiers purposefully led us a roundabout way to ensure the secrecy of their campaign, driving some of us closer to madness. As we gazed down at the village, every once in a while, passing villagers, trying to fulfill their curiosity, would stop and stare. Sadly, and as surprised as they were, their attention was diverted away by the slew of stolen animals that would be sold to them for a few gold pieces, an insult to their worth.

Well beyond the sight of the long-gone village, we then set up camp at the onset of nightfall. Whoever had them pitched their goatskin tents on the exposed northern rocks of the mountain. Demoralized and defeated, I listened to the nonstop cries as I tried to understand day one of this everlasting saddening experience. How would I possibly explain this? Where would I begin? Who would I tell? Maybe the colonel was right. Who would even believe us? As the kerosene lamps around the campsite lit like fireflies in the sky, I, of course, continued to ask questions. I had every right to do so. At that moment, though, as so many times before, I had too much to focus on; I couldn't think enough to begin arranging anything. Not in this condition. Hunger had spun my mind around an untraceable spool, and thirst had weakened my ambition. Having absolutely nothing in this horrid deficiency, Vartan and I thus sat beneath the canopy of a short tree at the outskirts, resting our heads against the bark, staring off in different directions. As strong as we claimed to be, undeniable exhaustion had us expired. We didn't say much to each other. We were starving. Our lips were swollen, and our tongues were dried. We were dehydrated. The intense sun and eternally dry and dusty journey had cracked our tanned and torn skin, and the kilometers of walking had bruised our already swollen feet. It was an unremittingly terrible circumstance, but at the mercy of the sunless night, it felt good to rest, just enough to get us through day two.

33

"Just weeks prior to our exodus," old Armen explained, seated in his chair, "it's true that the Ottoman Turkish government passed a temporary law legalizing the deportation and relocation of thousands of families. Introduced by Mehmet Talaat Pasha, the Law of Deportation, called the Tehcir Law, was passed in the Ottoman Parliament by the Committee of Union and Progress on the 27th of May 1915. Even though the official document from the time does not explicitly mention the

Armenians, it authorized all officers of the Turkish military to deport, as individuals or collectively, all who were *sensed* to be a threat to national security and defense, all who were *sensed* to oppose the Turkish government, her orders, and all who were *suspected* of treasonous acts and espionage against the state. And since they were granted the right to deport any Ottoman civilian from any background, abuse of this biased law was commonplace. So yes, to answer your question, the colonel didn't lie. It *was* an official order from Constantinople to evict us from our homeland. The government had successfully and unofficially, through this temporary written law, made it illegal to be Armenian. It, however, stated nothing about the legalization of the murder that followed thereafter or the continuation of deportations well after it was deemed unconstitutional."

"What about their houses and the things that were left behind?" Armen's granddaughter asked.

"Well, on the 13th of September, 1915, months after we were deported, the Ottoman Parliament also passed, in conjunction with the aforementioned temporary Tehcir Law, another temporary law called the Law of Expropriation and Confiscation, solely to deal with that subsequent issue. The law stated that all possessions, including homes; any building, including churches, schools, and banks; land; personal property; livestock; and all funds that had been abandoned were to be turned over to the government to be *protected* until the Armenians returned. It was never protected nor returned to us. They had legalized theft after a forced and involuntary abandonment by Armenians, using the confiscated possessions to pay their politicians and resettle Turks onto Armenian land, even going as far as renaming the cities. It quickly and effectively made everything Armenian, simply put, Turkish. As of the telling of this story, fifty-six years later, this temporary law remains in full effect.

"Let's continue."

34
Day Two

Before the sun's rise, the soldiers yelled for us to get up. Unable to catch up from any lack of sleep or even see the path ahead, Vartan and I began our march with the others in the cover of darkness. All around us, those who weren't careful lost their footing and fell, spraining and even breaking their bones on the bare rock. Unable to keep up, they were killed or left behind.

When the sun finally peeked over the horizon and slowly began heating the air, those who had extra supplies, or at least a humanly desire to share, began a system of helping those who didn't. Like a charity, they gave food, sips of water, shelter in the form of blankets or animal skins, and extra shoes for those walking barefoot. Even a man that I saw offered to carry a baby girl and a small roll of goods to give her tired mother a break. Gratefully accepting, the mother handed the child and roll to him as he walked alongside. It was relieving to see the strong defending the weak and the fearless helping the fearful. It was the purest unity of an exploited people, and it sparked a hope that would eventually expand to a limitless rule.

In time, we approached the top of a rocky ravine that had a small stream running through it. Through the undisturbed cracks of its walls, bushy plants grew out of the face like a beard on a man. With a direct command, the soldiers told us to make camp at the top of that rocky ravine. Not yet mid-day, we thus settled down onto the ground. There, I contemplated removing my boots to give my feet a chance to breathe but didn't want to be caught barefoot when we started moving again. So, I sat with my dirt-filled eyes and watched my surroundings and all that it was, until the sting of the blisters on my feet pressing against the thick leather echoed into my brain. As I tried moisturizing my drying mouth with my own saliva, I realized that I couldn't keep my boots on any longer. I therefore stretched over and loosened the leather laces. Carefully then, I slipped off my boots and dropped them next to me. Feeling the cool air drying the sweat, I wiggled my toes and gently began massaging the arches when the soldiers made an announcement.

"Any man who wants a drink of water," they yelled to our part of the caravan, "follow us!"

Quickly, everyone arose, even the women, finally relieved, but the soldiers sat them back down with their rifles.

"The men only!" they repeated.

Solely focused on the mention of hydration, I grabbed a boot and carefully, with the utmost of care, slipped it on, trying not to rupture my blisters. By the time I grabbed the other boot, a group of two hundred or so men had already gathered ahead of us, some carrying containers for others, to begin their short trek towards the soldiers.

"Hurry up," Vartan said, standing, waiting over me.

Moving as efficiently as I could, I tied my laces and stood up in a way to try to conserve energy.

"Let's go," I said.

As we followed the group, a younger soldier, one that I'd never seen before, stopped us cold. He was distraught. I saw it in his face.

"Not you two," he said, grabbing our arms.

Vartan turned around and tore the soldier's hand off his wrist by twisting out his thumb.

"What do you mean not us?" he argued. "We're thirsty."

The soldier took a step back and pointed his pistol at us. "It's not your time," he said. "Now move back."

With a daring stare in Vartan's eyes, we moved away from the younger soldier and walked back to where we were just seconds ago with the women and children. There, he stood guard over us as we watched the rest of the men with a helpless glow, most of whom I recognized from the prison, line up at the edge of the ravine. The soldier then paced near us, walking in percussive steps, preventing us from drinking.

"Now remove your clothes," the soldiers ordered the men lined at the edge of the ravine.

Curious and just as confused as us, the men stood for a while, questioning the direction.

"In front of our women?" a man asked a moment later.

A soldier pointed his rifle at him. "They are not your women anymore," he answered. "Take them off."

As odd as the request was, the men thus removed their torn shirts and pants and casually threw them towards the row of thirty or so soldiers. A handful then raked through and collected the garments by hand, while they stood, facing them, naked, waiting for the promise of life.

"Now turn around," they said, "if you want water."

As thirsty as the man next to them, every single one of them turned around, peering into the rocky ravine.

"Aim!" a soldier commanded.

The soldiers raised their rifles.

"Fire!" he screamed almost immediately.

Through the blast, the bullets left the chambers and into the backs of the naked men, dropping them collectively as a group into the shallow stream below, making an unwelcome splash at the bottom. Those who tried to evade their looming end leaped prematurely onto the jagged rocks only to be met by the bullets streaming from above at those who still moved.

Immediately, the women burst again with their cries. The screams, my God, the agonizing screams. They never stopped.

At that moment, a second blast of gunfire from another part of the caravan echoed against the walls, cursing the air. The soldiers then slung the weapons back over their shoulders and walked back towards us. On the way, one soldier bent down to the ground. He had found something. He poked through the dirt with his finger and grabbed a handful of soil, dumping the contents onto his other palm. Subtly waving his hand sideways, he sifted through the loose dirt and rock, letting the larger pieces fall through his fingers. He then let out a short burst of laughter while holding up a ring made of gold, laughing fully in celebration of his find.

"My reward!" he said. "This is our reward!"

Drawing the attention of other soldiers, he then searched the ground for more as the others quickly turned to the caravan in its entirety, at first rummaging through boxes and wraps, and eventually stripping the women of their clothes, looking for their treasures. Through the escalating ordeal, they stole everything, stuffing their canvas military bags with anything of value—gold, jewelry, and currency, ravaging and killing anyone who resisted.

"Go ahead," they answered to the resistance, "tempt us, and we'll call for reinforcements!"

To combat the robbery, many of the women buried their valuables, in hopes of a return, or, as a more common practice, swallowed them whole. If I ever had the urge or wanted to experience living in the land of lawlessness fueled by violent greed, this would be it.

While they carried canvas bags of gold and jewelry and draped them over their horses, the soldiers started us up again, marching us farther into the wilderness towards the desert.

As we continued our ever-slowing pace, five or six soldiers, I noticed, stopped to speak to Colonel Barçin. With their goods over their horses, they did so for a few minutes until the colonel pointed south, ahead of the caravan. Just as his hand relaxed, the soldiers saluted and dismounted. They removed all the gear from their animals, including the bags, then leaped back on, riding their horses full stride in his pointed direction, creating a blinding fog of dust. I coughed a dry and burning cough as the particles lingered in the air around us and even closed my eyes in a desperate attempt to sleep as I walked, but even that didn't help.

By the time nightfall arose, it was time to make camp again. Away from us, the soldiers set up their tents and placed the valuables and gold next to the containers of kerosene they used to make fire. There, they ate lavishly in the warmth, laughing aloud, boasting about their day, while Vartan and I sat against a lone, smooth rock in the cold of the night with nothing to eat for the third day and nothing to drink for the second. My eyes burned, my head pounded from the inside out and the outside in, the scrapes on my body stung from the salt of my sweat, and I could barely speak. It was at that moment that a damning thought ran through my head.

"I think I'm dying," I told Vartan.

Not immediately responding, he let my words process.

"No, you're not," he said as if he were out of breath. "Don't say that."

"Well," I began, with a shift of my thoughts, "I feel like I am. I've never been this thirsty or hungry. I'm so hungry... so tired. Look how skinny we're getting."

Vartan didn't answer. He looked depressed, understandably so. We had to do everything we could to conserve our bodies, even if it meant not speaking. I knew, however, that there was more to it, and it made me think enough to put myself in Vartan's boots in order to think like him. I raced through his mind, collecting any information I could. Just when I thought that even thinking was draining my limited energy, I suddenly realized why Vartan was so desperate to know the answers to so many questions, why he always seemed to be in a panic, why he always seemed to be in deep thought. It wasn't deep at all, just solitary. If Vartan and I were going to work together, we had to understand each other.

"Vartan," I started, saying only what I, myself, could recognize, "don't worry—you'll see her again."

Realizing my understanding, he awakened, rediscovering an old connection.

"I didn't—I never even said bye," he confessed.

Before he could elaborate, a thin, bearded figure approached us. I stood up in defense, fueled by adrenaline.

"Who's there?" I called out in Ottoman Turkish.

Vartan stood as well.

The figure stopped.

"It's me, Hovahness," a man answered in Armenian.

"We don't know a Hovahness," I retorted.

"Yes, you do. We met the other day, informally. I came to apologize for my outburst."

"Sara's husband?" I asked, remembering his pregnant wife.

"Yes. Please," he invited, "join us in our tent. As my offering."

"Is there food?" I asked bluntly. "We're hungry."

"Yes."

"And water?" I asked again.

"Yes," he confirmed.

Vartan and I exchanged glances. Neither of us had any outright objections, so, unanimously, we accepted his offer and followed him a few yards to his tent—a thin tarp held up by three tree branches and dimly lit by a tiny kerosene lamp. As we entered the surprisingly large interior, Hovahness introduced us to his family seated on a large, handwoven textile, atop a colorful carpet made of wool, common to the cause.

"This, as you know, is my wife Sara, and her mother, Lorik."

"Pleased to meet you," we each greeted in Armenian as we sat down on the large carpet covering the ground while Lorik massaged her swollen ankles.

"I'm Armen, and this is my brother, Vartan."

"Again, I would like to formally apologize for losing my temper earlier. This, in combination—"

"I understand, Hovahness," I interrupted. "You did nothing wrong. We weren't insulted by any means. This is a terrible time for all of us, and I would like to say thank you for sheltering us. Right now, excuse my bluntness, but we're starving and very thirsty."

"Very well," he smiled, "and call me Ova."

"So nobody knows anything, right?" Vartan started again. "I mean, we're just being relocated?"

"Basically," Ova responded as he casually reached into his bag and took out a leather water sack the size of a man's head, complete with a leather shoulder strap.

I followed its movements with intensive eyes.

"Help yourselves," he said as he handed it to me.

I popped out the cork plug, letting it swing freely by the leather cord. Before helping myself, though, I handed it to Vartan.

"No," he refused, holding up his palm, "you go ahead."

Without a second's pause, I tilted my head back and held

it up, slowly tipping the wooden nozzle. From it came the source of my life. Water. Although warm, it moved down my throat like liquid silk and refueled my deprived body, partly washing away my headache. Well aware of the limited supply, I resisted the urge to continue and stopped a short time after, breathing a sound of satisfaction in response. I then handed the sack to Vartan, who drank from it as well.

"Now that you've drunk," Ova predicted as I wiped away the excess between the hairs of my lengthening beard, "you're going to be even *more* hungry."

Reaching into the same bag, he then carefully removed two small bundles of brown burlap, the same type of material that covered the floor of our barn. He placed the bundles in the center of our circle and carefully unwrapped each one. In the first bundle were raisins, and in the second, walnuts.

"Help yourself," he greeted again.

By instinct, I reached for the food, but Vartan held back my hand.

"We insist," he began, motioning to the meal, "the ladies go first. I'm sure they've eaten just as much as we have."

As a rare event, Sara and Lorik smiled before reaching in with their forefingers and thumbs, taking three walnuts and five raisins each. Vartan then offered them to Ova, who took the same portion. Finally, we, too, took our portion and ate them all the same. Humbled by their hospitality in a time when they didn't have to offer it, I felt my body attack the nourishment like a foreign enemy, absorbing it immediately. It wasn't roasted duck, but for the moment, it satisfied my needs.

And that was our dinner for the night.

"So," I began, wanting to know my rescuer, "where are you from?"

"From the city," Ova replied. "We lived in an apartment near the main square. And yourself?"

"We had a vineyard and apricot orchard in the outskirts."

"Good Lord!" he smiled. "Do you know Garo the winemaker? My God, I swear he makes the best."

An overwhelming sadness pushed me over. My body heated as I heard Garo's laugh and saw his smile, and the lump in my throat swelled.

"Yes," I answered, "I do."

"Is he here? With us?"

"No," I answered.

"Oh?"

"He… didn't make it. Neither did his family. He was killed… in a slave camp."

Ova took a moment to himself. "Son of a bitch," he swore as he made the sign of the cross. "I apologize for my language, but Garo was a great man."

"I know," I agreed.

"He's in a much better place than here. This, around you, is corruption at its worst. I'm sorry, but none of this makes sense. You know, we ought to plan something, a *real* uprising."

"Oh," Lorik, Ova's mother-in-law, uttered, not amused, "you and your revolutions! You have a better chance at living if you just sit still!"

"Just look around you," he continued, ignoring his mother-in-law. "There are tens of thousands of us and less than a hundred soldiers. We just have to, you know, come together." He passionately interlocked his fingers to make a ball with his hands.

My ears wiggled. My eyes liked what they saw. He had my attention now.

"But they have weapons, swords, and rifles. We're dying with barely sticks for fire," Vartan explained.

"Yes, but that's not the point," he reasoned, cutting himself short. "Ah, what am I saying," he continued. "I have no idea. Just a thought."

"Exactly," Lorik affirmed, "just a thought."

Ova paused.

"So… which one of you is older?" Sara pointed to the two of us, changing the subject.

With the recurring theme fresh in my mind and an unaccustomed sense of meeting another person so intrigued by the world around him, I didn't respond. Who was this man? This Ova, who shared my visions? This man, with a bearded, European face, elongated head, chiseled nose, and proportional body, seemingly carved from a block of marble. This thinning simpleton. Who was he? Where did he come from? How did he get here?

"Well, uh, I'm almost eighteen, and Armen is sixteen," Vartan answered after noting my silence.

Ova was very peculiar to me. He didn't say much, but just enough to show that he was a visionary, a man of principle. He was ambitious and curious, and his ambition and ideas, not strangely enough, fed into mine. I knew what he meant. He knew what he meant. It made sense in his mind, and it made sense in mine. He just couldn't put it in words enough for others to understand.

"Two brothers," he responded, "very nice."

We just have to come together, I repeated to myself, still fixated on the thought. Did I finally meet someone who saw the world as I did? Did I finally find hope in this desolation? If Ova was capable of thought like this, then more would be, too. Immediately, I imagined the shocking effects something this powerful could produce. I imagined how an idea this audacious could spread like disease. Something so powerful that it could become unstoppable and change the course of history. Something stronger than any force on Earth. An infinite source of influence. A victory that could defy all odds.

That was the answer.

Unity.

A deep instinct, an innate force that all humans are naturally born with. The uniform and undying determination of the man next to you to see it through to the end. The need and the want, like Ova said, to come together. I watched him hopefully as he stood up to sit next to his wife, Sara, an absolute gem. Her long, black hair, black eyebrows, dark-brown eyes, and unreal exotic appearance. I watched him, now as a man of other men. I watched him as he slid behind her and held her in harmony, completely unaware of the potential he just described, and placed his hand gently on her pregnant stomach. I watched him, thinking about the unfolding future, planned from a poor man's tent, until Vartan, now entirely uncomfortable from the sight, stood up and left, disrupting my valuable, infinite train of thought, taking my focus with him.

"Excuse me," I spoke on his behalf as I followed him out.

"Hey!" I called out to him. "What are you doing?"

"I can't be here anymore! We can't do this," he expelled. "This isn't the way it should be!"

"You have no—"

"She doesn't know where we are; she doesn't know where we're going; she doesn't know for how long, and the worst part is neither do we. I can't send her a letter, and I can't even leave! When will I see her again? *How* will I see her again? I'm so—I just don't know what to do. This is tearing me apart. How did this happen? How did we *let* this happen?"

"Vartan, you'll see her again! But not now. We're here now. We have to do what we can with what we have. Just remember, Nadia's safe. Keep telling yourself that."

"I try to, but it's so hard. My God, how do I know you're right?"

"Those people are good people. You saw what they did for us."

"I know, but what if she's not there when I get back? What if she left? How will I find her?"

"You will," I said, just as a faint whirring sound filled the night air from the distance. "Trust me."

"I'll tak—"

"Shh… shh," I breathed, interrupting him. "Do you hear that?"

The strange yet familiar sound grew louder, riding flawlessly atop the wind. It whistled through the air, rattling like hollow bells made from a thin metal.

Vartan put his ear to the wind.

"Yeah," he replied.

Confused, I stood still and continued to listen as it

uniformly grew louder.

"It sounds like—"

"*Shh!*" I interrupted again.

Slowly, I put my ear to the ground, followed by the soft touch of my hand. The earth was rumbling. I felt it.

Noting the same disturbance, the other refugees began emerging out of their tents. Immediately then, the source became clear—clawing hooves and neighs, now mixing with that of the bells and whistles. I stood erect, realizing the approaching threat.

"Get back in your tents!" I screamed.

Not a moment later, the sudden onslaught of mountain Kurds ran through the caravan with decorations hanging over their animals, disrupting the night. Like savages, they rode in every direction, screaming and yelling, going around Vartan and me so close that our shirts caught the wind of their passing. Mesmerized by the confusion and the sudden mayhem, we yelled all around us, warning the others. If these intruders wanted to kill us, they would have done so by now. Thus, with complete disregard of our presence, I realized that these were thieves of a different kind.

Like bears searching for honey, the Kurds then dismounted and began tearing away the tents with their swords. They threw the coverings carelessly to the side, ignoring the food and leaping past the money. When they finally found what they came for, an easy task, they dragged out the prettiest of their prizes and placed them atop their horses, illuminating the reason for this uninvited tirade.

They were here for the girls.

"Vartan," I yelled, "get back!"

Fully complying with my request, we ran back to the torn tent, now in useless pieces on the ground. There, I pulled the wool carpet out like a tablecloth under fine dinnerware.

"Quickly," I ordered, "Sara, you and your mother, hide under here."

As scared as they could be, they crawled under the carpet as I threw branches and twigs over it, even dirt, using anything to mask the colors. I then joined Vartan, and we stood guard amid the turmoil, using every primitive part of our minds to protect the unprotected.

"Any girl that passes," I instructed Vartan and Ova. "Get them and hide them!"

They acknowledged.

"Over here!" we called out in Armenian to the passing girls. "In here!"

Hearing the familiar language, three ran to us, and we guided them under the same wool carpet. I even reached out and grabbed a young one's arm, pulling her to safety.

As we stood in defense against the ravishing horde encircling us, as our girls were being stolen away into the mountain caves and valley dwellings, and even as the Turkish soldiers now joined the riot and took them into their own tents, I thought about what Vartan said. How had our lives withered down to this? How did this happen? How did we *allow* this to happen? From inception to now, all the events that led to hundreds of thousands of Armenians being relocated from the land they'd occupied for millennia worked seamlessly with each other. My grandmother was right. From the past to the present, from the Hamidian Massacres, to the massacre at Adana, to the stripping of our rights, to the blockades, the isolation, to the false charges of conspiracy, to the sudden occupation of our schools, the forced removal of our firearms, the elimination of our defense, the killing of our community leaders, the slaughters, the legalization of crime, and finally, the deportation for those who remained. All of it accomplished thoroughly over a course of time. She saw it coming. As Armenians, though, why didn't we? We shouldn't have been so naïve. We *should have* seen it coming. We should have seen this final chapter looming in our midst, using the past as a means to define the future, noting that each successive event had grown in severity from the one before it. Perhaps, though, we were blinded by our silly vision of prosperity. Perhaps our naïvety was sourced from our foolish goal of harmony, our irrational optimism during a time of violence. Perhaps, even, we wanted to aid the progress of a nation. Why didn't I speak up? Why didn't I voice my opinion? I was only a boy. Who would have listened? Now, though, as a man of all men, I had to be fair. I needed to take my own advice. Did it make sense to blame each other? Of course not. How could I possibly ask the Armenians to foresee their own fate? What about the abusive government? Ara was right. We should have never trusted them—the lies and broken promises, the deception, the robbery, and the depravity of the Young Turks, who, instead of working with the Armenians to unite a broken empire, instead of granting us our deserving rights, instead of being the driving force to a prosperous and harmonious future, decided to totally eliminate the source of their jealousy and, at the least, throw their economy into complete ruin. After all, we were the inventors, the bankers, the merchants, the tillers of the land, the doctors, the forward thinkers, and the teachers—the economic and intellectual steam engine. But now, we were being driven out like cattle in a deportation.

A slow march to the death.

There was no safe zone. No promised land. The soldiers weren't taking care of us. They never were. There was no food, no water, and no protection. We were defenseless and bare on this infinite march to hell. To an end far worse than any massacre. To a death through torture, starvation, thirst, sadness, disease, anger, and madness, completely deprived of all units responsible for human survival. To a place built of falsehoods, disguised purposefully as truths and hidden behind the curtain of shame. A place that would ultimately challenge our faith, our will to survive, and our ambition to dream. What was happening here was happening everywhere, an attempted annihilation of millions of people across the Ottoman Empire—the murder of Armenia. Hundreds of thousands of helpless women and girls, each on one of hundreds of death marches, each of whom forcefully dropped everything of their day in an attempt to arrange for this mysterious and momentous journey to an undisclosed location for an undisclosed amount of time. Drastically altering their lives, with no time to organize adequate supplies or even food and water, with no instruction on how to pack or what to bring, I couldn't imagine the stress and the hardship they must have endured, especially after facing the bestial slaughter of their husbands and molestation of their families. Now, alone, they spent their days marching through all the elements, through dust and fire, fighting rape, kidnapping, and insanity, crying pitifully, wearing barely but their disheveled hair and torn dresses, now carrying only the items they needed to survive. Over treacherous terrain and under the torturous sun and drying heat of the rocks, they faced the biggest challenge of their lives, knowing eventually the day would come that would force them to decide who would live and who would die: them or the ones who walked alongside, dreadfully hungry and thirsty, no longer laughing or playing, now starving and dying—their children. And thus, as I stood in defense for those who couldn't stand on their own, for those under the hidden carpet, and growled at the passing mountain Kurds, summoned and armed by the soldiers who marched ahead, informing them of the approaching defenseless race, as I stood guard over that wool covering, protecting six girls from death, united next to the one who I trusted most and a man named Ova, I screamed inside through the flame, feeling my heart speed up once again to an abysmal rate. And so, the more I thought and the more I saw, with each passing sight and each passing sound, the screams, the cries, and the desperation, with so much inhumanity and so many thousands of charred, maggot-filled bodies scattered along the path of these two unassuming brothers, I realized that I had only seen the world through the eyes of an idealist. Now, though, I began to see it as my grandmother did. I began to feel as my grandmother felt. Against my own nature, against my own acceptance of myself, I understood now what it meant.

I began to hate.

35
Day Three

On the third day, Vartan and I awoke next to Ova, lying on the edges of the wool carpet, holding it down securely with our bodies. Realizing the new light, I quickly scrambled up and pulled it up, sending the dust in all directions. To my immediate consolation, I exhaled a sigh of relief, feeling the hair on my growing beard tickle my nose. Sara, Lorik, and the four orphan girls were all right. Relieved, I wiped my face free of the dirt and, with Vartan and Ova, helped gather what remained of their belongings. It was time to march again. As a way to try to occupy their minds, the four girls, too, joined in on the work ahead of us.

They were mortified. I saw it in their faces.

"Please," I said, grabbing the youngest girl's wrist, "don't lift another finger. You need to rest."

Turning her head up at me, she locked her innocent eyes with mine. In that little moment, she began to cry. Then, with a compelling lunge, before I could even react, she wrapped her arms around my torso, barely reaching my chest, and hugged me, harder than I've ever felt, causing me to drop the small items I had in my hand.

"Thank you," she cried. "Thank you for what you've done."

I didn't say anything. What could I have said? I simply returned the gesture and held her for as long as she wanted, until she let go.

"As long as we look out for each other," I stated a moment later, "we can survive anything. Promise me you'll do that for the rest of your long life."

Crying still, she nodded her head in my chest. "I promise."

The other girls then came in and gave me, Vartan, and Ova their gratitude, thanking us each with their blessings, including Sara, with a quick yet passionate kiss to her husband. With our arms knit around each other, we then carried on. With each step, with each limp, we continued our march, staying true to the mundane process.

Not an hour later, a groan, a painful grumble from behind us, caused me to turn around and look. It was Lorik, Sara's mother, sobbing in pain.

"Please, Sara," she called out, "my ankles are swelling again. We need to stop."

Using Ova for support, she leaned over and began massaging them with her thumb as I looked around for any soldiers. There weren't any. So, after a short walk back, I knelt down to take a look. Her ankles were the size of small cantaloupes, and the swelling had traveled down to the top of her feet. Lorik wasn't a small woman, but no ankle should've been that large. Gently placing my finger on it, I felt the undrained joint.

"Ay!" she cried in agony. "Oh my God, my God, this is too much."

Her eyes began to tear from the pain.

"Mom, you need to move," Sara advised. "Please get up and walk. We'll carry you if we have to."

"Sara, I love you," Lorik cried softly. "Go on ahead of me. Let me be."

Refusing to accept her mother's request, Sara responded.

"No, Mom, this is the heat talking," she explained. "I'm not going to leave yo—"

"You have a child to raise," she interrupted. "I've lived my life already. I've watched you grow and marry a handsome man. This is the end of my road. You must continue without me. Look at me." She pointed to her ankles. "I'm useless. All I will do is hold you back."

"What? Mom—"

"Lorik, you're talking nonsense," Ova interjected. "Now get up before the soldiers find you."

Continuing to cry like a tired baby, Lorik sat on the heated gravel as the caravan passed around us, watching with barely enough energy to see.

"No, no, no, no," she cried. "I'm done. I'm done. This is it."

"If you don't walk, we'll carry you," Ova said as he leaned over. "With God as my witness, I'll die before I leave you behind."

He placed his hands underneath her body, and Vartan

and I leaned over to help pick her up. Just as we did, two soldiers quickly spied us and hit us out of the way with the butts of their rifles.

I didn't even see it coming as we fell just meters away.

"Get up!" they yelled to Lorik as they took a step back and pointed their rifles at her.

Yelling from the ground, Sara, too, began to cry uselessly as I placed my hand on my forehead and felt the warmth of my own blood trickling down my face. Firmly claiming her position, Lorik remained where she sat and began to pray. Just as she started, the soldier lowered his rifle and slung it back over his shoulder. From my dazed state of mind, I thought, through a miraculous discovery, that his human side had taken over.

I was, unfortunately, wrong.

Instead, the soldier unbuckled his holster and quickly pulled out a smaller weapon, his pistol, and pointed the barrel at her temple.

"I am not telling you again," he repeated as he cocked it back with his free hand and held it firmly in place. "Get up!"

Suddenly then, Ova jumped in and knelt in front of the soldier, placing his head between the weapon and Lorik.

"We will carry her," he pleaded softly, quivering.

The soldier stared at Ova, who followed the barrel's position with his head, then looked at his comrade, who nodded in approval.

"Good," the soldier agreed as he uncocked the pistol and placed it back into the holster at his side. "Carry her or you'll be food for the dogs."

"Thank you," Ova whispered with a slight bow of his head. "Thank you."

Simply then, as if on a mere stroll, the soldiers left but watched us from the distance. Thus, by that mid-morning, Vartan and I, each with barely enough energy to carry ourselves, staggered up and helped Ova carry Lorik. Through the nonstop dust and heat, even as my legs burned and my fingers ached, even when I couldn't keep my eyes open, and even as the sun slowly dried the life out of us, we dragged our feet over the dirt, doing what we had to do, carrying a woman whom we'd previously never met.

Through my hazy eyes, I then noticed a large group of people marching towards us in the opposite direction. I watched the dust being kicked up like a storm until they passed right in front of us—a cluster of fifty or so men, each tied together in groups of six or eight being led away by four soldiers. As they passed, as we carried Sara's mother, I looked at their faces; we looked at their faces—each one of them as sullen as the next, yet dreadfully peaceful. Down into the shallow valley behind us, they marched beyond our line of sight, succumbing to the abuse, barefoot, hands tied. Just seconds later, a ring of gunshots echoed, scaring off the birds. I couldn't even turn around to look, but only the soldiers returned to join the colonel ahead.

"Sir," one began, "we have orders from Constantinople to bury the dead. The orders are quite clear."

The colonel began to laugh. "That's what I hear. They keep reminding us. Why can't we just leave them? They'll be the fertilizer for our new Turkey."

The other soldiers laughed, but the one persisted, "Sir, they're diseased. The soldiers are falling ill because of them."

After finishing his laugh, the colonel began to say something further but fell silent and thought for a moment, now understanding of the need. "We'll stop here," he said, followed by his next orders.

Fulfilling the colonel's next request, a team of soldiers then stopped the caravan, weaving through the clumps of refugees, and picked men at random, forcing them to leave their families and walk ahead of them at gunpoint. Among the chosen were Vartan, Ova, and I. Rifles high, they forced us to place Lorik on the ground and walk ahead to a small spot of thick, newly sprouting trees. We did so in silence. There, we met with nearly two hundred other men. Throwing fifty shovels with short, wooden handles, the soldiers ordered us to begin digging a long, rectangular ditch. In the heat of the day, Vartan, Ova, and I thus began throwing the rocky dirt over our shoulders and into the small forest, creating a blanket of fine particulates that lingered in the space around us.

It was there, not too far away from the rest of the caravan, that I met Joseph, a man in his early twenties, digging with his bare hands, scratching and clawing at the ground.

"The suffering, the suffering," he kept mumbling to himself, "must end the suffering."

Exchanging glances of pity, Vartan, Ova, and I kept our thinning heads low as we listened to his unending repetition, until finally, well into the night, the soldiers ordered us to stop digging. With bloodied and scraped hands, we and whoever hadn't fallen dead from exhaustion thus dropped the shovels and scrambled to our tentless camp to sleep as survivors of the third day.

36
Day Four

Covered with dirt, I awoke at sunrise unsure as to how we were still alive. It had been days since we'd eaten a decent meal. As I looked around me, seeing the grisly display of abandoned infants and rotting corpses, I noticed how much smaller the caravan had become. Most of the men had been killed, with death and disease now as plentiful as the dirt upon which we walked. Numbed, I tried to shake off the clay, pasted on me like glue, as I sat with Vartan, Sara, and the four orphan girls while Ova tended to Lorik's ankles, which had showed significant signs of improvement from the break.

Without delay, the soldiers roamed through the caravan, just as the day before, and began rounding up men at random. Pulling them up from their shirts or underarms, they forced them back to the ditch as I sat, waiting, in hopes that they wouldn't come by. My wishful thinking, once more, had proved useless. Swiftly, two lingering soldiers approached our settlement from behind and aggressively pulled Ova up to his feet by his upper arm, pushing him to join the others, leaving Vartan and me behind.

Crying in desperation, we reached out, trying to pull him back, but the soldiers kicked us down and dragged him away. Everything that could've been said had already been said, therefore creating a sickening silence. With an extended glance back at us, Ova studied the four girls, then looked at Lorik and finally, at Sara, one last time, understanding of the end.

Beginning again with the same tools, he thus continued scraping away the dirt with the other men, carving the hole deeper as the soldiers sat on guard atop their horses, inspecting their work. They continued the dreadfully slow process, carefully avoiding the dead, until mid-day, when their laborious efforts created a ditch a meter deep, perhaps two meters wide, and forty meters long.

"All men drop your shovels," the soldiers then announced multiple times to the overcrowded assembly.

Relieved from the break, the men straightened their bent postures and threw the shovels out to the feet of the horses, wiping the tiny amount of salt water from their brows shortly after. There they stood, in the ditch, covered fully with the same reddish-brown dirt, and watched as the Turkish soldiers collected their tools. From my vantage point, I saw their panting chests, the tops of their shoulders, and their heads, including Ova's, as the soldiers positioned themselves at the edge. Behind them, the colonel then raised his hand into the air, and the soldiers raised their rifles. Quickly, I leaped, covering Sara's eyes, in anticipation of the brutality. With a drop of his arm, through the punishing sound, Ova then fell out of sight as they shot their rifles, killing some and injuring the rest. They then began reloading, but the colonel interrupted their actions, cutting them off.

"No more," he screamed, initiating a cease fire. "Conserve your bullets!"

"But they're still alive," one pointed to the bleeding mess.

The colonel peered inside, confirming his underling's concerns, then slapped the reigns of his horse. Making no attempt to slow down, the colonel rode the beast towards the ditch. Just at the edge, however, the horse stopped voluntarily, sliding powerfully to a halt, and neighed. Contrary to the colonel's commands, it backed up away from the pit of wounded men as the soldiers watched their leader, confused, yet intrigued, all the same. Once again, the colonel slapped the reigns, and again the horse refused, disobeying its call of duty.

Angrily, Colonel Barçin called upon a soldier. "Come here," he ordered, "and slap its rump."

With a wild swing, the soldier landed his palm on the rump, scaring the horse. Unwillingly, it thus jumped into the ditch and trampled the survivors like twigs on a forest floor, crushing them beneath its immense weight. The sound of it, combined with the neighing of the frightened animal, caused a matrimony of screams from those who watched, from those who needed to look so they could believe it, from Sara, Lorik, Vartan, and me, and all the others.

And thus, in a shallow, unmarked mass grave, somewhere in the mountains near a small forest, Ova perished under the hooves of an unwilling beast through a grossly unwarranted death.

Without a moment's pause, as impossible as it seemed, we were then ordered to get up and continue our march. At this point, being so tired, hungry, and thirsty, I was unable to distinguish between reality and wherever else I could have possibly been. I couldn't believe it anymore. I couldn't fathom the death, the scale of it.

It truly felt like the end of the world.

As brothers, Vartan and I took it upon ourselves to overcome our own adversity and ensure the well-being of the women, of Sara, Lorik, and the four orphan girls who cried the entire way, never once stopping, forcing us to become immune to the sound. We tried every method of consolation, but there was nothing we could have done to dampen their emotions. They were unbelieving of the malice, just as I was. Only until the late afternoon did a familiar sound occupy our ears anew.

The sound of renewal—flowing water. We had begun our approach to the Euphrates River.

Crying with what came across as a sudden joy, the

women of the caravan staggered their way over, some still in their now oversized dresses, some naked, and impatiently threw themselves at puddles of water leading to the banks. Then, as the thunderously flowing river came into view, they shrieked as the corpses of the ones who marched behind us floated downstream like boats as plentiful as the droplets upon which they rode, drowned as a group. Becoming stuck in the brush, their swollen bodies partially clogged the river, forcing an overflow of the banks. The sight and sound of gushing water within our reach, however, presided over the nerve-wrecking sight of the hundreds, likely thousands, of bodies, becoming a salvation to our deprivation. Thus, despite the diseased water, most ran up to the small opening in its bank still, causing a menacing and confusing stampede, to try to get their fill.

Seeing our rush, the soldiers met us with swings of their scimitars, scaring us away, quenching their insatiable appetite for power as we tried to quench ours for water.

"Those who want to drink must pay," they announced. "Ten gold pieces a cup!"

Quickly, the caravan began searching for their currency. They looked high and low, digging through bags, pockets, even searching under the dirt, only to remember that it had been stolen by the soldiers just the other day. Unbelieving of the cruelty, Vartan and I guided our group and sat under the shade of a tree. As I looked around me at the humiliating ordeal, I noticed a group of soldiers relaxing under the shade of a different tree, speaking to the colonel. Just as before, after finishing their conversation, they left the caravan and rode far ahead. Just when I returned from my distraction, to those with whom I sat, I realized that through the mayhem of the stampede, we had lost something valuable.

"Where's Sara?" I sprung up, searching around.
"My God," Vartan said. "I don't know. Where is she?" He joined me with the search.
"Sara!" I called out. "Lorik, have you seen Sara?"
Sobbing softly, she shook her head no.
"Sara!" I called out again, running through the caravan.

"Sara!" Vartan called out.

Running through the thousands of people wearing similar clothes over the same skeletal frames, Vartan and I continued calling out her name. We didn't find her; we *couldn't* find her.

And I began to panic.

....

Down the northern banks at a smaller opening, a group of women stood, lined up at the edge of the Euphrates River, some holding their babies. They cried, saying their last words and praying their last prayers. Choosing to die rather than continue on the perilous journey, they, one by one, jumped into the tumultuous and foaming current, immediately being swept away. Among them, to the southern end was Sara, facing the water, sharing the same hopelessness as the rest, crying at a lonely end near a tree. Behind her, a young Turkish soldier slowly approached the scene, witnessing the ordeal, scaring more women into the water.

"Stay away from us!" Sara screamed as the water splashed all around her.

"No, no!" The soldier edged forward, placing his palms ahead of him. "I'm not here to hurt anyone," he explained. "I'm going to throw my weapons away."

He then reached across his body with his left hand and took hold of his rifle, showing Sara, and threw it into the river.

"Stay back!" she screamed in agony as she now clung to the overhanging tree.

The soldier stopped. "All right. I won't move any closer," he complied. "Please, just stay there."

With the same left hand, he unholstered his pistol and unsheathed his sword and, once again, showed Sara as he threw them equally into the water.

"I'm begging you," he started again, "don't do this."

The women around her continued to jump in, shrieking slightly with each plunge.

"What difference does it make?" Sara cried, slightly turning her torso, revealing her pregnant body. "I'd rather die at my hands than at yours!"

The soldier noticed her bearing. "If you do it for anyone, don't do it for me. Do it for your unborn child. You're pregnant!"

"When did that stop you? I've seen you cut them right out of us!"

"No," the soldier began tearing up, "that's not me. That's not who I am. I'm not *them*."

He began creeping towards her again, now extending his right hand.

"Why should I believe you?"

"I'm sickened by what I've seen. I didn't join the military to do the devil's work. Every day, this cruelty haunts me. Every day, I carry this burden. If I had the power, trust me, I would go back and change all this, but I can't undo what's been done. For the sake of the same God above, please, just take my hand."

With one hand on the trunk and another slung over an extended branch, Sara didn't take it, but further slid herself farther over the turbulent and raging river as he continued his slow approach to the noisy spectacle.

"Here," he said, stuffing his hand into his pocket and showing her a few gold pieces, "take this as my token. Please don't jump. There's enough death around us."

She clung firmly onto the slippery branch, crying, feeling the water jump up at her body, her hair, and her face.

"I'm begging you," he cried again. "I'm *paying* you to stay alive. I don't know what else to do. You have to trust me when I say I'm not like the rest. I need to release myself from this time just as you do. Believe me when I say I love Armenians. I love your people. I love your culture. I love your food, your dance. I don't want to see it die and especially not in a river.

"Have mercy on me," he begged persistently. "Just take my hand. As long as I save just *one more* Armenian, I can free myself from the bond of this sin. Please."

He stopped and knelt just short of her, keeping his hand

extended.

"Sara!" I screamed with my approach.

As soon as I saw the soldier, however, I stopped.

He turned to look at me, stunned, still kneeling in his place, and watched me as I tore a hole through his head with my eyes. I analyzed the situation. I saw Sara, far from me, draped over a slippery, cracking branch, the tips of her toes barely on the banks. I saw the women who continually leaped to their deaths, including the lady with the purple top and brown skirt from day one. Then I saw the soldier, merely a man's distance away from her. I saw the gold in his hand and his extended arm. Then I saw his lightened waist, his empty holster. I knew a threat when I saw one, and this wasn't it.

The soldier stood up.

"I'm trying to help her," he pleaded in Ottoman Turkish as he tore off the shirt of his uniform, sending the buttons flying. "I'm bare. I pose no threat. I've offered all my gold. I've tossed my weapons into the river. If you have the power, please do what I cannot."

"Sara," I said calmly, fixated on the younger soldier, who I now remembered as the one who'd stopped Vartan and me just the other day, "do you hear me?"

She nodded her head.

"Do you trust me?" I asked again.

She nodded once more.

"Then please," I pleaded, "take his hand."

The soldier, seeing my backing, put the gold back into his pocket and reached out to Sara, whose tears dropped into the river as frequently as the women around her. Still holding onto the branch, she looked at him, his extended hand, then back at the tumultuous and raging water. Then, as the branch cracked once more, she shrieked and reached out, extending herself to the bank as he extended himself to the river. Thus, Sara was immediately pulled to safety, and without a pause, she ran to me, leaving the soldier behind as he knelt to the ground in relief, hearing the final splash near him.

"Thank you," he murmured as he hung his head.

"Thank you, thank you, thank you."

He then stood back up, being reminded of a detail, and ran towards us. I turned to face him and pushed Sara behind me. He stopped.

"This gold is hers," he told me as he took the pieces of gold back out of his pocket.

Feeling a jolt of needed warmth ring through my heart, I took the shiny metal pieces then put my arms around Sara's petite frame, guiding her back to camp, never finding a need to speak of the foregone events.

At sunset, as we tried recuperating from the day's events, as we sat in a daze eating our walnuts and drinking the warm and bitter Euphrates water bought with the soldier's gold, I tried once again to accept this life but fell short, continuing to be unbelieving of the heartlessness, even after the deed of the good soldier. Therefore, with a mind desperate for healing, I placed my head down on the uncovered ground and slept, fully exposed to the cold air of the night.

That night, I had a dream.

I awoke, standing in the center of *Soorp Asdvadzadzin*, our church. It was a vibrant, sunny day. From the high windows, the heat of the light beamed down mightily, reflecting off the inner stone walls, and warmed my cold body. Around me, the early congregation, in formal attire, laughed and talked among each other, waiting for the service to begin. From the entrance, a steady stream of people cheerily added to the ones already inside. This time, I could move. I stood in my spot and turned in a circle to view my surroundings. I saw my friends and their families and their friends and their families. Even though it was Sunday, I didn't know why I was there. I was too tired. As I turned back towards the front doors and completed the circle, two golden knights with golden helmets hiding their faces, each with a golden spear four times as tall as them, marched inside between a break in the stream. They were the gatekeepers. Clanking loudly, the sound of their armor overpowered that of the hundreds of speaking voices as they took their first and last steps inside, standing guard on either side of the doors. Just at their heels hit the final spot on the floor, the doors behind them closed as one and were held shut by a single, golden chain through its handles and locked with a single, golden lock through the links.

"Hey," I screamed at the knights, sensing imminent danger, "unlock the doors!"

Simply, though, they remained motionless.

Just then, a quick roll of thunder from afar echoed faintly into the chamber, diverting my attention to the high windows. As if a powerful storm had rolled in, the light of the sunny day turned into the black of the night as a dense set of dark clouds blocked the sun. Not seeing the knights or the coming storm, the congregation kept their conversations strong as the candles inside the church lit up, reinstating the visibility.

My inner feelings had slowly begun to twist in on themselves. Something was wrong.

"Hey," I screamed again to the knights, "don't you hear me? Open the doors!"

And yet, they remained motionless.

Fed up with their inaction, I took a step to open them myself. However, two chains each of three links, each half the size of my body, shackled each of my legs to the stone floor, freezing my foot mid-stride. Jerking my knee forward, I felt the cold metal against the skin of my ankle but couldn't evade the grasp of its burden. So, I sat where I stood, keeping my eyes on the knights, and picked and pried at the metal cuffs with the tips of my fingers. To no avail, I screamed out loud in frustration and rose back to my feet.

"Get out!" I screamed to the congregation, trembling nervously, as a cold gust rushed in. "Something is wrong!"

And yet, nobody heard me.

Feeling the weight of something materialize in my shaking hands, I peered down at a single golden key resting in my palm. I leaned over to check the shackles around my ankles, but there were no breaks in the metal, no seams or keyholes of any kind. The key wasn't for me. Booming again, the thunder reverberated much louder than before, this time shaking the walls.

And yet, no one took notice.

Then, through a golden tune, a swift call of golden trumpets played a sound as sweet as honey. As beautiful as it was, however, I knew it came as a frightful warning.

I needed to hurry.

"Hey!" I yelled again, reaching and grabbing, trying to give the key to anyone who would take it. "Take this! It unlocks the door. You'll be free!"

And yet, even as the golden trumpets played the golden song, even as I held the golden key that unlocked the golden lock, nobody saw me. I waved my arms in fury, trying to gain their attention, but they continued their conversations. I was invisible to them.

Anticipating the yet looming danger, I paced in my limited freedom, continually trying to grab their attention. For the third time, the thunder boomed, now violently shaking the ground, knocking everyone, including me, clear off their feet. From above, the fine pale sand rained down, followed by a few, small pieces of the stone ceiling. The congregation finally took notice. Staggering up to their feet, they instinctually ran to the exit. The golden knights, however, lowered their massive golden spears, barring their only means of escape.

Suddenly then, from directly above us, the deafening roar of a lion combined with the bark of a dog rumbled the air, loosening more stone fragments from the walls and the ceiling. To satisfy their curiosity, the congregation looked up just as a large hand with long, slender fingers and talons of an eagle punctured through the stones of the roof and tore it away entirely as if a tornado had struck, felling giant boulders to crush the fortunate. The maddening cries of panic instantly induced a chaos. Through the enormous hole in the roof, I then saw a demon. It had four arms, the horns of a ram, skin like a reptile, and the face of a man. With a swoop of its first arm, it reached through the opening of the ceiling and snatched the gatekeepers away from their post and dropped them outside. Raising his second arm, the demon then smashed the two golden knights with a large rectangular hammer, causing the earth, once again, to rumble.

Realizing their newfound freedom, the congregation immediately ran around me, back to the newly unguarded doors. Without the gatekeepers, they pulled and pried at the handles, but when they failed to open, they turned to the stone of the walls, pounding and chipping at the cracks. They were, however, trapped inside.

Needing to fulfill my purpose, I knew I had to escape. I had to free these people. I pulled and kicked at my chains, but the sharp edges of the shackles dug themselves deep into my skin, cutting it open.

"Take the key!" I cried out in vain.

However, even as I cried and yelled and pulled and kicked, no one heard me. They were indifferent to my pleas.

"The windows!" screamed the panic-stricken men in their last desperate attempt. "Take them to the windows!"

In their final moments, they organized themselves at the base of the western wall, holding each other's shoulders, underneath the largest window. As they clung together, the women and children climbed onto their backs and reached for it. Seeing this, the demon raised his hammer and pounded the ground with another thunderous blow, knocking the women and children down from the walls and back onto the floor.

With a sweep from its third and fourth arms, the demon then reached back into the church and plucked two handfuls of people. It then opened its human mouth, revealing its crocodile-like teeth, and swallowed them whole, roaring in delight once again.

As the men persistently organized themselves together once more, a whirlwind suddenly whistled outside, throwing leaves, papers, and debris in all directions. A bolt of lightning then struck the clouds, cracking the sky in two. From the rift in the heavens, it then began to rain fire. As it streaked across the blackened sky, the fiery rain crashed into the people with explosive impacts, catching them ablaze. Instantly, they screamed as they burned, continually scratching at the walls, as the women and children climbed higher up on their shoulders.

Within the wrecking storm and burning fire, I cried and screamed and yelled as a witness and threw my hands in the air to protect myself from the debris.

As we all continued our attempted escape, as my ankles continued to bleed, the church then began spinning as if I were a drunkard. It spun around me, shaking at first, then spun so fast that it forced me to tightly close my eyes. In the few seconds of the dizzying flurry, the wind died, the lightning died, the fire extinguished, the roaring ceased, and the screaming stopped. The church was silent, as calm as a steadily flowing stream. The church, too, slowed to a halt, stopping its turmoil. Carefully then, I opened my eyes, unaccustomed to the eerie calm, and blinked them clean. Through the opening in the roof, I saw the sun, shining as bright as the day began.

The demon was gone.

As I took in a few calming breaths, I looked at the golden key that I held so reverently as it turned to coal and crumbled between my fingers to the broken shackles that held me, then to the floor.

I was free.

Thus, I hesitantly clambered over the rubble and stones towards my freedom and noticed the charred inner walls with endless scratches and the mounds of heaping ash against them. I finally climbed over the severely burned and disfigured doors, quickly exiting the church and fully into the bright light. Just before I took another step, however, a recognizable figure stood in front of me, blocking my path. It was Der Kourken, alive and well. In one hand, he showed me the old, crooked branch that once held his head, and in the other, the golden chain with the locked golden lock still locked through its golden links.

"Don't be sad," he reassured with a bearded smile. "Everything will be all right."

He then leaned over and placed the chain around my neck. As I felt the weight of it pull at my shoulders, I tried seeing beyond him to the field, but he blocked my view, only allowing me a partial glimpse of what lay beyond, bolting his eyes securely with mine, following my every move.

"*Der Hayr*," I explained, "but I need to leave."

"No," he whispered. "Wake up. Now."

Then, in a calming demeanor, I opened my eyes and awoke, gazing at the cloudless night to the billions of saving stars. I stared up at them in serene wonder, thinking that, even for a moment, I was in an apricot tree on my farm, that I had just awakened and that I'd smell my mother's cooking, hear my father's work, or eat those delicious orange fruits. I even thought that Tavit could be riding over or that I'd be called for my own chores. I then felt the chain of the gold crucifix around my neck, the one my grandmother had given me. That part, I knew, was real. Whether I dug it up while at the well or whether it came to me through my dream, it was now as real as the screams of the caravan, which quickly pulled me back to a place I didn't want to go.

And thus, I sprung up, remembering my whereabouts, realizing the mountain Kurds had returned. Running through the caravan, they joined the soldiers and chased the girls all the same. Becoming evermore greedy, they came this time with a killing purpose. Swinging their scimitars, they butchered and hacked until, from my stance, I saw one tear open a woman at her belly, felling a gold coin that had been swallowed from before.

"Gold!" he screamed as he picked up the bloodied element. "There's gold inside them!"

Thus, as a prompt incentive to the others, the rest, including the soldiers, aimed at the bellies for more, inducing a wound not so quick to kill. Ruined by the sights and through the spectacular mayhem, I then heard a sound, something that I'll never forget, a beautiful voice, unique with distinctions of silk, calling my brother's name. It shocked my system to overdrive and heightened my status.

"Vartan!" it screamed.

It couldn't possibly be true, but it was.

"Oh my God, Vartan!" I screamed out loud as if it were the last scream of my life. "*Vartan!*"

"What?" he answered.

"Listen!"

Placing his ear to the wind, amid the violence and the screams and the sounds of death, he, too, heard the same golden tune.

"Vartan!" the voice called.

He scrambled around more energetic than I've ever seen, as if a new life had been given to him. Ignoring everything around, he called out a response.

"Nadia!" he screamed feverishly. "*Nadia!*"

"Vartan!" she called again.

"Nadia, where are you!"

"I'm here!"

Turning around, Vartan immediately found her and lunged at her like a man in a race. In that moment, they embraced each other through an infinite fusion, becoming as one in a striking reunion.

"Oh my God, Nadia, Nadia," Vartan cried. "You kept me alive. You kept me alive. Are you all right?" he cried in a panic as he searched her head and shoulders for any signs of struggle.

"I'm all right," she replied. "I'm fine."

"Why did you come back?" he questioned as he gave her a kiss. "How did you find us?"

"The stars," she answered with a heartfelt cry. "I heard a caravan moving south, and I followed the stars to you."

"Under the carpet!" I screamed out to them despite the excitement. "Let's go—get under the carpet, *now!*"

"Quick," Vartan instructed, "you need to hide."

"What's going on?" she cried, desperately afraid and confused as Vartan grabbed her hand and pulled her to the wool covering.

"You have *no* idea what this is!" he yelled with a sudden crossness. "Why did you come back?"

"What else," she cried. "What else was I to do?"

Thus, as she sat under the carpet with the other girls, Vartan put his hands over his face and paced all around. "You are to stay under that carpet!" he yelled, emotions running rampantly.

With the covering firmly in place, Vartan and I then covered it again with dirt and returned to our positions. Standing near death, we screamed and cried in a blood-lust rage, watching as the horde slaughtered the remaining, cutting them to pieces just for gold. My stomach churned, my head spun, and I felt the immediate urge to leave my post, to protect those who couldn't protect themselves. I wanted to do something beyond my control, feeling the need to do what was right, but I fought it and remained where I stood, defending the girls at all costs for the second unending invasion.

Finally, when it was over, when the Kurds left, I fell to the ground and cried, pounding at the dirt with my weakened fist, asking the question I already had the answer to.

"Why," I muttered, "why is this happening?"

Quickly raising the dusty covering, Vartan fully exposed the girls, including Nadia. She stood up, pale from the endless scare and leaped to Vartan as they embraced once more in a tearful joy.

Kneeling still, I suddenly had an infinitely sinister taste on my tongue. I inhaled, trying to compose myself, then stood up and joined the girls who clung together closer than ever. With a slight dip, I, too, sat, still on high guard, when Nadia, debilitated by the calamity, removed something that had been draped across her chest and over her shoulders. I looked through the darkened air curiously, realizing that it looked familiar—the way the rod and loop fell perfectly into each other, the way the brown patina shined.

It was my satchel.

Lifting the floppy brown flap, she reached in and pulled out an apricot and handed it to the little girl as a way to distract her from the grisly aftermath. She smiled through her tears and bit into it, then offered it to the next girl.

"No need for that," Nadia said as she pulled out a second and gave it to the next girl, then another to the third, then finally enough for all of us. Before I took my bite, I looked at that small orange fruit and felt the tears roll down my face. At that point in my life, I didn't feel like I deserved it.

"Go ahead," said Vartan, "it's real."

Hesitantly then, I bit into it and felt the sweet sugary taste mend my darkened mouth and melt down my throat, energizing my muscles. With that act of thoughtful kindness, I knew full well that Nadia quite possibly saved us again.

"By the way," she said as she took the satchel off from over her head and extended it to me, "this is yours."

With a casual reach, I lightly took hold of it, then examined the broken strap, which had snapped in the middle. I then stuck my right arm through the opening, followed by my head, so that it would drape equally across my chest. It rode a little higher now that the strap was shorter, but it felt more secure.

"Thanks," I said warmly, happy that I had at least another item from my past.

For the rest of that night, Vartan and I, despite our deteriorating health, kept awake, watching over the girls huddled together under the carpet, to ensure they survived. Thus, that night, the fourth, I didn't sleep. Not at all. I couldn't, because I knew day five was among us.

37

How much can one man endure? I remember thinking to myself at the rise of the morning sun. How much can he endure before he breaks? What happens when all hope is lost? Then what?

Today would be my day.

By the end of it, I would get the answers to the questions I should have never asked. I would exhibit just how remarkable and resilient the human spirit really is, just how much it can tolerate, what it can do, how it can accept, and how it can recover. I would realize just how far and how long a man can be pushed into a corner before he begins to push back. This day would prove to me who would fight and who would let go. Who would live and who would die. By the end of it, I would learn that every detail that had been thrown at me, every lesson that I soaked in, was done so for a reason, and I would see its culmination used to its fullest potential so that it could be propelled through my body for a greater good. And when it was done, I would think back, even remembering a time when I knew who I was.

Today, I would learn my final lesson.

I would find my purpose, my significance, who I'd become. I would discover the core of the innate mind, what it truly means to be human, why we persist in this life, why we force ourselves to find our purpose, why we tirelessly search for our meaning, trying to justify our existence. And I would learn the answers to these questions through the contrary.

What would happen if we didn't?

The last day.

Day five.

As we dragged our dying bodies, keeping our heads low under the unending dangers of the mid-day sun, as we pushed past the dried timber, small patches of grass, and thin desert shrubs, I closed my eyes. I closed my eyes and thought of the days past and how I wished for them. Now only as a fragmented illusion, as I now heard only the frequent hollow thuds upon the ground, I nearly forgot what it was like. They seemed so far away.

With a shake of my head, I opened my eyes. The heat was playing games with me. Next to me, Lorik limped nearly on her own, blessed by the slow pace of the caravan. On my other side, the four orphan girls and Sara walked close together while Vartan and Nadia behind me held onto each other in the endless struggle. Asking all the questions she had, Nadia tried to understand the purpose of this massive transit. We did all we could to explain as she soaked the sights of a dying race barely pushing their feet, looking as if they'd been washed ashore from a lost voyage at sea, even detailing the soldiers and their daily killing squads who systematically murdered groups of men at random, justifying why some boys wore dresses. We explained how Vartan and I had escaped death thus far, how neighboring

Armenian villages were pushed and added into our deportation, how we rescued the girls, why people ate flour and grass pies, and even our developing place in history. We explained everything except for the constant rapes and how Ova died. We couldn't do it.

Then, Nadia explained her own journey to us, how she left in the middle of the night, reminding her sisters to be patient with their new family. How she stopped at our farm for apricots, explaining that a Turkish family had occupied our home. How her horse later broke its leg and had to be left behind, forcing her to continue by foot through the wilderness. How she hid during the day and traveled by night. She shared her story and we shared ours, digressing from the anguish fairly quickly and focusing on the norm. Through it all, Nadia became quite familiar with Sara, realizing a connection on many different levels. They shared their passions, their hobbies, and even their tastes in food. They talked, speaking about their villages, their families, their clothing, and their personal struggles, eventually keeping the conversation solely between themselves, making the most of what they could.

I wish I could've done the same.

With my newfound satchel draped across my chest, tied in a knot from where it broke, I tried to focus on the road ahead, away from my hallucinations, to the end of the parade. Just then, a different familiar voice cast a reel over my name. I slowly turned around at the surprising call. It was Joseph, the man whom I met as we dug the ditch. He had survived. Dirtied and bearded, he hobbled to me with a grandiose smile across his face.

"Armen, want to see something?" he asked.

"What is it?" I responded.

"Come here." He motioned, forcing me to deviate away from the group.

Promptly noticing, Vartan immediately became perplexed by the request but was too far away to hear.

"Look," he said with a smile as he unraveled a torn piece of canvas, revealing a pistol.

Astonished and immediately paranoid by the find, I quickly covered it with my hands and pushed it down, peering around nervously.

"Joseph!" I reprimanded. "Where did you find that?"

"I stole it," he laughed. "I took it from a soldier. It only has one bullet. See?"

He held the small metallic cone between his forefinger and thumb. I reached for it, but he grasped it in his palm, pulling it away from me.

"Joseph, keep that hidden," I advised as I covered the pistol with the canvas. "Do they know?"

"No," he laughed yet again, "of course not."

"Does *anyone* know?" I specified.

"No, only you," he laughed more excitedly.

"Well, you can't possibly do anything with that," I explained. "They'll kill you, then us, and then they'll send reinforcements. Don't use it. From one Armenian to another, just don't."

Joseph laughed. "Isn't it great? This is so exciting!"

"Stay close to us and don't wander away," I said as I put my arm over his shoulders, guiding him back to our group. "Come with me here."

"Vartan," I called with my return. "Vartan, Joseph has a pistol."

"What?" he asked as he took his arm off his fiancée and glanced at the young man. "Are you serious?"

"Yes," I explained.

Joseph wandered away, laughing.

"Hey, Joseph!" Vartan reached out. "Come back here!"

"We need to keep an eye on him," I whispered. "He's going to get us all killed. He only has one bullet. He thinks he can make a difference."

"Can he?" Vartan asked with a weakened eye still planted on him. "We're all dead anyway."

I looked at him in bewilderment, insulted by his cynicism, as Joseph wandered back.

"No," I affirmed, "he can't."

Just then, a team of soldiers approached us, leading another four groups, each consisting of eight men tied together with thick, braided rope. We stopped our words short and held our breath until they passed, lowering our heads, until they reached the top of the nearby hill to our southwest.

"That's going to be us one day," Vartan eyed, still on his path of self-defeat.

"Don't say that!" Nadia hit him.

"I'm just trying to be realistic. If Joseph has one bullet, then that's one more that we didn't have before."

Joseph smiled thrillingly. "They don't even know. They walk right by and don't even know."

The sound of gunfire then permeated the air, saturating our senses and disrupting all talk. As the echo carried afar, the women cried louder as Nadia, unaccustomed to the new violence, jumped at the sound. Ahead of us, the colonel quickly searched around the landscape as if someone called his name and galloped towards the source of the shots.

"Are you all deaf?" he reprimanded the troops newly climbing down the slope. "Conserve your bullets! That's why you have swords. Here," —he threw a tank of kerosene up at them— "use this and take care of it."

Sighing, the soldiers picked up the tank then turned around and returned to the scene. In an instant, a thick black smoke rose high above the tree line as the bodies caught fire like dry firewood on a cold winter day.

"See," the colonel reassured as he watched his troops march back down, "that's much easier than digging."

Then, with a slight change of direction, he rode ahead, sighting us along the way, as we helplessly marched ever more slowly. He glared at us with his rotten eyes, at Vartan and Nadia linked together. From atop his horse, the colonel sat unnaturally quiet, as if he were thinking, remembering. Even when his troops approached him, he quieted them instantly so as to not disrupt his process. With a hasty dispersal, they let him be for the rest of the day.

Just before the sun set, he called them back to carry out his final request, one final command—a direct order to split the men from the women, the boys from the girls, regardless of their relations to each other or even their age. It was during that late afternoon that hell became one with the Earth.

On their mission, the soldiers approached us from all angles, quickly surprising us, and beat us with the butts of their rifles. Most fell to the ground, including me. Upon the dirt, from the searing pain, I felt like a drowning man. Breathing heavily, with no feeling left, they then forced us up, rifles pointed. Instantly, they grabbed us by our torsos and fervently tore us away from each other. They split Vartan, Joseph, and me from the girls, pushing us into one group, and Nadia, Lorik, Sara, and the orphans into another. They split whole families, husbands from their wives, brothers from their sisters, making it the worst experience of my life. With each separation, with each pull, everyone screamed. The women cried their last cries, and the few men said their last words. They then picked eight men, including Vartan and me, and walked over with a thick, braided rope. With a rounding swing onto the ground, they began tying us together as the groups of men and women continued exchanging their words of love, crying and screaming to each other, for one another. Merely minutes from death, some didn't have the strength to stand, and thus, within the turmoil, they simply lay on the ground, confused and mentally buried. I looked at them, the fallen, seeing the imminent death, and wriggled like a worm in the soldier's grasp, refusing the time, refusing to be one with the dirt. It was useless. They had me tight. Just then, from across the blockade, Nadia, from a sudden rush of unattainable vigor, screamed for Vartan as she, too, fought and kicked in defense of the unfair gap. The soldiers, however, held her just as they held me.

This was the end. Our time to wake.

Seeing her struggle, Vartan, as if being met by the same invigorating rush, twisted out of the ropes and fought his way back to her, punching a soldier along the way. Keeping the pistol at his waist, the soldier then unsheathed his sword, but I used my bound hands and hammered it down with my fists, using my spent and falling body as a weapon. The soldier then hit me with a force back to the ground then thrust the bayonet of his rifle at my body. I rolled away and the point stabbed into the ground, breaking off cleanly.

"Hey, get over here!" the others screamed to their comrade.

Realizing a more important task, the soldier staggered over to them, forgetting about me entirely. It took him and five other soldiers to pull Vartan away from Nadia and five more to tie him down. He fought like I've never seen a man fight, until the muscles on his bony frame swelled and his blood boiled. Every single one of his veins bulged over him like branches on a tree as they tore him away.

Across the new blockade, they held Nadia as she yelled and cried. She, too, fought like I've never seen a girl fight. She was a tough girl, Nadia. Moving as quickly as possible, the soldiers then picked a group of seven girls, including Sara, and isolated them from Nadia, Lorik, and the four orphan girls. They pulled and pushed them, preventing those seven girls from breaking free, even tearing off their clothes. Lifting their tanks of kerosene, they then began pouring the fragrant liquid over their heads as they whimpered, tasting the sour, bitter taste.

Nadia, in her last and final fight, in her last struggle to stand for justice and exemplify what it means to be alive, broke free from the soldier's grasp and jumped into Sara's small group, intentionally pushing her soaked body out of the way with a violent drive to the ground to a place just behind a large, sheltered boulder. Just then, a powerful sound burst through my ears, deafening them into a high-pitched squeal.

Nadia saw it coming.

I readjusted my jaw, surprised at the sound so close to me, and looked around. With his untied hands, I saw Joseph kneeling next to me, shakily holding his newly fired pistol, just as terrified as I was.

In the midst of my prolonged silence, I then watched as Vartan screamed in a silent, uncontrollable cry as I knelt there, unable to hear anything beyond my own muffled breath and insane beats of my heart. Scaring even the soldiers, I watched him as he yelled like I've never seen a man yell. He yelled so loud it turned his face red, until his neck swelled. He then roared and clawed at anything that moved, at the soldiers who maintained their firm grasp, trying to break free, forcing his hands apart even as the rope dug into his wrists, until he bled, to get to his love.

He tried and he failed.

As my hearing quickly reunited with my brain, I then watched as Nadia's lifeless body, like an angel, fell elegantly to the dry and cracking ground, followed thereafter by the distorted reality that consumed us all like the plague—the screams of the men, the cries of the women, and the laughing of the Turkish soldiers.

"*No!*" I screamed and cried in an infuriating and painful disbelief. "Joseph, dammit, Joseph, why did you do that?"

"I'm sorry, my friend," he replied as he dropped the discharged the weapon. "No more suffering."

He then sprang up and ran a pathetic hobble away from us, easily being chased down by the soldiers in an effortless rundown.

"Take them away," the colonel ordered.

Thus, in order to finish what they started, the soldiers tied us to one another in the same group of eight. They pulled us to the base of a small and very shallow hill to the west, overlooking a valley. Behind me, Vartan cried and cried like I've never seen a man cry. He cried so hard that he shook, until he trembled, until he fell to the ground with no life left to live. As I cried along with him, as they dragged my brother over the rocky ground, as I used my might to pull his body, I felt the heat of a blazing fire erupt behind us, creating a sound unlike any with a feeling that no man will ever forget.

Then, I said something that I couldn't have said alone.

"Vartan," I shouted behind me, "get up!"

Unhearing of my request, he had already accepted the nearing end and continued to bawl as the soldiers pulled us uphill over the rocks and dried sprouts of weed. Noticing the new anchor in the back, one soldier from up front then trekked towards us. Thus, as I scraped my knees and felt the tug of my satchel catching on the rocks, as useless as it seemed, I did all that was left to do. I prayed. Reciting the Lord's Prayer, I begged the Lord to give my brother the strength to continue, to give us the hope to survive. Even in my sickness, I used all my energy to fulfill this miraculous feat. I prayed to let us live to see another rising sun. I prayed for the ability to recover, for the opportunity to rise.

He finally listened to what I had to say.

"Hey!" another soldier called out to the one walking back. "Forget it, we're nearly there."

With a simple shrug, he turned back around, and moments later, we reached the top. As the other captives, dazed and defeated, rehearsed their final words, the soldier swung his scimitar, murdering the man in the lead. He then kicked the headless body into the valley and let it swing by his tied hands. I felt the force of his pull on my wrists from the rope that still tied us to each other. As if he'd had enough with Vartan, the same soldier then returned to the back, where Vartan lay on the ground, and pulled him to his knees.

"Vartan!" I screamed. "Look at me. *Look at me*!"

He sagged his head in defeat.

"Get up!" I cried. "Get up. Get it out of your head. Fear is in your mind!"

Kneeling still with his tied hands and closed eyes, he fell back to the ground in useless pity. I knelt with him and took hold of his head.

"Please, no!" I begged as I felt the pull of the rope tighten again, pulling me closer to the edge. "Don't—this is my brother!"

I then looked at Vartan, into his eyes, his closed, teary eyes. The eyes of a dead man. He clenched his teeth as the soldier took out his pistol and pulled him back up by his long hair.

He then pointed the gun at his head.

With a single squeeze of his finger, the soldier pulled the trigger, and I screamed.

Yet, nothing happened. Just a click.

With my bright red eyes, I looked at the weapon in

astonishment then continued to Vartan. If anyone could convince him to keep moving, to survive, if anyone could do it, I could.

"Vartan, please! We can't die," I cried. "If we do, all this was for nothing. Please, Vartan. Get up. I need you. If there's anything left in you, anything at all, you'll fight! Do it for Mama, for *Hyreeg*, for Tavit, for Garo, Ana, Ara, and Mary! Do it for everyone else before us. Please," I begged. "Get up. Say you're not afraid. Say it with me, Vartan. I'm not afraid! Tell Nadia you're not afraid! Vartan," I yelled. "I said get... *up*!"

Then, with a raise of my arm and the drop of my merciless and untamed hand, I slapped him, sending an electrifying shockwave through his face and down his neck, burning his cheek to a deep sparkle. And suddenly with my hit, just as my hand touched his face, I felt a jolt electrify my *own* face, followed by an instantaneous vision—the old man from my dream years ago still standing in the metallic room. He had slapped me the same. Cowering away in disbelief, I placed my palm upon my own cheek, feeling my thinning, leathery skin.

The soldier then looked at his jammed weapon, shook it, and once again, held the barrel against Vartan's head. As if coming back from a meaningless existence, my brother looked at me as the soldier cocked it back once more.

"I'm not afraid," he whispered as I repositioned myself from the effect of the mystifying force.

The soldier pulled the trigger once again.

Again, nothing happened.

"Oh my God, Vartan," I said as I crawled back to him with a newfound hope. "Say it!" I screamed. "Say it again. I'm not afraid. You told me that. I'm not afraid!"

"I'm not afraid," he said a little louder.

"I'm not afraid!" I screamed as the tears continue to fall.

"I'm not afraid!" he yelled to the ground with a remarkable power.

And then, it happened.

From the deepest pits of my chest, an explosion burst through my ribs, stemming from the same intense flame that burned inside. If change is what I wanted, then I had to go and change it myself. Nobody would do it for me. I realized through all the odds that I needed to *choose* to be the change. I had no choice. I felt the warmth of the flame feed me a glorious meal and drink me a glorious drink. Like a vine, it fed into my veins as I channeled its power, feeling the force work its way through my body, rattling my bones and thumping through my skin. There was nothing I could do anymore. I did nothing to suppress it. Knowing that it wasn't going to leave, I thus allowed it to consume me entirely, letting it expand and work through my body *forever*.

The soldier then raised his weapon for the third time and stuck it against my brother's head. I felt the tension of the rope suddenly ease, freeing my weighted arms, and so I leaped like a hare and knocked the pistol out of his hand as it shot into the ground with a deafening echo. I then fell, spilling the contents of my satchel, revealing the one last chance I had at survival—a recognizable, sharpened piece of metal with an ivory-colored handle. There was no turning back now. I wasn't going to stand back and do nothing. I couldn't. Not anymore. If I wanted to overcome adversity, no one would pull me from under its grip but me. The flame inside now controlled me. It spoke to me, revealing those words, and bubbled out through the pores of my skin like boils on a leper. It seared out of my eyes and out of my ears. It ripped through my arms, to my fingers, and through my legs, then out my feet. I was now filled entirely with a hatred, an infinite hatred, that only society could have built, and I cried, not through sadness anymore, but from a blood-hungry rage working through my hands. Now, with the strength to do what I was destined to do, it was time for me to do what my father told me to do.

Save us.

Thus, I thrust my body against the dagger and grabbed a fierce hold of its handle, feeling it instantly fuse with my palm. With a powerful jab, I stuck the soldier in his throat and roared like a dragon. I then cut the rope that bound my brother's hands, and he unraveled mine.

Seeing the failure of their comrade, the soldiers from the lead unholstered their weapons, but Vartan, like a starving hyena, sprung up and attacked their legs, dropping them to the ground. I followed suit and had the soldiers meet the fury of my will working now with a weapon. I then kicked them over the edge and stood over the valley, crying in anger, and listened to the voices of the remaining four captives behind me, very well alive, begging me for their freedom. They, too, now felt the contagions of the addictive flame seeping into their souls. Without a moment's pause, I cut the ropes that bound them, momentarily freeing them from their misery.

But it wasn't over.

From the thickening wall of smoke and fire, through the nauseating scent of burning hair, a man crawled up from beneath, panting and deeply agitated. Quickly, I threw myself behind a low-lying bush, placed the bloodied dagger against my chest, and closed my eyes tightly, blocking all sounds. I focused on the crunching of grass under his boot, his heavy breathing, and finally then, his voice.

"I told you," he yelled, "don't waste your bullets on Armenian—"

Before he could even finish his sentence, I hurled myself through the frail plant and pounced on him like a rabid tiger from hell, driving myself to an uncontrolled state, feeling my soul take a barbaric stance of defense, and knocked him to the ground. I then thrust the dagger straight up into his bearded chin as I looked deep into his face, his cowardly face, with the tip now coming out of his eye.

With a locked jaw, he growled, unable to speak, uttering incoherence, and stared into my eyes as I stared back into his. I didn't say anything to him; he knew what I would've said. Instead, I slid the dagger out and thrust it deep into his chest. Atop the shallow hill overlooking a valley, the man grumbled and gasped a few short breaths, then closed his eyes one final time.

The colonel was now dead.

With a shivering roll, I pushed myself off and stood to face the others as they gawked at me in bewilderment.

"A hero," one whispered under his breath. "This man's a hero!"

"Sent from Jesus," another exhaled in a shallow state of shock. "He was sent from Jesus!"

They smiled joyfully, laughing in celebration as I focused on the women down the hill.

"Sara! Lorik!" I screamed to the ones now hiding together behind the sheltered boulder, feeling the searing heat burn my eyes. "You're free. Get up here, *now*!"

Using the smoke of their burning sisters and the scattered confusion as their cover, nearly four hundred women who'd been waiting for death, including the four orphans, limped with each other to the top of the hill, passing the colonel's body along the way.

They were drenched in kerosene.

Hurriedly, they joined us as we climbed down into the valley and ran between the trees and over the rocks, escaping now as free Armenians.

38

The clock on the wall read 12:04. Four past midnight. Armen sat in his chair with his right leg crossed neatly over the other. Seated in front of him, his family, mesmerized and humbled by what they'd just heard, whimpered. They glanced at their grandfather, Vartan, seeing him now as more than just a man lying in a hospital bed.

"Believe it or not," old Armen stated, "this story does have a happy ending. I'm almost done. I've come this far; I might as well go the whole way."

His family listened on.

. . . .

After a seemingly infinite escape, we stopped a few hours from sunrise to rest at a grassy clearing between some high trees. It was time for an attempted recourse. That night, I watched as Vartan walked alone to lay on his back in the comfort of the flowing plain, not far from the rest of us. There, he didn't close his eyes. Instead, he stared up at the stars while I approached him cautiously, thinking of what to say, of all that we'd been through. Silently then, I pitched a blanket next to him and placed the dagger upon the dulled colors and sat down, noticing my boney kneecaps. However, before I said a single word or made a single sound, Vartan took charge.

"Armen," he said sullenly.

I removed the satchel from over my shoulder and placed it next to the dagger, then paused, waiting for him to continue.

He didn't.

"Yes?" I asked.

"I can't cry anymore. I have no tears left."

My heart sank.

With a shift of my weight, I repositioned myself through the crushing sadness to lie down next to him, and I, too, stared blankly into the night sky.

"We… We've been through a lot," I replied as I gazed at the same stars. "We just have to… move on. That's all we can do."

My brother echoed a sound of approval.

"Here," I continued, "this is yours. I don't want it."

Without hesitation, I passed the dagger to Vartan. With a slight turn of his head, he took a light grasp of its unstained ivory-colored handle and lightly passed his thumb over the carvings.

"You know," he started as he studied the craftsmanship, "we never did have that rematch, did we?"

I smiled in response to his surprising call. "No," I answered. "I would've won anyway."

He chuckled, followed by another delay. "My God," he exhaled a moment later with a subtle shake of his head, "so much has changed for us. So much has changed."

"I know," I agreed somberly.

"But why?" he said barely. "Why did God do this to us?

Don't you wonder?"

I turned my head to face him, realizing again that he was no different than me. "Yes, I do," I replied plainly.

"So why? What's the reason?"

I then faced the stars once again. I knew I had an answer, but it didn't immediately come to me, so I thought, using my sights as an inspiration.

"God didn't do this to us," I responded a few moments later. "The devil did."

He paused.

"Then why didn't God protect us? Why didn't He stop this? Where is He?"

"He's here. With us."

"After all this? How can you say that?" Vartan whispered with a slight crack in his tired voice.

"Well, He is," I persisted.

He rolled his head and looked at me from his deeply hollowed eye sockets. "How? How do you know?" he questioned, barely coherent, almost unbelieving of my faith.

"Because," I explained, "we're still alive."

Vartan didn't respond.

"Just promise me," he mentioned a little while later, "that you'll never speak of what happened here."

My eyes swelled, but no tears came out. I, too, had none left. "I promise."

Then, with an overdue closing of our eyes, the conversation ended, and we slept, but not by choice.

Day five was over.

....

It would be a fool's game to go through life and not learn from the world and experiences around us. In 1913, I had a lot of faith in the Young Turkish government, and so did a lot of others. We all hoped that we could have lived together in peace, discovering a way to set aside our differences. I tried to keep an open mind, but by June of 1915, I knew it wasn't the case. My experiences were too much to ignore, creating judgments that I didn't want to make and feelings that I couldn't erase.

Like I said, the more I knew, the more I understood.

By the time I was sixteen, I thought of myself prior to my initiation into the muddle of genocide. I had grown tremendously, faster than I would have ever imagined. Perhaps too fast. From time to time, I think about the man I became as a result of the previous set of events. I had accepted myself and became satisfied with that man because I chose to shape my life the way I wanted it. It's true that I was always destined to be who I am now regardless of the circumstances that surrounded me. If I had to do it again, I would've done it the same way.

I'm sure of it.

I, Armen Hagopian, have learned from every lesson in my life—some were easy, some were hard, but all came eventually. By the end of 1915, I had learned everything that I needed to know about what it means to be human, what it means to exist. I learned that in order to be found, I had to be lost. In order to be fearless, I had to be scared. I learned that in order to be big, I had to be small, and in order for me to be powerful, I had to be powerless. And only after I truly knew what it meant to hate, did I learn how to love.

Vartan taught me that.

Because with that developed hatred came a purpose at a time when I needed it most, a purpose to undo what had been done to me.

My final lesson.

....

After being awakened by the sun a miserable few hours later, we walked together to a nearby Arab village who took us in. There, they kept us until we recovered, until we felt safe enough to continue. For most, it never happened.

After a few months, by September of 1915, Vartan and I decided to take a chance. With Lorik, Sara, Sara's new baby boy, and the four orphan girls, we thus boarded a steam train, a new transportation system of the time, to Jerusalem, a place rumored to house and protect tens of thousands of victims of this crisis upon humanity. When we arrived, we quickly found an Armenian orphanage designed and opened specifically for the purpose of our housing. Regardless of the newfound safety that I felt within the stone walls of the ancient city, it didn't take long to come to a further realization that Vartan and I needed to be with the only family we had left—little Margaret and our Uncle Mesrob, who never left Ohio. So, as our final call, we decided to go to America.

In order to buy tickets, we ran bags of salt for a local vendor until we saved enough for two. After securing the girls in the orphanage and in our hearts, we kissed them each, knowing that we'd see each other again, and let them be with their newfound mother, Lorik. Thus, on November 3rd, we took our first steps onto the ocean liner at Port Said in Egypt and boarded the monstrous metallic vessel, lined at the seams with steel bolts, filled with other Armenian victims just like us.

It was at that moment, the moment I stepped foot onto that deck, that I realized that all that had been done to me, all that had been stripped from me, could be fixed. That's when I realized that hope hadn't been lost, and the hate, that languishing hate, that I carried with me for so long, indeed had a cure. For, sitting alone on a crate on the deck of that ocean liner was a girl, an Armenian girl, wrapped in the aura of salvation. Anahid, my beacon of light. It was at that moment that I knew I was capable of loving again.

"Hi," I said to her, still not fully understanding my instinctual actions.

"Hello," she responded shyly.

My heart quivered. I was nervous, and I wasn't sure why.

"May I sit here?" I asked. "Next to you?"

"Of course."

Thus, with a short slide, we unknowingly began the first chapter of a new era.

In the hospital room, Anahid smiled through her unending tears, vividly remembering the events in her life that'd led up to that moment. She remembered her own family, her own struggle, and what she'd endured just to sit upon that crate.

Old Armen smiled at her.

"Your great uncle Vartan, however, never got it in himself to love again. He couldn't. With Nadia's death came the death of innocence as he knew it, as we all knew it. She was as mysterious as she was beautiful and deceptively strong. She saved Sara and her baby, just as Joseph tried to, but in a very different way. And through Nadia's selfless action, she, too, became one with the flame, the ultimate force that drove us all to each other. And, through the genocide, Vartan never let go of that force of many faces that burned so passionately within his own soul, one brought to him by Nadia. Not once did he let go of that shapeless entity that became crucial to his survival, his purpose, the one he discovered so soon, knowing early on that hate is simply a weak manifestation of the mind, just as fear.

"Therefore, with Nadia's passing, Vartan stayed with her in the only way he knew how, through *her* love, *her* passion. He made the stars his obsession, taking it with him onto that ship to America, where he studied the science of it all, astrophysics, quickly becoming a respected expert of the night sky. He did it all for Nadia, all to impress her, so they could always be together through this knowledge."

The family looked at Vartan, still comatose in his bed.

"Wh-what happened to the dagger?" old Armen's grandson asked.

Old Armen didn't immediately answer.

"There are many lessons here, I know. But if there is one you should take from this, it's that no matter what happens to you in this life, you must always persist. You must always continue," he stated. "It will take courage and determination to do so, but in this life, you must continue through all perils regardless of the challenges you may face. Erase the fear and the hatred, the greed and the jealousy. Separate yourself and distinguish between what's important and what's not. Look after your brothers and sisters, your friends and families. Make time for them, for anyone who needs it. Work together, not against each other. Become leaders, thinkers, and be the voice of those who can't speak. Find people to know, people to care about, and people to love. Grow, expand, and reflect. Do that and your time here, our time here, will be better.

"That dagger now sits on the mantle over Vartan's fireplace. Every day for nearly sixty years, he kissed that piece, thanking it. Every single day."

No one made a sound.

"For decades, I thought and analyzed those agonizing years growing up. I thought about the events that led up to that point. How did things become so gruesomely violent in such a short amount of time? With all that I learned, after love had overpowered my seemingly impenetrable feelings of hate, I realized something important, something truly profound. I realized that the Ottoman Empire was never our enemy. The Turkish people were never our enemy. The officials at Constantinople manipulated the minds of their own people, purposefully breaching the public trust to satisfy their unfulfilled agenda, to justify their crime through ignorance and tyranny and exemplify the last two stages of genocide: assimilation, as it happened to Nadia's two sisters and nearly to us, and finally, denial. The Armenian Genocide was the Young Turkish government's cruel game, built solely upon the lies and deceit of corruption, and channeled through their people as an attempt to wipe us free from this Earth.

"They did not succeed.

"What they did to us still haunts me to this day. It is inexcusable and unforgivable," old Armen continued. "In 1914, at the start of World War One, over two million Armenians lived in the Ottoman Empire. By 1922, less than four hundred thousand remained. Nearly one million Armenians were murdered by the Young Turks in 1915, and nearly six hundred thousand more were forcibly displaced and deported into the deadly Syrian desert as an attempt to erase an entire race of people from the histories. If, by September 1915, when the few arrived in Aleppo, the Armenians didn't die of starvation, dehydration, disease, or insanity, if the Turks didn't kill them, their broken hearts did. They were never the same.

"At its onset in 1915, Vartan and I witnessed merely thousands of those deaths, including the form of torture used on Tavit called *bastinado*. Yet, by our escape, we had only gone to one funeral. Even our animals received a proper burial. Our experiences were so terrible that it only felt right to make that promise to each other to never tell the story you just heard.

"We couldn't bear to relive it.

"In the years that followed, World War One ended, and Britain, without hesitation, tore the Ottoman Empire apart in October of 1918 for siding with Germany. Thus, joining the war became nothing more than a catastrophe for the Young Ottoman Turks. Soon after, Mehmet Talaat Pasha, one of the supreme orchestrators of the genocide and avid members of the Committee of Union and Progress, fled to Germany, a place where he thought he could find refuge from his guilt and the death sentence issued to him by the very government in which he served. There, he was killed by an Armenian in 1921. After allowing for his arrest, Soghomon Tehlirian confessed to his crime, citing the unspeakable violence committed by the former leader and his government as explanation for his actions, and was found innocent by the courts of Berlin, subsequently being acquitted of the charges brought against him. Another member of the committee and orchestrator of the genocide, Ahmed Jemal Pasha, was killed in 1922, in Georgia, by a group of three Armenians, all part of Operation Nemesis. A third, Enver Pasha, died in battle, also in 1922.

"Then, decades later, before even the start of World War Two, a man named Adolf Hitler rose to power. Being inspired and influenced by the German military's eyewitness report of the Ottoman Empire's destruction of Armenia, the methods of extermination including the slave camps, dehumanization of the Armenians, mass burnings, primitive gas chambers, stolen land, meaningless laws, burning of books, and the erasure of family records, he led his own party to carry through with yet another genocide in the twentieth century. The Holocaust. Only during that time, in 1944, did a man named Raphael Lemkin create the word especially to describe the atrocities that had befallen us and his own Jewish people, using the Armenian Genocide as culprit of undeniable influence for future affairs.

"However, in order for a higher thinking, before I went insane, I had to be hopeful. I had to find the sliver of light. Despite the catastrophic consequences of not learning from the past, I've witnessed and I've seen, many times, the strong mercy of the few overcome the malevolence of the many. I've seen the strength of humanity. I've seen the compassion and the sympathy at a time when I needed it most. I've seen the truth. I've seen the right in a world of wrong. I've seen the good, and I saw it when I was blind.

"So, in the end, we *are* like the sheep, like the cranes. We are in this life, not for ourselves and for no other reason but for each other, for other sheep, for other cranes. I'm certain of it. That is our purpose, why we are born, why we exist, for the sake and survival of everyone else, as just one basic instinct sewn into our existence, and that is the *only* way we survived extinction—because of this endless support for each other, to one another—this force, this flame. Only until we were alone did we learn how to work together. Without question, had it not been for the camaraderie that was such a defining way of life, I would not be telling you this, my account.

"If you haven't noticed by now, I'm a thinker. I wasn't always like this. I must admit, I was naïve about the world around me. I accepted things as I saw them from the outside. I never saw behind the curtain, the thoughts, the framework of society, as I do now. I never analyzed my surroundings—people, situations, events—like I do now. I never probed for a deeper understanding, like I do now. With my old set of eyes, it's become impossible to stop analyzing and impossible to stop questioning. The more I knew, it proved, the more I understood. This was the result of finally finding what I was searching for—*my* purpose, *my* place. The thought alone and the opportunity to find what I sought was enough to put my heart at ease. And through the analysis and the questioning, the aging, ever-influential flame, with the same insane power, continues to pound at me from the inside out—a natural connection—the bridge that Nadia epitomized so purely, so naturally, connecting us to one another. It seeps continually through the stitching of my soul and works through my everyday actions. With each passing experience, it claws and roars like a pack of lions roaming free. Nothing holds it back. It pulsates from deep within my heart, only growing, becoming ever more controllable. It's in my hands as a force that I now know how to control, a force that I now understand.

"The story I just told you was solely of my own as just one of millions resting beneath the ground, resting forever as a reminder of man's inhumanity to man, as evidence of an attempted recourse of history.

"Most of which will never be told.

"My name is Armen Hagopian. You will remember my name. I am from Kharpert. I am from Van. I am from Bitlis. I am from Erzerum. I am from Sivas. I am from Dikranagerd. I am from all the provinces and all the villages within, all that was, and all that will be.

"I am from Armenia.

"My name is Armen Hagopian. I am Vartan, I am Tevos, I am Hasmig, I am little Margaret. I am Armenian. I stand for truth and for justice. I stand for what is right, to make a difference.

"I do it because I can.

"This is my story. This is your story. This is our story. We are all of the same, of the strong, of the weak, and together, we will rise."

Epilogue

The day was done, and the story was over. The family left, as did old Armen, rendering the hospital room empty for someone else. The old professor now stood with Nadia in the great kingdom above, rejoicing in an everlasting bliss, free from the bondage of existence.

He was seventy-three years old.

In a simple neighborhood, over a cracking, unkempt street, old Armen drove slowly. With a careful turn of the steering wheel, he guided his rattling Bel-Air into the driveway and shifted it into park. For a moment, he sat in the car and looked at the small, freshly painted white house in front of him. He didn't have many thoughts. The day was just starting. With a pull of the handle, he creaked open the door and placed his feet down onto the ground and hobbled, ever so slightly, over the sidewalk and to the front door. With a slight twist of the unlocked knob, he stepped into his brother's home and slowly walked through the short hallway decorated with many photos of his family upon its walls. At the end, he turned into a room, a library, filled endlessly with books on every subject and staggered to the fireplace. There, he stopped and rested his large palms against the stone mantle, fixing his eyes upon the dagger. He didn't pick it up. He didn't touch it, but studied it, curiously, as it sat silently. Peacefully. He then shifted his eyes to the unlit firewood and shook his head with a heart-warming smile.

"We did good, Vartan. We did good."

The list below denotes some books that helped me re-create the lifestyle and mentality of the time and provide a historical base for my plot and characters. I have not included the endless newspaper articles I read (≈1894–1923), the websites I used, or the family interviews I conducted, all of which also helped me illustrate the terrible history of the Armenian people.

Aivazian, Aram P. *Armenia: Usurped by Genocide and Treachery: Documentary—Protest of a Survivor.* Willowdale, ON: Aram Aivazian, 1992.

Balakian, Peter. *The Burning Tigris: The Armenian Genocide and America's Response.* New York: Harper Collins Publishers, 2003.

Douglas, John M. *The Armenians.* New York: J. J. Winthrop Corp., 1992.

Graber, G. S. *Caravans to Oblivion: The Armenian Genocide, 1915.* New York: John Wiley & Sons, Inc., 1996.

Institut Für Armenische Fragen. *The Armenian Genocide: Documentation, Volume I.* Germany: Buchhandel-Service Dietrich Prehl, 1987.

Kuper, Leo. *Genocide: Its Political Use in the Twentieth Century.* New Haven, CT: Yale University Press, 1981.

Miller, Donald E., and Lorna Touryan Miller. *Survivors: An Oral History of the Armenian Genocide.* Oakland: University of California Press, 1999.

Morgenthau, Henry. *Ambassador Morgenthau's Story.* London: Sterndale Classics, 2003.

Nazer, James. *The First Genocide of the 20th Century: The Story of the Armenian Massacres in Text and Pictures.* New York: T. & T. Publishing, Inc., 1968.

Riggs, Henry H. *Days of Tragedy in Armenia: Personal Experiences in Harpoot, 1915–1917.* Ann Arbor, MI: Gomidas Institute, 1997.

Sarafian, Ara (ed.). *United States Official Documents on the Armenian Genocide, Volume I: The Lower Euphrates.* Watertown, MA: Armenian Review, 1993.

Terjimanian, Hagop (ed.). *The First Holocaust: The Genocide against the Armenian Nation, 1915–1923.* Ottowa: Arax Publishing House, 1982.

Toomajan, Harry J. *Exit from Inferno: The Odyssey of an Armenian American.* Waukegan, IL: H. J. Toomajan Estate, 1955.

Toynbee, Arnold J. *Armenian Atrocities: The Murder of a Nation.* New York: Tankian Publishing Corp., 1975.

Fable inspired by the works of Mkhitar Gosh (1130-1213)

64983256R00261

Made in the USA
Lexington, KY
26 June 2017